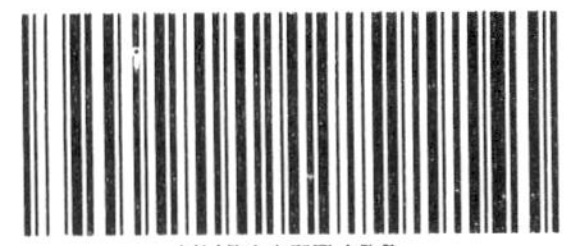

THE SECRET DOOR

A PHANTOM OF THE OPERA NOVEL

J. M. Smith

ISBN: 1495922766
ISBN-13: 978-1495922763

DEDICATION

I would like to dedicate this book to my dear friends F.P. and E.M.C. who helped me tremendously during its creation. Without your thoughts, contributions, and editing skills, I never would have finished this book. The laughs we shared during the writing process are treasures I will always carry with me!

I would also like to dedicate this book to my dear husband. Thank you for your patience, your support, and your encouragement as this story took over my life for the better part of a year. I love you! Forever!

CONTENTS

ACKNOWLEDGMENTS

While obviously being a Phantom of the Opera novel—and thus, inspired by Gaston Leroux, Susan Kay, Andrew Lloyd Webber, and all the other wonderful authors who have woven tales of the mysterious masked genius living beneath the Paris Opera House—this story was also inspired, in large part, by the song "The Secret Door" by Evanescence. That beautifully haunting melody conjured up images in my mind of dimly lit passageways, red roses, and a dance in the dark. What would one find if they opened The Secret Door? This story has been an effort to find out.

1 COLLISIONS (PROLOGUE)

1884

Erik ghosted through the secret tunnels of the opera house, his cloak billowing behind him. Having just gathered supplies at the kitchens, he was making his way back to his home beneath the world when he heard the sound. It was a low wail, a keening bellow, and Erik found that he *had* to move toward the pitiable moan, to ascertain if perhaps some innocent wounded animal had made its way into the Palais Garnier in search of kindness. He knew, if that were the case, the creature was unlikely to find benevolence above, and while he was truly not in the market for a damaged pet, he had never been the type to allow mistreated innocence to go unaided.

He walked in the direction from which the sound was issuing, and as he got closer, he realized that this was no poor animal yowling in pain, but a girl... Erik almost turned back upon his way once the realization had been made. He would attend to abused innocence, but rarely had he been able to find any such blamelessness in the realm of men. And yet, the cries were full of such...*anguish*—an emotion with which he was very familiar. He had almost reached the source, and so concluded that he might as well investigate the origin of such a bitter dirge.

When he was certain he had reached the point of the cry's provenance, he determined that he was behind the walls of the chapel. Stealthily, he slid to the tiny crevice between the stones, through which he could peer into the room unobserved. There, on the cold, hard floor, hunched over on her knees before a glowing candle, was sorrow itself. Clad simply, in a white dressing gown, her long dark curls fell forward to shield whatever face she possessed from his view. She was still weeping, and her heaving back showed tangible evidence of each sob that escaped her tiny frame. As she shuddered to draw in a shaky breath, she lifted her head to look upward, and he could tell that she clutched a framed photograph to her chest. Her face, though tear stained and red from her wailing lamentation, still possessed a delicate beauty, and it seemed entirely wrong to Erik for tears to ever fall from those eyes—which were now such an iridescent blue from her crying.

"Papa, I miss you," she entreated to the air around her, in a voice thick with tears, "Why did you have to go? Why did you leave me here all alone, in this place that is not my home?" She looked down again, her hair once more obscuring her face. "I *have* no home." Her body shook anew with excruciating sobs.

Erik was consumed by the scene before him. As he gazed at the girl in her sorrow, he was certain that he was witnessing not *just* a girl, but a desolate angel fallen from the celestial heights. Surely there could be no other explanation for her boundless misery, which pierced through his very heart with its sharpness. He ached to reach out to her, to offer her some measure of comfort, and indeed he felt his hand reach yearningly toward the switch which would open the chapel wall. He longed to let her know she was not alone—that she could live in *his* home, if she would only agree to share it with him. But he knew that he could do nothing to ease her pain. An angel could not be comforted by a monster. Any attempt he could make to console her, would only grieve her further.

And so, his fingers curled and his hand fell to his side. And though it seemed as if his feet had transformed into stone—locked to the very spot on the floor where he stood watching—Erik somehow managed to turn from this tragically beautiful fallen angel, to make his way home—once more, into the abyss.

❧

2014

Jenna retrieved her purse and slammed the door of her locker shut, wincing once she did so, as it made the pounding in her head even worse. She had been scheduled to work a sixteen hour shift, but she felt the beginnings of the flu coming on, and luckily her charge nurse was able to find her coverage. After clocking her first eight hours feeling miserable and grumpy, she was definitely ready to go home.

It was raining when she put her old Chevy in gear and pulled out onto the road. Even at this late hour—after eleven at night on a

Tuesday—New York didn't sleep, so there was more traffic than she really wanted to maneuver through to get to her little apartment. She comforted herself with thoughts of peeling off her scrubs, crawling into bed beside Jake, and just drifting off to sleep. She would shower in the morning—although if she still felt like this tomorrow, she was calling out sick.

When she opened her front door, after climbing two flights of stairs, thanks to a broken elevator, she was greeted by the welcoming "Mreooows" of her cat Red.

"Hey, Buddy," she said, gently, scratching his soft head as he began to purr. It was odd that he was out here. Jake was surely asleep by this time, since he had the early shift tomorrow, and since Red was the most spoiled cat in the entire universe, he always slept in bed with them. Maybe he had simply sensed her coming, and wanted to greet her at the door, like the human child he thought he was. Jenna picked him up, and nuzzled him close to her face as she made her way to the bedroom.

As she got closer, she heard muffled noises coming from her room. Had Jake fallen asleep with the TV on again? She noticed the door closed, and once again thought it odd, since they always left their door open at night. She quickly shoved it open and then wished she hadn't.

There, in the middle of her bed, was her boyfriend with some blond. And they were… and he was…

Jenna turned her head away in disgust. "Oh God," she groaned, tossing Red down to the carpeted floor. She shielded her eyes with her hand and staggered from the room, feeling as if she would throw up.

"Jenna…" she heard Jake call after her, and then, apparently to his *date* for the evening, "Get *dressed*, will you?" His voice raised, as he called after her again, "JENNA!"

Jenna shook her head. There was a pit in her stomach and her head pounded a thousand times worse than it had earlier. No, she could not deal with this right now. Not the way she was already feeling.

She grabbed her keys and purse, just as Jake made it out of the bedroom, jeans unbuttoned, no shirt. "Jenna," He reached out toward her, but she backed away before his hand could touch her arm. "Let me explain…"

"NO!" She held up her hand to cut him off, fighting back the tears that were threatening to break loose. "I'm a big girl, Jake. No explanations necessary." She put her hand on the door handle.

"Jenna, come on..." he continued. "Where are you going to go at this time of night anyway?"

"Goodbye, Jake." She pulled open the door and stepped out of her apartment, "I'll be back for Red." And for the second time that night, she slammed the door.

She bolted down the stairs which led to the garage for their building and hopped back into her car. She didn't know where she was going as she turned the key in the ignition, and she didn't care. She just knew she had to get away. Away from Jake. Away from the string of disastrous relationships that had plagued her life since...well... forever. "You're so smart, Jenna," people had always told her. "You'll do great things in life." She snorted in self-derision. *Wow, if they could just see me now!* she thought. *Supreme idiot, capable of doing nothing but picking loser after loser.*

She turned on the radio in frustration. The loud guitars which immediately started blaring out of the speakers matched her state of mind nicely, even if they did nothing for the screaming pain in her head. She had thought Jake would be different. He was intelligent, and sexy, and funny. They had seemed to bond instantly—a whirlwind romance that had taken her breath away, and had her moving into his apartment much sooner than she had initially thought was prudent. But hey, love was love, right? Apparently not.

The tears were flowing freely now as she thought of how sure she had been that she had finally found the right guy. They were around the same age, had about the same level of education, worked in the same field—those things were supposed to matter, right? It was no big deal that he sometimes scoffed at her interests and never seemed to want to spend time with her friends. They were good *together*, and that was all that really mattered, right?

Wrong.

Jenna's head had had enough of the guitars, and the pounding rhythm was really more than she could take. She changed the station to something she hoped would be a little more relaxing, trying to calm the storm in her mind. The music now on the radio was from one of her favorite Broadway musicals—the one about the deformed madman who lived under the opera house. Even though they lived in midtown Manhattan, Jake had refused to take her to see a performance—just another one of those interests of hers that he'd always ridiculed. As she listened to the swell of the strings in the soothing song, she remembered how she had seen images of the heroine fainting into a dead sleep at the end of this song. Oh, how Jenna wished she could do the same. Her eyelids were heavy, her head was still pounding, and she ached all over. Sleep would be so comforting—and for awhile she could forget what had just happened. But like the poor heroine in the play, she knew that in the morning, she would awaken to an unmasked horror, and she would have to deal with the shards of another broken relationship.

Looking out her side window, she realized she was down by the river, which looked rough and choppy in the rain. How had she already driven this far? She was going to have to look for an exit soon, so that she could find a place where she could stay for the night. She was so incredibly exhausted…

The oncoming headlights and blare of the horn startled her to consciousness—but too late. Jenna swerved to avoid the oncoming vehicle, and in her panic, stepped hard on the gas. She heard a scream as her Chevy left the road and headed straight toward the river below. Right before the sickening splash, when blackness of the night water took her, Jenna realized that the scream was her own.

2 WAIT, I THINK, OMID, WE HAVE A GUEST!

Erik tied the boat to the makeshift dock on the lakeshore, immediately ascertaining that he was not alone. "Daroga," Erik called in a singsong tone to his uninvited guest, "I'm *home*."

"Good evening, Erik," Omid Javed said, looking up from the book he had pillaged from Erik's bookshelf.

"I had hoped it *would* be," Erik responded sarcastically, unfastening his cloak as he made his way to the sitting room. "But it appears I must entertain *company*." His tone did nothing to belie his annoyance as he draped his cloak over the leather chair. "Although, truly, if you continue making yourself comfortable in *my* commorancy while I am not even present, I may have to begin charging you francs for the privilege."

The Daroga let loose a maddeningly cheerful laugh, and Erik sighed deeply, taking the small sack he had carried from boat and moving toward the kitchen to put away the supplies he had procured. "Oh, come now, Erik," Omid began, following close behind, the corners of his brown eyes crinkling in amusement. "I am responsible for your flight from Persia, so you know I must keep tabs on you."

"Oh," Erik agreed in a sardonic whisper, rolling his eyes. "You must." He began stocking cupboards and drawers with the necessities he had acquired on his trip.

"After all," the impossible man continued, "it would not do to have the Angel of Death running loose unchaperoned around Paris with his Punjab Lasso!" He finished his thought with a chuckle and Erik turned slowly to scrutinize the man before him. Swarthy and dark, as most Persians were, Omid Javed could be said to be the closest thing that Erik had ever had to a friend. That did not, however, make him any less insufferable—especially with that self satisfied smirk spread across his features.

"You should know, Daroga," Erik began, his voice a menacingly soft whisper, "That I have not used the Punjab Lasso since my arrival in Paris, eighteen years ago. Although that is *not* to say," he allowed his voice to trail a bit as his mismatched gaze sharpened, "that I have not been *tempted*."

Omid Javed averted his eyes from Erik as he cleared his throat with a cough. "Yes, well…" He began awkwardly trying to shake off the momentary discomfort that Erik's tone inspired. It was difficult to do, when the visible half of Erik's mouth had so obviously curled into a disconcerting smile. "Where have you been? Your supply trip seems to have taken longer than usual, and I expected you would be home when I arrived."

Erik recalled the sorrow he had witnessed in the opera chapel, and he silently cursed the Daroga for ruining the fun he was having threatening him. "There appears to be a new arrival in the dormitories," Erik said in a guarded tone. He turned back to arranging his cabinets. He truly did not wish to speak of the somber figure he had spied on his return trip. He had not been able to stop thinking about her until he had found the Daroga rudely sprawled upon his reading chair, but now when directly questioned about his activities, he was reminded of the heartbroken angel and his mood, if it were possible, soured even more.

"Which new arrival is that?" Omid asked, reaching past Erik to the bowl piled with apples. As he made to snatch one, Erik gave him a sharp glare over his shoulder. Was there no end to this Persian's familiarity with his belongings?

"Please, help yourself to an apple," Erik hissed, acerbically. When Omid did precisely that, Erik added, "I do not know the *arrival's* name—only that she seemed quite…grieved."

"Grieved about what?" the Daroga asked, mouth half full of apple.

Erik looked at him once more in disgust. "I do not know *why* she was grieved." He could not very well have told the Persian that her grief was about a fall from Heaven. "And honestly, man, have you *no* manners? *Must* you speak with your mouth full of *my* apple?"

Omid looked at the half eaten apple and back at Erik. "Want it back?" he asked, proffering the fruit to his irritated friend.

"What?!" Erik started with a huff, "NO!" He was just about to throw the Daroga out of his lair once and for all, promising to set new traps, when they heard a crash from somewhere back by the lake and an accompanying scream. The two men looked at one another, and in silent agreement, made toward the sound, Erik stopping near his cloak long enough to obtain his lasso. They had to walk a bit down the lakeshore, partway into a cavern before they found the presumable source of the noise. There, sitting on the banks of the lake, filthy, bleeding from the head and clutching her ankle, was a girl—apparently another new arrival at the Opera House. When they stopped short at the sight, she looked up at them, a look of complete confusion on her face, and said, "Where am I?"

❧

"We've got a crash victim, Traumatic Brain Injury, non responsive," the paramedic said efficiently as they quickly rolled the stretcher into the treatment room. "Uneven pupils, blood pressure elevated, pulse and breathing slow."

The ER nurse walked alongside the stretcher, jotting down notes as she went.

"Actually works here, believe it or not," The paramedic continued, "Genevieve Wilson, ID said. RN up on the 5th floor."

The neurology resident looked up from the chart he was perusing and rushed over to the patient, readying his stethoscope for use. His week on ER rotation had been relatively uneventful, but this seemed like a serious case. Jenna Wilson? He knew her. Well, he knew *of* her. He'd seen her around the hospital quite a bit since he'd started his residency. She always seemed a hard worker, with a vibrant smile and a "can do" attitude. He had not had a chance to actually talk with her, since it seemed she was always busy—always running from one room to another—but he had definitely noticed her beauty and her charm as she had helped with a few of his patients.

As he listened to her heart and lungs for himself, he examined her for signs of injury. Her color was pale. There was significant bruising under her eyes and behind her ears, and blood trailed into her reddish blond hair from a gash on her forehead. "What happened?" he asked the paramedic, as he lifted her eyelids and shone a light into her eyes. Nothing.

"Drove her car off the side of the road into the Hudson River,

Doc. Head hit the windshield on impact with the water."

The doctor's brow crinkled in surprise. "Let's get a tox screen and call radiology. We're going to need a CT scan of the brain stat." The doctor's face took on a look of concern as he wrote his orders on her chart. "Any next of kin?"

"Police ran her vehicle registration. Lives in Midtown—apparently with a Jake Trudeau. They contacted him and told him we were bringing her here."

"Good," the doctor said nodding, all the while still looking at his patient with concern. "Alert the OR," he said to the nurse. "Depending on what the CT shows, we may need to go in and relieve some pressure."

"Yes, Doctor," the nurse said, as she went to the desk to start scheduling the ordered tests.

The doctor walked over to the shelf of supplies behind him, pulled on a pair of gloves, and grabbed some antiseptic and gauze. He carefully began to clean the wound on her forehead, assessing the need for stitches. She looked so fragile, so frail, so different from the way she had looked when he had seen her on the floor with patients just earlier today. True, she had seemed maybe a bit under the weather then, but still so full of life compared to this. He reached out and took her hand in his. It was cold through his gloves, yet for some reason, he was compelled to squeeze it gently, as he promised, "We're going to get you better, Miss Wilson. I promise."

3 ANGELS OF MERCY

"Where am I?" The intruder repeated, looking frantically around her. "What is this place? Who… who are *you*?"

"Who am *I* Mademoiselle?" Erik repeated her question with raised eyebrow. "I am the owner of *this place* so I believe the better question is who are *you*?"

"I…" she began, still surveying her surroundings in a panic, "I…Where *am* I? How did I get here?"

Erik sighed in exasperation. First the Persian arriving uninvited, and then the wild ravings of this hysterical woman—would this day never cease in its irritations? "You are in *my* domicile, Mademoiselle, and as to *how* you accomplished entry, it would be in your best interest if you would quickly enlighten us as to your methods."

Omid glanced with incredulity at his friend, and then at the girl, whose eyes merely blinked in utter bewilderment at Erik's statement. Kneeling down, so that he was at eye level with the girl, and taking a deep breath, Omid began. "What my friend was trying to say," he ignored the disgusted grunt that Erik released at hearing word *friend*, "is that this is his home, and he was wondering how *you* managed to get in, since not many can find the entrance unaided."

The girl looked down, and took a few deep breaths herself, blinking her eyes several times, as if trying to awaken from some bizarre dream. When she realized her surroundings hadn't changed she began, slowly, "I…I am not entirely sure. I was driving…and it was raining…and I saw lights, and then…" her breathing quickened, and she shut her eyes tightly "The river. Oh God, I drove into the river." She covered her eyes with her hands and shook her head back and forth.

With narrowed eyes, Omid sought to confirm what she just said, "You drove a buggy into the Seine?" He suddenly started looking around, and Erik glared at him when he heard the Persian ask, "Where's the horse?"

The girl looked up and met his gaze as if *he* were the lunatic. "NO!" her voice raised in consternation, "I drove my Chevy into the Hudson!"

Erik and Omid's eyes met with guarded expressions. This girl was undoubtedly an escapee from the asylum. It was obvious, simply by her attire—a loose fitting shirt and trousers which were filthy, torn and damp. Her words, however, made it abundantly clear that she was not firmly entrenched in reality. It had not rained in Paris for days and where on earth was the Hudson? It was certainly *not* in Paris—was it even in France? Women did not drive, and certainly not some strange… *thing*… called a Chevy. And yet, she did not appear to be a threat of any sort. She looked weak, and helpless, and *terrified.*

"Oooooh," they heard the girl's dismayed groan, as she looked at her trembling hands for the first time, "I'm bleeding."

And she was obviously hurt.

Erik sighed with an irritated huff, and walked over to the girl. "Come," he said, leaning over to take her hand, "we must tend to your wounds." Erik pulled on the girl's hand in an effort to help her up, but as she tried to rise, she stumbled, her eyes starting to flutter, and Erik could tell that she was about to fall. "Owww! My ankle," she moaned loudly, "my *head*." Quickly, he reached out to steady her, placing his hands on her shoulders. Realizing that his sitting room was much too far a walk, if merely standing up made her dizzy, Erik grudgingly lifted the girl into his arms, and carried her toward the Louis XVI-style sofa, instructing Omid to grab a throw to toss over it. Silently lamenting to himself that it could not be helped, he placed her wet, grimy person on the settee lengthwise, so that her offending ankle could be elevated.

He knelt beside her, and examined her head. There was a great deal of blood, but the wound would have to be cleaned before he could tell how bad it was. Judging by her dizziness a few moments prior, he assumed it was at least moderately severe.

Erik rose and commanded Omid to stay with her as he went to the kitchen to fetch a basin that he filled with soapy water and a sponge. Upon his return, Erik dipped the sponge into the warm soapy water and wiped the girl's brow free of the grime and blood that had so marred it, carefully assessing the severity of the cut as he did so. It was several moments before he realized that his visitor was looking at him intently.

"Has no one told you that it is rude to stare?" He inquired, not meeting her gaze, but focusing his eyes on the gaping laceration on her head. Now that it was clean, Erik could tell that the cut was not overly large, but would indeed require stitches to heal properly, as it was already beginning to bleed again.

"I'm sorry, I…" the girl spoke quietly, still staring at him. "I was just looking at your mask."

"Daroga," he called sharply to the Persian who was watching over him intently. "Come, make yourself useful." When Omid knelt down next to Erik, he noticed a defensive set to Erik's jaw, and Omid knew the girl had done the worst thing she could possibly have done by drawing attention to his mask. Still, Erik put a few pieces of clean linen into the Persian's flustered hand and then pressed his hand to the girl's forehead, looking at Omid, but not the girl. "Now, hold this here and apply pressure to the wound until I return."

"I can do that myself," She protested. "I'm a nurse…"

"Well then," Erik said, deciding to simply indulge her delusions to move this process along, "*As* a nurse, you are aware that we must avoid the risk of infection. And as your hands are still…" his nose wrinkled in disgust, "filthy, you must allow the Persian to do as I instructed. Last I checked," he added dryly, "He didn't make a habit of biting."

Omid glared at Erik as he rose from the floor and exited the room with a huff, but he did as he had been commanded, turning back to the girl and offering a sheepish smile. Upon his return, Erik was carrying a needle and a length of thick black thread.

The girl's eyes widened in fear. "What is that for?" she asked, her voice rising about an octave in pitch.

"Again, Mademoiselle," Erik huffed "As a *nurse*, you must recognize that a wound of such a gaping nature would require closing."

If possible, her eyes grew even wider. "And *you're* going to close it?" she shrieked.

"Well, I would allow the Persian, but he hates the sight of blood," Erik returned dryly, glancing at Omid as he pulled the thick black thread through the needle's eye.

"Wait! You have to sterilize the… " her voice trailed off as Erik held the tip of the needle in the flame of a candle for a few moments, meeting her eyes.

"I know," he said, simply, drawing close to inspect the wound once more. Erik removed the linen Omid had pressed to the wound in his absence. The bleeding had already begun to abate, but the skin still gaped, so Erik readied himself to lay in the first stitch.

"This *will* hurt, Mademoiselle," Erik informed her in a soft tone that might have been meant to be soothing.

"I know," she practically whimpered, closing her eyes once again and trying hard not to flinch.

"Would you at least like some cognac, Mademoiselle?" Omid offered, once again, displaying his maddening familiarity with Erik's belongings. When she nodded, Omid took two glasses from the small wooden liquor cabinet Erik kept and poured some of the deep amber liquid into each of them. He handed one glass to the girl and kept one for himself, immediately tossing his head back and drinking deeply. Erik shook his head back and forth at the Persian's sheer audacity and vowed to add a lock to the cabinet at his first convenience. But he was pleased when the girl also drank, and then placed the glass on the little side table next to the settee. At least *that* was a good idea on the Persian's part.

Erik turned his attention back to the wound. As he touched the needle to her skin, he could see her hand squeezing tightly on the arm of the settee and he realized she was trying to remain brave in the face of the pain. As he worked, he tried to engage her in conversation, to distract her from the discomfort.

"So you never answered my question, Mademoiselle," he began in a velvety tone.

"Which one…OW!" She could not suppress a yelp at the sting of the needle. "Was that?"

"The question of how you got here," he murmured softly, choosing to overlook her little shriek. "*Beyond* jumping into the river, that is." He began to hum quietly as he continued to sew up her wound, waiting for her answer.

"I…I don't know, exactly," she answered, only wincing slightly, as he worked. "I remember driving into the river, and then, somehow, suddenly I was walking in this… tunnel? I don't know…it was dark. And at the end of the tunnel, there was a… door." She opened her eyes once more and looked at him. "When I walked through the door, I was there by the lake, where you found me. I heard the door slam behind me, but when I turned to go back, I tripped and twisted my ankle, and that's when you came."

Erik looked at her silently a moment longer. "You walked through a door right there, by the lake?"

"Yes. The one right behind where you found me."

"Hmmm," Erik responded, assessing her answer. "And how far did you walk before you tripped?"

"I had only walked about two or three steps away from the door before I heard it slam." She watched him nod silently before asking him, "Why?"

"Well, because, Mademoiselle," Erik told her, calmly trying to keep his voice velvety soft, "in the precise location where we found you, there *is* no door."

"It has been a long time since I have seen you act as an Angel of Mercy, Erik," Omid spoke quietly, as Erik washed his hands. Omid had been enthralled by Erik's ministrations to the girl, who was now resting, comfortably on the settee. It reminded him so much of when Erik had cared for his own poor Aziz before he had succumbed to the illness which had first claimed his mother.

"I would greatly appreciate it if you kept this to yourself," Erik said, drying his hands with a kitchen towel. "I have a reputation to uphold as the Angel of Death."

The Persian chuckled a little at Erik's ever-present sarcasm, while his manner had displayed such care for his patient. "Where did you learn such skills?"

"I have always had to care for myself, Daroga," he said, replacing the towel on the hook above the counter. "Certainly there has never been anyone willing to tend *my* wounds."

Omid looked at the back of his friend's head in sincere regret for the cruelty and loneliness that had filled Erik's life and driven him to such a solitary existence. Were he simply shown a bit of kindness in the face of his bizarre disfigurement, the gifts he could have bestowed upon the world were many. But time and time again, he had been confronted with man's great *inhumanity*. Erik had been abused, and then coerced into *heaping* abuse upon others. It was rare that he was ever given the opportunity to treat another human being with kindness—but apparently he had not lost the capacity. "Have you yet to discern her name, Erik?" he asked, seriously.

"No," Erik answered, in a low voice, "but I persist in my belief that she is an escapee from the asylum."

"Shall we return her?"

"And have her chained to the wall, beaten, and nearly *starved?*" Erik asked, cynically, turning to face Omid. "I know of the *methods* by which the insane are treated as well as the conditions in which they are kept. I would not subject a rabid animal to such cruelty, much less a confused girl. Does she look *that* dangerous to you?"

"Well, *no*, but what shall we *do* with her?" Omid asked, confused.

"*We* shall do nothing, Daroga," Erik asserted. "*I* shall allow her to convalesce on my settee until such time that I can decide the best course of action."

Omid smirked. "Maybe she can dance! Madame Giry is always looking for new ballet rats. Didn't you say they got a new arrival just today?"

Erik was reminded of the ethereal beauty he had spied in the chapel—so alone, so afraid. How he wished he could see her again. How he longed to stroke her cheek and whisper to her that she was not alone—that *he* was with her. But no—it was not for monsters to commune with angels. He was destined to be eternally alone.

As the thought entered Erik's mind, a rueful smirk spread across his face, for at the moment, he was *not* alone. No, presently, he was burdened with an annoying Daroga in his kitchen and an unidentified mental patient on his sofa. He sighed and shook his head, wondering what he did to deserve this day.

"Has anyone come to see Miss Wilson yet?" the doctor asked a passing nurse, as he tied off the last of his patient's stitches and applied gauze to cover the wound. The CT scan results were not as severe as he had feared, and he was hopeful that Jenna would wake soon. There appeared to be no reason for pressure-relieving surgery, so he placed the stitches to close her wound. He had been certain that by the time he was done, there would be a frantic boyfriend begging to see her. In truth, he had hoped for it—it was widely believed that coma patients were aware of what was happening to them on some level, and sometimes it was the voice of a loved one, or a comforting touch, that was that final push they needed to be coaxed awake.

"No, Doctor," the nurse informed him. "When we tried to call upon her admission, the boyfriend asked about her condition and said that he'd stop by in the morning—that he has early shift anyway."

The doctor was taken aback, by what seemed to be a rather callous way to feel about a woman with whom one *resided.* But instead, he simply asked the nurse, "Oh, does he work here too?"

"Yeah, he's a physical therapist. That's how they met. Of course, if you ask me, he's a little too friendly with *all* the nurses, if you know what I mean."

The doctor's eyes narrowed and he nodded. "I see. Thank you, Maxine."

"You're welcome." She left with a smile.

The doctor turned back to his patient and gazed at her quietly for a few moments longer. With her wound cleaned and dressed, she looked much better than she had when she came in, but she was still so frail and so…alone. It was 7 a.m., the end of his shift, and he was exhausted. He had to work again that night, so he knew he needed to get home and get some sleep, but a part of him did not want to leave her there with no one on her side.

He reached out and took her hand again in his. "I have to go home now, Miss Wilson. But I promise I'll come see you later. By that time, I bet you'll be in a room of your own. You rest, and work real hard on waking up for me, alright?" He smiled at her, even though her eyes were closed, and squeezed her hand once before leaving her side.

4 WHAT IS THIS PLACE

Jenna's head was swimming. A voice was saying her name, and there was pressure on her hand. Unfocused light and colors floated before her eyes—blues, browns and greens—too blurry for her to distinguish. She was close enough that if she just reached out, she could almost touch…

Her eyes fluttered open at the call of a song, and she was in yet another dream world, but this one was in focus. The warm glow of candlelight danced all around her, casting soft shadows on cold stone walls and rich wooden furniture. She was lying on an old fashioned couch in some type of fancy parlor, a soft throw draped over her legs. The floor was covered with a Persian style rug, richly patterned in red and black and gold. Before her, a stone hearth, filled with warm, dancing flames, was flanked on the left by a small dining table, with four chairs, and on the right by a tall bookcase, just bursting with hardback volumes and stacks of loose paper. A rich burgundy leather reading chair sat between the bookshelf and the settee, and a black grand piano presided over the other half of the room. Seated at it, playing a lush, rich melody, was a man.

He was impeccably dressed in a white button down shirt and black slacks. His hair was dark, a few clumps falling forward over his …*mask*? Yes, he was wearing a mask. A smooth white mask which covered only half his face.

Suddenly, a rush of memories came back to her. The accident—her car going into the water—the certainty that she was going to die—the long, dark corridor with the old wooden door—the two men discovering her—the man in the mask, carrying her back to this room, cleaning her face, humming to her as he stitched her wounds. He had seemed a little perturbed when he first found her, but he had shown her nothing but kindness and gentleness when he was tending to her injuries. But who *was* he? And why was his mask so *familiar*?

Erik's eyes peeked over the piano's open lid as the girl awoke. He watched her take in her surroundings, her eyes darting all about. When her gaze finally fell on him, he saw her flinch. He felt a sardonic smirk appear on his face. He was well acquainted with looks fear being directed toward his person—it was the standard first reaction to his presence. And why should it not be? He was, after all, a monster. He took a deep breath and sighed.

"Good evening, Mademoiselle," Erik said, by way of greeting as he ended his song.

"Where am I?" she asked again.

Erik rolled his eyes and said, "Again, Mademoiselle, we have already established that you are in my home." As he watched her, she lifted a hand to the stitches in her head, a look of recollection seeming to wash over her features, and he was relieved that he did not need to add amnesia to her symptoms of dementia. "Does your head hurt?" he asked.

"It's a little foggy," she admitted, nodding her head gingerly. When Erik saw her wince, she added, "And a little achy." She looked at him hopefully, "Do you have any Tylenol or Motrin?"

Erik raised an eyebrow at her, realizing that the rest had done nothing to improve her delusional state. "No Mademoiselle. I do not."

She looked down in disappointment, holding her head in her hands.

"Am I dead?" she croaked, not certain that anything she was seeing before her was real.

Erik's brow wrinkled in surprise at her question. "Do you think your head would hurt so much if you were?"The girl shook her head, wincing again. "It might, if I were in hell," she groaned.

Erik smirked again, in ironic amusement. "Though I have often felt as if I *were* residing in hell, I assure you, Mademoiselle, that you live." Erik watched her, and realized she needed something to lessen the pain she still felt in her head. Following Omid's lead from earlier, he crossed over to his liquor cabinet and poured her another glass of cognac. "Here," He said, unceremoniously handing her the brandy. "This should help dull the pain."

The girl took the glass from him cautiously, trying to determine his intentions, meeting his gaze, for the first time. It was then that she noticed his eyes were of two different colors. The right eye, peeking out from behind his mask, was a striking, icy blue, the left one a brown so rich, she felt as if she could see forever in its depths.

When Erik felt her gaze lingered a little too long on his mask, he turned away and walked over to his reading chair. She was going to *have* to learn to stop staring!

"So, where *is* this place?" she asked again, in a shaky voice as she took a small sip of the liquor. She raised a hand as if to stop him from interrupting when she saw him let out yet another frustrated sigh, which seemed to be his favorite way of dealing with her questions. "I *know* it's your home. But, really, *where* are we?"

"We are in Paris, Mademoiselle," Erik supplied simply, not willing to divulge the full details of his home's location.

"Paris?" she asked, a look of shock on her face. "That's impossible!" She felt a knot form in the pit of her stomach. Obviously, her night had just gone from bad to worse. Regardless of his beautiful "home," and his intriguing eyes, this man must be some kind of loon who had delusions of New York being a grandiose European city.

"I assure you, Mademoiselle, that we are, in fact, in Paris."

"If we are in Paris, Sir," she asked, not able to stop herself from trying to make him see reason, "why are we not speaking French?"

Erik looked at her quizzically for a moment. "Mademoiselle, we *are* speaking French," he informed her—in perfect French.

"What?" she asked incredulously, her voice rising a bit, "*Of course* we're not speaking French. I don't even know *how* to speak French."

Erik sighed deeply once again, running his hands through his hair. Where was that blasted Persian when he needed him? It seemed he could never be rid of the Daroga when he didn't want him around, but now, when he had a lunatic houseguest, the man could not have taken his leave fast enough. While he was grateful to have finally found some method of deterring unwanted Persians, what he really needed right now was some help.

"Well, Mademoiselle, if we are not speaking French," Erik asked in his most long suffering voice, "what language are we speaking?"

"Eng-lish," she said slowly, as if she were speaking to a child.

Erik tried his hardest to hold on to his last shards of patience, but they were leaving him quickly. "Mademoiselle, I speak English quite fluently, and you, are *not* speaking it."

"You really *are* crazy," she said in a soft voice while staring at him intently.

"*I'm* crazy?" Erik snapped, at the end of his patience. "You are the one who has obviously escaped from the mental asylum! Just look at the way you're dressed!" he threw a hand out, pointing to her scrubs.

"Ok," she nodded simply with a smile, placating him, not wanting to upset his fantasy for fear that he might become angry. Or violent. Of course, he had to be crazy, she thought. What other kind of man goes around wearing a mask? Unless he didn't want his identity known because he was some kind of criminal. "Listen," she began, in a sickeningly sweet voice, looking around the room once more, "Can I use your...um... cell?" She didn't care what had just gone down with Jake. He was *going* to come get her out of this mess, even if it was the last time they ever saw one another. After all, it was his fault she was stuck here in the first place.

"Cell, Mademoiselle?" Erik raised an eyebrow. "I'm sorry, I don't know what you're talking about."

A look of worry entered her eyes. "Your *cellphone*," she repeated, her voice rising slightly. "I just want to call my boyfriend"—could she still use that term for Jake?— "to come get me out of here.

"Mademoiselle," Erik began calmly, putting on the pretense of a smile, but realizing that that was probably not the most comforting expression, given his mask, "I do not know what a cell phone *is*, and I certainly do not have one myself." Maybe dealing with a mental patient was going to prove more difficult than Erik had expected.

"Look," she began, her voice rising slightly again as a panic slowly seeped into her veins, "you can't keep me here against my will by pretending you don't have a phone!"

She shifted on the settee, and began to push herself off. Her ankle giving out from under her, she landed on her knees, a moment later, with a howl of pain.

Erik stood before her, looking down where she remained heaped on the rug, his arms folded across his chest, "By all means, Mademoiselle, you are free to leave whenever you wish." When she looked up at him, he waved a hand in the direction of the cavern in which he had found her, a smug look across his face.

She took her own deep breath. She was getting annoyed with this stranger's attitude, as well as her own body's refusal to cooperate. "Look, if you don't want me to use *your* cell, can you just give me my purse? I'll use my iPhone."

"You were not carrying any purse when you arrived, *uninvited*, in my home, Mademoiselle," he spat the words out at her, irritated at her brazen demeanor. "Perhaps it is still floating in the Hudson—along with your *Chevy*—or failing that, it may be lying in the *tunnel* which you say you traversed to get here." He could feel that his brow was wrinkled in annoyance. He felt obligated to help this injured girl, but he was finding that he tolerated her much better when she was silent.

At his mention of the tunnel, she recalled the passageway that had led to that strange door. It had been long and dark, cool and damp. She remembered wrapping her arms around herself to block out the cold. The corridor had seemed to go on forever, but finally, at the end she had seen a door. It was a simple door, made of wood, curved at the top. She could finally make out some light glowing between the boards, and when she reached its threshold, she eagerly grasped the old black door handle and turned.

The door had opened easily before her, and she found herself in a cavern. The light she thought she had seen through the slats of wood was softer and more distant than she imagined it would be. She had tried to walk toward it, but she tripped on something and twisted her ankle just as she heard the door slam shut behind her. It had not seemed like such a simple door would have been able to make such a loud sound, but the crash of its closing echoed through the cavern. And that was when the two men had found her.

Had she somehow gotten into the subway system? She knew the urban legends about secret tunnels and abandoned stations that were no longer used, but as she looked at her surroundings, she could hardly imagine that such an elaborate dwelling could exist under the streets of New York. And if they *were* beneath the city, where were the rats?

"I just want to go *home*!" she insisted, forcefully.

"Well, if you would simply tell me your *name*," the masked man said in exasperation, "it might be easier to get you to your home."

"My *name* is Genevieve," the girl spat out.

"Genevieve…" the man repeated, in a hushed, silvery tone. It was, surprisingly, a beautiful name, and he let the syllables play slowly upon his lips.

"Yes, Genevieve Wilson," she repeated, feeling slightly self-conscious. "But I usually go by Jenna. Who are *you*?"

"I am Erik," he said, a tight smile spreading across his lips in the face of this girl's impudence. Despite her lovely name, suddenly, getting her *home* sounded like a very good idea. Surely the asylum would capture her again, but at least she would have a chance. "Where do you live?"

Jenna looked down, remembering the scene that had transpired before she went out for her ill-fated drive. "I don't even know anymore," she said, sadly, covering her head in her hands. Erik watched her silently. For all of her irritating tendencies, she seemed so very troubled about something.

He raked his hand through his hair and sighed. How had he gotten himself into this? Was he not the dreaded Angel of Death, who had tortured and executed so many poor souls in Persia? Was he not the mighty Phantom of the Opera, who could strike fear into incompetent managers with a simple note or cause a stir among superstitious ballerinas with a quiet "boo"? How did *he* manage to find himself in the role of nursemaid to an ill mannered mental patient who babbled mindlessly about such non-sensible things like *cellphones*, or *Tylenol*, and who thought she had driven into a river which didn't exist and walked through a door that wasn't there? Her head and her ankle were obviously damaged, and needed time to heal, not to mention the questionable state of her mental faculties, but that was *not* his problem.

Of course, *none* of this was his problem. In fact, the few unfortunate fools who had entered his lair uninvited were usually met with a very unpleasant welcome in one of the many traps he had set to defend his home. Ultimately, this girl was nothing more than an interloper—a trespasser on his property. He had every right to treat her as such. And yet, he found that he couldn't. He knew it went back to his inability to abide innocence suffering needlessly. But up until this point, that had meant he would occasionally set a bird's broken wing, share a scrap of food with a hungry cat…put a final end to the torment of a prisoner begging him for mercy with tortured eyes. As he looked at the girl once again, he remembered that though he was far from innocent, he himself knew how it felt to be damaged.

After a moment, he reached out a hand to her, which she grudgingly took. He helped her up and settled her back onto the settee.

"Thank you," she said, grateful to be off the cold floor. She looked up at him and continued, "I live in Midtown Manhattan. If you could just tell me how to get there from here, I can be on my way."

"Mademoiselle Wilson," Erik began, trying hard to keep his voice calm and his tone patient. "The only Manhattan I know is in New York."

"Yes, that's right," she nodded

"In *America*," he said the second word very slowly, as if hoping some type of grand revelation about that fact would sink in to her addled brain.

"Yes, of course," she answered in exasperation. For the first time since high school, she was tempted to add a well-placed "duuuuh!" to the end of her phrase.

"Mademoiselle," he informed her, sounding exhausted, "that is an ocean away."

"Miss Wilson," the doctor said in a cheerful voice, as he entered her room. Since his last shift, Jenna had been moved out of the ER and into her own room. Based on the scan results from last night, he had hoped for at least some improvement in her condition. There was no reaction, however, when he called her name, and with a concerned look crossing his brow, he took a glance at her chart. The tox screen had come back clean, showing no evidence of any drugs or alcohol in her system. The nurses had noted no change in her condition over the last shift.

He approached her bed and once again examined her pupils with a penlight. There was no tracking, no reaction whatsoever. He sighed, "Miss Wilson," he began, sitting down at the corner of her bed. "Are you *still* resting?" he asked, taking her hand once again in his and squeezing. "Can you feel that, Miss Wilson?" Once again, there was no response, but he continued anyway. "It's a beautiful day outside. The rain has stopped, and the sun is shining in through your window. Can you hear the birds singing?" He looked toward the window and smiled. "In fact, there are two little birds hopping around out there, right on your windowsill. They're quite funny." He chuckled a little and looked at her once more. "You should really wake up to see them yourself." She lay there, still not moving, still not reacting.

He could not believe that he had never spoken with her before her accident happened. Yes, they had had brief exchanges when they shared a common patient, but nothing more riveting than medication levels and lab results. He wished he knew what kind of music she liked, or the title of her favorite book. These details might help to draw her out of her coma and speed her recovery. He had a sudden memory of her aqua colored eyes, and the way they flashed when she smiled. He wished he could see them again right now, as her lids lifted from their heavy slumber. Would he ever again get to hear her bell like peals of laughter ringing out from the break room as she quickly grabbed lunch with her co-workers? She had always seemed so confident and vibrant, and so full of life. He had been meaning to introduce himself. Would he still have the chance?

He sighed in exasperation at himself and squeezed her hand once more, promising to see her again later. Rising, he replaced the chart in its holder at the foot of the bed, and made his way to the nurse's station. "Mrs. Richards?" he called out to the nurse in charge of Jenna's case.

"Yes, Doctor?"

"Has Miss Wilson had any visitors today?" he asked hopefully.

"Well, a number of her co-workers from the 5th floor came by earlier," she chuckled kindly to herself, adding, "They all love her up there."

The Doctor smiled, and nodded. "That's great. What about her boyfriend?" he asked. "Has he been in to see her yet?"

A look of disgust washed over the kind nurse's face. "Oh, yeah, he was here this morning—for all of five minutes. Came in, asked us how she was doing, went into the room, like I said, for about five minutes, and then left again, to start his shift. Said he'd be back later, but I haven't seen him since." She rolled her eyes and gave an indignant huff.

"Hmmmm." The doctor considered that information. "And he works here, right, Mrs. Richards?"

"Oh yeah. He's in physical therapy. That's how they met," she said, shaking her head.

"I see. Would you happen to know his name?"

"It's Jake. Jake Trudeau."

"Thank you, Mrs. Richards." He smiled at her warmly before he walked toward the elevators. "Take good care of her. I'll be back later."

"I know *you* will!" the nurse answered, before continuing on her rounds.

5 CELESTIAL ASPIRATIONS

Erik silently crept through the passage behind the costumery. This was an area of the opera house he had never thought he would need to traverse, but his resident mental patient had now made it a necessity. She had expressed an inclination to wash herself, and while he greatly approved of her desire for cleanliness, the clothes she was now wearing were fit only for a fire. Re-dressing in such grimy attire would simply defeat any purpose of bathing in the first place. And so, after hopefully convincing his guest that she would simply not be able to swim all the way back "home" to Manhattan, and getting her settled back on the settee with a book and a bite to eat, Erik departed to find some clothing that would be suitable for her to wear for the remainder of her convalescence.

He slipped into the room through a small opening behind the clothing racks. There he found rows and rows of dresses, some of them duplicates, from which he could choose. It occurred to him that he had no idea as to what Mademoiselle Wilson's size was. He knew she was taller than most of the ballerinas who graced the stage—though still shorter than him by about a head—and she did not seem to be quite so rail thin as the ballet rats either. That was fine, he thought, as he was not looking to dress her in a tutu. Perhaps though, he reasoned, he should choose slightly larger sizes, as she could simply cinch the dress if it was too big on her. Erik was quietly going through the dresses, holding a few up to himself, to gauge the length against his own height, when he heard the door open and then slam shut. He crouched low, and peered through the racks of dresses, not breathing, to determine who had entered the room.

He saw the bright red frizzled hair of Carlotta Giudicelli, the opera house's Prima Donna. She was carrying a dress in one hand, and she was dragging along a smaller, hapless girl with the other.

"I need this gown mended in half an hour, *little toad*!" she bellowed, continuing her tirade in her native Italian.

"It shall be done, Madame," the girl responded, looking to the floor. Erik looked at the girl more closely, at the familiar sound of her dejected voice. It was his angel—the one he had found in the chapel—that this cow of a diva was so mistreating. Erik's blood boiled as he saw the miserable woman toss both the girl, and the dress to the ground.

"See to it, that it *is* done, and done *right* this time!" she demanded in a huff, and turned on her heel to leave. "And return it to me—in half an hour and not one moment later!" She left the room with a flourish, and Erik curled his fingers into a fist to keep himself from wrapping them around her miserable neck.

Believing herself to be alone, the girl wiped a few stray tears from her eyes before gathering herself and the gown up from the floor and moving over to one of the sewing machines. She was garbed in gray working attire, and her glorious chestnut curls were tied back from her face with a black ribbon. A few errant curls, however, escaped the ribbon, and Erik had an almost uncontrollable urge to brush them away from her face. She sniffled a bit as her hands separated the layers of the dress, apparently searching for the tear, and Erik's heart blackened with thoughts of the Italian diva. The Phantom was going to have to pay *her* a visit very shortly.

As the sewing machine whirred to life, Erik heard his angel begin to hum. He listened to the soft, sweet melody, and could not suppress a smile when her humming turned to singing.

I once heard the tale of an angel
Oh, how I wish he'd appear

Her voice was soft and youthful, and yet so clear and pure. There were no pretenses in its character, no flourishes, just a simple, clear tone, and a sweet, innocent delivery. Erik wondered how she would sound singing an aria; certainly, she would be a breath of fresh air after the highly dramatic strainings of La Carlotta, whose theatrical flairs and heavy vibrato did little to disguise a voice that was harsh in tone, and lacking in precision.

And with his wings, soft and gentle,
Take me far from here…

He heard her singing trail off, and once again, his angel was speaking to the air around her.

"Oh, Papa," she sighed, still sewing the sow's ugly dress, "will you *ever* send me the Angel of Music? Will he ever allow my song to take flight and lift me out of here? I *hate* it here so much, Papa. This is not my home. I long for *our* home, where I could sing, and dance, and you would play…Oh Papa, *why* did you have to leave me?" She looked down at the dress, as once again, tears began to fall.

Her plaintive words once more pierced Erik's heart. She should not cry. She was all that was beauty, and sweetness and light, and tears did not become her. He wished, once again, that there was something he could do—that there was some way he could comfort her. But how? She cried for a father whom he did not know. She cried about her miserable state of existence that he could not change. She cried for an angel whom he could not produce. An angel of music.

Erik's breath caught within his chest. Perhaps he *could* produce that angel. What was an angel, after all, except an incorporeal being who was sensed, but not seen? And what would an angel of *music* do? She'd said it herself. An angel of music would make her song take flight, and lift her out of her current existence. And how could one do that? By teaching her the proper way to sing!

Had he not himself just been moved by the purity and the clarity of her voice? Had he not wondered how she would sound singing an aria on the opera stage? She would never do that, if she did not receive proper training, but how could she ever *hope* to achieve that training while working as a seamstress for a bovine like La Carlotta?

He could teach her. Music had been his first and only love from the time he was a child. It had wiped away his every tear, caressed his every heartache. He had become a virtuoso on any instrument he had ever attempted to learn. His singing had long been able to enchant those who had been blessed—or cursed—enough to hear it. He had nearly driven his own wicked mother out of her mind with his voice. These thoughts were not conceit on his part, but merely facts that he knew to be true.

His thoughts raced with how *he* could become her angel of music. He could remain hidden, behind the wall, and speak to her. She would never have to see him, and know that in truth, her angel was more like the devil himself. No, he could *teach* her in kind, encouraging utterances, and build her voice to the greatness of which he knew she was capable. In so doing, he *could* lift her out of her wretched state, only for her to alight again as the First Lady of the Stage, eclipsing that sorry excuse for a singer Carlotta in the role. He *could* do this for her, and then perhaps the tears she cried would be tears of joy, no more of sorrow. Perhaps by being *her* angel, he could help *his* angel to find her wings.

Once again, Erik heard the door to the costumery open. "Christine!" he heard the little blond ballerina, Meg Giry, call as she entered the room. "Christine. La Carlotta is on the stage *bellowing* about her gown."

Fitting Erik thought. Cows *do* bellow.

"Already?" his angel asked, shaking her head. "It has not even been the half hour she demanded."

"You *know* she is unreasonable," Meg answered. "Is it done?"

"Only just," his angel returned, tying off the thread that had made the repairs, and liberating the gown from the sewing machine.

"Well, come on, then, Christine, let's go," Meg asserting, grabbing onto her hand and urging her toward the door. "We don't want to keep the *diva* waiting." They exited the room in a rush, closing the door behind them.

Erik released the breath he had been holding as he'd watched the two girls leave. "Christine," he said in a throaty whisper, and never had a word sounded so sweet on his lips.

He hastily grabbed the few gowns he had chosen for Miss Wilson as he turned to go with a flourish of his cape. He was giddy to get back to his home and deliver the gowns, knowing now what he could do to help his angel, and he chuckled darkly when he thought of the other delivery he would soon be making.

❧

The elevator stopped at the 8th floor, and the doors opened out into the physical therapy department. The young doctor made a quick visit to the desk to inquire whether Jake Trudeau was still in. He was directed to the employee lounge, where, apparently, Mr. Trudeau was just getting ready to clock out for the day.

"Mr. Trudeau?" The doctor called to the shorter blond man who was standing at his locker.

His head shot around as he slammed the locker door, and he looked over at the doctor before saying, "Yeah, Doc? What can I do for you? I'm about to clock out, though, so unless it's urgent, can it wait 'till tomorrow?

"It's not about work," the doctor said, extending his hand to the lab tech, who shook it warily, "It's about Miss Wilson. I'm her doctor."

"Oh, yeah," the man said, chuckling a bit nervously. "Hi, how are ya?"

"I'm fine," the doctor returned with a tight smile. "But Miss Wilson could be better." When the blond man said nothing in return, the doctor continued, "I know it must be difficult for you to see her like this, Mr. Trudeau, but coma patients can greatly benefit from the support of loved ones. I was hoping you could come by and spend some time with her on your way out tonight. I'd like to talk with you about some things you might be able to do to encourage her to wake up."

The man's face contorted in a regretful expression, "Ah, Doc, I'd love to, but you see, I've got plans right after work, and I don't really have time to stop by right now."

The doctor looked at the man, taken a little aback. "Your girlfriend is right downstairs in a coma, and you don't have the time to *stop by* and see her?"

"Look," the man said, a little defensively, "I don't know what you think you know about our relationship…."

The doctor's eyes narrowed suspiciously, as he cut him off "I know that you live together."

"Well, we *did*."

"You *did*?" he asked, eyebrow raised. "What is *that* supposed to mean?"

"We did live together, but I'm pretty sure Jenna was going to change that…you know how it is…" he said, chuckling nervously.

"No," the doctor said, looking down to meet his eyes with a sharp look. "I don't."

"Oh well," the man's face reddened a bit, in embarrassment, "it didn't exactly end well, if you know what I mean."

"No," the doctor said again, still holding the man's gaze, his jaw set in a taut expression. "What, precisely, *do* you mean?"

"Well, she…she didn't exactly take it well."

The doctor was getting very tired of Mr. Trudeau's hemming and hawing. "She became upset when you informed her you wanted to end your relationship?" He told himself that only reason he was continuing to waste breath on this loser because this could be important in explaining Jenna's mental state leading up to the accident.

"Well, I…" the man began again, haltingly. "I didn't exactly tell her."

He tried to remain professional—he really did—but knowing that Jenna was lying comatose in a hospital bed while this sorry excuse of a *boyfriend* was having such a hard time finding words to express himself was making it truly difficult. His voice raised a little as he said, "Mr. Trudeau, will you *kindly* tell me *what* exactly happened?"

"She, uh…" the man began, looking away from the doctor's withering gaze. "She walked in on me and Mindy…while we were…uh…" Jake allowed his sentence to trail off.

The physician's gaze turned to one of disgust as understanding dawned on him. He raked his hand through his hair in aggravation looking at Trudeau with disdain. It was all he could do to keep himself from punching the fool, but instead, he paced a little back and forth before asking, "Was this right before she had her accident?"

"Yeah," Jake answered. "So she may not exactly want to see me right about now."

"Oh, really," he snapped, sarcastically, "Would you blame her?"

"Hey Doc," Jake began, defensively. "What's any of this to you, huh? How is it any of your business?"

"Miss Wilson is my patient. *That* makes all of this my business," he said, angrily, looming over Trudeau. "I've done all the tests, and I cannot find any good medical reason why she is not waking up. I need to find a way to motivate her—to make her *want* to come back to us—and obviously, that motivation is *not* going to be you!" The doctor slammed his hand against a locker before storming away, taking the staircase instead of the elevator.

6 ALONE IN THE DARK

Jenna closed the book she was holding in her hands after having read the same paragraph about five times and still not knowing what it was about. Though the masked man had tried to make her comfortable when he stepped out, supposedly to get her some clothes, she was anything but relaxed in this strange, windowless home. Yes, for all of its elegant beauty, Jenna had finally realized the home was without windows. Absolutely no natural light made its way into the rooms, the only illumination coming from the flickering glow of candles and the flames in the fireplace. It was at once both warm and creepy, but without the company of the masked man—Erik, he'd said his name was—the balance was definitely leaning in favor of creepy. Strange that the company of an ornery masked man—who was most likely crazy as a loon—served to dispel some of the gloom of the dark surroundings, but Jenna found that without him, she could hardly stand being in this room at all.

She glanced around the room again, until her eyes fell upon the lake. When she had walked through the door into this strange place, she remembered she had been by water. If she followed the lake's path now, would it lead her back to the door? Would she be able to find her way out of this place, and somehow get home?

Jenna brought her legs around so that they touched the floor. Gingerly, she began to stand up. Her ankle screamed in pain, but she found that if she leaned most of her weight on her other leg, she was able to stand. She took a step, keeping her arms out to steady herself. Still standing. She took another one. Even though it was very uncomfortable, Jenna found that she was able to walk, as long as she favored her injured leg. Slowly, very slowly, she made her way to the lake. As she got close to the shore, she remembered to take a candle from one of the candelabras to provide some much needed light.

The flickering flame cast an eerie glow on the green water of the lake. She watched the ripples on the water as it flowed in the direction of the cavern in which she had been found. Jenna hobbled along with the lake, wondering if it was somehow fed by the Hudson. If so, she couldn't be that far from home. Certainly not in Paris!

She continued on into the cavern—the farther away she got from the little sitting room with the settee and grand piano, the more difficult the terrain. The ground was rocky and uneven, and there was less and less of it, as the lake began to widen. It was no wonder to her that she had tripped immediately upon emerging from the door, but, holding her candle out before her, and peering further into the cavern, she could not see actually *see* the door. No, the cavern seemed to go on for a while longer, until the roof of the cave just appeared to curve down into the floor, the lake slipping out a small opening in the ground to continue on its watery journey.

"No," she murmured to herself. "There was a door." She took a few more steps forward, her head beginning to throb. "There was a tunnel, then a door." Her voice began to rise, and become a little dismayed. "Where is it?" She started moving forward a little faster than she should have, groping aimlessly, searching for the door which she was sure she should have found by now. When she heard a voice echoing from the direction of the sitting room, she startled and fell, with a scream, into the lake.

Omid heard the scream and knew that someone was in the cave. "Erik!" he called, rushing toward the cavern. "Erik!" A loud splash, followed by the sounds of a water struggle and cries for help were the only answers he got. "My God!" Omid said to himself, eyes widening. "Erik is drowning the mental patient!"

Omid ran toward the sound, grabbing a lantern from Erik's table. When he found the source of the noise, he saw the girl, quite alone, splashing wildly in the water.

"Mademoiselle," he called, "Take my hand." He crouched down carefully, on the narrow lakeshore and extended his arm out to her, pulling when he felt her grab on. When she was once again on the ground, shivering and dripping wet, he put his hands on her shoulders to steady her, before asking, "Did Erik do this to you?"

The girl flinched backward a little bit, giving him a quizzical look. "NO! Why on earth would you ask that?"

"Well, I…" Omid began, but allowed his sentence to trail off. No reason to taint her opinion of Erik with his more dangerous side if she had not yet seen it. Truly, his friend *had* been doing so much better since arriving in Paris. "No reason, Mademoiselle. What *were* you doing?"

She huffed in annoyance as the man changed the subject. "I was looking for the door," she said.

"In the lake?" Omid asked, his eyes narrowed in confusion.

"No, not in the lake!" she snapped in irritation. "I was walking along the lake *shore*, looking for the door, so I could get home, and I accidentally fell in."

"Which door, Mademoiselle?" he asked, still confused.

"The door I entered through," she insisted. "Or are you going to tell me it doesn't exist too?"

"I… do not *know* of any door…"

"Oh forget it!" she huffed, wrapping her arms around herself against the chill of the cavern.

"Come, Mademoiselle," Omid said, gently nudging her in the direction of Erik's sitting room. "Let's get you back in front of the fire."

Jenna limped back toward Erik's parlor, the cold water having made walking on her bad ankle temporarily easier. When she made it back to the settee, she wrapped the throw around her now dripping form and sat back down.

"Where's Erik?" Omid asked, looking around for the masked man that only moments ago he had been so sure was committing murder.

"He said something about going to get me some clothes," Jenna replied, in irritation.

"Ah, well," Omid began with a smile, gesturing to her dripping clothes, "that will come in handy."

Jenna rolled her eyes. "I don't understand why he won't just let me go home."

Omid raised his eyebrow. He and Erik had been so convinced that this girl was an escaped mental patient, they'd never even considered the possibility that she might have a home and a family that was looking for her. "Do you live nearby, Mademoiselle?"

"Yes," she nodded, and then hesitated, "I mean I think so…"

She looked confused for a moment, and Omid felt a great wave of pity for her. "Have you told Erik?"

She huffed and the confusion on her face was replaced by irritation again. Omid smirked a little, thinking that it was fitting she should scowl at the mention of Erik's name. Everyone else did. "Yes, I told Erik!" she spat.

"And what did he say?" Omid probed.

"*He* said that we were in Paris." She rolled her eyes and shook her head.

"Well, we *are*, Mademoiselle," Omid answered, confused.

"Oh great. You too." Jenna let out a noisy sigh. "Erik sure seems to have been gone a long time," she said, pulling the blanket closer around her, and trying to huddle nearer to the fire.

"Well," Omid agreed. "He does sometimes forget himself when he goes above. But since there is no performance tonight, I am sure he will be back soon."

"Goes above?" She repeated him in confusion. "Performance? What are you talking about?"

"Mademoiselle," Omid smiled, his eyes sparkling. "Has Erik not told you *where* in Paris we are?"

"Daroga, I see you've returned." They heard a soft voice coming from the lake behind them.

Omid and Jenna turned at the sound, only to see Erik walking from the shore carrying several dresses draped over his arm. When he arrived before them, he placed the dresses on the chair and took one look at Jenna's dripping form before turning to Omid and demanding, "Were you trying to drown our guest?"

Omid held his hands up, as if in defense, beads of sweat running down his face. "Erik, I only helped her out of the lake, honestly." He reached into his pocket, grabbing his handkerchief, to wipe his brow. "I had nothing to do with how she got there in the first place."

Erik glared at Omid before turning to Jenna. "And why, Mademoiselle, were you *in* the lake?"

"I..." she stumbled a bit over her words at the intensity of his gaze, "I fell in. I was looking for the door, and I..."

"Looking for the *door*?" Erik cut her off. "Do you mean to say that you went into the cavern *alone*? With your bad ankle?"

Jenna didn't like the tone in his voice. "Yes, I went into the cavern alone. It's not like I'm some helpless...*invalid*...who can't do anything for herself."

"And yet," he pointed out with a sarcastic smile, "you fell into the lake."

"That's because it was dark and the footing was uneven—" she began defensively.

"Which is exactly why," he cut her off, his voice raising angrily, "you should not have gone into the cavern alone searching for some door that I have told you doesn't—"

"Well, *you* weren't here!" she yelled, rising from the couch, her voice as loud as his now, meeting his gaze without reservation. "I was alone and it was dark. Do you have any idea what it's like to be left alone in the dark?"

Omid was frozen as he watched the tense scene between the Erik and the girl. Once again, the mental patient had said perhaps the worst thing she could possibly have said. Erik knew better than anyone what it was like to be left alone in the dark. He had spent his entire childhood in a room with boarded-up windows, locked away by a mother who couldn't abide his face. He had spent his young adult years retreating into shadows to hide from the ridicule and derision he faced from the pointing crowds at the gypsy fair. He had risen to prominence in the courts of Persia, by imparting the most twisted forms of torment in the bleak torture chambers he was forced to design—only to fall prey himself to the blackness of addiction. And here in Paris, he had learned to take solace in the obscurity of eternal night, seeking its comfort against the garish cruelties of light.

Erik stared at her in silence for a moment. When he answered her, his voice had fallen to a hushed whisper. "Indeed, Mademoiselle. I do."

In the moment Jenna saw the shock of indistinct emotion flicker in Erik's mismatched eyes, she knew that she had said something wrong. Being alone only for a short time in the candlelight and shadows had seemed almost oppressive to her. But if this was his home, then *this* must be his life.

"Erik," she said in a penitent voice, reaching out for his hand. "I'm sorry."

Erik looked down at where her hand touched his. No one had willingly just taken his hand before. Yes, she had clasped his hand when he had helped her up, but this touch was freely given, and it felt so different. The awareness of it had almost caused him to miss the fact that she also used his name, another thing that few—other than the Daroga—ever did.

Erik cleared his throat and extricated his hand from her grasp. "Did you further aggravate your ankle, Mademoiselle, in your travels through the cavern?" he asked, still not looking at her.

Now that the cold of the lake water was wearing off, Jenna could feel her ankle beginning to ache again, but she wasn't going to complain, since she knew it was entirely her own fault. "I'm fine."

"Of course," Erik returned, and the half of his mouth that was unobstructed by the mask turned up in a small smile. "Well, since you are now dripping all over my rug, perhaps you would like to take this opportunity to enjoy that bath you had asked about and change into some dry clothing?"

Jenna felt her own mouth turn into a smile. "Yes, Erik, thank you." She hobbled over to the chair where he had left the pile of clothes, quickly going through them. After rifling through the entire pile of unfamiliar clothing, she looked up once again and asked in confusion. "Gowns and corsets? Really? Could you not *find* any jeans or t-shirts?"

Omid looked at Erik questioningly. Erik met his gaze and, shaking his head, muttered, "Mental patient."

The doctor watched as Jenna shifted and flailed in her hospital bed, even making some soft moaning sounds. He knew that sometimes coma patients experienced these involuntary movements, and that it did not mean they were any closer to waking up, but he couldn't help being hopeful. These were the first movements he had seen from Jenna since she'd come in. He would take them.

"That's right, Miss Wilson," he said, encouragingly, "Get angry. Fight your way back to us if you have to, but *do* come back to us." He watched her agitated movements a few moments more before he reached out and gently took her hand. He couldn't help but smile when she reflexively squeezed his hand and held on. Her other movements ceased, and she was peaceful once more, but she did not release his hand. He reached out with his other hand and smoothed her strawberry blond curls away from her face. "Please come back," he whispered again, as her mouth relaxed into a serene expression. "For me."

7 PLANS

Jenna eased her head back to rest against the old-fashioned, porcelain tub. A warm bath was exactly what she needed right about now to soothe her aching muscles and calm her rattled nerves. So much had happened in the last...had it really only been one day? It was so hard to tell in this place that was ever shadowy and always dark.

She thought about Jake and how he had betrayed her. How could she have been such a fool? She was always falling for the wrong kind of man—the flashy kind that made her feel like she was something special, only to use her and then dump her like yesterday's news. Did he even know about her accident? Did he even realize she was missing? Would he begin to care only when she did not return to get her things and they began to get in the way of his new girl? Would she ever be able to get out of here and retrieve her belongings? Or *Red*? He was the only male in her life who was always loyal and never betrayed her.

She allowed herself to sink deeper into the tub, wishing the water would just wash all her troubles away. But then again, it was water that had helped get her stuck in this situation in the first place. What had truly happened when she drove her car into the river? She did not remember anything after the initial splash—only that she was suddenly in that passageway leading to the door, the door that she had not been able to find, even after she had thoroughly searched the cavern where she had entered the day before—the door which everyone kept telling her simply did not exist.

Maybe she *did* die, she thought, closing her eyes. Maybe the accident *had* killed her and she was now stuck in some type of limbo where nothing was real. That would certainly explain this strange windowless house, the cold dark passageway, and the door that had disappeared.

But it did not explain Erik. Erik was real.

She began to run a soapy cloth over her arms and neck, wiping away the dirt and filth that was covering her skin. Erik was *very* real. He was somehow so familiar, almost as if he had always been a part of her life. Those thoughts were ridiculous, she knew, as she allowed water to cascade over her back, rinsing away the grime and the suds. Surely if it were true that she had known him, Erik would know *her*, and he would be able to get her home. But even though she knew he was a stranger, when she looked at him, something inside her almost…*recognized* him. Even the fact that he wore a mask did not seem incredibly unusual to her. That too was almost expected. It was if she *should* know him, but somehow, something was holding her back. Her fingers reached up and brushed the stitches on her forehead. Maybe that head injury had knocked something loose, for it was almost as if there was a physical barrier blocking any memory she might have had of Erik from before the accident. She snickered mockingly as she reached forward and rubbed the dirt from her legs. "Maybe *that's* where my door went!" she quipped to herself. "Maybe it's in my mind." She would be entirely ready to believe this whole experience *was* in her mind, if it had not been for the presence of Erik.

Jenna stopped washing as she remembered how stricken his eyes had looked when she had yelled at him about being alone in the dark. She felt a wave of guilt wash over her for that. Despite the fact that his notions were as crazy as they come, and his demeanor was a bit…ornery… he had treated her with nothing but kindness. He had closed her wound, and had seen to her comfort. He had even gotten her some clean clothes to change into—never mind his very strange choices. And if she were honest with herself, she had missed him when he was gone. Despite his sarcasm and eccentricities, like wearing a cape and not knowing what a *cellphone* was, she found his presence oddly comforting. "Sheesh!" she said to herself in disgust "Pretty quick to be developing Stockholm Syndrome."

For the truth was, she knew, as she began to rub suds into her tangled, matted hair, no matter how kind or comforting she found Erik to be, neither he nor his friend Omid had done anything to help her get home. In fact, they continued to insist that she was somehow in Paris—speaking *French* of all things! And yes, Erik had provided medical care for her wounds, but what he *should* have done was take her to a hospital! "Surely, they must have hospitals, even in France," she muttered out loud to herself. Somehow, she knew, she was going to have to find her own way to get home—and wandering around the back cavern, looking for the way she got in and almost drowning herself in the lake was obviously *not* going to work.

Maybe she should play along with Erik, she thought. Perhaps she should stop talking about getting home, stop telling him where she lived, and just pretend that she was satisfied to be right there with him. After all, as oddly charming as he was, it wouldn't be so hard. Then, the next time he went out, she could perhaps join him—and then maybe she could figure out where she was and find her way from there. And then she could send help, because the idea of Erik living here, all alone, truly upset her. Maybe he *was* insane, she thought, but that was no reason to leave him alone in the dark.

"So I see you have not told your guest where you make your humble abode," Omid said, once Jenna was in the bath.

"I told her we were in Paris," Erik said, apathetically, pouring the Persian a glass of Cognac.

"Really?" Omid challenged, taking the brandy Erik offered. "And you think that is sufficient?"

"She doesn't even believe that," Erik told Omid, raising his shoulders slightly, as he took a seat in the reading chair across from the settee. "*She* thinks she's from New York."

"New York?" Omid asked confused, taking a sip of his drink.

"Yes, as in America," Erik clarified. "She refuses to accept that we are in Paris. She doesn't even believe she is speaking French."

Omid shook his head, trying to wrap his mind around what Erik was saying. "What does she *think* she is speaking?"

"English," Erik answered, rolling his eyes.

Omid shook his head again. "That's very…perplexing. Still, with all of the traps you have set around this lair of yours, don't you think you should give her some more details about her surroundings? She already got herself into trouble today while you were gone."

Erik envisioned what further tumult might have occurred if the mental patient had decided to explore other areas of the house and shuddered. "You have a point, Daroga. The traps could be very detrimental. I shall just have to lock her in the guest bedroom in the future when I am away."

Omid rolled his eyes. "Oh yes, that's certainly the most logical course of action."

"It would be for her safety," Erik insisted, artlessly.

"You *could* just acclimate her to her surroundings," Omid offered sensibly. "It worked with me. I can enter your home freely, and I never trip the alarms."

"Don't remind me," Erik muttered, dryly. The Persian was the only person, beside himself, who knew how to enter the lair without becoming entangled in his labyrinth of traps set against intruders. Erik frequently rued the day he taught the Persian the correct route, since the man could not seem to help himself from using it at will. He supposed it would be safest for him to simply explain to the girl the more nefarious features of his home, so that she did not harm herself in the traps. Still, the alarms had been silent at her arrival. It made Erik wonder how exactly she had gotten into his home in the first place. He knew she insisted that it was through some sort of secret door in the cavern at the end of the lake. But Erik knew that door did not exist, for no one kept secrets from the Phantom. No, he was certain that the door was merely a fabrication of the girl's hysterical mind, and yet, the fact remained, she had gotten into his home somehow.

"So, how was the trip above, Erik?" Omid asked, taking another sip from his snifter and disturbing Erik's pondering. "Your visitor seemed to think you were gone a long time."

Erik's spirit leapt at the mention of the opera house, as his thoughts turned to the beautiful Christine. "I saw the new arrival of whom I spoke the other day, Daroga," He said, his eyes taking on a sparkle Omid had not seen before. "She is working as a seamstress in the costume department."

"In the *costume* department?" Omid repeated. "I had assumed she was another ballet rat."

"Oh, not a rat, Daroga." Erik shook his head, with a look of absolute awe on his face. "Surely, if she *were* a dancer, she is possessed of enough elegance and grace that she would be none other than the prima ballerina."

Omid raised an eyebrow at Erik's effusive praise. He had never seen the man quite so rhapsodic about another human being before.

In truth, it was rather disturbing.

"But she is not a dancer?" Omid asked when Erik's voice seemed to trail off.

"No, as I said before, she is presently working as a seamstress. And further, she was being quite horribly abused by La Carlotta—that swine!" Erik scowled and Omid noticed his fingers curl into a fist. Well, at least that was characteristic of the Erik he knew. Carlotta had been vexing him since she had started at the Opera House, and Erik had long enjoyed tormenting her in subtle yet distressing ways as he took on the persona of the ghost.

"But I am going to fix that, Daroga," Erik asserted, and Omid once again noticed the worrisome gleam in his friend's eye.

"Erik, what are you planning?" Omid questioned, nervously.

"I shall be taking her on as a pupil," Erik said in a self-satisfied fashion.

Omid coughed a bit on his cognac. "Carlotta?"

"Christine!" Erik huffed, impatiently.

"Christine? Who's Christine?"

"Daroga!" Erik snapped. "Do try to keep up! Christine is the new arrival who is being abused by Carlotta."

"And you are taking her on as a pupil?" Omid asked in disbelief. "What are you going to teach her? How to haunt conceited divas?"

"No, I'm going to teach her how to sing."

"To sing? I thought you said she was a seamstress."

"No," Erik corrected him, "I said she was presently *working* as a seamstress. There is a difference."

"Oh," Omid threw his free hand up into the air, "of course."

"I heard her sing, Daroga," Erik explained, his eyes taking on that faraway glint that made Omid so nervous. "She has the voice of an angel. With proper training, she will rise to the status of first lady of the stage—and finally that fraud Carlotta will fade into oblivion."

"And *you* are going to provide that training?" Omid asked, skeptically.

"Of course," Erik said simply.

"Where, Erik? Are you going to bring her here? Perhaps she and the mental patient will take lessons together?"

"No, Omid," Erik said, in annoyance. "I will instruct her in the opera house. She will never even have to see me. She does not need to see my face to hear my voice." *And she will never know that she is being taught by a monster*, he thought to himself.

"You're going to teach her as The Phantom?" Omid was incredulous. He had never seen Erik act quite so impetuously.

"No," Erik said in a whisper, almost as if talking to himself, that faraway look once more in his eye. "I am going to teach her as an angel."

"*WHAT*?!" Omid cried out, in absolute astonishment.

"Oh never mind!" Erik growled in irritation. "It is no concern of yours, and I do not even know *why* I am telling you anyway."

"What about the girl, Erik?" Omid reminded him of his unexpected houseguest who was still currently in the washroom. "You were supposed to be deciding upon the best course of action for her. Have you yet decided, because it seems awfully foolhardy for you to be taking on this seamstress—"

"Pupil!" Erik broke in to correct him.

"Whichever!" Omid dismissed Erik's correction and continued with his thought. "It seems awfully foolhardy for you to be taking on a second girl when you haven't even determined what to do with the first."

"I admit I do not know what to do with the mental patient, Daroga." Erik let out a troubled breath. "She is quite puzzling, indeed."

"She speaks of wanting to go home, Erik. She has never once mentioned a mental hospital. Do you think it is possible that we were wrong? That she is not a mental patient? That she has a family out there that is looking for her, trying to get her back?"

"She thinks her home is an ocean away, Daroga," Erik commented. "While I concede it is possible that she is not actually an escapee from the asylum, I hardly see how it can be possible that she is truly from New York. And once again, she is a conundrum."

The two were silent for a few moments, Omid savoring his Cognac and Erik lost in his thoughts. The only sound in the lair was the quiet rush of the lake waters as they made their never-ending journey out the opening in the cavern. When the door to the bedroom opened softly, two sets of eyes looked up to meet the sight laid out before them.

The girl no longer looked anything like a mental patient. She had chosen a long sleeved mint green day dress, with white lace lining at the collar and the cuffs. The wraparound neckline, though properly demure, revealed a bit of the creamy skin which stretched over her collarbone. While the dress was a bit large on her, as Erik had feared it might be, she remedied that problem by tying the waist tightly with its darker green sash, and the bodice accentuated her curved form quite nicely. Her hair, now clean and still slightly damp, fell in reddish blond curls at her shoulders, and while there was a distinct look of self consciousness in her aqua blue eyes, in truth, the girl's transformation took Erik's breath away.

"You look lovely, Mademoiselle!" Omid declared loud enough to make the girl flinch. His attention was now fully upon her, and he beamed at her brightly, a smile spread wide over his face.

"Much improved," Erik grunted, quickly averting his eyes to the floor when he saw her gaze shift to him.

"Thanks," she managed to mutter over her own discomfort at being dressed so foreignly.

"Are you hungry?" Erik asked, desperately trying to divert the attention from the girl's newly attractive appearance.

"*I* could happily eat," Omid heartily replied. "I had a light lunch."

Erik glared at the Daroga once again. "It seems that it will be three for dinner, then," He huffed with a tight smile. Jenna watched him quietly as he quickly exited to the kitchen to prepare the meal.

"Come, Mademoiselle," Erik heard the Persian's voice trailing behind him. "Don't mind him and his moods. Sit before the fire and chat with me while we wait."

"So what does she like? Is she a reader? Does she have an interest in a particular type of music?" the doctor asked Jenna's charge nurse curiously. He was still encouraged by the movements he had seen Jenna make the night before, and he wanted to capitalize on any progress she might be making toward consciousness. He realized, however, that her boyfriend—ex-boyfriend, he reminded himself—was going to be of no help. When she was admitted, her family history had revealed that her mother was dead and father unknown. She had no brothers or sisters, and her only family was an aunt who lived several hours away. If anyone was going to work with Jenna and try to draw her back, it was going to have to be him.

He'd lain in bed the night before, cursing himself once again for not having gotten to know her when he'd had the chance. He realized, however, that if he was going to make any kind of meaningful connections with her now, he had to learn as much about her as he could. He had gone in early that morning, hoping to visit with her for a while before starting rounds, but the nurses had been bathing her. So instead, he went to speak with Jenna's charge nurse, to learn a little more about her before his shift began.

"Well," the older woman answered thoughtfully, "I know she liked animals. She had this big yellow cat she talked about all the time. And reading…yes, she often had her nose in a book in the break room. And she definitely loved music. She was always talking about some concert or another that she wanted to see. "

"So…rock and roll? Pop? Classical?" he fished for more information.

"Oh, definitely contemporary stuff. But I think she liked some Broadway stuff too. I remember her complaining one night about Jake not wanting to take her to some musical she wanted to see."

He made a non-committal humming sound. It didn't surprise him one bit that Jake refused to take her to a show on Broadway. What a fool! A delicious dinner at one of the city's finest restaurants, followed by a Broadway show seemed like the perfect night out with a woman like Jenna. Of course, they would cap the evening with stopping by a street vendor so he could buy her a rose after the show. Then they would walk home hand in hand in the moonlight, or maybe enjoy a carriage ride around the park.

"Doctor…"

"I'm sorry, yes?" he looked at her, blinking, when he realized the nurse had been talking to him.

"You seem to be taking quite an interest in Jenna," she said in a leading fashion. "I didn't realize you two were close."

Close? He thought ruefully to himself. *If we'd been close, I wouldn't have to ask these questions. I would have made it my business to know her every interest, fulfill her every desire. If we had been close, she wouldn't have come home to find me entertaining another woman in our bed. She would have been the only woman for me, and instead of crashing into the Hudson, she would have spent that night wrapped safely in my arms.*

He shook his head quickly back and forth to clear his mind. What was he thinking!? This was not about dating Jenna. This was about helping her come out of a coma. Nothing more. He had not been close to Jenna. He had never even had the courage to introduce himself to her. He doubted she even knew his name.

"I don't really know her, Miss Miller," he responded professionally to the charge nurse. "But right now, I'm her doctor and I intend to see her get well." Because right now, he thought, he was all she had.

He smiled politely and thanked the woman for her help before going on his way.

❧

"That was delicious, Erik," Omid said, standing after he had finished his bowl of soup and hunk of bread. "A real pleasure."

"The pleasure was all yours, Daroga, I assure you," Erik said with a crooked smirk.

Omid rolled his eyes, and made his way to Jenna. "Mademoiselle, do try have a good evening," he said, giving a little bow, "present company notwithstanding."

Jenna chuckled a little as she caught Erik glower at Omid. In truth, Erik could not wait for the Persian to go. His endless prattling during dinner was getting on Erik's final nerve. In fact, as soon as he had gotten over the shock of the mental patient looking, well, less like a mental patient, his mind had wandered back to his earlier trip above and his intended voice lessons with Christine. He had hoped to have a quiet evening, to work out the perfect way by which to approach Christine as her Angel of Music, but the Daroga's nonsensical chatter with the girl and her responding laughter was distracting him from his ruminations and making it quite impossible for him to think. Besides, he had another errand he had to do before he could rest tonight, and he was eager to get to it.

Jenna helped Erik clear the table after the Persian had taken his leave. "Omid was right, Erik," she commented to him sweetly. "The soup was *very* good."

"Thank you, Mademoiselle," Erik practically mumbled, looking down, not used to receiving praise. "It was a very simple recipe." He took the dishes from Jenna's hands.

"Erik, can't I help you do the dishes? After all, you cooked."

"I would rather you rest your ankle, Mademoiselle," he answered, still looking down. "Putting too much weight on it too soon is not a good idea. Perhaps you should settle yourself in the sitting room with a book and I can brew a cup of tea while I am scrubbing the dishes."

"Um, alright, Erik," Jenna said, "If you're sure."

"I am, Mademoiselle."

Jenna retreated to the sitting room and chose one of Erik's many volumes from his over filled shelf. She made herself comfortable on the settee and began to settle into her book.

"Mademoiselle," Erik said softly, as he entered the room once the dishes were scrubbed. He handed Jenna her cup of tea. "Is there anything else that you require?"

"Well…no…" Jenna responded, looking up from where she was seated on the settee. "I'm fine, Erik." She was about to ask if he would join her when Erik nodded and walked into his bedroom. When he emerged a few moments later, he was wearing his cloak, and was carrying a wide brimmed black hat in his hand.

"Are you going out?" Jenna asked in alarm, when she saw him.

"Yes, Mademoiselle." Erik answered, again not meeting her eye. "I have a matter to which I must attend. Please try not to drown while I am gone." He began to turn toward the lake. "I doubt the Daroga will return tonight."

"Erik, can I come with you?" Jenna called before he could get very far. This could be her chance—if not to break away, at least to see where they were located.

Erik turned finally to look at her. He had avoided meeting the girl's eyes, since she had emerged from the washroom, but he did now, and could not help but notice the trepidation in her gaze. "Mademoiselle, is there a problem?" Erik asked, in a soft, whispery voice.

"No. It's just…" Jenna began, wringing her hands nervously. "I don't want to be alone again—in the dark."

Erik looked at her. There were plenty of candles lit in his home, not to mention the fire in the hearth. One could not truly call his chamber, as it was right now, dark. But Erik understood that darkness could take many forms, and for all of the girl's independence and bravado, she was in strange surroundings, and she was scared. Erik knew the feeling all too well. There had never been anyone in his life to consider *his* feelings about being alone in the dark, but that did not mean he had to treat this girl as callously as he had always been treated. After a moment, Erik silently returned to his bedroom, and this time when he emerged, he was carrying a second black cloak. “Let us go, Mademoiselle. It's late.” He tossed the cloak to her and continued walking toward his boat. Jenna quickly reached out and caught the mantle, wrapping it around herself as she hurried to catch up. “Is your ankle going to be alright to do some walking, Mademoiselle?” Erik asked, not looking at her, but getting into the vessel and reaching for the oars.

“I think I'll be fine,” She answered, trying to favor her aching ankle just a bit.

Erik did hold his hand out to steady her when she climbed into the boat. One fall in the lake was quite enough for the day. She grasped onto his hand without hesitation and took a seat on the bench across from him. He began to row as soon as Jenna was settled. Before long, the house by the lake was no longer in sight, and the two traveled down dark passageways that twisted this way and that. “There are many things that you should know about my home, Mademoiselle.” Erik confessed to her, as they wound quietly down the lake, his lantern casting eerie shadows on the rocky walls as they went. “But the most important thing to remember is that, if you do not know exactly where you are going, you could get terribly lost…or hurt.” Erik's eyes met hers with a flicker of warning, and Jenna seemed to understand his cautionary message.

“Erik, where are we going tonight?” she asked, breaking the silence that had fallen between them when her curiosity finally got the best of her.

“Tonight, Mademoiselle,” Erik responded, and Jenna thought she could almost see the curl of a smile on his face and a glint in his eyes that pierced through the darkness. “We are going hunting. For toads.”

8 THE FROG PRINCE

Erik and Jenna traversed the lake in the little boat, following its twists and turns, the lantern hung at the front of the boat casting a misty glow on the water's surface. When they came to a wall, Jenna saw Erik reach his arm briefly out of the boat and touch the surface of the stone. Instantly, the barrier moved aside, releasing them into the fresh night air and scores of twinkling stars above.

"How did you do that?" Jenna asked in an awed whisper, a look of amazement on her face.

Erik glanced at her, a crooked smile spreading over his features, and said, "I have my ways, Mademoiselle."

They took the boat a short way further where they docked by a small wooden post that had been embedded into the lakeshore. After securing the boat, Erik helped Jenna out of the vessel, making certain that she was steady on her feet, before leading the way down a winding dirt path to a wooded marsh.

"Why exactly are we hunting toads, Erik?" Jenna asked as they got deeper into the woods.

"Because there is a…*woman*…above," Erik began, saying the word *woman* as if it left a bad taste in his mouth, "who is in the habit of mistaking poor seamstresses for the webbed-foot amphibians." He continued onward, reaching out before him, pulling branches out of their path. "I simply thought to give her some examples of what a toad actually looks like, to enlighten her on the difference between the two."

Jenna looked at him silently for a moment, then smiled. She noticed the mischievous glint in Erik's eye, and she liked it.

As they continued on their way, Jenna felt emboldened to ask him a question that had been on her mind. "Erik, when you say *above*, what does that mean, exactly?"

Erik stopped where he stood and turned back to look at her, before saying, "Mademoiselle, you may have noticed that my home has no windows."

Jenna nodded, admitting, "I had actually been wondering about that."

"Hmmm …" Erik regarded her a moment more. "Inquisitive thing, aren't we," he asked, and Jenna saw his eyebrow raise. "Well, it has no windows because it is underground." He turned at that point to continue on their journey. Jenna tried to ask exactly *what* ground it was under, hoping to glean their true location in a roundabout manner, but Erik moved quickly and she had to follow, for she had no desire to be lost in the woods without him.

Finally, they arrived at a small pond, the shore of which was covered in moss and riddled with tall grasses and overgrown reeds. Jenna could hear the low hum of flying insects all around her and the deep croaks of frogs. Erik held his forefinger up to his mouth as he looked at her intently in the dark.

"Now remember, Mademoiselle—and this is very important," Erik instructed with a solemn expression, looking directly at her. "You must hide the lantern within your cloak. Remove it only when I give the signal, and be sure to shine it right in their eyes. Keep it steady until I tell you to conceal it again. The light will stun them and make it easier to get them in the net." He lifted his left hand, extending his first finger, and warned, "And most of all, you must be *silent.* They have keen hearing, and we do not wish to frighten them away." Erik continued to look at her with an expectant expression until Jenna nodded once to indicate understanding. He reached inside his cloak and produced a small black sack, crouching down to moisten it in the water. He took a few more silent strides until he apparently spotted something of interest. Kneeling low, he withdrew a long handled net from his cloak and looked back at Jenna, who was watching his skulking movements with fascination. He pointed toward what she could only assume was his prey of choice, and she removed the lantern from her cloak, shining it in the direction he indicated. She beheld the scene before her as he quickly thrust his net forward and, with an expert flick of his wrist, entangled the frog beneath the mesh. He stretched his other arm out silently, lifting the frog from its perch on the rock and gently placing him in the sack. When the deed was done, Erik glanced back at Jenna with a wickedly satisfied gleam in his eye, and she found that she was breathless as she hid the light of her lantern so that he could obscure himself once more as he searched out new quarry.

Time and again, the scene was repeated, and with each attempt, another toad was added to Erik's sizable collection. Jenna felt utter delight at his every conquest. He was amazing to watch, with his leonine grace and hunting skills—the absolute portrait of stealth and dexterity. Part of what held Jenna's rapt attention was his obvious thrill in the chase. He seemed to become more and more energized with each new acquisition, his eyes glowing with some internal light. From the way Jenna could feel the blood racing in her veins, she knew his excitement was contagious.

After a time, Erik dipped the bag again into the water, to ensure the soggy comfort of his newly captured friends and began to tie off the drawstrings, when he heard a loud, rumbly *ribbit*. He looked up at the noise, and Jenna could just make out his eyes narrowing as he peered across the pond to detect the source of the sound. A huge bullfrog was perched on a water lily leaf, near the center of the pond. Jenna caught the flicker in Erik's eye, as he began to move, once again, toward the water. Even though she had been admonished at the start to be silent, she reached for his arm, whispering, "Erik, no. Don't get greedy. He's too far, and we have enough."

Erik rolled his eyes and waved off her concern, as he signaled for her to make ready with the lantern.

Jenna tried once again to make her case. "Erik," her whisper was now more urgent, hoping that he would listen, "You'll never reach him!"

Erik's blazing eyes met her gaze directly as he whispered, "Watch me!"

Once again, he positioned himself on the loamy ground near the pond. At his signal, and with extreme perturbation, Jenna exposed the lantern in the hopes of stunning the bullfrog into place. Erik got low and stretched the arm that held his net, hoping to reach the frog. But it was too far in, and he had to extend his torso over the water in order to span the distance. Confident that the frog was stupefied by the light, Erik brought down his net, only to have the frog, at the very last second, jump straight at him with a thunderous croak. Erik lost his precarious balance and landed in the shallow water with a loud splash.

Jenna immediately set the lantern down and ran to help Erik out of the pond. She extended her hand as he struggled to right himself from such an embarrassing position. When he turned to face her, she tried to hold her laughter, she truly did, but when she saw him—hair wet and tousled, white shirt filthy with mud, and the disgruntled expression on his dirty and disheveled face, she couldn't help herself. She let loose with a snort of laughter, which only intensified as Erik looked straight at her and blew an unruly lock of hair out of his eyes with an upwardly directed puff.

"I'm sorry, Erik," she expressed her contrition between fits of giggles, "I really am. I just…"

"Told me so," he supplied in an annoyed tone of voice.

Jenna took a deep breath and her giggles calmed, although she still wore an amused smile upon her face. "I was *not* going to say that."

"Which is why *I* did," he returned, self-deprecating humor now clear in his crinkled eyes.

Jenna's smile grew brighter as she noticed a smudge of mud on Erik's face. She reached forward with her finger to wipe it away, only to have Erik catch her hand with his as she touched his cheek. He did not brush her hand away, but simply held it, a look of surprise in his eyes. The intensity of his gaze made her look down, and she slowly extricated her hand from his grasp and lowered her arm to wrap it, and its partner, around herself in embarrassment. "I'm sorry," she said quietly as she studied the ground. "You had some mud on your cheek."

Erik drew a shaky breath and responded, "I'm sure my appearance is disastrous beyond imagination after my impromptu swim." He joined her a moment in her scrutiny of the dirt beneath their feet, before asking, "Shall we go? It's time we get back, since our friends have a busy day tomorrow."

Jenna looked up at Erik once again and saw only kindness in his eyes. She smiled at him as she nodded her agreement, and they retrieved their belongings and began to make their way back to the boat. As they walked, Jenna was filled with a sense of well-being. She and Erik had truly made a great team that night—even though she did not really know for what cause they were teaming up. She thought about the fun she had and how much she had enjoyed assisting Erik in this caper. She decided to ask her unvoiced question from earlier—the sense of camaraderie having grown between them during their toad-hunting adventure.

"Erik, you said earlier that your home was underground," she began easily. "What exactly is it under? And where do you go when you go above that has seamstresses, and mean women, and…old fashioned dresses?" she gestured to the green dress which she wore under her cloak.

Erik stopped their progress to look at her, feeling his heart begin to beat rapidly in his chest. Would it be a mistake to tell her? He had never before revealed the location of his lair to another human being—except to the Persian, and *he* hardly counted. He knew that her understanding of her surroundings was paramount to her safety, but surely explaining the dangers of the tunnels would be enough. Was it required of him to reveal their exact location? If she had heard stories of the Opera Ghost… But no, he reminded himself, with a deep breath. That shouldn't be a problem. For in her mind's addled state, she believed she lived in New York! Certainly tales of his misdeeds had not traveled that far.

"I reside beneath the Palais Garnier, my lady," he told her with a resolute look upon his face. "In the fifth cellar, to be exact."

"Beneath the Palais Garnier?" Jenna echoed in response. This was the first clue Erik had given her to their exact location, and that name sounded somehow familiar. She knew that he was under the impression that they were in Paris, but surely there must be some equivalent to the Palais Garnier in New York. She felt her brow crease as she worked her brain trying to remember that name, when suddenly it was like a fog lifted and she blurted out, "The Paris Opera House!"

Erik froze at the recognition in her voice. Perhaps she had heard of the ghost, and telling her their exact location had broken through the dementia in her brain. "That is what I just said, Mademoiselle," he confirmed in breathless trepidation.

Jenna surmised that if Erik thought they were living under the Paris Opera House, then that could mean he was truly making his residence under the Met. She marveled to think such an amazing underground world could be hidden beneath Lincoln Square. Was the lake by his house somehow connected to the pond in Central Park? It wasn't so far away, and certainly, that must be where they were now, for in the concrete jungle that was Manhattan, where else would there be such forested land?

Erik must have noticed the intense look on her face, because she heard nerves in his voice as he inquired, “Mademoiselle, are you alright?”

Jenna looked up at him and smiled. “I'm fine, Erik,” she said, with a warm tone. “Now let's get these frogs ready for their mission.”

Erik smiled back at her, but there was a definite look of disquiet in his eyes. They turned to continue on their way when Jenna asked, “So what *is* their mission, Erik?”

Erik began to haltingly explain his plan for the frogs. Jenna listened in amusement as they retread the winding path back to the lake, every now and then letting loose a giggle. She noticed that with each little chuckle, Erik's voice increased a bit in confidence and before long, they arrived at the makeshift dock where they had left the boat, both laughing at the prospect of playing a prank on Carlotta—who sounded just awful to Jenna.

Erik placed the sack with the toads carefully in the corner of the boat and climbed in himself, reaching out a hand to steady Jenna's entrance. Just as she was about to take his hand in hers, Jenna heard a noise. She realized in that moment that the sound meant there were other people nearby.

She looked at Erik, who was still gazing at her expectantly, his hand outstretched toward hers. She glanced behind her at the sound of civilization, calling her toward her home—her life. She felt herself take a few steps backward, while looking at Erik, seeing his face fall in confusion. She found she didn't want to leave him—not after the kindness he had shown her, not after the fun they had had together that night. But she knew this could be her only chance. She felt a moment's regret, as she looked in Erik's bewildered eyes, and mouthed *I'm sorry.* At the last moment, he must have realized what she was going to do, because he lunged forward to grab her arm, but he was too late. She dashed away, out of his reach, and off in the direction of the clamor, hearing him curse in the darkness behind her.

❧

The doctor looked through the patient library and realized that the selection was truly dismal. He thumbed through volume after volume of grocery store romance novels, with bodice ripper covers that featured artificially well muscled men with long, flowing blond hair—

often wearing a kilt. At their feet, sprawled in some sort of prone position, were scantily clad, simpering heroines—blond, brunette, or ginger, it didn't matter. He had hoped to spend his upcoming break reading a bit to Jenna, but coma, or not, he could not bring himself to read her this trash. He knew the hospital relied on donations to build their patient library, but if this collection was any indication of the kind of donations they accepted, they were going to have to become more selective.

Having no luck in the adult section, he made his way down the shelf to the pediatric selections. Here, there were similarly disappointing offerings. He sincerely doubted Jenna's interest in Spongebob Squarepants finding a Crabby Patty or in what would happen If You Gave a Mouse a Cookie. "How 'bout we put the cookie in a mousetrap and find out?" he muttered under his breath in exasperation. He wanted to read to Jenna to stimulate her brain, not to bore it into a deeper state of unconsciousness.

Finally, for lack of anything else even remotely appropriate, he signed out a thick volume of old fairytales and made his way to Jenna's room. At least they were classics, he thought. And he could always embellish them if they seemed too simplistic.

He knocked on the door when he reached Jenna's room—mostly out of habit, but he had to admit that a small part of him wished she would somehow answer him, even if it were to tell him to go away. He opened the door and found her laying in her bed, as always, her strawberry blond curls fanned out behind her, those vibrant aqua eyes shielded by lids lowered as if in sleep. How he wished she would awaken. His heart beat a little faster as he fantasized about seeing her waking first thing in the morning—her lids fluttering open, as sunlight poured in through the window, and her lips turned up into a grin. She would whisper his name sleepily, and he would reach for her, placing gentle kisses on her forehead before he closed his eyes and…

Read! He told himself, pulling up a chair and sitting down alongside her hospital bed. He opened the book to a random page and looking down, read out loud, "The Frog Prince." He rolled his eyes once again at the lack of selection in the library and began to read.

"Once upon a time, there was a prince who was enchanted by an evil sorceress. She changed him into a frog and forced him to live in the palace garden under a bush, near the pond. After many years, the sorceress died, but still the frog remained, living in the garden, under a bush, near the pond. One day, a mighty King moved into the palace, and his daughter, a beautiful angel of a girl, with golden curls and blue-as-the-sky eyes," the doctor smiled at her description and looked again at Jenna, as she listened tranquilly to his tale, "went to play in the garden with her golden ball. When she lost the ball in the pond, she became very upset. Upon hearing her cries, the prince—who was still a frog—hopped out from under his bush and asked her what was wrong. She explained that she lost her ball, and he assured her he could find it for her, if she would only promise him one thing.

"'Oh, anything at all!' declared the girl, certain there could be no promise the frog would demand that would be too difficult for her to keep.

"The Frog hopped into the water and in no time had lifted out her little toy, and she took it, overjoyed at having her treasure back. When she thanked him and asked him what favor he would ask, he said simply that he would like to be her friend.

"The girl thought it was strange to have a frog for a friend, but she had made a promise, and so she agreed. Every day, she returned to the garden and spent time with her new best friend. They would play with the ball, and talk under the tree, and sometimes, he would present her with a lily that had grown on the surface of the water, where he made his home. Before long, the little girl truly loved her froggy friend, and felt sad that she got to live in the castle, while he was forced to live alone in the pond.

"That night, when it was time for her to return to her home, she lifted the frog, and took him with her to the palace. She introduced him to her maids and butlers as Lord Froggington of the Land of Toad. She set him beside her at the table, allowing him to nibble a bit of food from her plate. And at bedtime, she set him gently on the pillow next to hers, and tucked him in with a handkerchief so that he could sleep. Before darkening the lamp by her bedside, she leaned over and bestowed on the frog a goodnight kiss, and was amazed when there, in place of her frog, was a handsome prince, who leapt from the bed and knelt down before her, taking her hand.

"'My lady, your kindness has banished my ugliness and your sweetness has revealed my true princely nature that has been hidden under the guise of a toad. I asked for your friendship, and you gave me your love. And now I ask for the treasure of your hand in marriage, because truly, my lady, you have already stolen my heart.'

"The princess leaned forward and kissed the prince once more, to seal their bond. They were married the next morning, and the King handed them the keys to his kingdom as a wedding gift. They all lived happily ever after."

He sighed as he read the final words of the story. "Such drivel," he muttered under his breath. "Fairy tales never come true." He closed the book loudly and looked up at Jenna. She was smiling. It was a radiant smile—the kind she would bestow on him in his dreams—and he realized it took his breath away. Unaware of what he was doing, he began to lean in closer to her, mesmerized by her beauty.

Suddenly, he saw her hands begin to blindly reach out for something. He watched her intently, amazed when her hand found his cheek. Without thinking, he reached up his own hand, to hold her palm against his face. He loved the feel of it, and he turned his face into it slightly, leaning a little into her unknowing caress. "Wake up, Jenna," he entreated, breathlessly, his eyes closed at the delight of her touch. "*Please* wake up." He opened his eyes and gazed at her intently for a few moments more, willing her with all his being to open her eyes.

But she did not. Her lids remained closed, and eventually the smile faded from her face, and her hand grew limp and he placed it gently at her side.

He would not give up on her, he thought, as he worked to return his breathing to normal. He told himself it was because she was his patient, and she was relying on him to get her well. He reminded himself that she had no family, no friends she could count on so the burden of her recovery fell on him. But he knew that he would keep trying for a different reason—however unprofessional that reason might be. Though medicine may not be able to pull her out of this coma, he was sure now, more than ever, that she was aware of what was going on around her. Kindness and caring could coax her back to them, and he planned to show her as much kindness and caring as he possibly could. For he knew after today, that he could not stop caring for her if he tried.

9 REALIZATIONS

Damn her! Erik fumed as he scrambled his way out of the boat. *How could he have been such a fool?* No sooner had he revealed his secrets to that cunning charlatan, that false deceiver, than she had run from him—to betray him, no doubt, to the managers. Perhaps this whole thing had been a farce—perhaps Moncharmin and Robert' had hired her to pose as a helpless little convalescent to cause him to let down his guard and expose his vulnerabilities. And it had worked! All she'd had to do was bat her eyes and flash a little smile, and he had divulged the hidden mysteries of his home. *This* is what came of trusting other people. *This* is what came of believing that there could be more for him than a life of solitude. *No one wants to befriend a monster, Erik,* he goaded himself. *No princess ever really kisses the toad.*

He hurried off in the direction in which she ran, calling after her, yet knowing she would not turn back. Before long, the little clearing gave way to the city streets of Paris, which, even at this time of night, did not truly sleep. The carousers were always immersed in inebriated celebration, the seedy *gentleman* always engaged with *ladies* of the night. The soft thuds of his boots pounding the soil transformed into the loud cracks of them striking the sidewalk, as Erik rounded a corner and was met with a sight that stopped his heart. The girl was standing in the middle of the road, looking as stunned as the toads, while a fast moving carriage was bounding straight for her!

"GENEVIEVE!" He bellowed as he launched forward from the sidewalk and into the street, shoving her out of the way just as the carriage barreled past. As they flew toward the opposite sidewalk, Erik wrapped his arms around her, cushioning her head from the impact of the fall. When they landed, with her beneath him, he pulled back slightly, holding her still by her shoulders and frantically scanning her shocked form for injuries. When he was satisfied that there were none, his look of concern turned to a glare. "Was near drowning not enough for you today, Mademoiselle?" he seethed at her through clenched teeth. "Were you so eager to be rid of me that you wished to add being crushed and mangled to your evening activities?" He roughly released her shoulders and thrust her away from him, as he pulled himself up to a sitting position.

Jenna pushed up to support herself on her elbows, still breathless, both from the near accident and from Erik's obvious fury. "Erik, please," she began in a brittle voice.

"Please what?!" He growled at her, his eyes flashing with anger. "Please tell you more of my secrets so that I can give you additional ammunition to betray me?"

"Erik, no," she whimpered, shaking her head pathetically.

"Please take you further into my confidence, so that your deceptions can fuel even greater destruction?" he spat, his voice thick with emotion as he rose to his feet and raked his fingers through his hair, pacing back and forth.

"Erik, stop," she pleaded, tears filling her eyes.

"I *should* have stopped!" he turned on her, towering over her imposingly, "before I told you where I live. Before I revealed to you the secrets of my existence."

Jenna just shook her head from side to side, the tears spilling silently down her cheeks.

"I can never even rest in my own home now, knowing that you know—knowing that you have the power to destroy me."

"Erik…" she wept, imploring him to listen.

He leaned over her, and bringing his face so close to hers they were almost touching, he shouted, "You could have *died* tonight! Is that what you wanted?" When she flinched away from him in fear, he stood once more, pacing the ground. "I *trusted* you," he hissed, his own eyes shining with unshed tears of rage.

Jenna looked down and her body was wracked with sobs. She curled into herself, resting her head on her knees, wrapping her arms around her legs as she sat there and violently wept.

Erik looked at her in disgust, as she rocked slightly back and forth, her back heaving with sobs. *Well, she has only herself to blame for her tears*, he thought, as he stalked the ground, his ire not allowing him to be still. He had shown her every kindness, tending her wounds, giving her shelter, even allowing her to accompany him on his outing when he could have simply locked her away. He had treated her as a guest when she was nothing more than an intruder! And the first chance she got, she had betrayed him—putting herself in grave danger as she did so! He had every right to yell at her, the way he saw it. She had almost *died,* and once again, he had saved her, thinking nothing of his own safety in doing so! *Why is she still crying in a heap on the ground?* He wondered, his fingers tangled in his hair. *She should be thanking me! I saved her life after she betrayed me! Why will she not stop crying?*

He stopped again to look at her, certain that his brain would explode if he had to endure her sobs much longer, and suddenly, it was as if the wind had been knocked out of him. *He* had done this to her, he realized. And for what? Some imagined slight on her part that may not even be true. *He* had *decided* that her intent was to betray him—yet he saw no evidence of it. He'd seen no proof, and still, he painted her a Jezebel. The only thing he knew for certain was that, when she had the chance, she had run from him. Given the fact that this was the most natural reaction in the world when confronted with a monster, in truth, she had committed no sin.

He silently crouched down next to her, lifting his hand to comfort her in her sorrow. But as his hand hovered over her back, he found that he could not make contact. He had done enough this night to hurt her. He would not allow his touch to taint her as well.

"Mademoiselle," he said, his voice tentative—quavering, "That carriage was seconds away from running you down in the street. Would it have been worth it," he asked, trailing off into a guttural whisper, "just to get away from me?"

Her head lifted and her sorrowful eyes met his vulnerable ones. "I… I was only trying to get home, Erik," she asserted, her voice strangled with tears. "I was not trying to get *away* from you. I just wanted to get my life back—but I didn't necessarily *want* to leave you." She broke down at the end of her phrase and threw her arms around him, burying her head in his chest.

Erik looked down at the woman who was presently blubbering into his shirt and wondered how on earth he had managed to get to this point. He had set out to catch frogs, and had wound up terrifying his houseguest. He had wanted only to protect her, and yet, he had managed to make her cry.

Erik finally allowed his hands to gently pat her back. "There, there," he said, awkwardly, "It's alright, Jenna. Everything is going to be alright."

She looked up to meet his eyes. "I'm sorry, Erik."

"I know," he said calmly, hoping an even tone would convince her to stop crying.

"I wouldn't ever betray you," she said to him with such earnestness, that he felt ashamed he had ever thought it of her.

"I know, I know." He said again, because he truly did not know what else to say.

"I really only wanted to go home," she said again, and he felt pained to hear the anguish in her voice.

"I *know*, Mademoiselle. Please, hush." He tightened his grip around her, desperate to make her stop crying.

"But now I realize that home is very far away."

"She became very agitated, Doctor," the nurse explained nervously, as Jenna's doctor furiously unfastened the leather restraints that had been placed on her arms. "We had to restrain her for her own safety."

"Really? For her own safety?" he fumed. "Did anyone try to just sit in here and *talk* to her? Sometimes the sound of a familiar voice can help quiet a coma patient's agitations. Did it ever occur to you to try to treat her like a human being, instead of tying her up like some dog?"

"We're sorry, Doctor," the nurse began again, trying to make him see reason, "but the restraints are standard protocol when dealing with coma patients that have become violent."

"Violent?" he asked, having to remind himself to remain professional.

"Yes, Doctor. She was flailing her arms about and convulsing—we were afraid that she could fall off the bed."

The doctor looked down at Jenna now that all the restraints had been removed. She was no longer agitated, but she did not look exactly right. There was something tense in the way she was laying there, but he couldn't quite put a finger on it. "In the future, please call me or have me paged if she becomes agitated again—*before* you apply the restraints."

"I'll make a note on her chart, Doctor."

"Thank you."

"Do you need any assistance with her, Doctor?"

"No, I'll be just fine."

The nurse nodded as she quickly left the room.

"Jenna," He began in a gentle voice, taking a seat next to her and grasping her hand in his. "What's got you so tense? Rough day at the office? Come on," he smiled, as he stroked little circles on her hand with his thumb. "Kick back, relax, and tell me *all* about it. I promise I'll be a good listener…" he paused for a moment, not really knowing why, but compelled to give her at least the chance to respond. "No? OK, I'll go first. It's been a long day for me! So many patients, such little time! But still, if the nurses had just called me I never would have let them…" The doctor stopped mid-sentence, as he looked up to see silent tears falling from her eyes. "Jenna," he whispered, wiping her tears with his fingers, "It'll be alright now. I'm here…everything will be alright."

When her sobs had quieted to occasional hitched breaths and her tears had finally ceased to fall, Erik pulled away slightly to look at her. With her blotchy face and red-rimmed eyes, she was a sad sight to behold, and once again, he was reminded that he was an ogre. To have caused her such agony with his unfounded assumptions and unchecked rage… No wonder she had run away from him!

And that was the crux of the issue, was it not? Looking at her pitiable form, he knew his suspicions had been absurd. If the managers and they had inserted her into his lair, then they already knew everything she could have told them. And truly, they were not competent enough to concoct such a devious plan to ensnare him anyway. No, revisiting the situation logically, he knew that there was no way she could have betrayed him in the manner of which he had accused her. But still, she *had* run away.

After the time they'd spent in the marsh, he had begun to think that perhaps she enjoyed his company—that there was a chance he would not always remain lonely. But when she ran, he recognized the folly of hoping that she—or *anyone*—would ever be inclined to do something other than flee his presence when given the chance. It had always been thus, so how could he even *think* it would change?

Without a word he pulled her up and began to lead their way back to the dock. She clung to him as they walked, leaning her head lightly against his shoulder. Occasional hiccups in her breathing illustrated her still unsettled emotional state, and Erik desperately hoped she would not start crying again.

This time, Erik lifted her into the boat before deftly untying it and setting them on their way. There was silence between them as Jenna stared blankly before her with hunched form and glassy eyes. Was she so despondent at the prospect of being returned to the demon's lair?

When they reached his home, he lifted her from the boat and she once again leaned on him for support as they made their way to the settee. After depositing her there, Erik retreated into the kitchen, only to return a short time later with a cup of hot tea. When she still only stared, unseeing, ahead of her, Erik bent to put the tea on the side table, and turned once again to leave the room.

"I'm scared, Erik." The tiny voice stopped him in his tracks. In the short time she had been a visitor in his home, he had heard her sound brash, confused, amused, and insane, but he had not yet heard her voice sound this defeated. He cursed himself, once again, for being the cause.

"Mademoiselle," he began in a guarded tone, forcing himself to face her, but unable to quite meet her eye. "I did not mean to frighten you, but when I saw that carriage…"

"Why wasn't it a car, Erik?" Jenna asked, cutting him off.

Erik looked at her in confusion. "A *car*, Mademoiselle?"

"Yes, a car!" She repeated, with growing exasperation. "Where I'm from, it would have been a car."

Erik sighed again, and shook his head. "Mademoiselle, I don't know what a *car* is."

"That's just it, Erik." She looked at him with a worried look on her face. "You *should*."

"Mademoiselle, I…" He began, but she cut him off.

"You should know what a cellphone is too. You should *have* one. And a television. And a computer. And…*electricity*!" She stood up and pulled on the skirts of her dress. "And I shouldn't be wearing clothes like this. I should be in a t-shirt and jeans. I bet you don't know what those are either." She paced a little back and forth, reminding Erik of a female version of himself. "I thought you were just eccentric, Erik.

Actually, I thought you might be a little crazy." She clarified, apologetically, as Erik marveled that she thought *he* was the crazy one. "I figured that was why you didn't have any of these things—but tonight, Erik..." she paused and shook her head. "A horse-drawn carriage? They haven't been used as general transportation in well over a hundred years. And the driver, Erik, his clothes—they were so. . *old-fashioned.* And cobblestones on the street? Erik, where was the asphalt? This is not the New York I know."

New York again! Erik sighed in exasperation. It was apparent that her grasp on reality had not improved. The things she was speaking of now were complete gibberish and were beginning to make his head spin. He had, however, thought that they were at least making some headway in her acceptance of their geographical location. Had she not been the one who recognized that he was living beneath the *Paris* Opera House? "I have told you, Mademoiselle," he repeated once again, rubbing his temples with his forefingers, "we are *not* in New York. We are in *Paris.*"

"What year, Erik?" She asked him.

"What year?" he repeated her question. *Certainly*, he thought, *she must already know this.*

"Please, just answer my question." She asked again, more forcefully. "What year is it?"

"It is 1884, Mademoiselle," he answered, deciding to placate her. Jenna put a trembling hand to her mouth as Erik heard her exclaim nervously, "Oooh Toto, we're not in Kansas anymore!"

Erik shot up and the last remnants of patience tumbled from his mouth as he blurted, "Oh, come on now, Mademoiselle, who the *hell* is Toto, and what is this sudden talk of Kansas? Weren't you just going on about New York?"

"You're going to think I'm crazy, Erik, " she warned him.

"I wouldn't begin to fret about that now, Mademoiselle," he answered dryly, knowing that he had thought she was crazy from the moment he'd found her.

"It's supposed to be the year 2014."

10 INTOXICATING TONES

She was crazy. Erik knew this. First, all of these made up inventions, and now to claim it was 130 years into the future? Erik had hoped that as her head wound healed her senses might clear, but to listen to her rantings, they were just getting worse.

But her eyes…they were bright and they held the fire of intelligence. They were not vacant or wild, like those usually possessed by the deranged. No, the windows to *her* soul were alert, and sharp, and emotive and…*not* reflective of insanity. As Erik stared into her wide, sincere, but utterly terrified eyes, he was finding it difficult to simply dismiss her fears.

He took a seat on the settee and motioned for her to join him once again. After a moment, she did and they faced each other for a short time, not speaking, until Erik finally said, "Mademoiselle, I cannot pretend that what you say makes any sense to me."

Jenna looked down, "I knew you were going to think I was crazy."

"Well," Erik responded with the hint of a crooked grin, "you just admitted you thought it of me."

Jenna glanced at him, and immediately felt a little of the tension ease. "I did." she admitted again, adding sheepishly, "I'm sorry."

"Oh, you aren't the first." Erik continued with the self-deprecation, since it seemed to be calming her down a bit, and he wanted her to be calm for the conversation he wished to have. "The Daroga has been denying my sanity since the day we met—but to be fair, I think his mental faculties are the ones that should be called into question."

Jenna actually heard herself giggle a bit. "Yes, that's an interesting friendship you two have."

"Oh, I wouldn't call it a friendship." Erik began, thoughtfully. "I think of him more as…an *affliction.* An irritating one. Much like a rash."

Jenna laughed fully then, and Erik could not help but smile at the sound. "Oh Erik!" she giggled, her eyes crinkling endearingly at the corners. "How have you managed to get me *laughing*, in the midst of one of the most terrifying, confusing experiences of my life?"

At her comment, Erik sobered a bit. He couldn't believe he was actually going to do this, but it was necessary, and it was…right—and while doing the right thing didn't always matter much to him, in this case, with this *girl*, it did. He took a deep breath and looked her straight in the eyes and said, "I apologize, Mademoiselle, for my behavior on the street. It was unwarranted and I regret being the cause of your terror and confusion."

An unfamiliar emotion clouded Jenna's eyes, and Erik was surprised to feel her touch his hand. "Apology accepted, Erik. Your temper did scare me a little, but that's over now, and I have much bigger things to worry about."

Erik just stared at her in shock. After the boorish way he had treated her, he could not imagine her dismissing his rage so simply. And there was still the matter that she was touching his hand. "I…thank you…Mademoiselle for your…forgiveness…" He stumbled, unsure of what words to use to accept forgiveness, since he had certainly never asked it of anyone before.

Thankfully, Jenna interrupted his pathetic attempt. "I do have one favor to ask, Erik."

"What is that, Mademoiselle?" Erik asked, grateful for the distraction from his pitiful loss for words.

'*Please* stop calling me Mademoiselle." She smiled when she saw his brow furrow in confusion. "Even if you're screaming it at me, I would much prefer you call me Jenna. That's what all my other friends call me."

Erik felt a blush—an actual blush—creep over his cheek at her words. Her *other* friends? The way she said that, did it mean the girl—*Jenna*—thought of him as a friend? "Is that what we are?" Erik asked in disbelief. "Friends?"

He thought he detected a bit of a blush enter her cheeks now as well. "I would like to be, Erik," she admitted, averting her eyes from his.

"As you wish," Erik croaked in a gravelly voice, "Mademoi—*Jenna*."

They both laughed a little at his near slip. "Thank you, Erik." She said with a smile.

"Well, *Jenna*," Erik began with a little smile, steering the conversation back to his original intent, "like I said earlier, I cannot yet make sense of the things you told me." When he saw the crestfallen look in her eyes, he quickly added, "But I *want* to understand. What more can you tell me about the night of your accident?"

Jenna nodded and took a deep breath before answering. "It was dark, and it was raining…and I was driving…a *car*, that is," she added, realizing her words needed some explanation. "It's kind of like a carriage, but it's powered by an engine, not a horse."

"Ah," Erik responded, nodding. "Very interesting." He was sure that he'd like to hear more about these *cars* some other time. "Please, go on, Jenna."

"OK, well, like I said, I was driving and I was…upset. I had come home early from work and found…" she stopped for a moment and swallowed hard, "my boyfriend in bed with another woman. And I…I *had* to get away. "

Erik felt his fingers tighten and his fury rise at Jenna's words. He imagined this fool *boyfriend* of hers had much to do with Jenna's accident. "I had been driving for awhile, and before I knew it, I was down by the river. And I had had this horrific headache all night, and I was so tired. I…must have nodded off—fallen *asleep*—briefly, because the next thing I knew, I heard a loud horn, and there were headlights coming toward me—headlights are how we light up our cars at night, so we can see each other on the road." Erik nodded his understanding, encouraging her to go on. "I swerved to get out of its way, and I wound up going over the guardrail and into the river."

"And what happened next?" Erik asked, leaning a little in to her, eager to hear this part of her story. "What precisely do you remember after you swerved into the river?" He knew this had to be the key to what had happened to bring her here.

"Well…" she paused as she stared off into the distance, delving deep into her memory to attempt to answer his question. "I remember falling into the water. I heard the splash. But then everything went black. The next thing I knew, I was in the tunnel I told you about that led to the door which opened into your cavern."

"Good, Jenna. Now, can you describe the tunnel?" he pressed gently, urging her for more detail.

She tried to remember but was met with a terrible pain in her head. She shook her head back and forth, in frustration. "It was dark, Erik, I couldn't see much and I…"

He saw Jenna becoming agitated and realized that if he wanted to get any information from her, he was going to have to calm her down once more. Erik hated the idea of using his voice to manipulate her. He had driven many an enemy to unwitting deaths with his masterful vocalizations alone. His carefully crafted inflection had gained him the obedience of the most unlikely servants. His voice, lauded in the courts of Persia as almost akin to that of a god—or a demon—could bring about great delight, but could also be his deadliest weapon. Nevertheless, he allowed his intonation to take on that hypnotic quality which had mesmerized so many others to their very souls.

"Try to relax," he adjured, in that voice like liquid gold, squeezing the hand that was still inexplicably clinging to his. "Try to concentrate. For *me,*" he added, in an almost seductive whisper.

She closed her eyes and expelled a long, shuddering breath, feeling herself falling into a trancelike state, induced by Erik's mellifluous tones. "Well, like I said, it was dark, and cold…and damp."

"What were the walls like?" His voice was dripping with honey, enticing her to look deeper into her mind's eye. "What about the floor? Any details at all will help."

"I…I thought the walls were made of dirt—as well as the floor. But…"

"But what, Jenna?" Erik said her name like it was a song, sending her deeper into the dream he was trying to conjure.

"Well, now that I think about it, they almost seemed to…undulate…they sort of…*rippled.*"

"Rippled, Jenna?" Erik's low murmurs washed over her.

"Yes…almost like waves."

"And the floor? Did that move too?" He coaxed, gently.

"Well…" Jenna paused, sinking deeper into the lush feeling of being wrapped in his voice. "*Yes.* Almost like the sand beneath your feet when you're in the ocean. The floor was solid, but bits of it seemed to crumble away with every step I took."

"Was the tunnel long?" he prodded, beginning to use his deft fingers to trace small circles on her still lingering hand.

"It seemed endless—it was so dark and cold. But then there was the door."

"Tell me about the door," that velvet voice commanded. "What was that like?"

"It was…" she sighed. "It was made of wood—but not solid wood. More like…planks. And they were tied together by some kind of rope. I could see light shining though between the planks, and its top was curved. When I turned the handle, it opened easily."

"Now, think, Jenna," he whispered, slow and smooth, continuing his ministrations on her hand. "This door—did it move too?"

"The door it…" Jenna stopped, as Erik's voice broke through each barrier in her mind and she had a vision of the door before her. Only this time it wasn't the solid object opening from corridor into cavern. Now when she saw it, it too oscillated and flowed, the light between the wooden slats shimmering back and forth. She saw herself reach for the door handle, but this time the door didn't open. It dissolved. "Oh Erik," she said, breathing heavily, her entire body suddenly shaking as she began to awake from the stupor Erik had been purposely creating. "It wasn't a door! I can see it—I can see it now. It didn't open and lead me here. I touched it, and it disappeared!" Her eyes were wide and terrified once more, and she shook her head back and forth. "Erik, what is happening to me? It seemed so real. The door was *so real.* But it wasn't real at all!" Her voice became shrill, as she shook even harder, "How can I know what *is* real? What if *nothing* about this is real? Erik, I just don't know *anything* anymore."

Though Erik had never known loving comfort in his own life, when he saw Jenna so near to another breakdown, he instinctively let go of her hand and wrapped his arms around her. "Shhhh," he whispered soothingly in her ear, pulling her close, stroking her hair. "It's alright. It's going to be alright." He pulled away a little to look her in the eye, pulling her out of the last vestiges of the trance he had woven around her. "Jenna, look at me. I'm here," he said, "and *I'm* real! I promise you, we are going to work this out." She leaned toward his chest again, and he allowed her back into his embrace. "Everything is going to be alright."

❧

It had been another long shift, but that did not stop him from going to visit Jenna for a few moments before leaving for home. As he expected, when he entered her room he found her alone. He walked over to her bedside and sat once again in the chair, taking her hand in his and stroking it gently. "Hello, Jenna," he said, in a sweet, whispery voice. "Do you know what time it is? It's almost midnight. The moon is out, and the stars are shining, but it's so hard to see them with all of the city lights twinkling everywhere. You know what New York is like. It never sleeps—and the lights never go out in the city either." He smiled a little as he looked at her. "It's time for me to go home—it was a long shift, and I'm exhausted. But I couldn't leave without saying goodnight." He reached up to smooth the hair away from her face and he stood to tuck her blankets in a little more tightly. "Have pleasant dreams, Jenna. Maybe you'll dream of the Frog Prince," he paused, searching his tired brain for other possibilities, "or of puppies or kittens or anything else that makes you happy." He took her hand again, "But remember your dreams, Miss Wilson. When you wake, I want to hear all about them." He squeezed her hand again and smiled as he whispered, "Good night. I'll see you in the morning."

He turned and walked out of her room, hoping tomorrow would be the day that she would open her eyes. Jenna's nurse shook her head and smiled as she watched him go.

Erik held Jenna until she had finally stopped trembling, and shortly thereafter, she was asleep. For a moment he marveled at the fact that this girl—in truth, that *anyone*—could be so comfortable with him that she could rest in his arms. But in recalling the events of the day, he realized it was likely that exhaustion had simply rendered her able to sleep anywhere at that moment. Gently, he rearranged her in his grasp so that he could carry her to the spare bedroom—the one made up with his mother's old furniture. He laid her carefully in the grand feather bed, and for the first time, he was glad he had kept it. All these years it had confounded him that he felt so compelled to retain the possessions that his mother had valued so much more greatly than she had him. For the memories they held, these sticks of wood and lengths of fluffed fabric deserved to be on a funeral pyre instead of in his spare bedroom, but tonight, he was grateful for his mother's incessant desire for beauty and comfort. He knew Jenna's troubled mind would be eased by the warm bedclothes and her depleted body would be refreshed by the soft cushions. Erik stayed long enough to be sure that she remained sleeping, then soundlessly crept from the room, closing her door, but not completely, so that a shaft of candlelight would illuminate the darkness of her boudoir.

Erik made his way once more to the settee, staring blindly at the final throes of the fire in the hearth. Although he now had more reason than ever to believe Jenna was mentally impaired, he no longer did. No, something unfathomable was happening to her—something that was without reason. But somehow, he *had* to find the explanation. *2014*. That was the year Jenna claimed it had been when she had her accident—the year her *boyfriend*—why did he find himself seething at the word?—had grieved her so unforgivably, and caused her to drive her…*car*…into the river—in New York. And yet, when she surfaced, she was here, by his lake, in the year 1884. How had it happened?

He searched his brain, trying to think if he had ever read of similar scenarios in his scientific volumes. He knew that instances of time travel had appeared in stories and legends since the earliest days. But they were simply constructs—fictional devices that were used to create interest in a text that was merely the expression of an author's imagination. He needed to find something that would reveal *how* a person could travel through time—and surely novels and myths could not be the answer.

Water. Erik was certain that water had something to do with Jenna's journey. It had started in a river and ended by his lake, and the interim was spent in a tunnel with a door that ebbed and flowed like waves on the ocean. Yes, water had to have something to do with this—but what?

Erik tossed the matter round and round in his head until he felt his own lids droop as the final flames in the hearth began to die away. Sleep was calling him, as it rarely did, and because he knew his muscles would punish him in the morning if he reposed all night on the settee, he dragged himself up and staggered to his bedroom. He went into the washroom attached to his chamber, to wash the grime from his face and hands, quickly divesting himself of his soiled clothing when he returned to his room. He replaced them with the black silk pajamas he had taken to wearing since his time in Persia. Pulling aside the black sheets, he crawled into bed, placing his mask on the bedside table before he, himself, succumbed to sleep.

11 MORNING DELIVERY

Jenna wanted to rest for a hundred years. Her sleep had been dreamless and deep, and as she felt wakefulness tickle at her senses, she protested opening her eyes. She was lying on a warm and cozy cloud, wrapped in a billowy veil of cotton, but there was a funny sound in her ear, and a slight cool spot on her chest. As she tried desperately to cling to the last remnants of slumber, she felt the spot move and heard the funny sound once more. What was it? A creaking…a rumble…. Her eyelids fluttered open to see two golden eyes, with black slits across the middle, bulging out of a flat, olive colored head. As she slowly registered what she was seeing, the bottom of the head opened and out came a low, rumbly *ribbit.*

"ERIK!" Jenna bellowed

Sure enough, he appeared out of the shadows of the room, laughing guiltily at her alarm. He came forward to lift the frog from her and cradled it gently in his hands. "Good morning, Jenna."

"Good morning?" she questioned, as if it was anything but. She hurriedly drew the blankets up around her and glared at him. "Erik, how *could* you?"

"Well, Jenna," he said, a smile still spread across his face. "You were sleeping so soundly,"

"You know," Jenna interrupted him in an annoyed tone, "Most people follow that phrase up with 'and I didn't want to wake you'."

"Well," Erik's eyes went wide with feigned innocence, "*I* didn't want to wake you. But our friend here," he continued, patting the frog on the back of his head, "was just itching to make his debut in La Carlotta's dressing room, and thought the only way to hurry that along was to rouse you from your slumber."

Jenna huffed, "You're *wicked*!"

Erik made a little bow, "Guilty." He bit back a snicker when he saw Jenna roll her eyes. "Now make haste. The rest of your dresses are hanging in the armoire. We must hurry to get to La Carlotta's dressing room before rehearsals start."

"*We?*" she raised her eyebrows at him.

"Of course!" he answered, with almost boyish excitement. "After all, you're already an accomplice—don't think you're getting out of this now! I am certainly not willing to leave you here alone. Look at what happened yesterday."

Jenna rolled her eyes again. "You're not going to let me live that down, are you?"

"Certainly not." Erik retorted, his eyes still glistening. "Now, hurry, Jenna. We really don't have much time to lose." His eyes took on just a touch of apology, "I really did let you sleep as long as I could." And with that, he left the room, still stroking his little frog's head.

Alone once more, Jenna blew some errant strands of hair away from her eyes and shook her head. "Apparently," she said to herself in a sarcastic tone, "mischief makes him *giddy.*" She reluctantly rose from the decadently comfortable four-poster bed and took in her surroundings. She was in a richly appointed bedroom with plush cushions and luxurious fabrics gracing the delicately carved rosewood furniture. She crossed over to the graceful armoire and pulled on the dainty handles to reveal the dresses that Erik had procured for her yesterday. She rifled through the selection of gowns once again, this time taking in the fine fabrics. She chose a royal blue gown with black velvet adorning the neckline and blue eyelet lace at the waist, sleeves and hem. There was a soft bustle all tied up with a bow in the back. She felt like she was going to a Victorian costume party.

She was fastening the last of the black velvet buttons when she felt a sudden chill run down her spine. The realization hit her that Erik's choices had not really been that strange after all. The furniture surrounding her was not antique, but the current trend in fine furnishings. The dresses in the armoire were not vintage styles—they were high society fashions that were worn in the best of circles. Erik's lair was not lit with candles because he liked the smell of burning wax—it was because he had no electricity. No one did. *1884.* How could it even be possible? Would she ever find her way back home? Jenna felt a little dizzy, and held onto the wall a moment to steady herself.

There came a knock on her bedroom door.

"Yes, Erik," Jenna called and the door opened.

When Erik saw Jenna standing by the armoire, head lowered, hand resting on the wall, he rushed over to her. "Are you alright?"

She nodded, "I am, I was just thinking…I saw this type of furniture in antique shops and museums growing up—these dresses were pictured in history books. But now…" she trailed off, not really knowing what more to say.

"Jenna," Erik said softly, looking into her troubled eyes, "I promised you last night that we would figure this out, and the Phantom always keeps his promises."

Phantom, she thought. *I do know that name.* Jenna swayed on her feet as she suddenly felt a little light headed and foggy, destroying any hope she had for recollection.

Erik grabbed her shoulders to steady her, immediately regretting his slip of the Phantom title. What if she somehow knew of his reputation? Of course, he doubted there could be any chance his name would live for over 130 years. Still, the way she reacted…maybe it was her injury? "Jenna, are you absolutely *sure* you're all right?" his gaze was full of concern. "How is your head?"

"I'm *fine*, Erik," she assured him, not certain herself what was going on.

"Well then," he let go of her shoulders awkwardly and led the way out of her room, "Follow me."

Jenna followed him out to the lake. Once again, he helped her into the boat, where she saw a large blue dress box tied with a black ribbon and bow. She smirked as she remembered Erik's plan from the night before.

When they were underway, Erik reached into his cape, and produced an apple. "Here," he said, handing it over to Jenna. "You were lightheaded a moment ago, which likely means you should eat."

Jenna smiled as she took it from him, "Thank you, Erik." She took a bite from the crisp apple as they turned down an unfamiliar canal—one they had not traversed the night before. After a short time, they were tying their boat to a new post. Erik retrieved the box and took her hand with his free one, to guide her as they entered a tunnel.

"Follow my footsteps, Jenna." He glanced over his shoulder to meet her gaze. "Believe me, you do not want to go off course." Erik began to slowly move forward, keeping to the left side of the tunnel.

"Why is that, Erik?" Jenna asked, curiously.

"Well," Erik answered as he carefully navigated them through the labyrinthine inclines to their goal. "There are many traps in these tunnels."

"Like mouse traps?" Jenna asked confused.

Erik snickered lightly, "Well, I would say *rat* traps, but truly, their quarry is even bigger than the oft-maligned long-tailed rodents."

"I don't understand." Jenna continued to prod.

Erik sighed. "Jenna, they are traps for those who might try to enter my home uninvited."

Jenna stopped, causing Erik to stop as well. "Why would you need traps for people?"

"There are those," Erik began carefully, "who would not be happy to know that I was living here."

"Well, why *are* you living here?" Jenna asked. Truly, with everything else she was processing, it had not struck her odd until that moment that he lived beneath an opera house.

"This is my *home*, Jenna."

"Yes, but *why* do you make it your home?"

Erik sighed. "I built this place. The Palais Garnier. I worked right beside the architect—much of the design is mine, and my blood and sweat are in every stone. I built my home below as well, because I…" Erik paused with a faraway look in his eye. "I no longer wanted to be a part of the world above."

Jenna thought she sounded like a broken record as she once again heard herself ask, "Why, Erik?"

"Because the world above did not want me." He answered curtly, beginning to walk, giving Jenna no choice but to follow. "And so I live in the bosom of my greatest love—music. And I have learned to be perfectly happy alone—with only the errant Daroga darkening my door once in a while."

"Don't forget the wayward time traveler."

Erik glanced back to her with a crooked smile spreading over his face. "I will not forget you, *if* you promise to keep up." He gave her arm a playful yank as they continued on their way, causing her to stumble just a little, but not to fall. "Now we're almost to Carlotta's dressing room. Remember, keep quiet—watch and listen. It's not every day you'll see such a show!"

In a few moments, they stopped again and Erik looked at her once more, putting his finger to his lips. He let go of her hand, indicating that she should stay right next to him. He reached up and pressed a spot on the wall that looked like any other spot on the wall, but suddenly, the surface moved aside and opened onto a window of sorts, which revealed an extravagantly furnished, but very untidy dressing room. There were racks and racks of opulent dresses and shawls and shelves full of shoes, at least two rows deep. Every flat surface in the room was scattered with baskets of bows and ribbons and hairpins, and on the opposing wall was a shelf full of mannequin heads bearing wigs and headdresses and the most ridiculous hats Jenna had ever seen. Many of the heads also bore ostentatious necklaces, and boxes brimming with jewels cluttered the dressing table that was already crowded with lipsticks and powders and rouge. Affixed to the wall near the table, to the side of the oval mirror, was a plethora of yellowing newspaper articles with titles of "La Carlotta's Triumphant Debut" or "Carlotta Giudicelli Graces the Paris Stage."

Erik moved the window aside, and entered the disorderly room and Jenna followed only to realize their entry way was the full-length mirror. "A door in the mirror, Erik?" Jenna asked.

He glanced back at her. "It is the only place she has not jumbled up with her *accoutrements*, is it not? She enjoys looking at herself too much for that," he shuddered as if the thought disgusted him. "It certainly looks as if a brothel regurgitated its contents in here!" Erik commented, looking around the chaotic changing room for a place to lay the box. He settled on the chaise lounge, strewn with furs and cushions.

"Erik," Jenna asked as they made their way back to the crawl space behind the mirror, "Are you sure she'll even notice the box, with everything else in there?"

"I'm sure," Erik replied as he pulled the mirror opening closed, leaving the inner wall of the passageway open, so they could spy on any activities that might take place in the dressing room. "Carlotta's vanity is rivaled only by her laziness."

They settled themselves behind the mirror to wait. "Do you do this type of thing often?" Jenna whispered since there was still no one in the dressing room.

"Only when I feel it necessary to ensure the quality of my opera house, or the obedience of my staff," he whispered back. "Carlotta has long been unnecessarily cruel to those she deems *beneath* her. It's time someone taught her a lesson."

At that moment they heard a noise at the door, and they both fell silent, so as to not alert Carlotta to their presence.

"I shall be at rehearsal when I am ready," they heard the heavyset diva call over her shoulder. "And not a moment before." She shut the door and sashayed to her racks of clothing, muttering under her breath, "Silly fools. Thinking they can rush perfection!" She thumbed through the selection of dresses, smiling when she found one that met with her approval. She walked toward the mirror, unbuttoning the first two buttons on her bodice. Jenna had to stifle a giggle with her palm when she saw Erik make haste to cover his eyes, only peeking through slightly parted fingers when he heard Carlotta exclaim, "Che cos'è? What is this?"

They watched her walk over to the chaise, and sit down next to the box, quickly untying the black ribbon and lifting the lid. All at once, several frogs jumped up and out at her, releasing loud croaks as they did so. Carlotta screamed, dropping the lid of the box. She immediately jumped up and ran out of the room, sputtering in Italian the entire time. She slammed the door behind her, and they could hear her stumbling down the hall, calling for the managers.

Erik quickly motioned for Jenna to remain quiet. He speedily re-entered the dressing room, scooping up the harmless frogs that had jumped out of the box. He placed them back in, closed the lid and tucked the box under his arm. In its place, he left a handwritten note, which said,

Perhaps you will no longer mistake poor seamstresses with toads, now that you have met a few of the latter in person.—O.G.

He then rejoined Jenna, closing the mirror and the wall behind it, and grabbing her hand, as they began their sojourn back down toward the lake.

Jenna did not make a sound until they were safely within the boat, sailing toward Erik's home. Once they were, their eyes met, and they finally let loose the guffaws they had been strangling since the diva had opened the box.

"Erik, did you see her face?" Jenna howled with laughter.

"Unfortunately," he responded, chuckling. "I was afraid, for a moment, that I might see much more."

Jenna snorted. "Oh yes! You looked terrified!"

"I was!" Erik agreed, "I had never seen a cow undress before, and I did not want to start today."

Jenna giggled, as she gazed at him. Pure amusement lit up his unmasked features, and she realized at that moment that what she could see of his face was really quite handsome. Without thinking, she said, "I like your smile."

The smile in question immediately faded from Erik's face, as he coughed in a start at her statement. "You um…" he began, his voice obviously flustered, "probably shouldn't grow accustomed to it." He coughed again, his throat suddenly very dry. "It doesn't appear very often."

Jenna once again wanted to ask him why, but realized she had already said something wrong, as Erik would no longer look at her. Instead, they made the rest of their way back to the lair in an uncomfortable silence, the mirth from just moments before completely gone. It was almost a relief when Erik noticed the arrogant form of the Daroga sprawled once again in his reading chair.

"This is becoming a habit, Daroga." Erik called to him once they were ashore. He helped Jenna out of the boat, still not meeting her eyes, and immediately walked up to the Persian. "Did I not tell you yesterday that I was going to start charging you rent if you kept occupying my domain while I was out?"

Omid rolled his eyes, "Yes, yes, Erik. You always do your utmost to make me feel welcome."

"I *must* attempt to remedy that." Erik quipped.

"Mademoiselle," Omid smiled and extended a hand to Jenna as she approached. "How has our friend been treating you?"

Jenna smiled, glancing quickly at Erik. "Very well, Monsieur," she answered as she took Omid's proffered hand.

"Please, Mademoiselle," Omid spoke, giving her hand a gentlemanly kiss, "you may call me Omid."

She nodded, "And you may call me Jenna. In fact I would prefer it."

"Well, now that you two are on a first name basis," Erik interrupted, looking as if her were about to jump out of his own skin, "I am reminded that the cupboard is nearly bare."

"But, Erik, you just…" Omid began, before Erik cut him off.

"Why don't you two…*friends*…catch up, while I go out to gather some more supplies and let the frogs loose." He turned back to the boat, without waiting for reply.

"But Erik, I thought I would accompany you to release them." Jenna objected.

"I see no need for that, Mademoiselle." Erik continued to the lake, without turning back.

"Erik, it's daylight." Omid began to protest.

"I am wearing my hat, Daroga. It shields my mask. I shall be fine." He was in his boat, pushing off shore before calling, "Enjoy your visit, Persian! Do make it a short one. I would not mind you being gone before I return."

12 ANGEL OF MUSIC

Omid and Jenna watched helplessly as Erik sailed away in his boat, not two minutes after their initial return. When he was out of view, they turned their heads to look at one another. At the same time, they each blurted, "What just happened?"—"What's *with* him?"

"*You* were with him, Jenna," Omid pressed. "What got him into such a foul temperament?"

Jenna thought for a moment. She shook her head, at a loss, and answered, "I don't know."

Omid rolled his eyes and sighed. "Ahh. I see our friend is being crystal clear about his inner thoughts once again."

Jenna sighed too. "I just don't understand. We were laughing, and having such a good time, and then he just…" She shook her head and shrugged.

"Well, my dear," Omid said, "that explains it. He has always had an aversion to good humor."

Still exasperated, Jenna suddenly remembered her manners. "Um, would you like some tea…or …something?" she asked, figuring that despite what Erik said, she could probably find some items with which to be hospitable in Erik's kitchen.

"Oh don't trouble yourself, Jenna," Omid waved her off. "I'll take the *or something.*" He proceeded to walk to Erik's liquor cabinet and pour himself some cognac. "Would you care for some, Jenna?" He asked, holding the bottle out to her.

"Oh, no thank you, Omid." Jenna shook her head and went to sit down on the settee.

Omid replaced the stopper on the bottle and returned it to the cabinet. "You know," he said amiably, taking his seat on Erik's reading chair once again, "I have never seen Erik actually drink any of his own brandy. I think he keeps it here especially for me."

Jenna smiled at that thought. For all of Erik's bluster, she could tell he enjoyed Omid's company. At the very least, it gave him someone to complain about.

"So," Omid began, conversationally, "what have you two been doing to occupy your time since I last saw you?"

Jenna thought back on the events that had happened since dinner time last night and was overwhelmed with how much had happened. "So much…" she said out loud, as she remembered the frog hunt, the near miss with the carriage which led to Erik's terrible display of temper, and then their talk last night when they realized she had slipped backward in time, not to mention their adventure in Carlotta's dressing room. How could she ever hope to explain all of that to Omid?

"Well, where were you returning from just now? Obviously you had not gone to stock the cupboards, and did Erik say something about frogs?"

"Oh, yes, "Jenna began. "We had been to Carlotta's dressing room."

Omid's eyes widened, "Carlotta's…" He abandoned his words, suddenly feeling the urge to take a long drink from his brandy. "What on earth were you doing there?" he asked in a choked voice, after swallowing hard, feeling the burn of the whiskey as it passed down his throat.

"Oh, Erik wanted to spook her with some frogs we had caught last night," she said nonchalantly. "It worked great, too," she smiled, remembering the startled look on the rude singer's face. "She ran out of there, screaming in Italian. It was so funny. We laughed so much once we were back at the boat."

"*Erik* laughed?" Omid asked in wonder. It had been ages since he had seen his friend laugh—truly laugh. It had to have been before his sweet Aziz passed. When his little boy had died, so had Erik's laughter—or so Omid had thought.

"*Yes*," Jenna exclaimed, "he laughed *so* hard." Omid saw her eyes go far away. "And his smile…He looked so *happy*, Omid." Suddenly, she looked right at him. "Does mischief always make him that way?"

"He does tend to enjoy it," Omid confirmed, "but I confess that I do not think I have ever seen him quite as elated by it as you've described. What happened to sour his mood?"

Jenna's face looked troubled. "Like I said, I don't know." Her eyes narrowed as she struggled to remember. "It all seemed to turn when I said I liked his smile."

"Ooooh yeah," Omid finished his drink and placed the glass noisily down on the side table. "That'd do it."

"What do you mean?" she asked, confused.

"His smile is part of his face, Jenna." Omid replied. "And Erik never likes there to be any attention paid to his face."

Jenna considered that quietly for a moment. His face. He was sensitive about his face. That must be why he constantly wore that mask. He did seem a little perturbed the other day, when she told him she was looking at it. But *why* does he wear it? What was he hiding? Gathering her courage, she looked Omid in the eye and asked, "Why does he wear the mask?"

Omid looked at her silently for a long moment. "Jenna," he reached for his glass to take another sip, before remembering that the liquor was gone. "Are you sure you don't want any cognac?" he asked, going back to the cabinet for a refill of his own drink. She shook her head again, and when Omid was once again seated, drink in hand, he began.

"Erik was born with a deformity. The right side of his face, Jenna—the side he keeps masked—it's…hideous. Some have described it as looking more like a corpse than a man."

"Oh, please, Omid," Jenna began to protest, "I hardly believe it could be that bad."

"Well, whether you believe it or not," he replied, "it's true. His own mother could never look at him, and she forced him to wear a mask from birth—that was after she came to terms with the fact that she had to keep him alive, since killing him would condemn her soul to eternal torment."

Jenna gasped in shock at Omid's words. "No, surely his own mother…"

"She was horrible to him," he drank another sip of his brandy, trying to wash the image of his friend's pain away. "She never touched him, except to beat him if he ever sought affection. She told him his face was a poison, and that he would destroy anything he ever touched. She told him he would never be loved because his face made it impossible."

"What an evil woman," Jenna said in outrage. "To treat her own child so cruelly."

"She was the first to treat him cruelly, it's true," Omid agreed, "But she was not the last. Erik's life has been full of people who beat him, mocked him, and treated him like some kind of freak because of his face. He has known more than his share of savagery in his life. That's why he lives here, beneath the opera. He no longer wanted to be in the world because…"

"The world did not want him," Jenna quietly finished Omid's sentence, which was an echo of Erik's earlier words.

"Yes. That's right," he nodded, taking another long drink from his glass. "The truth is," Omid continued, "it's the world's great loss. Erik is a genius. He built this opera house, did you know that?"

"He told me," she nodded.

"He apprenticed with a master mason in Italy—quickly surpassing him in skill." Omid began to list Erik's many areas of expertise. "He is a master architect and artist. He speaks several languages fluently. He has a solid grasp on the science of medicine. Hell, he's even a magician! And have you heard his music?"

"I have heard him play…a little."

"Oh, Mademoiselle," he said, falling back to the formal greeting, as his voice took on a tone of awe. "You should hear him play a *lot.* And you should hear him *sing.* He could make Allah himself weep at the beauty of the sound."

Omid's expression darkened once more, and he finished his tale, "And yet he lives here—hiding his many talents—because humanity cannot handle his face. They seek to destroy him because they do not understand him. He plays at being a *Phantom,* bullying the opera managers with pranks and threats into doing things his way, when by rights, they should simply obey him because he is their intellectual better."

Jenna was deeply troubled by the Persian's words. It saddened her to hear that the man she had come to know as gentle and witty had been treated with such barbarism by others around him. "But Omid," she said, still confused about one thing. "I was not cruel to him. I joined in on his game. I laughed with him. I complimented him."

"You *accepted* him, Jenna," Omid corrected her. "And that terrified him, because he has never truly known acceptance." At the look of bewilderment in her eyes, Omid added, "But you did nothing wrong. Erik will come around. He just needs time."

Jenna nodded. *Well,* she thought to herself. *He's got all the time in the world.* It wasn't like she was going anywhere anytime soon.

❧

As soon as he had finished his morning rounds, the doctor hurried to Jenna's room. He had purposely left her as his last patient, wishing to spend a bit more time with her, but that had not been his smartest idea. He had found himself distracted while tending his other patients. He could not wait to get to her room to see how she was doing. Perhaps she had awakened? Tomorrow, he told himself, he would have to come in early, so he could check on her first thing.

When he approached her door he found that she was not alone. Jake Trudeau was there, and the scoundrel was holding her hand! The doctor felt the wind being knocked out of him. Had Trudeau finally realized what an imbecile he had been? Had he finally realized what his disgusting behavior was doing to the beautiful woman that loved him? Had he returned to her side to once again claim her as his own?

The doctor knew he should be happy. Isn't this exactly what he had encouraged the buffoon to do from the beginning? Visit Jenna? Spend time with her? Coax her back to consciousness? This was good. Obviously, his own attentions had not been enough. Finally Jenna had the support of someone she loved. So why did he feel like he was being punched in the gut?

He was about to turn away when he saw Trudeau release Jenna's hand and place it on her chest. He pulled back her bed sheet, and touched her bare calf, giving it a squeeze, and drawing his fingers up and down the length of it. When Trudeau's hand moved up to her thigh, the doctor had had enough.

"Excuse me, Mr. Trudeau," he interrupted in outrage, taking long strides to arrive at Jenna's bedside, his lab coat flaring out behind him. "But what the *hell* are you doing?"

The smaller man looked up, startled, "Uh, my *job*. You ordered physical therapy to prevent muscle atrophy, remember, Doc?"

He *had* ordered physical therapy, and now he felt like a moron. "Oh…um…yes," he coughed a little to cover up his mortification, wishing that he was not, at this moment, feeling his face turn bright red. "That's right. I…um…had forgotten you worked here."

"That's uh," Jake started, looking at the doctor like he was a madman, but then remembering that he had been hoping to talk to him. "That's alright, Doc. Listen...I've been meaning to ask you about Jenna's condition."

"Well," the doctor hedged, wondering if perhaps some of Trudeau's feelings for Jenna were returning after all. Still, there were privacy laws... "I do not know how much I can tell you. You aren't her husband, and since you two are no longer...involved," he watched Trudeau's face for any sign of rebuttal, but he found none. "HIPPA prevents me from ..."

"No, no," Jake said, waving his hands in front of him and shaking his head, "I don't need any major details or anything. I just was wondering how long you thought she might be out?"

"Out, Mr. Trudeau?" he asked, questioningly.

"Yeah, out," he said, emotionlessly. "You think she's going to wake up any time soon?"

"Mr. Trudeau," he began calmly. This was a fair question, even if it was delivered in an irritatingly odd manner. "It's very difficult to predict when or even *if* coma patients will emerge from unconsciousness." As he heard himself saying the words, he felt his heart sink as he recognized the truth in his own statement. She might *not* wake up. And the thought filled him with dread. "At this point, all we can do is spend time with her and hope for the best." When Trudeau continued to look at him expectantly, he added, "and wait."

A look of disappointment came over Trudeau's face—or was it discomfort? "You see, Doc...when Jenna left that night, she left her cat with me. Now, normally, I don't mind taking care of the cat," he insisted in a whiny tone of voice, "but, you see, I'm about to leave on vacation in a couple of days, and..."The doctor was once again incredulous. "You're leaving on *vacation*?"

"Yeah," he chuckled a little, "Mindy has to go to Paris for her job, and I figured I'd tag along. I got a cousin, Lucas, who lives there. I figure I could hang out with him while she's working. Take in the sights with her at night. I mean, I've been through so much lately, I could really use a getaway."

"Obviously." the doctor answered, dryly.

"But I don't know what to do with the cat. I don't really want to pay for a pet sitter—since that's expensive and he's not mine—but I don't know what to do. Should I take him to a pound or something? I mean if she's not waking up ..."

"You are a fool!" the doctor snarled.

"Huh?" Trudeau was taken aback. He looked at the doctor with squinted eyes.

"Never mind," he huffed. "Bring me the cat."

"You serious, Doc?" Trudeau looked surprised.

"Yes. I don't have any pets at the moment and the cat may bring her comfort."

"Oh, yeah," Trudeau smiled, "that's a great idea, Doc! Why didn't I think of that?"

"I guess *her* comfort just wasn't on your mind," he raised an eyebrow at him. "What, with, Mindy and the trip to France and all."

"Yeah, you know how it is," he smirked. "*Relationships.* They do kind of take over."

The doctor smiled tightly and nodded. In truth, he didn't have a lot of experience with relationships. He had always been too busy with studies to spend much time dating. The one woman he'd dated in medical school had been little more than a glorified study partner. Even now, he often couldn't find the nerve to ask a woman out—as evidenced by his shyness around Jenna before her accident. It irritated him to no end to realize that this idiot in front of him had not only been with Jenna, but had had no trouble moving on to another girl, and would probably move on from that one too.

"OK," Trudeau got back to the question at hand. "You gonna be here tomorrow? I can bring Red by."

"That would be fine," he muttered. "Just page me when you get here."

"Hey, do you mind if I bring some of her other stuff too? You know, just to get it out of the apartment? Mindy wants to start leaving stuff at my place, and she says having boxes of Jenna's things around really creeps her out."

He had to resist the urge to strangle the weasel. "That would be fine, Mr. Trudeau."

"Cool." Trudeau turned back to Jenna and reached for her leg again.

"Um, Mr. Trudeau," the doctor interrupted him. "I can take it from here. You are excused."

"Oh," Jake said, surprised. "Thanks, Doc!" He walked out of the room, never looking back at Jenna.

The doctor glared after him, shaking his head. "Really, Jenna," He asked, turning back to her, and manipulating her leg back and forth to complete the therapy he could not bear to see Trudeau perform. "What did you see in him? You deserve so much better." He paused for a moment, moving around to her other side, lifting her arm above her head and moving it in wide circles. "No matter. I will note on the chart that I do not want him performing your therapy in the future. Besides the conflict of interest, he's simply an idiot!"

❧

Erik wandered through the tunnels behind the opera house walls. He had not seen anyone on his trek to release the frogs to their natural habitat, and each one had happily returned to the marsh with a grateful croak. Somehow, however, the successful mission had done nothing to improve his darkened disposition. There was no good reason for his mood to be so bleak. He had achieved his objective of harassing the bovine soprano whom he loathed. Her shrieks had been satisfying, and he could only assume that the note he left had clearly made his point that she was not to continue to bully innocent young girls in the future. He had accomplished his goal exactly as planned. *Well*, he thought, feeling himself sink deeper into a foul frame of mind, *he had not exactly acted alone, had he? They had carried out the plan together.*

Jenna. He was forced to admit that his guest was the reason he was so ill spirited. It was not that she had done anything wrong—on the contrary, she had followed his instructions to the letter, she had marveled at his ingenuity, and she had shared in his sense of triumph. Though she had never met Carlotta and had only his word from which to form her opinion of the cow, she was clearly on his side. Once again, she had given him the impression that she enjoyed his company. Erik shook his head and scoffed at the idea. *The last time you thought that, she ran,* he remembered. *She will run again*, his inner voice warned. *She told you herself—her greatest desire is to get back home.* And her home was more than a world away—*it would take longer than a lifetime to get there.*

"I like your smile," she had said to him with a smile of her own. *Maybe she really is insane,* he thought. *How could she—or anyone, for that matter—like anything about this face?* His mother had loathed it from the moment of his birth. The slave girls in Persia recoiled from him, preferring death at the hand of the Shah over one night spent next to his inhuman form. Luciana had leapt to her demise rather than confront the countenance she had begged him to reveal. No, there was nothing to *like* about this hideous visage with which he had been cursed. The girl did not know that about which she spoke. If she did, she would denounce him for saving her from that carriage—surely preferring the crush of horse's hooves to being forced to bear his repulsive ugliness.

He paused a moment, reaching a hand out to the wall, to steady himself against the wave of sorrow which threatened to overcome him. He could not trust her words of friendship because he understood that if she knew him—really knew the beast that he was—she would hate and despise him just like everybody else. He knew that he was destined to be forever alone, with only the occasional company of that insufferable Persian to temporarily interrupt his loneliness. He had come to accept it He had learned how to tolerate a life lived alone. But now Jenna spoke of friendship—and yet she yearned to leave.

His heart was twisted with his own confusion when he heard the soft cries of another. He opened his eyes to his surroundings and realized that, once again, he had wandered behind the chapel. He located the fissure in the stone, and his heart first leapt, then broke apart to see the Angel, *Christine*, weeping again, alone on the floor.

"Oh, Papa, it was awful, simply *awful*," she whispered through tears. "She…she *struck* me!"

Erik felt the rage fill him. As he gazed upon Christine, he noticed that, indeed, her cheek was reddened. Who had struck her? Who dared to lay a hand on this poor, innocent Angel?

"She accused me, Papa, of being aligned with the *Phantom*." Christine continued on. "She claimed I had gotten him to plant toads in her dressing room! *Toads*, Papa!"

Erik's rage was replaced by guilt. His ridiculous plan had backfired, and now, the one he'd longed to avenge was bearing the brunt of his folly.

"Oh, Papa, she is just a vile human being!" Her voice sounded angry now, still thick with tears, but stronger. "An evil, stupid woman! I did not put those toads in her dressing room—I'm sure it was no ghost! She is awful to everyone, and she has made so many enemies! Anyone could have done it. I am not the first girl she has called a toad! Besides," Christine had spent her temper now, and her voice was back to the soft sad tones that so squeezed his heart. "there is no such thing as ghosts." She paused looking down, "Or angels." Her sobbing started anew, "Oh Papa, I am so lonely here, and the Angel of Music—he will *never* come."

Erik heard his voice before he was cognizant of what he was doing. "I'm here."

Christine looked up at the sound of the voice that was soft as a whisper on the wind. Had she had spent so much time talking to her dear, departed father, that she was now imagining him talking back? "Papa?"

Erik inwardly cursed himself, realizing at that moment that he *had*, in fact, spoken out loud. *Don't answer her, Erik! Let her think she was imagining things. Let her think her emotions simply have her overwrought.*

"No, my child. It is your Angel." His lips loosed the silvery words as if on their own accord. "Your Angel of Music to whom you pray." *Good God! He was the one who was insane!*

"Angel?" Christine spoke, her blue eyes, full of awe, beginning to turn toward the wall behind which he stood. "Have you at last found me? How can this be?"

Erik realized that in his haste, he had forgotten to throw his voice. Damning himself again, to the deepest bowels of hell, he threw his voice to the opposite wall, purposely taking on the ethereal quality that he knew could so easily influence others. "I have heard you call, and I have come to show you that you are not alone."

Her head whipped around again, looking in the direction from which he had made the sound emanate. "Oh, Angel!" She exclaimed, her voice filling with joy, "Papa swore he would send you. He swore you would come."

Erik let a little mirth enter his own voice now. "He did, my dear." He made his voice bounce from wall to wall and seem to come at her from all around. "And I have." He recalled his original goal in posing as her angel. "And I will lift your voice to great heights, and make it soar to the heavens."

As Christine spun round and round, trying to locate the precise source of that divine utterance, Erik caught a glimpse of the wonder on her face, and it took his breath away. Caught up in her rapture, she suddenly began to sing the sweet, soft melody he had heard her sing before. She called him her angel, her guide, her guardian. She implored him to grant her his glory—as if he had any glory to give.

The sound of her voice was pure heaven to his ears, and Erik closed his eyes so that he could more fully delight in her song. Yes, she was untrained, but the clarity and the purity that her vocals naturally possessed were enough to make his heart thrill. Once her voice was developed by his tutelage, she would easily be able to bring him to his knees with a single note. And he almost yearned to kneel powerless before her.

"Angel?" she had stopped singing, and called out to him once again, and Erik realized he had to make some answer.

"I am here, Christine." And as her name left his lips, he marveled at how it was perhaps the most beautiful sound he had ever uttered. "And I *will* be here. I will teach you. I will guide you." And then he added, in way of warning, "But you must keep me your Secret Angel. Speak of me to no one. They will never understand."

"I promise, Angel." She was facing his wall once again, and he could see that her eyes were wide with sincerity. "I will not tell a soul."

"Good," Erik responded, "for I am yours, and I am yours alone."

13 YOU WIN

"OK, next up is the case of Ms. Genevieve Wilson," the Chief of Neurology, Dr. Kenneth James, began, looking up from his notes to address his team. The weekly staff meeting was a forum where all his doctors could share and discuss their cases, gaining each other's perspectives on critical aspects of healing. It was a valuable part of the team's weekly routine, both for patient care and physician growth. Dr. James just wished that sometimes these meetings didn't take so long.

"She's mine," the young doctor rose to give his report. Dr. James didn't really know him well. He was new to the team this year, and he was quiet. Still, he had had a successful internship and had a reputation for making sound judgments, even if he did seem a bit idealistic at times.

The resident began his report. "She's 27 years old, suffering from Traumatic Brain Injury. She came in Monday night after a car accident. Upon admission, her pupils were non responsive, BP elevated, and breathing slow. Tox screens showed no alcohol or drugs in her bloodstream, and CT scan did not show significant intracranial bleeding. She was unconscious upon arrival and remains so. Recent exams show her vitals to be normal, breathing better, pupillary reaction to light returning to normal. She has exhibited some simple movements. I have hopes of her waking soon. And…that's about it." He began to sit.

"What is the level of family involvement?" one of the other doctors on the team asked.

The resident slowly returned to a standing position. "There has been no family involvement. She has no nearby family."

"Friends? Partners?" Another of his colleagues asked, as they all made notes on their patient lists.

"Her co-workers have visited," he explained. "She has no romantic partner."

"Hmm," said Dr. Blaine Charleson, an obnoxious 3rd year resident. "She works on the 5th floor, doesn't she? I could have sworn I'd seen her around with that PT guy—you know, the short blond one?"

He swallowed before answering, "Apparently, they have ended their relationship."

"Man!" Dr. Charleson commented, shaking his head. "Wish I'd known! Jenna's hot."

When the department chief noticed the younger resident's gaze grow dark, he cut in, "Dr. Charleson, keep it professional."

"I apologize, Doctor," the senior resident responded to his boss, before asking, "So why do you think she's still in the coma?"

Still distracted by Charleson's classless display, the new doctor asked, "Excuse me?"

"Well, Doctor, you paint a very rosy picture of her condition, yet the fact remains, she's still in a coma. So what's your best guess?" he played with a pencil, looking up at the young doctor with a smirk.

"I…" he cleared his throat, not exactly knowing what to say, because it was puzzling to him as well that Jenna remained unconscious. "You know, Doctor, that coma patients are very unpredictable. It's hard to say why they remain unconscious or why they awaken. We just have to give them the finest care possible and hope for the best."

"I see no evidence of pressure relieving surgery in her notes." Charleson commented, looking down on the sheet in front of him.

"That is because it was not performed." He glared at the senior resident while trying desperately to hold on to his professionalism. "The tests did not indicate that it was necessary."

"Dr. James," Charleson asked, turning to the chief, "may I ask why such a low ranking resident was assigned to a young girl with a traumatic brain injury? Don't you think she might have benefitted from having a doctor with a little more medical experience? Maybe someone who would be able to use his own intuition to better interpret the findings of the tests?"

"Dr. Charleson," our resident asserted before Dr James could answer. He leaned in toward the obnoxious physician, hands spread on the table before him. His irritation was obviously winning the battle with his reserve. "I have been with Miss Wilson from the moment she was admitted. I have the utmost experience with her case—which is why *I* am treating her in the best manner *I* see fit."

"Which is how, exactly?" Charleson calmly challenged.

"She receives preventative physical therapy. We monitor her vitals closely. We provide sensory therapy, reading to her, talking to her…" his voice trailed off in frustration. *Damn.* Even to his ears, it certainly sounded like he wasn't doing much.

"Who reads to her?" Charleson asked, meeting his eye. "Talks to her? You said yourself she has no family. Do we have paid R.N.s sitting and reading to patients now?"

"I do," he answered, a little more loudly than necessary. When he was only met with silence from those around him, he added in a quieter voice, "She *has* no one else."

The tension that followed was broken when his pager went off. The doctor looked at the message and sighed, "I apologize, but I have to go." He reattached his pager to his belt and turned toward the door.

"Highly irregular to leave in the middle of a briefing, isn't it, Doctor?" Charleson goaded.

He looked toward Dr. James, hoping for understanding. "It's Miss Wilson's ex-boyfriend. I arranged for him to bring her cat. I was hoping a visit with the animal might help her."

Dr. James looked at the young man, who truly did not deserve Charleson's posturing. "Go, Doctor. We can talk later."

The resident shot out of the room hastily, as Dr. James turned to Dr. Charleson, saying, "*We* will talk now."

❧

Erik returned to the lair, looking far more relaxed than he had when he'd left it. He gracefully exited the boat and practically floated over to the sitting room where Omid and Jenna were hunched over a friendly game of Bezique. It did not go unnoticed by Omid that his friend had arrived completely empty-handed. So much for stocking the cupboards—which, as Omid knew, were perfectly well stocked to begin with. "Good evening, Jenna," Erik greeted her with a polite smile, which she returned, happy to see him looking a little more like the man she had come to know.

"No supplies, Erik?" Omid could not help but prod. "Were the opera's kitchen cupboards bare as well?"

"Daroga, I see you're still here too," Erik remarked with a raise of his eyebrow. "How delightful to know that you have not yet learned to take a hint."

"You know I require plain speech, my friend," Omid teased, taking a sip from yet another glass of Erik's liquor.

"Well then, in that case, Daroga, get…"

"Erik!" Jenna interrupted their banter with a little chuckle. "How did it go with the frogs?"

He looked at her a little puzzled, "The frogs?" he asked. "Well, they did fine, of course. Hopped right out into the marsh, with little prodding from me."

"Well, where have you been, all this time, man?" Omid asked. "You obviously were not at the kitchens, and I'm sure the frogs did not take this long to *hop out of the box*! Why, you were gone so long, I've just about finished your bottle of cognac."

Jenna shook her head back and forth, laughing at how Omid incessantly provoked Erik.

"It's a good thing, then, that I have another bottle," Erik replied, calmly, taking a seat at the table between Jenna and Omid, looking over their card game to determine that the state of the battle was not in Jenna's favor.

"You do?" Omid asked, perplexed, for he had only seen the one bottle in the cabinet. "Where is it?"

Erik absentmindedly reached over and plucked a card from Jenna's hand using it to trump the card Omid had just played. "It is hidden."

"Hey!" Omid protested, though whether it was in response to Erik's move, or his answer, was not clear. "That isn't very nice!" Omid held his cards closer to his chest to protect the secrecy of his hand.

"When have you known me to be nice, Persian?" Erik asked, smoothly playing another of Jenna's cards. Jenna smiled at the way Erik so effortlessly took over a game that had been quite perplexing to her. He was obviously a master at the diversion, being able to continue his banter with an ever more flustered Omid as he decisively crushed him in the contest. When Erik mercilessly counted up the points at the end of the match, he leaned over to Jenna and grinned, "You win." The rakish way he said it had her suppressing an urge to hug him, as she recognized the same twinkle in his eye that had been there when he was capturing the frogs. The tension from earlier in the day, however, somewhat held her back. Still, she could not resist arching an eyebrow at him and asking, "*What* do I win?" Erik discerned a slight shift in the air between them and swallowed, staring back at Jenna, not exactly knowing what to say. He was almost grateful when he heard Omid clear his throat and comment, "My my, your mood has changed. What happened to lift you out of your gloom? Did Carlotta break a vocal cord?"

Jenna noticed the mischief return to Erik's eyes as he turned toward Omid to answer, "We should be so lucky. She seems too busy breaking ear drums to worry about vocal cords." The mischievous twinkle left Erik's eye, only to be replaced by a faraway gleam. "I saw her, Daroga," he said on a sigh.

"Who? The diva?" Jenna asked this time, wondering if Erik had any more news on how their prank had been received.

"No," Erik responded, still staring into space. "The *Angel*." Omid had already begun to roll his eyes and Jenna looked at him strangely until Erik whispered the name "Christine."

Jenna stared at him in confusion, "Who's Christine?"

"Oh, weren't you listening, Mademoiselle?" Omid asked, sarcasm dripping from his every word. "She's the angel!"

The Persian's jest made Erik snap out of his reverie, sighing. "Christine is the seamstress I was telling you about, Jenna. The victim of Carlotta's wrath."

"Oh," Jenna said, finally understanding.

"But she is so much more than a seamstress." Erik rose from his seat, and began to extol her virtues. Omid took a gulp of his drink as Erik began, after once again offering the glass to Jenna, to see if she required the same liquid fortitude he did to get through Erik's imminent speech. "She has the voice of a lark and the soul of an angel." Coming back to earth momentarily, he looked at Jenna and asked, "Do you know that…cow, that…*pig* had the nerve to blame her for our actions! She *struck* her!"

"Oh no," Jenna answered.

"Uh oh," Omid responded, peering down into his now empty glass, trying desperately to spy at least one last drop of amber relief.

"But fear not!" Erik continued, pacing as he resumed his oration.

"I wasn't," Omid muttered, and Jenna slapped him gently on the arm.

If Erik heard Omid's remark, he expertly ignored it. "Christine shall have her revenge. With her voice, and my training, she will become the greatest Prima Donna in the land, and then that… *goat*…will not even be fit to sew Christine's hems!"

"Your *training*?" Jenna questioned, still thoroughly confused.

"Oh, yes," Omid answered with a bright smile. "Didn't you know? *He's* an angel too!"

"You're drunk, Persian," Erik glared at Omid.

"No, I'm not," Omid disagreed, "but I *should* be. Are you watering down my alcohol, Erik?"

"*Your* whiskey?" Erik responded, incredulously. "Do you mean *my* whiskey, which you *steal* without permission every time you enter my home—also without permission?"

"Well, Erik," Omid pointed out pleasantly, "you stole it first."

When Erik just glowered at Omid, speechless, Jenna took the opportunity to cut into the conversation. Erik had been in such a fun mood when he returned, and she was somewhat annoyed at Omid for bringing him down. She was not in the mood to witness another one of his displays of temper.

"Erik," she asked, drawing his attention back to her. "What is he talking about?"

Realizing Jenna had not yet heard of his plan to displace Carlotta, Erik sat back down at the game table, turning distinctly away from the Persian, and told her. "Christine has a lovely voice, Jenna, but it is untrained. I have told you that music is my greatest passion. I know how to sing, so I am going to teach her, and once she has had the proper training, she will far surpass Carlotta in skill, since she already has such lovely raw material with which to begin."

Jenna heard Omid snicker but ignored him. "So she has agreed to lessons, Erik?"

"She *has*." He smiled, contentedly.

"Then you will bring her here?" Jenna asked, excitedly. "It will be wonderful to have another girl around here."

"Well, no," Erik said, a little discomfort entering into his expression. "I cannot bring her here. She cannot know me."

"But I…thought she already knew you?" Jenna once again heard confusion enter into her tone. "How could you have discussed lessons with her if she didn't know you?"

"*Angel*, remember?" Omid interjected. Erik glared, while Jenna kicked Omid under the table to shut him up.

"I will teach her in the opera house from behind the wall of the chapel." His eyes were clouded once again, and Jenna felt her spirit fall.

"But Erik, why?" she asked him, sadness coloring her tone.

"Is it not obvious, Mademoiselle?" He rose and began pacing once more.

"If it were obvious, Erik," Jenna responded, "I would not be asking you."

"She expects that it is an angel that will be teaching her," Erik said. "The Angel of Music, to be exact."

"Well, why would she expect that?" Jenna questioned.

"Because that's what he told her," Omid added in.

"*Because*," Erik corrected him, "that's what her dear, *departed* father promised would happen. He said he would send her The Angel of Music to make her song take flight. She truly believes in what her father promised her. She was despondent that the Angel had not yet come.

"I saw her crying for her angel, so I told her I was him, and that I had come to teach her. She believes her angel has come to lift her out of her despair. Why would I shatter her illusions?"

"Especially when they work out so well for you," Omid retorted.

"Why are you still here?" Erik turned to him and asked.

"I cannot resist a good drama," Omid said with a smile. "And you, Erik, are full of it."

Erik turned away from him once more and concluded his tale, "Regardless, it will work. She does not need to see me to hear my voice, and she *will* learn, and one day grace the stage of this very opera house."

"When will you start lessons?" Jenna asked.

"We have already begun." Erik smiled at the memory. "She sang a bit for me today. But we will meet every evening, so there is much I need to prepare." Erik started to walk toward the bookshelf, gathering papers and taking them with him to the piano. "I trust you two can prepare your own dinner?" Erik called to them, already thumbing through the sheets of music before him. "There are plenty of provisions in the kitchen."

❧

It was late when he walked into her hospital room, carrying his lab coat over a bundle in his arms. "Jenna," he called quietly, "I'm back. And I brought you a visitor." He closed the door behind him with his foot, gingerly balancing the bundle on one arm and using his free hand to remove the coat, revealing a very spoiled, very cuddly yellow cat wearing a red collar. As soon as the coat was removed, the cat let loose a loud "MEEERRROOOOOOW" and rubbed his head against the doctor's chin. He chuckled, saying, "I know, I know, Red. You're happy to see her too." He walked over to Jenna's bedside and sat in the chair next to her bed. "So I have a new roomie, Jenna. Nice guy. Talks a lot. Furry. I think you two know each other," he said, with a smile, rearranging the cat so he was closer to Jenna. "Would you like to hold him?" When he gently placed Red beside Jenna on the bed, the cat immediately started to purr, bumping his head against Jenna's hand, as if asking for a pet. The doctor reached out for Jenna's hand and softly placed it on the cat's back, which seemed to make the feline purr even louder. "Awwww, see?" The doctor said sweetly, "He likes you. I knew he was a good judge of character." He continued to watch Jenna's face for any sign of a reaction, as he reached out and pampered Red's head with a few lazy pets. Suddenly, his fingers brushed up against Jenna's, and he glanced down to see her slowly stroking Red's fur. "Jenna?" he asked quietly. "Jenna, can you hear me?" he asked again, but got no response. "I know you're in there, Jenna. I know you can hear me. Why won't you wake up? What are you waiting for?" He sighed in frustration, his head hanging low. "What am *I* doing wrong?"

After a moment, he felt soft fingers on his head, and he realized that Jenna's hand had moved from stroking Red's fur to his hair. He glanced up at her face, and once again saw that serene smile cross her lips. He felt his heart jump a little, thinking her smile could only be more beautiful if her eyes were open.

"I know I've said this before, Jenna," he said in a somewhat shaky voice, "But I'm not giving up on you. I *know* you know I'm here, and I know you can hear me." He closed his eyes, and breathed deeply, taking in the feeling of her fingers in his hair. "I just hope that one day soon you'll answer me."

14 GENIUS

"Finally!" Jenna said to herself, as she opened the last kitchen cabinet to find the tea. A simple dinner had come and gone, Omid had taken his leave for the evening, and still Erik was at his piano, preparing for tomorrow's lesson with his *angel.* He did not actually play much—mostly running scales and short passages of songs here and there, making copious notes on sheets and sheets of paper. It had gone on for hours, and though Omid had hinted earlier at Erik's genius, there was only so much plinking and plodding that Jenna could take. She had decided that though he had not eaten dinner, it seemed a very *singer-ly* thing to do to drink tea, and since his mind was on voice lessons tonight, the tea might be just the thing to distract him—at least for a few moments.

She removed the lid from the ornate metal box and found…dirt. "What the…" she muttered to herself, realizing after a moment that they did not have teabags in 19th century France, and of course, she was going to have to use loose tea. She had never made tea this way in her life—and though she looked all over the little box, there were no instructions. "Hmmm. I guess brewing tea from tea leaves should be common knowledge right about now," she said to her self. She hesitated for a moment, wondering if perhaps she should ask Erik if *he* would make *her* tea, but she got the distinct impression she would dry up from dehydration before he would separate himself from his piano.

Letting out a loud huff of air, she mumbled, "Well, it can't be that hard," as she began to scoop several spoonsful of the very fine mulch-like substance into two porcelain tea cups while she waited for the kettle to finish boiling. When the water bubbled, she poured it over the leaves and let it sit for a few moments while she gathered the sugar bowl and a little container of cream, not knowing how Erik preferred his tea. She set these things, along with two silver teaspoons and two cloth napkins on a tray she had found in one of the cabinets. Handling the delicate tea items, she felt, for a moment, very much like an elegant Victorian lady, and she decided she should simply embrace the part for the time being. After all, Erik was obviously too distracted by his *angel* tonight to figure out a way to get her home. With a satisfied smile on her face, she set out to carry her offering to Erik.

She stood there quietly beside the piano a moment or two with Erik not noticing she was there, so absorbed was he in tapping out notes and recording them on his sheets. She cleared her throat once, twice, three times, and still Erik's attention was entirely focused on the circles and lines he scrawled on the paper, coinciding with the tunes that were swirling around his mind. Finally her impatience won, and she called out "Erik," perhaps a little louder than she had intended.

With a start, Erik looked up and met her gaze. "What?" he asked, not noticing her tray at first, but then slowly realizing what Jenna carried in her hands. "Oh," he said with surprise, "you made tea?"

"Yes," she smiled again, finally received the acknowledgement she'd craved. "I thought you could use some."

"Oh, well," he began, as his eyes wandered once more to his music. "That…" he jotted down a quick note, absentmindedly, "that was very nice, but I have much to do to prepare…"

"You've been working for hours!" she interrupted him. "You didn't stop for dinner. Did you even notice that Omid left?"

"That *would* explain the absence of hot air in the room," he replied emerging somewhat from his music-induced stupor, a sardonic smirk teasing at his lips.

Jenna allowed him a grudging chuckle. "Well, that, and the fact that the fire's died down."

Erik glanced over to his hearth, to see only embers remaining where there were once roaring flames. "Ahh," he commented, nodding. "So it has."

"Five minutes, Erik," Jenna asked quietly. "You don't even have to get up from the piano. Just drink your tea and take a break for five minutes. After that you can go back to composing…or preparing…or whatever it is you're… doing, and I will borrow a book and go to my room and not disturb you. But I didn't want to go to bed without saying goodnight."

Erik sighed softly. He was not used to having anyone else reside in his quarters, and so his timetable had become his own. What did the rising and the setting of the sun matter to one who always lived alone in the dark? He ate when he was hungry—which was rarely—and he slept when his body gave out from exhaustion. He saw no real significance in either activity. But Jenna stood here before him, having made an effort to offer him some small nourishment and somehow feeling it important to acknowledge his presence before taking her leave from him for the night. "All right, Jenna," he nodded, realizing suddenly that his throat was a bit dry. "A cup of tea might do me some good." He acquiesced, as she set the tray on one of his side tables.

"Cream and sugar?" Jenna asked.

"No thank you," Erik waved the thought off. "I prefer my tea black."

Jenna smiled as she lifted a cup from the tray and handed it to him. "OK, then. There you go."

Erik smiled politely and took the cup she offered him. When she also had her own cup in hand, he took a drink of the still steaming liquid while looking up at her. He then promptly spat it out—all over the music he had been writing.

Jenna gasped, shocked at Erik's vulgar display.

"Oh," he gagged, "that was awful." He grabbed a handkerchief from his pocket and began to pat at the composition he had been working on. "Oh, don't be ruined…don't be ruined," he muttered at the papers in a worried voice.

Jenna reddened in a combination of embarrassment and irritation, and said, "I was only trying to do something nice for you!"

"Nice?" he repeated, unthinking, still blotting at his music. "How did you make the tea, Mademoiselle? By mixing lake water with dirt?"

"I used the tea that was in *your* cupboard," she answered back, her voice rising in indignation.

"Do they no longer make tea in 2014?" Erik shot back acerbically, "Because the tea in *my* cupboard never tastes like this when *I* make it."

Jenna could feel angry tears rise to her eyes, but she'd be damned if she would let him see them fall. "In 2014, we use tea bags—not the *dirt*, as you call it, that I found in your cupboard," she shouted. "And *you* did not make the tea, did you? You've been too busy isolating yourself at your piano, preparing music for a girl you have to talk to *through a wall.* You barely even noticed the living, breathing people who were here in this room *with* you tonight!" She yanked Erik's cup out of the limp hold his hand still had on it, placed it on the tray with the rest of the supplies, and hurriedly made off to the kitchen.

Erik stared at the place where she had stood a moment longer, mouth gaped open in stunned silence. Had she just *yelled* at him? The fearsome *Phantom*? In his own *home*? Because *she* had botched something as simple as making tea? Tea he had not wanted—had not *asked* for? Tea which he only drank because she somehow decided it was necessary for him to drink it?

He had been perfectly happy to sit here at his piano, composing, honing, perfecting the methods by which he would forge Paris' greatest soprano. He had his work—he had his music. He hadn't needed interruptions, or tea, or…or…people! And he definitely hadn't needed her to say goodnight.

But *she* had felt compelled to say goodnight to *him.*

Erik inwardly groaned as he covered his head with his hands and heard his elbows make a loud, discordant sound on the piano keys. She was *right.* Damn it, *again*, she was right! He had been so terribly wrapped up in his plans for teaching Christine, that he had forgotten that Jenna was here, all alone in a strange world, with no one to turn to except for him. Was her predicament really so different than his angel's? Jenna too was lost, out of place. But she strove to show *him* kindness, and he…? *He* had spent the entire evening completely ignoring her, thinking instead about Christine.

Erik rose from his piano bench and quietly walked into the kitchen. He arrived to see Jenna slam closed the drawer that held the teaspoons and begin to scrub furiously at the hardly dirty teacups. Without a word, he stood beside her at the sink. He poured some water into a pot and set it to boil. He then gently removed the teacups from her hands, rinsing them, and opened the drawer to retrieve the spoons she had just deposited. He reached into the cupboard and once again took down the box of tea.

"What are you doing?" Jenna asked, petulantly.

"I am making you," Erik said calmly, "a proper cup of tea."

"You don't have to do that," Jenna said, looking away.

"I know it is not required. I *want* to," Erik said calmly again. He reached for the cast iron teakettle she had used, and poured a bit of the boiling water into it, allowing the vessel to get hot, and then poured the water out. He scooped a few spoonsful of the tea leaves into the warmed kettle, and poured the rest of the boiling water over them. He covered the kettle, and allowed it to sit, as he went to the cupboard that held the cooking utensils and produced a strainer. When the tea had steeped for several minutes, Erik placed the strainer over each tea cup, pouring the rich brown liquid, letting the leaves themselves be caught in the sieve. He then placed the steaming cups, spoons, kettle, sugar and cream back onto the tray she had chosen and began to walk out into the sitting room. When she did not immediately follow, he turned back and motioned with his head for her to come with him. He then directed them to the settee, where he waited for her to sit before he placed the tray on the table and took a seat on the other side. He handed her a cup, saying, "Your tea, Jenna."

Jenna grudgingly took a sip and said, "This is good, Erik."

"Thank you, my lady," he responded, taking a sip himself. When the uncomfortable quiet around them lingered, Erik once again found himself with that awkward urge to repent from, atone for and be forgiven of his recent behavior. "Jenna," he began quietly. "I find it quite ironic that I had never apologized to a single soul before I met you, and here I am, expressing contrition for the second time in as many nights."

"Erik, you don't have to apologize," She said looking down.

"Of course I do," Erik insisted. "You tried to do something… kind… for me, and I was completely ungrateful, and ungracious. I am sorry, Jenna," he stated with a sheepish grin. "Again."

Jenna couldn't help but be warmed by his offering of remorse, and she smiled, saying, "It's ok."

Erik looked at her quizzically. "What does OK mean? Are you still upset with me?"

Jenna chuckled, "No!" she assured him. "I'm not angry. OK means the same as all right. I was simply saying that it was alright that you…reacted the way you did."

"No it wasn't," Erik shook his head. "But does that mean I have your forgiveness?"

Jenna was moved by the sincerity in Erik's eyes, and holding his gaze, she simply nodded and said, "Yes."

With a relieved smile, Erik whispered, "Thank you."

Quiet fell between them again. Eager to keep Erik in the talking mood, Jenna asked, "So how are your preparations coming? For your lessons?"

"I think…" Erik began, not really sure how to answer. In truth, his time at the piano had been a wild jumble of thoughts and inspirations, all converging on him at once into one glorious, yet completely disorganized heap. It would take time to unravel the insights that had taken root tonight, but in answer to Jenna's question, he simply said, "I have enough for a start," and chuckled. "I've never done this before—I never taught anyone how to sing. I just…want to be able to help her," he said, thinking of Christine. "She's so alone. She needs me." He looked at her as he emphasized his last words, holding her gaze. He saw her eyes grow somewhat distant as she nodded and said, "I know."

Once again, Erik felt the heat of shame build up in his chest. "Here I am again," he said, "thinking of her while I am talking to you." He looked at her slightly sheepishly and added, "I haven't forgotten about you, Jenna. I *will* find a way to get you home."

She averted her gaze from his and nodded. Truly, he had her a bit flustered. Maybe teatime wasn't such a smart idea.

"Do you miss it?" She heard Erik ask quietly, when she remained silent. Could it be that he too wished to keep talking?

"My home?" she asked.

"Your home," he nodded. "Your…family?"

"I don't really have a family," she told him. "I never knew my father, and my mother died a few years ago."

" I am sorry to hear that, Jenna."

"It's ok. It's just…my life," she shrugged and smiled a little, but Erik noted that the humor did not reach her eyes. "I have no brothers and sisters, and now…" She paused for a brief moment, thinking of Jake. "I don't have a man in my life either, so…yeah. It's just me." She gave a mirthless chuckle.

Though he did not act on it, Erik had the odd urge to reach out and touch her hand. He was consumed with a feeling that was entirely foreign to him. It was as if, even though Jenna's life had been lived over 130 years from now, he could understand her experience because it seemed somewhat…familiar. Certainly she was not a hideous deformed freak who had been continuously abused to the point that he now hid in a basement, but, somehow, she had also wound up alone.

"Your...*intended?*" he pressed on, recalling what she had told him the other night.

Jenna chuckled a bit at Erik's choice or words. "Well, he was *my* intended, but I certainly was not his!"

"Your...*boyfriend* then," he clarified, using the unfamiliar phrase she had used the other night. "He took another paramour, correct?"

Jenna gave a tight smile and nodded, "Yup, bingo!"

Again, Erik did not recognize the words she used, but the meaning came through crystal clear. She had been betrayed by the one from whom she expected only love. And yet, that man had *not* been her husband. He marveled at how such a beautiful woman could be, as yet, unwed. "How is it that you are not married?" When Erik saw Jenna's cheeks turn red he immediately regretted his loose tongue. "Oh, Jenna, there I go again. I apologize."

"No, Erik, it's a valid question. I know that women marry much younger in the 1800s—at an age when, in my time, frankly, we would consider them barely more than children. In the 21st century, women tend to marry much later. Most of them go to college and have jobs before they settle down with a husband and have children. But I..." She paused, taking a deep, uncomfortable breath, "I didn't really have a master career plan. I have just been unlucky. I always wanted to get married and have kids, but I've never been able to find the right man. I'm what they call," she made quotation signs in the air with her fingers, "a loser magnet." She shook her head in disgust. "I've always dated the guys who made me feel *special*—saying and doing all the right things until they got what they wanted from me, and then dumped me as soon as they found someone else they wanted even more," she said with a faraway look in her eyes. "Jake was no different, except that I moved in with him—which was a first for me." She looked down with a sad expression into her teacup. "At least my cat thinks I'm special."

"Jenna," Erik said in a hushed tone, instinctively reaching out and tilting her chin up with his hand. "You *are* special." Their eyes met, and for a moment, a palpable intensity passed between them. Not understanding why he was feeling so breathless, Erik cleared his throat, saying, "You even got me to apologize three times in two days. That is more than I have apologized to anyone in my life—and believe me when I tell you I have done some things to the Persian…"

Jenna giggled, "I can *only* imagine."

"Hopefully not!" Erik quipped and the mood was lightened. Once again, Jenna noticed that sweet, handsome smile light up the exposed side of Erik's face, and she felt such a strong urge to remove the mask and see the other half of that expression, regardless of what Omid had said. She reached out and let her fingertips graze the mask, as his eyes looked into hers questioningly. She knew that, no matter how strong her desire, removing that barrier was a venture for another day. So instead, she only allowed her fingers to trail down the porcelain outline of his cheek, recalling that other side of him that she did really long to know. So she asked, "Erik, will you play with me?"

Erik raised his eyebrows in surprise, "*Play* with you, Jenna?"

"*FOR* me," she corrected herself immediately, feeling her cheeks grow hot with embarrassment. "*For* me. Omid told me…" she began and immediately saw his eyes roll. She giggled a little as she continued, "that you were a musical genius, and I…"

"Certainly saw no evidence of that tonight," he said, with that self-deprecating humor that Jenna so enjoyed.

"Well, I'd *like* to," she smiled.

"Come," he said, placing down his teacup as he led her to the piano. He sat on the bench, and began to play, shifting from melody to melody. Many of the tunes were familiar to her from music classes she had taken in high school and college. Great masterpieces written by Mozart and Beethoven, Handel and Bach. But the notes were brought alive anew by Erik's virtuosity, and his passionate delivery made the old songs *breathe* again, as if Jenna were hearing them for the first time. After he had played for a while, Erik looked up at her with that confident twinkle that was becoming so familiar and asked, "Was that genius enough for you, Mademoiselle?"

"*Well*," she began with a smile, unable to resist the urge to challenge him just a bit more. "I don't know. I still haven't heard you sing."

"Sing!" Erik exclaimed, in mock outrage, "To be fair, Mademoiselle, you never asked me to sing."

"Well, now I am," she smirked and raised an eyebrow. "Sing for me! Come on, now, *Monsieur*. Your genius is on the line."

"My *genius*, Mademoiselle?" Erik responded, playfully. "Well, if it is my *genius* on the line, perhaps I should not sing you any old song, but one of my original compositions."

"Oh, I think that's an excellent idea, but *I* have one that's even better," her eyes sparkled with a mischief of her own.

"Indeed, Mademoiselle?" Erik asked, intrigued. "What could be better than one of my own compositions," he asked with exaggerated conceit.

"An original composition," she began, an impish twinkle in her eye, "completely improvised."

"What?" Erik was surprised by her demands. "Lyrics and melody, composed spontaneously?"

"Exactly," Jenna confirmed, looking directly in his eyes. "Or is that too much to ask of a genius such as yourself?"

That ambitious gleam glowed brighter in his gaze. "Hardly," Erik asserted, playfully brushing off her concern, knowing that she was simply giving him the opportunity to work through a bit of the tangle of inspiration that had hit him earlier. "Would you care to name a theme for the composition—a topic about which I should emote in song?"

"Love," she spoke before thinking, feeling mortified once she heard her voice say the word out loud. Oh, why had she said that?

Erik's took her suggestion in stride, however, simply stating, "Ah, I see you *are* trying to make this a challenge for me, suggesting a motif about which I know nothing."

"If you would rather…" Jenna began to backpedal, feeling horribly about her thoughtlessness.

"Nonsense," he replied lightly. "After all, a *genius* must strive to capture the essence of realities with which he has no experience." And with that, he pressed his fingers to the keys, playing the first sparse, hesitant chords of what would become his improvised song.

After a few gentle progressions, Jenna playfully reminded him, "Remember, *Monsieur Genius*. Music *and* words."

He knew she was trying to tease him good-naturedly, but since the lyrical concept had been dancing around his mind for most of the evening, he glanced her way with a crooked grin and opened his mouth to sing.

A suffocating hold
A dagger to the bone
Someone to invade your

Private space

"Erik," Jenna commented, jokingly as she listened to the words he sang, "I think you're singing about Omid!"

He chuckled as he played the next progression of chords, and the warmth of his laughter was still somewhat evident as he began to sing the next verse of words.

Always needing more
Vexing to the core
Intruding on your sanity
With a smile upon her face

Yes, Jenna thought at the reference to Erik's poor put upon sanity, *definitely Omid.* She found it funny that her demand for a love song had resulted in an ode to the friend that seemed to permanently reside under Erik's skin.

With the third verse, however, the song began to subtly build in intensity, and any resemblance to his friendship with Omid began to fade from Jenna's mind.

Someone to whom you can't say no
Who inspires gentility in storm
And no matter how much you hide from her
She'll want to know you. She'll need…to know you.
Suddenly you find yourself surrounded
With feelings that you never thought you'd know
And though at first, the thought is terrifying
She is with you. She's beside you.
You can tell that she is frightened just like you.
But you take her hand, because you know together
You'll make it through.

The song was not done, but that was all Erik had at the moment. He looked up at Jenna, expecting a witty remark, and saw that the light, teasing expression was gone from her face. Instead, her eyes were filled with emotion.

Jenna could not articulate her reaction to the words that had issued from Erik's mouth. His song was simple, it's true, but his voice had been so full of emotion, alternating between a rich strength, and a soft vulnerability. As the tension grew in the song, the understated poignancy with which he sang tugged at Jenna's heart, knowing what she did about his childhood, about his past and his present. Beyond the words, his voice was beautiful, and it *affected* her in ways she could not express. And while she knew he expected some reaction, she found herself unable to do more than stare at the amazing musician before her.

"Well," he asked, finally, his eyes looking at her expectantly.

"That was …beautiful," she whispered.

"It's not finished," he admitted, somewhat self-consciously.

"I'm sure it soon will be," she replied, still staring at him with astonishment.

"So am I a genius?" he teased, hoping to get back to that light banter he had enjoyed so much earlier.

"Without a doubt," She said with a peaceful smile, as the echoes of his voice continued to tease at her memory. She looked at him a moment longer, unable to think of anything else to say. So she whispered, "Erik, I think I'm finally going to say goodnight."

"Oh…all right, Jenna," he said, admittedly a little disappointed to see her go. He found that he was really enjoying their time together, but he had to remind himself that most people—apparently even those from the 21st century—needed regular sleep.

"Are you going to work a little more on your lessons?" she asked, looking for an excuse to convince herself she really should leave the room.

"Um…" Erik's mind was so far off the lessons, that he had to think a moment before comprehending what she'd said, "Perhaps."

"Ok," Jenna nodded. "Goodnight."

"Jenna," Erik called, as he watched her smile and turn to make her way toward the spare room. When she looked back to him, he reached out his hand, and giving hers a gentle squeeze, he whispered, "Goodnight."

Jenna smiled again, and, wordlessly, walked back to her room. When she closed her door, he stared, unmoving, at his piano for a moment, trying to recapture his earlier inspirations for the lessons. After a few long moments, finding it hopeless, he got up and moved to his bookcase, thumbing through the many volumes lining the shelves. "Time travel, time travel," he muttered to himself, "What do I have here about time travel?"

"I'm sorry, Jenna. I'm so sorry." He was as gentle as possible, as he used tweezers to lift the thread, carefully sliding the scissors beneath the knot to open the suture. He knew this should not be hurting her, but *he* could not help but wince each time he used the tweezers to pull the thread out of her freshly healed skin, the soft pink coloring reminding him how delicate she was at the site of her wound. He repeated the process with every stitch, apologizing each time, until all of her sutures were removed, and he was confident that she would not bear much of a scar to remind her of the ordeal. He tore open an antiseptic wipe from the suture removal kit and used it to clean the area where the wound had been. He stopped when he saw her suddenly grimace.

"What is it, Jenna?" he asked, his eyes crinkled quizzically. "You weren't complaining when I was removing your stitches. What is it about the wipe that you don't like?" He wondered if the antiseptic burned her somehow at the site of her injury, so he brushed the wipe against her arm, but he got the same response. "Ok, it shouldn't be irritating you *there*," he spoke out loud, still thinking. Taking a new wipe and rubbing it against his own skin, he felt the cool wet sensation and asked her, "Were you *cold*?" When, of course, he got no answer, he decided to try something he had read up on last night as he'd sat there, tickling under Red's chin before bed. He extended Jenna's right arm with one hand, and with his other, he ran his index finger slowly down the length of her arm. His touch was feather light, and when he felt her shudder, a smile broke out across his face. "Yes, Jenna," he exclaimed, repeating the contact again, and eliciting the same response. "That's good! That's good!" He chuckled, almost overjoyed that she was showing a response to the stimulus he was trying. "Keep it up."

He heard the knock, and turned to see Dr. James standing in the doorway.

"Dr. James, hello," he said, in greeting.

"Sounds like there's a bit of excitement going on in here," the Neurology Head said questioningly.

"There is, Doctor," he responded, his elation clear in his eyes. "She's responding."

Dr. James looked over at the patient who was clearly still unconscious. "How so, Doctor?"

"She shuddered at my touch," he blurted, only realizing how that sounded out loud when he saw the department head raise an eyebrow. "Um…that is to say, she shivered in response to a light stimulus I provided. I was doing some research on Coma Arousal Therapy last night," he barreled on, wishing to divert his embarrassment. "It's a therapy regimen of extreme sensory stimulation. It's thought to aid in activating the reticular system, which you know governs consciousness. It's been known to increase the number of meaningful responses that coma patients make, and can prevent sensory deprivation, which, as you know, retards recovery and can further depress already impaired brain function. I think she would be an excellent candidate for C.A.T., since she seems to regularly respond to touch."

"Excellent idea, Doctor," the senior physician responded, approvingly. "See if Physical Therapy or Occupational Therapy is equipped to provide that type of treatment."

"Actually, Doctor James," he interjected, "I was hoping to perhaps perform it myself."

"Doctor, I applaud your concern for your patient," the chief began, in a dissuasive manner. "However, we do have therapists for a reason. They have their areas of expertise and we have ours. That is what *you* should be focusing on."

"Understood, Dr. James," he pressed on. "But, in truth, I find the technique fascinating, and I was hoping to make a study of Miss Wilson's reactions, and perhaps present her case at the Neurological Symposium next fall."

Dr. James studied his subordinate carefully. He admired his determination and willingness to go the extra mile for his patient, but still, there was some cause for concern that he was taking the case too personally. "Are you certain, Doctor, that your interest in Miss Wilson's case is merely academic?"

"Of course, Doctor," he responded, cautious to keep his nerves at bay. If his boss thought he had anything more than a professional interest in Jenna, there is no way he would be allowed to stay on her case. He could not lose her as a patient, for the claim of doctor over patient was truly the only realistic claim he had on her. And he was not willing to relinquish that as of yet. "What other interest would there be?"

"Miss Wilson is a very lovely woman," Dr. James suggested, watching the young resident closely for any sign of emotion.

"A fact that Dr. Charleson made very clear at the meeting," he replied with squared jaw, looking his boss straight in the eye, the model of resolute professionalism.

With a deep breath, Dr. James allowed, “Alright, Doctor. Be careful. Take good notes.” With a parting nod, he left the room.

He waited until he heard his boss's footsteps fade away down the hall before turning back to Jenna. “Looks like we got approval to be lab partners on our little experiment, Miss Wilson,” he said in a playful tone, gathering up his supplies. “Now you just make sure to do your part and wake up. After all, you want me to get a good grade, don't you?”

15 LET THE DREAM BEGIN

It was early morning, but Omid knew Erik would not be asleep. The ghost rarely rested, which was one reason why he was so successful at haunting the opera house. He moved about and caused his mischief when respectable souls were sleeping. Then again, since Erik thought himself devoid of a soul, Omid supposed it was fitting. He brought with him a bag of fresh pastries, since he was also certain Erik would not have thought to provide Jenna breakfast, most likely expecting her to subsist for days on fumes like he was wont to do.

Fully expecting Erik to be composing or even out and about in the opera house, he was surprised to see him sitting in the leather chair, a book in his hand, and several strewn on the floor around him.

"Erik," he said, a bit taken aback. "What are you doing?"

"I would have assumed," his friend began, not even looking up from the page he was perusing, "that since you observe a book in my hand, you might have surmised that I was reading."

"You're in my chair!" Omid exclaimed, in mock outrage.

Turning the page he had just finished scrutinizing, Erik replied, "I do admit, Daroga, you've spent more time in it lately than I have. But, it still remains *my* chair."

"What has got you so enthralled?" He pressed, discounting the fact that Erik was completely ignoring him. "It's not like you to toss your belongings about like this," he waved his hand, indicating the books all over the floor.

"I am trying to find some information on our guest's predicament," Erik informed, finally looking up, "so as to help her get home."

Omid looked at him incredulously, "So you *are* sending her back to the mental hospital?"

"What?!" Erik was taken aback, and startled into looking at the Persian. "NO! As it turns out, Daroga, Jenna is not a mental patient after all."

"Are you sure?" Omid raised an eyebrow at him. "Then why is she here?"

"She is actually a time traveller from the 21st century," he said, in total seriousness.

"Really," Omid said, impassively. "Well, Erik, it is good to know that Jenna is sane—especially since you have obviously decided to let go of your already tenuous grasp on reality."

"I know it seems crazy, Daroga," Erik began, rolling his eyes and letting loose a heavy sigh. "But is it really so impossible? There have been tales of time travel from the very earliest of ages. I found mention of it in a Hindu myth dating back to 700 BC, and countless instances after that in the legends of many different world cultures—from the Celts to the Japanese to the Hebrew to the Norwegians. They all boast tales of time travel."

"But that's just it, Erik," Omid interjected. "They are *tales.* Fictional stories and myths."

"True," Erik agreed. "But when something is so much a part of the collective consciousness, doesn't it at least allow for the possibility that it *could* happen?"

"What made you all of a sudden start believing this, Erik? A few nights ago, you were completely convinced she was bereft of her sanity."

"The other night, Daroga," Erik began, "we were outside by the marsh. She…" Erik hesitated, as if what he had to say next was difficult for him. "Ran from me…but she was almost hit by a carriage." Omid was surprised to see a look of abject terror in Erik's eyes as he said this. "When she saw it, Daroga, she knew something was wrong, and she told me her fears. She asked me the date and when I told her, she said that she was from the year 2014."

"And that's when you decided she *wasn't* crazy?" asked Omid, shaking his head.

"I know we believed her mad. But I'm telling you, Daroga, she is not crazy. There's something in her eyes…"

Omid raised an eyebrow at Erik and asked, suspiciously, "Since when do you spend so much time looking in a woman's eyes?"

"We know Jenna is not from here," Erik continued quickly,

completely avoiding Omid's question. "And she speaks of things—things that seem so strange and wonderful—things that don't exist, and yet I wish they did. If she is not from the future, then she is a genius and a visionary. But…" Erik paused briefly, "I *believe* her, Daroga. And I have been trying to figure out how she may have traveled here and how I might help her get back to her own time."

Omid studied his friend closely. It was strange to see not the least bit of cynicism in his expression. Things with Jenna had certainly changed over the past few days. "Well," he asked, realizing he was not going to beat Erik, so he might as well join him. "Are you having any luck?"

Erik shook his head, a look of disgust coming over his face. "Not unless she was transported by fairies, enchanted by a harlequin, or visited by a guardian angel." He closed the book he had been holding with a huff. "It is all so maddening! The idea of time travel is so widespread, but understanding how it might be possible is proving harder than I thought. As much as I allow there could be something to the universality that the concept, it is also universally explained in ridiculous, fairy tales. I'm going to have to consider this further if I am to discover something that could be useful to Jenna."

"Erik," Omid began carefully, "Could it be that she *is* mad? Not every insane person is a lunatic. There are many who could pass as rational. There are even," he added, knowing that he was treading on dangerous uncharted territory, "those that are beautiful."

"This has nothing to do with her beauty, Persian!" Erik barked. "It has to do with the fact that she needs my help, and I am trying to give it to her. Just like Christine."

"Oh yes, the singing seamstress." Omid rolled his eyes.

Erik decided to take a deep breath and ignore the Persian's impertinence, even though his fingers were tingling again. "The only thing I can deduce is that Jenna's time travel had something to do with water. She drove into the river in her time and wound up here by the lake. I don't think that can possibly be insignificant."

Omid chuckled to himself a moment before earning himself a glare by declaring, "I would hope not! Otherwise, your ideas are *all wet.*"

❧

Jenna was back on her warm, cozy cloud, but suddenly, her arm, was freezing. She looked down to see soft little snowflakes alighting onto her skin, lingering the briefest of moments before dissolving into dew. She shivered against the cold, and with a flutter, opened her eyes. She was, of course, in the spare bedroom, surrounded by the pillows and blankets of the lush feather bed. Her arm had come free during her sleep, however, which would account for the chill that had woken her from the dream. She absently wondered if Erik had ever rebuilt the fire, and was mildly disturbed to find that the mere thought of him was making her feel warmer already. "I must still be half dreaming," she admonished herself, as she threw off the covers and walked over to the armoire to select a new dress to wear for the day.

When she left the bedroom, Jenna was surprised to see Erik and Omid huddled together over one of his books, talking in hushed tones. "Good morning," Jenna called out to them, with a smile.

"Good morning, Jenna!" Omid greeted her warmly, rushing over to her and giving her hand a quick peck in greeting. "I trust you slept well?"

"Quite!" She nodded and smiled sweetly at him.

"Splendid!" he exclaimed, with a bright smile. "I brought you some breakfast, because, considering Erik's lack of enthusiasm for food," he gestured toward Erik with his head, "I thought if I hadn't, you might starve!"

Jenna looked over Omid's shoulder and caught Erik's gaze. While he was not as ebullient as his Persian friend, she did notice a slight upturn of his exposed lip and a sparkle in his eyes that she found electrifying. When Jenna did not comment on the offer of breakfast, and her glance at Erik lingered a moment too long, Omid raised an eyebrow, saying, "I'll just go make some coffee to go with these, and then we can all sit down to eat." He made his way to the kitchen as he contemplated the information his friend had given him earlier, as well as the looks on Erik and Jenna's faces when they regarded one another. He almost felt as if he suddenly had ceased to exist as they'd gazed at each other from across the room.

Erik rose from his reading chair and slowly closed the distance between himself and Jenna. The moment she had emerged from the bedroom, a strange, fluttery feeling appeared in his chest, and Erik was surprised to realize that he was happy to see her. Not breaking her gaze, Erik asked, "Do you like coffee in the morning, Jenna?"

"I'm a nurse who often works twelve to sixteen hour shifts," she smiled. "I live for it!"

He raised his exposed eyebrow to her and asked, "Do they make coffee from bags in the 21st century too?"

Jenna remembered her mishap from last night and giggled, "Well, actually, some do. Some even use these little plastic things called pods too," she chuckled at Erik's horrified expression. "But that's not how I brew it," she assured him quickly. "I like freshly ground beans, myself."

"Agreed!" he sighed in relief. "I'm hoping you like your coffee strong, for that is how the Persian makes it." Erik rolled his eyes. "Of course, that should prove useful, since I'm sure he will be prattling on about something this morning. I always find I need extra help staying awake when he does."

As Jenna laughed at his joke, she remembered their playfulness from the night before. She looked down a little, suddenly bashful as she recalled the feelings his song had awakened in her. When she did, though, she suddenly felt Erik's long fingers brushing her forehead.

"Jenna, what did you do?" Erik asked, his tone cold.

She looked back up at him, confused, "What do you mean, Erik?"

"Did you think I was *not* going to tend to them?" Frustration entered his voice, laced with a hint of disappointment, as his hand returned to his side. "I know I was distracted last night, preparing for my lesson today with Christine, but I also assured you I had not forgotten your needs. "

"Erik," Jenna asked again, still perplexed by his sudden shift of mood. "I don't understand."

"Did you not *trust* me to keep my word?" the frustration was growing more heated, now, and Jenna saw Erik's temper begin to flare right in front of her eyes.

"Erik!" She spoke his name loudly, trying to get his attention back on her, and not on his brewing irritation. "What on *earth* are you talking about?"

"Your *stitches*, Jenna. They're gone."

"Mrrreeeoooowww!" Red the cat crawled over to him and bopped him in the head, rubbing his cheek against his forehead and kneading the mattress as he did so. "Red!" The doctor chuckled, as he stroked the cat's soft yellow fur, immediately eliciting a happy purr out of the cuddly animal. "I am *trying* to research ways to bring Jenna back to us, you know!" When the precocious feline proceeded to climb onto the book that was open in his lap, the doctor added, "You're not helping, Red!" *Purr, purr, purr,* was the feline's only response.

Knowing that reading time was over, at least for the moment, he lifted Red up into his arms and cuddled the cat while thinking about Jenna. "What's she like, Red?" he asked the animal absently. "Is she as sweet as she is beautiful? Does she like candies and chocolates? What's her favorite flower? What kind of music should I play for her? I've got to find someway to reach her. The books all say to try somewhat unpleasant stimuli to draw her back into consciousness, and if I have to, I will. But, really, Red," he said, looking directly at the cat's face. "Do you think she'd enjoy a drop of Tabasco sauce on her tongue? Or the smell of ammonia near her nose? Yuck. There have got to be better ways to reach her. I want to make her *want* to come back to me, not shy away.

"No, Red," The doctor continued, as he saw Jenna's face in his mind. "I don't want her to shy away from me at all. I want her to look at me with those amazing eyes, and I want her to run to me, and throw her arms around me, and kiss me…" He shuddered a little at the thought, and then sighed. "I'm a mess, Red. I want her to love me, when she doesn't even know my name. I know that's crazy. But I want it anyway. I want *her* anyway."

He looked over at the clock on his bedside table and realized that it had gotten quite late. He gave Red one last cuddle and placed him down on the bed. He went into the bathroom for his nightly routine and then returned to fall into bed and shut out the light.

When his eyes closed, she was beside him in his dream. They were walking hand in hand along a riverbed and the light was dancing in her strawberry blond hair. They whispered lovers' secrets to one another and laughed with joy, knowing at that moment, there was no one else in the world but each other and nothing more important than their love. Soon, they came to a blanket laid out on the mossy shore, and they sat down for a picnic in the sun. They dined on crusty breads and fine cheeses, and fed each other grapes and berries for dessert, their lips mingling in wine flavored kisses. When he leaned in and whispered in her ear, "I love you, Jenna," she kissed him, deep and full on the mouth, as if in an answering declaration of love. Their kiss ignited a blaze between them, and as they lay back, removing troublesome articles of clothing, he knew that nothing before in his life had ever felt so right. They made love to each other, on their blanket in the sun, the rush of the river mingling with the moans of their desire. And as that wave of passion finally broke over Jenna's body, she cried out his name as she clung to him, her arms tight around his back.

He awoke in a sweat, startling Red off the bed. He was breathing heavily and raked his hands through his hair. Yes, he thought, there was no longer any doubt. He was a complete and utter mess.

16 A NEW PET

"I should definitely bring you on my errands more often, Jenna," Omid said, the corners of his eyes crinkling in amusement. "You make shopping much more fun!"

Jenna laughed and smiled up at Omid. "It *was* a lot of fun, Omid," Jenna agreed. "Thank you for the treats," she said, gesturing to the bag of sweet dessert items on which he had splurged for her at the patisserie, after noticing how much she'd enjoyed the pastries from breakfast. *Just in case Erik once again forgets to cook*, Omid had told her. *Or to eat.*

Omid had been unceremoniously kicked out earlier that afternoon by a very frustrated Erik, for "*prattling on obsessively over nonsense,*" as Erik put it. Realizing that Erik was trying to work on his lessons for Christine, Jenna had volunteered to go along, to give him some peace and quiet. Erik initially protested, saying that it was far too dangerous for her to be out and about in a big city. Jenna had balked, reminding Erik that she was from New York and insisting that she could handle the city. Erik had then threatened the Persian to within an inch of his life if any harm should come to her, but finally relented that it might be a good idea for Jenna and Omid to go out for the afternoon.

The sights and sounds—and smells—of nineteenth century Paris had been a bit overwhelming for Jenna at first, but once she got used to the rumble of buggy wheels replacing of the honks of taxi horns, the city began to remind her of home. Bright colors swirled everywhere, as merchants standing by covered carts hawked their wares loudly in the streets. From baguettes to bouquets, household necessities to fanciful baubles, it seemed one could find anything on the congested Parisian streets. Jenna began to feel a sense of excitement and adventure as she explored the unfamiliar marketplace with Omid, who used his good-natured humor and adept navigational ability to guide them expertly through the strange, overcrowded streets. By the time they had stopped for a late lunch at a sidewalk cafe, Jenna found herself quite enjoying the experience of strolling Victorian Paris.

Still, as the shadows grew long and the daylight began to dim, Jenna found she was quite relieved to once again be approaching the Palais Garnier. She was very ready for Omid to lead her back down to the quiet stillness of Erik's lair, so she could rest her feet and relax after her eventful day. Perhaps Erik would even make her another cup of tea. She smiled once again at the memory of their previous evening.

"Meeeerrrroooow," came the tiny cry at Jenna's feet, and she looked down to see a fluffy Siamese kitten with creamy white fur, gray nose and ears, and bright blue eyes looking up at her.

"Ohhh," Jenna gasped, and bent down to pet the kitten, shifting the bouquet of fresh blooms she had gotten from the flower cart into the crook of her arm. "Hello," she said in a sweetly hushed tone, reaching out to stroke the kitten's creamy fur. Suddenly she remembered her dear Red. How she missed his soft yellow coat and his low rumbly purr. She felt a tear spring to her eye as she hoped that he was being cared for.

The kitten purred at Jenna's attention and rubbed her cheek against Jenna's hand. "Oh, Sweetie, do you have a home?" Jenna continued to speak kindly to the fluffy feline.

"Likely not, Jenna," Omid answered for the kitten, watching as it cuddled even closer to the girl, who had absently gathered the young cat, holding it close.

"Why do you say that, Omid?" she asked, instinctively looking for a collar around the kitten's neck. Finding none, she looked up at her escort.

"We have many strays in Paris, Jenna—both cats *and* people," he told her, sadly. "Most never find a home. They don't last very long on the streets."

"Oh no," she said in breathy reply. She looked at the little kitten again, as its blue eyes stared up at her. "Well then you're coming home with me," she determined, standing while still holding the kitten and walking once more toward the Garnier.

"Jenna," Omid questioned in a hesitant tone, "Are you sure this is the best idea? Erik…"

"Will never have problems with rats!" Jenna rationalized, continuing on, cuddling the kitten close.

Omid smiled and followed her. He liked Jenna's way of dealing with Erik. No nerves. No fear. No hesitation, even at the prospect of his considerable temper. It seemed that in this vibrant, sweet, possibly insane girl from another time, Erik might have finally met his match.

❧

"Good morning, Jenna," the young doctor said cheerily, as he once again entered her room. He was not officially working today, but he just could not wait to see her. Besides, he did not want to waste any time beginning this new form of sensory therapy. For it to be successful, all the research had indicated that it should be begun early after diagnosis and repeated often. He only hoped that he had not waited too long. "I'm back," he said, "and I brought your favorite visitor." He bent down and placed the cat carrier on the ground, releasing the indignant inmate with a flick of his wrist. For his trouble, he received a loud "Mrreeeooooow!" as Red swiftly ran out of the carrier and jumped up on Jenna's bed. He immediately began sauntering back and forth, tail held high, rubbing his face up against Jenna and purring contentedly just to be near his owner.

Smiling to himself at the precocious cat, the doctor just sat there a moment and observed their reunion. Jenna was still not awake, but he was sure he could detect a certain serenity on her face as the cat nuzzled her lovingly. Were her lips upturned slightly, or was it his imagination? Suddenly, his mind wandered back to the dream he had had the night before, when his imagination had completely run away with itself. The sensations of the dream had seemed so real—her lips so soft, her body so warm, her touch so…exhilarating. He shook his head back and forth to try to come back to reality. These types of thoughts were highly unprofessional, and he was ashamed of himself for entertaining them. A woman had never before affected him this way. Sure, he had had a few dates in high school and steady girlfriends for much of college and med school, but he had never been a "ladies man." When he had first seen Jenna, she had taken his breath away with her vitality and beauty—and he still cursed himself for not having made her acquaintance sooner. But he had been too shy, and she had been involved in a relationship—even if her idiot ex-boyfriend hadn't deserved her. And of course, even then, there had been professional decorum to consider. Now, however, she needed him, to help her get her life back—and he *needed* to help her get her life back, because he cared about her so much. *But what if she doesn't care for you when she wakes up?* asked an unkind voice in his head. *What if this connection you feel toward her will only ever be in your mind?* He took a deep breath against the apprehension he felt at the thought. It didn't matter, he told himself. She was his patient, and he was her doctor, and he needed to do everything he could to help her, regardless of what happens—or doesn't happen—later.

"Jenna," he said, clearing his throat, wishing it could be just as easy to clear his mind. "We're going to try something new today, ok?" He smiled, despite the turmoil he was still feeling inside. "We're going to play a little game of Name That Tune. Are you ready?" He paused long enough for her to answer, if she were so inclined. Jenna remained ever silent, but Red gave him a happy *Meeow!* "OK, Red, you can play too," he said, jovially, masking the uncertainty in his heart. "But don't give all the answers away, OK?" The cat gave a quick *Mr-reh*, and sat down next to Jenna to give himself a bath.

Reaching into his jeans pocket, he retrieved his iPhone and began to scroll through his music library. "OK, Jenna. I'm going to play some songs for you. If you know the name, feel free to shout it out," he joked with a smile. "But if you're not feeling very talkative at the moment, try to at least smile if you like the song—maybe squeeze my hand a little," he added quietly, loosely taking her hand in his.

He thought back to what Jenna's head nurse had said about her musical taste. "Contemporary…" he muttered to himself, "hmmmmm …" he chose a song with loud guitars and heavy drums. He placed the phone right next to her bedside table, turning the volume up a little louder than he would normally find comfortable, just to see if the music would have any effect on her. He continued to hold her hand as the song played, but there was no response. "OK," he said to himself. "Not a fan of that one. Let's try…" he said, choosing another, song from his library, this one a bit calmer, but still lively. "This one. Come on, Jenna. Try to guess the name. Red, no cheating."

"Mreow!" was the cat's only reply, as he continued to lick between his claws.

Again, Jenna gave no response. Song after song, he remained so hopeful, but Jenna's expression never changed. She never squeezed his hand—she never so much as flinched. She didn't stroke Red's fur either, as she had the night before. He began to feel completely dejected, wondering if perhaps, she had begun to slip too far under. He felt frustration clutch his heart as he scrolled through his musical library once more. *That could not be the case*, he admonished himself. There had to still be a chance. He stopped at a selection he had not considered before. The soundtrack to *The Phantom of the Opera*. He remembered, then, that the head nurse did say Jenna was fond of Broadway musicals. It was a long shot, but it did not hurt to try. After all, this one was the longest running musical of all time. Odds were, if she liked Broadway, she would like this.

He pressed play, not saying anything to Jenna this time, having grown so apprehensive. Once again, she had no reaction as the overture and then the first chorus number began to play. Completely crestfallen, he lowered his head and just let the music continue on. “I won't give up, Jenna,” he mumbled to himself. “I can't. I want you back too much.” *But what if she doesn't want you?* His thought from earlier echoed inside his head. He closed his eyes, “Somehow, Jenna. I'm going to find a way.”

The soundtrack had advanced until the fresh, young ingénue had begun to shakily sing her first aria. With a sigh, he began to reach across to the side table, to shut off his phone, but as he did, he felt a slight pressure on his hand. He froze and looked at where his left hand was still holding hers. There! Again! Her fingers were fluttering, gently squeezing, closing around his own. “That's right, Jenna!” he gasped. “That's right, that's right! You like this music?” Her fingers squeezed a little harder, and he looked up to her face, to see that her lips had definitely curved up into a smile. “Oh, Jenna!” He gushed, “Can you hear me?” and he felt her fingers tighten once again.

He felt his heart beat faster and his spirit lift in joy. “If you can hear me, Jenna, then hear this,” he asserted, his voice aflame with excitement. “If you like this music, I'll play it for you—every day if that's what it takes. And I'm going to keep trying, Jenna—keep trying to find ways to reach you. I will never give up on you, Jenna. I need you to come back to me.” He squeezed her hand tightly, as the music continued to play.

Erik waited soundlessly behind the wall to the chapel. He had arrived at his destination a bit early, and the trepidation and excitement in his chest were almost too much to bear. As he'd told Jenna, he had never had a pupil before, but he was eager to spend this time molding Christine's voice, helping her to achieve her full potential. She was not meant to be a lowly seamstress, pushed around by the likes of that farm animal Carlotta. No, she was meant to be lauded and praised, lifted up as first lady of the stage. That was his goal for her, even if it were not yet her goal for herself. He knew, just from the few sparse phrases of song he had already heard from her lips, that she was capable of conquering the hearts of the music loving public. And he was eager to show her how.

He had spent much of his blessedly quiet afternoon working on his lessons, practicing the techniques he would endeavor to teach Christine, making notes of the methods that he intended to use. This was, of course, *after* he had ejected the intolerable Persian from his home—which was not to say that the afternoon was without its preoccupations. Jenna had elected to go along with the nuisance Daroga to leave Erik distraction-free. If he were honest with himself however, his mind had wandered, more often than he cared to admit, to her situation.

Ever since the morning, when he had noticed her stitches mysteriously gone from her forehead, he had felt a strange sense of foreboding. She'd sworn she had not removed them, and he had obviously not done so himself, so their absence was a mystery. They could not have simply disappeared on their own, especially not at the exact time he himself was considering removing them. The entire affair was exceedingly bizarre.

Jenna had somehow transported from 2014 back to 1884, water had somehow been involved—he was sure of it—and now her stitches had disappeared. He could not shake the feeling that it was all connected—that something was happening that was even more incomprehensible than time travel. Was such a thing even possible? And even if it were possible—time travel, or this *other* thing, whatever it was—why *his* lake? Jenna was not only from the 21st century, but also from New York. Even if she were to travel back through the centuries, why would she also travel across the sea? None of it made sense, and as Erik had tried to focus on his lessons for Christine, the mystery of Jenna's circumstance kept creeping back into his consciousness, drawing his attention from the task at hand. He had always been a very focused man, so this distraction was enough to make his head spin and then throb with a dull ache. He was just grateful the Daroga had gone, for if *he* had still been in the lair, jabbering on incessantly about absolutely nothing, Erik was certain his long idle lasso would have found a purpose once more.

There was a quiet creak as the door opened across the small space, and Erik saw Christine enter the room, her cheeks pink, as if from running, her rich sepia curls bouncing freely around her shoulders. Erik suddenly wondered how soft and springy they would feel in his fingers, and an almost irresistible urge to touch them had Erik's arm reaching out before him. When he made contact with cold, hard stone, he was reminded of his foolishness. *You can never touch her, Erik,* he chided himself. *She can never even see you. Be grateful that you are nothing but a spirit to her—an angel. She would never wish to be in your presence otherwise. Get ahold of yourself.*

Erik took a deep breath and released it on a sigh, and Christine looked up and all around, as if she'd heard.

"Angel?" she asked, quietly, eyes wide with a hopeful, expectant expression.

"I am here," Erik responded, remembering to make his voice take on that ethereal quality whereby it seemed to arise from out of thin air.

Erik watched as a smile spread over Christine's face. "I *knew* you'd still be here!" she positively gushed. "I'm sorry I was a bit late," her voice turned somewhat apologetic, "La Carlotta needed more alterations on her costume—I dare say she wouldn't split so many stitches if she didn't insist upon having her bodices sewn so tight! And just as I was leaving, Meg had a tutu emergency. I never realized such things were even possible before working here. And I ran as fast as I could, and…"

Erik was a bit amused by her tale of mishaps. "Fret not, *Mon Ange'*. You're here now."

She looked around once more, searching in vain for the source of the celestial voice. "*Mon Ange'*?" she repeated the appellation in confusion. "Why would you call *me* that? *You* are the Angel. Not I."

"Ah, but my dear," Erik responded, his voice both otherworldly and warm, filling her with a sense of heavenly affection, "You sing like an angel. And while I am *your* angel, as long as you sing, you will always be *mine* as well."

If possible, her smile got even wider, and Erik felt the air leave his chest at her beauty. Oh, she was just exquisite—as magnificent as he was foul. And her beauty dispelled all rational thought from his brain, making it seem possible—even if for just a moment—that he could, in fact, be an angel for her.

"Then shall we sing, my Angel?" she asked him sweetly, bringing him out of his daze.

"We shall, *Mon Ange'*," he whispered, tenderly. "But first, we must learn the proper way to breathe." Feeling himself a bit breathless in Christine's presence, Erik realized that he too could benefit from such a lesson.

17 SOMEDAY MY PRINCE WILL COME

Erik practically floated on air as he made his way back to his home. His eyes were faraway, the corner of his mouth turned up in a half smile. His heart felt light in his chest. The lesson with Christine had been filled with mostly breathing exercises and a little light vocalization, but every time he had heard her voice, his heart had skipped a beat. Christine was truly the most delicate, angelic, simply perfect woman he had ever laid eyes on. He recalled the sparkle in her azure eyes when she reached a previously unattainable note, and how her lush, sable curls danced wildly around her face when she giggled in satisfaction. And her voice. Oh her voice made him, for the first time, believe in heaven, for truly there could be no other source for such beauty. Crystalline and pure, her voice, even when simply running through scales, touched him in a way he had never been touched before. It reached directly into his soul and held him tightly in its grasp. And though he knew he could only ever be a figment of her imagination, a celestial being shaping her voice for splendor, he knew that she would always be the one to hold *him* under her spell.

He arrived at the shore of his home, quickly securing the little boat in place, and was immediately met by flavorful aromas wafting from the kitchen and the sounds of conversation hushed by the closed door. There would be time for the evening meal, but neither the promise of sustenance nor the thought of company appealed to him at the moment. His heart was filled with a tide of music that threatened to overflow if he did not sit down promptly and commune with his piano. His long fingers began their tarantella with the ivory keys as his mind set forth on an imagined journey, foreseeing great possibilities for his dear angel. The Prima Donna on opening night, Christine would easily earn accolades from the adoring crowd, a cavalcade of flowers strewn at her feet, ovation after ovation after ovation. Her voice would be her majesty—and he would have the private glory of knowing that his spirit was entwined with her song, giving it fullness, beauty and life. His darkness would magnify her light—would enrich her singing—and he would see her praised as the greatest soprano ever known. Christine. Dear Christine. *His…*

"MMMREEEOOOWW," he heard as the keys sounded with a jarring dissonance. Erik gasped in surprise when, without warning, a ball of white and gray fur bounded upon the keyboard. He gawked in astonishment as the furry interloper traipsed along the keys, trailing an untuneful melody behind it, discordant tones issuing from its fumbling paws.

Jenna and Omid swiftly emerged, unnoticed, from the kitchen as they heard the cacophony from the piano and guessed its cause. Ready to intervene to save the little kitten's life, Jenna was stopped in her tracks by Omid, who put an arm out to stop her when they saw Erik reaching out and taking the kitten gently in his grasp. "Wait, Jenna," Omid leaned close to whisper in her ear. "Let's see how the lunatic reacts."

Jenna looked at him, aghast. "But Omid, the kitten!"

Omid rolled his eyes. "He's not going to kill it, Jenna." A glint of mischief lit up Omid's eyes, "But the temper tantrum might be good for a few laughs."

"What's this?" Erik asked in a hushed tone of voice, holding her up so that her little blue eyes flashed at his mismatched ones, "How did you get here, *peesh-ee*?" he questioned, using the Persian diminutive for cat.

"Mreeeow!" she mewled again, in a high, thin tone, squirming just a bit as Erik held her out, dangling over the piano.

"Oh, Erik," he heard Jenna's voice, as she began to rush over to collect the kitten from him. "I'm sorry she disturbed you." She reached out to take the cat from him, but he did not hand her over.

"Who *is* she?" Erik asked, still looking with wonder at the kitten.

"Well," Jenna began cautiously, lowering her arms back to her sides. Erik seemed to be somewhat intrigued by the little cat, but he was so given to mood swings, she could not be sure. "I found her on our way back from the market. She was hungry and alone. She had nowhere else to go."

"So now it appears my home has indeed become a shelter for the needy and unfortunate," he commented drolly, still looking at the little kitten. "I suppose that *is* why the Daroga is here so often."

"You *do* take such good care of me, Erik," Omid exclaimed with an indignant huff, leaning up against the wall and folding his arms across his chest at his friend's snide comment.

"I had a dog once," Erik commented, shifting the little kitten, so that she could rest a bit more comfortably on his arm, stroking her fur with gentle fingers. The cat closed her eyes and began to purr as he did so. "Her name was Allete…" Erik's eyes took on a wistful look, as he voice trailed at the memory.

"I'll do all the work to take care of her," Jenna promised quickly, still somewhat dumbfounded at the sight of Erik petting the kitten. She had been prepared for him to put up a fight, but his immediate tenderness with the cat had caught her off guard. Still, for some reason she felt the need to justify the cat's presence. "And I'll take her with me when I go home. Red could use a friend."

For the first time, Erik looked up at Jenna. Since his lesson with Christine, he had not thought once about Jenna's situation. He felt a slight twinge of displeasure in his chest at the reminder that he was supposed to be helping her find a way to return to her own time. He brushed it off, however, choosing instead, to comment on the apparent name she had just uttered. "*Red*, Jenna?"

"Yes," Jenna answered, giving Erik a slight smile. "Red is my cat, back home."

"Red," Erik began in a condescending tone, "is a hue, not a name. *I* shall be taking on the task of naming *this* little one," he said, once again looking at the kitten who was still purring contentedly in his arms. "So as to ensure that she has a proper designation, not a *color*."

Jenna opened her mouth to defend her choice of name for her beloved cat, but Omid merely snickered.

"Samineh," Erik called the kitten in a hushed tone. "You shall be named Samineh."

"Erik," Omid chimed in, "You have merely called her Delicate One in Persian."

"It is fitting, isn't it, Daroga," Erik insisted, looking over at Omid. "She is small, and dainty, and oh, so elegant. She is a very *delicate* lady who deserves a name as graceful as she is." He finished his commentary with a slight smile.

"I think it's a beautiful name, Erik." Jenna said, feeling her heart swell at his sweetness with the kitten happily asleep in his arms. "Much better than Fifi."

Erik wrinkled his eyes at her. "Fifi? *Really*, Jenna! How revolting!"

"Pardon me! That was *my* suggestion," Omid corrected him, pretending to look miffed.

"Oh, well *that* doesn't surprise me!" Erik commented rolling his eyes to heaven. "You've never been one for grace, Daroga."

Omid chuckled again, ignoring Erik's insult. Instead, he asked, "So how was your lesson, *Angel*?"

"Unless you mean for me to become your angel of doom," Erik began, glaring at the Persian, "*You* will not call me that again, Daroga."

"Oh all right, Mighty Phantom," Omid corrected his choice of appellation, throwing his hands up in the air in a defensive gesture. "How was your lesson with Christine?"

Erik shook his head in disdain at the Persian, but answered anyway, his tone once again becoming wistful. "Christine," his eyes stared straight in front of him at some unknown vision, his fingers still absently stroking Samineh's fur, "was exquisite. Even simply running scales and vocalizing, Daroga, she possesses the most beautiful voice I have ever heard—already far superior to Carlotta. It is simply her meekness and the management's incompetence that prevents Christine from taking her rightful place in the spotlight."

Jenna listened to Erik extol Christine's virtues and felt a pit begin to form in her stomach. The way Erik talked about Christine—it was obvious he felt more for her than simply the admiration of a good singing voice. She remembered the night before, when she had heard Erik singing, and how *his* voice had made her feel. It was clear he was feeling somewhat similarly for Christine. He was becoming infatuated with her, and for some reason, that knowledge made Jenna feel a little queasy.

But that was ridiculous! Jenna shook her head a little as if to rid herself from the thought. Jenna did not belong here, and Erik had promised that he would help her find a way home. It's not as if either of them wanted her to stay here permanently. So what if he was becoming interested in the seamstress that he was teaching how to sing? It's not as if he could possibly be interested in *her*!

There you go again, Jenna, she scolded herself silently, *falling for the wrong guy. And this one's not even from your century.* Plus, he has some pretty terrible mood swings and is *very* quick to rush to judgment. And of course, there *was* the mask. What was he hiding behind the mask? Regardless of what Omid had said, all *she* could see were two very beautiful, but very guarded eyes. And she sighed as she remembered the half smiles that she had seen light up his visible features. How she wished she could see the rest of his smile. And that voice…

STOP it Jenna! she mentally screamed at herself. These kinds of thoughts could not possibly end well. Especially since he's got a thing for the seamstress that he has to talk to from behind a wall! *Behind a wall!* Who could possibly fall in love with him from behind a wall? *Of course*, her traitorous mind pointed out to her, *you're starting to fall for him from behind a mask.*

"UUUGGGH!" Jenna growled out loud, grabbing her head with both hands, trying to get her double-crossing brain to stop.

Omid and Erik ceased their conversation at once. "Jenna, are you alright?" Erik asked her, releasing the kitten and immediately hastening to her side, his voice tense with concern.

She mentally cursed herself for groaning out loud and looked straight in Erik's worried blue and brown eyes, assuring him, "I'm ok, Erik. I was just thinking…"

"Did it hurt?" Omid interjected, earning him a dark look from Erik. Omid looked back at him innocently, causing Jenna to chuckle a bit at his well-placed joke.

"…that dinner was getting cold," she finished her thought with a smile. "Come on, Gentlemen. It's time to eat." She said, removing herself to the kitchen, Samineh scampering behind her, tail held high in the air.

"I hope you bought yourself some good liquor at the market today, Daroga," Erik said, making his way to the kitchen to help Jenna carry out the meal.

"Of course not, Erik. That's what I have you for, my friend!" the Persian responded, taking his place at Erik's small dining table. "After all, I don't exactly stick around here for your charm!"

❧

Red was once again curled up at the foot of Jenna's bed. The iPhone was playing the Phantom soundtrack, and Jenna's doctor was about to try his next experiment. "Sense of smell," he muttered out loud to himself, as he set his scent samples out on her bedside tray, which he had rolled across the room, so that she could deal with one smell at a time.

"OK, Jenna," he said, approaching her bed with the first in his arsenal of aromas. "I am thinking about switching aftershaves," he said, reaching the small bottle of green liquid under her nose, and wafting the scent toward her. "What do you think of this one?" Jenna made no indication that she smelled anything, so he held up the bottle with the blue liquid and asked her, "Do you prefer this one? Please don't make me let Red decide," he noticed the cat's ear twitch at the mention of his name. "I'm not sure his judgment in this case would be very sound. After all," he grimaced "he seems perfectly content with the smell of his litter box." When she still made no response, he did not allow himself to get discouraged. He knew that the sense of smell was a difficult one to stimulate for coma patients, so he was just going to continue and hope he could get her to react to something. He reminded himself of that exhilarating moment when she had grasped his hand while listening to the music. That had proven to him that she was still in there, and he would just keep trying different things to get her to respond.

"OK, you're unimpressed. I will figure out the aftershave question myself." He walked back over to the table and picked up a small bowl of crushed garlic. "Time for the vampire test," he joked as he returned to Jenna's side. "If you recoil from this smell, you might just be one of the undead." He made his voice low and tremulous as he said his last word, going for a spooky effect. Red opened one eyeball at the comment and grumbled as if in disdain. "Hush you," he said to the outspoken feline. "No comments from the peanut gallery." He placed the bowl under her nose and waited for a reaction. Nothing. "Well, Jenna, apparently you pass that test." Red yawned, as if to say, "I told you so." He sighed, and went back to the table for the spicy mustard. He dipped his finger in it and extended his hand to her face, his fingers gently brushing her lips as he did so. He shivered a bit at the contact, and admitted to Jenna, "OK, I don't have a cute line for this one, Jenna. But if you can smell it, can you let me know in some way? Crinkle your nose, turn your head away…slap me! Just…something." He watched her closely for any hint of a reaction. He thought he did see a slight scrunch of her nose, and maybe a slight attempt to pull away. "Hmmm." he thought. "We may have gotten somewhere there."

He looked around the room, and his eyes settled on a bouquet of red roses and white carnations that was on her windowsill. He walked over and reached for the card, thinking it strange that she should have received flowers, wishing it had been him who'd sent them. *Get well soon, Love Aunt Penny,* he read the card aloud. "Ahhhh," he said. "Your aunt sends her best wishes." He reached into the arrangement and picked out one of the roses, carrying it over to Jenna. "Well, let's see if her flowers can help." He held the rose out to her and he was certain he noticed a small smile on her lips. "Oh," he said quietly. "You *like* the scent of roses." He kept the fragrant flower by her nose a moment longer, *imagining her dressed in a beautiful evening gown, arms outstretched toward him as he gave her an entire bouquet of red roses, tied together by a silky ribbon.* "Roses *do* have a beautiful smell," he said to her, his voice taking on a husky quality as he *imagined her moving into his arms, stretching up on her tiptoes to thank him with a kiss,* and he began to trail the flower down to trace her lips. "But they feel beautiful against the skin too, don't you think?" *In his mind the bouquet was placed on a table as he wrapped her tightly in his embrace.* He continued to glide the petals of the rose slowly across her cheeks, her eyelids, her forehead, his own lips slightly open, watching intently for her reaction. "I had meant to only work on your sense of smell today, Jenna," he whispered, as he saw her slightly shudder in response to the delicate touch of the rose. *In his fantasy, she was shuddering at the gentle probing of his tongue* and he once again brought the rose downward toward her slightly parted lips. "But you seem so much more sensitive to touch." When his flower reached her chin, Jenna's head fell slightly back, and he felt himself trembling as he continued the rose's trail down her neck, *imagining branding a path of hot kisses down the elegant length of her throat.* "Jenna..." he rasped as her saw her take in a sharp breath at the teasing of the rose.

"Interesting therapy session you're holding there, Doctor."

He dropped the rose on Jenna's bed and whirled around to see Dr. Charleson leaning up against the now open door to the room. He must have been too distracted by his fantasy to notice Charleson knock—*if* he had bothered to knock. "Good evening, Doctor," he said, stretching his mouth into a tight smile which he was sure was fooling no one. "What brings you to *my* patient's room?"

"Oh," Charleson began, as he slowly approached her bed. "When you missed the staff meeting this afternoon," *Dammit*, he thought to himself. He had completely forgotten about that stupid meeting. "I was…concerned. I asked Dr. James if you were alright." Charleson arrived at Jenna's bedside and reached out to take the chart at the foot of her bed, raising an eyebrow when Red hissed at him and jumped to the floor. "He said he was sure you were just swamped with your patient load, and the extra research project you had taken on." Charleson flipped open the chart, perusing it as he continued, "I told him I hadn't heard about that, and he explained that you were going to perform Coma *Arousal* Therapy on Miss Wilson."

"Yes," he agreed, tracking Charleson's every move. "That *is* what the technique is called."

"Uh huh." Charleson nodded, continuing to peruse Jenna's chart, looking completely unconvinced. "Well, please, enlighten me." He closed the chart and casually leaned against Jenna's footboard, looking at the young doctor expectantly.

He really wanted to wipe the smug look off of Charleson's face, of course, but being the senior resident, Charleson had every right to question him about his technique."It's simply a matter of intense sensory stimulation, in the hopes that enough of it will actually incite the brain back to consciousness."

"Ah, I see. And have you had success at *stimulating* her, Doctor?" Charleson asked, sarcasm dripping off his every word. "Has she been *aroused*?"

"Dr. Charleson," he said, taking a deep breath, desperately trying to maintain a professional demeanor, Charleson's double meaning not lost on him. "Would you care to step outside the patient's room with me, so we can discuss this further?"

"Oh, I'm quite comfortable right here, Doctor," Charleson answered. "Please answer my question."

"Miss Wilson might hear us discussing her case, Doctor," he tried again to get Charleson out of the room before he lost his cool.

"But that would be good, right?" Charleson countered. "Hearing about her condition would be rather *stimulating* for her, don't you think? Of course, you are the expert on *arousal*."

In a clipped tone, he answered. "Miss Wilson has shown some limited response to sensory stimuli."

"Such as…" Charleson raised an expectant eyebrow.

He huffed as he said, "She has squeezed my hand when directed, has wrinkled her nose at aversive smells, and has shivered at gentle touch."

"Oh yes," Charleson commented. "I think I walked in on her shivering. You too."

He had had enough of Charleson's implications. Pushing his lab coat open and setting his hands on his hips, he demanded, "OK, just what are you getting at Charleson?"

"That you are playing a dangerous game, Doctor," Charleson responded, keeping his cool gaze locked on the young resident at all times.

"What do you mean?"

"Your interest in her has gone beyond the professional, Doctor, and you know it."

"Dr. Charleson," he began through gritted teeth. "I must demand that you step out of the room if you intend to make such unfounded accusations. I do not need your baseless allegations to agitate my patient."

"No," Charleson retorted, standing up to his full height. "Fondling her with a red rose will agitate her enough. Or was that what you referred to as *stimulation*?"

"Please leave, Doctor," he demanded, towering over Charleson at his own full height, jaw set, eyes blazing.

"I'm going," Charleson said, beginning to make his way toward the door. "But I'm watching you," he said, turning back to face him, before leaving. "And I have no problem reporting you to Dr. James if I feel you've crossed a line." He walked out of the room, saying "Good evening, Doctor."

He sat down heavily on the edge of the bed, his head buried in his hands. After a moment, he felt Red jump back up to rub against his forehead as if to ask what was wrong. He reached out absently to stroke Red's fur, but looked toward Jenna, who seemed to be slumbering comfortably in her bed. "Oh, Jenna," he said, "I really *really* hope you wake up soon. We may be running out of time."

❧

Erik sat down at his piano again, after the Daroga had gone. Jenna had graciously offered to clean the dinner dishes so that he could have some more time to play. Little Samineh had taken up residence on his settee. He coaxed song after song from the piano, but none of them sounded exactly right to his ears. His mind was once again divided. He would think about Christine, so pure and lovely in her innocence and her talent, yet without warning, his mind would be on Jenna, and her unexplainable situation that had brought her to his domain. He would glance over at the kitten, so soft and peaceful as she slept on the settee, enjoying her new home, and without realizing it, his mind would wander to the promise he had made to Jenna, remembering that if he was successful, she would be leaving. He felt the ache from earlier in the day begin to creep back up into his head, and he was grateful, when he saw Jenna emerge from the kitchen carrying a tea tray. Remembering the previous night, however, he groaned in dread, and he felt the pulsing in his head intensify.

"Jenna...you made tea?" he asked, the uncertainty in his voice completely apparent. "Again?"

Jenna smiled and said, "Yes, Erik. I made it the right way, this time," she assured him, as she set down the tray and poured him a cup of the steaming brew and handed it to him. "I watched you last night, and I'm a quick study."

Erik wordlessly looked into the cup in his hands and then back up at her. "Drink it," she commanded him with a smile. "I promise, you won't spit it out."

I promise to do my best, he thought, fortifying himself for what could very possibly be another exceptionally unpleasant experience, *but that doesn't mean I won't want to.* He dared to take the smallest sip of the piping hot liquid in his teacup. Rich and soothing, it was delicious. "Well, Mademoiselle," Erik allowed himself a brief smile, and Jenna thrilled at the look of approval in his eyes. "You certainly *are* a quick study—as you say. This is very good."

"Thank you, Erik," she smiled and took a sip from her own cup, agreeing that her tea making skills had improved greatly overnight. Erik shifted over a bit on the piano bench, making room for her to take a seat next to him, since his settee was currently otherwise occupied. They sat in silence a few moments, sipping their tea, having discussed the events of the day earlier, over dinner. It was not an awkward moment, though. Erik seemed simply content, and that contentment did much to calm her own heart. When Erik was finished with his tea, Jenna took his cup and set it back on the tray.

She looked at him and said, quietly, "Thank you, Erik, for letting Samineh stay here."

Erik glanced over at the little feline curled up on his settee and responded, "I have long appreciated animals, Jenna. They are not judgmental and unkind, as many humans tend to be."

"I think animals do judge, Erik," Jenna countered him. "But they judge based on character, and they can sense a good soul immediately. Look how quickly Samineh warmed up to you."

Erik glanced back at Jenna and gave her a little crooked smirk. "Obviously, her sense of judgment must be a bit off."

Jenna rolled her eyes at him. "Take my cat Red, for instance…who, by the way," she said as an aside, remembering his earlier jab at the moniker, "was named, for his tendency to look simply dashing in his red collar, thank you very much." Erik nodded and held his hands open in a sign of appeasement. "When I first introduced him to my boyfriend Jake, Red hissed and scrambled away from me. I should have known right then," she chuckled, "that Jake was not a good idea. *Listen to the animals* my mom always used to say. *They know*." Jenna looked off into the distance, a sad smile on her face, as she finished her thought.

"Then why didn't you?" Erik asked softly, completely absorbed by what Jenna was saying. Whether it was the tone of her voice or the sad look in her eyes, he could not say. But suddenly, he really wanted to know why she had agreed to be intimately involved with someone who obviously did not deserve her.

Jenna closed her eyes and shook her head. "I don't know, Erik. Like I told you last night, I always wanted to be a wife and a mom. I always dreamed of finding that one man to spend the rest of my life with—who would love and adore me, and put me first in his life. But it was so hard. My mother never married my father and went through a string of guys while I was a kid. None of those relationships ever ended up happily. I always thought I would be different. That *someday my prince would come…*" She looked at Erik then and whispered, "But he *didn't*."

Jenna looked away again and continued, "I started to believe what everyone said, that *Mr. Right* only shows up in fairy tales, and it is unrealistic to expect that kind of devotion in real life. So I guess I stopped waiting around for my prince and decided that my expectations were too high. I allowed myself to become involved with guys who seemed great on the outside, but really turned out to be shallow and self-absorbed toads. Only I was always the last one to figure that out." She looked back at Erik with a sheepish smirk. "Even my *cat* could see it, before I did."

Erik looked at the false humor in her eyes and could see the sadness lurking beneath it. For a moment, she reminded him greatly of Christine, whose eyes were also often filled with sadness, when he knew they were made for joy. "Jenna," he said, his voice soft and soothing—not in artifice, but in a show of the true emotion he was feeling at hearing her pitiable tale. "I admit I am not sure I fully understand this concept of *Mr. Right*, as you put it. But a woman of your beauty and sweetness," he began, thinking that, in those ways too, she was much like Christine, "should be considered a rare treasure, indeed—and treated as such. A woman like that would make any prince richer, Jenna, and any man *worthy* of her *would* put her first in his life."

Jenna felt her face redden at his beautiful words, and she struggled against the lump that had suddenly appeared in her throat as she made her breathy response. "We don't appear too have many princes any more in my time, Erik."

"I don't believe that, Jenna," He said swiftly and firmly, looking her directly in the eye. "I admit that it is always far easier, even now, to find the scoundrels. But sometimes you have to wait longer and look harder to find the prince. And remember, you never know who is searching just as hard for *you* Jenna. I hope that when you return you to your own time, you give him a chance to find you."

Jenna bit her lips together and took a deep breath against the tears that threatened to form in her eyes. Oh, why couldn't she have been born 130 years earlier, so that *this* man could be *her* prince? How could she ever hope to find anyone like him once she found a way to return home? The urge to reach out and hug Erik was so strong, and yet she knew she should not do it. It would do nothing to quell the surge of feeling she was experiencing, and she would more than likely completely humiliate herself. Instead, she did something that was probably equally unwise, but would at least provide a sort of diversion.

"Erik, would you sing for me again?" she blurted quickly, still battling to get her emotions under control. "Like you did last night?"

"Last night…" Erik said quietly, remembering the challenge she had issued to him. "Still unconvinced of my musical genius?" He asked, lightly, a smirk playing on the exposed part of his lips.

"No, I know, but…" Jenna stammered, a little slow to pick up on his attempt to lighten the mood. When she caught his little smirk, though, she realized she should play along. "What have you done for me lately?"

Erik laughed out loud at her response—a deep, lush sound that Jenna found just wonderful. "Honestly, Jenna," he said, the humor rich in his voice, "sometimes you say the strangest things!"

Erik's laugh was infectious, even if it was at her expense, and she joined him, throwing her arms open and saying, "Hey, what can I say? I am here for your amusement."

Erik smiled and readied his fingers over the keys. "Is there anything in particular that you would like me to play, Mademoiselle?"

"No, just…" She was about to say he could play anything he wanted, but then she recalled that there *had* been a song stuck in her head for most of the day. "Well, actually," she began, "I have been hearing this melody in my head all day. But I don't know its name."

"Can you sing it for me?" Erik asked, intrigued.

"No, Erik," Jenna shook her head, horrified. "I can't sing."

"Well, I can't read minds," he countered. "Can you just hum it for me, Jenna? If it is a tune I know, I should be able to recognize it pretty quickly."

"OK," she said, trying to call the melody to mind once more. "It goes something like, *La la la…La la la LA la, La la la LAA la."*

Erik looked at her quizzically. "I don't think I know that melody, Jenna. But could you hum it again?"

"OK," she said, and proceeded to do so.

Erik, eyes crinkled, looked at the keys of his piano with great concentration. He plinked out the melody that Jenna had just hummed one note at a time. "Is that it?" he asked her.

"YES!" Jenna agreed, excitedly. "What IS that song?"

Erik shook his head, "I don't know." He played the melody again, this time adding supporting chords that matched the lushness of the tune that Jenna had heard in her mind.

"Yes, Erik! That is perfect!" she exclaimed. "And you've never heard the song before?"

"No," he shook his head, playing the tune once again as he spoke, adding a bass line with his left hand. "Never. But I like it. Can you hum some more?"

"Sure," Jenna hummed the rest of the melody, which seemed at once familiar, but illusive, and found herself amazed as Erik brought the song in her head to life.

18 THAT VOICE WHICH CALLS TO ME

Erik worked at his piano late into the night—long after Jenna had retired into the guest bedroom. As he toyed with the tune Jenna had hummed, Erik's two great passions of music and architecture converged to create the structure of a song. He erected opulent chord progressions around the simple frame of melody, fortifying the theme with buttresses of lush harmonies and embellishing it with intricate ornamentations of trills and flourishes. Finally, he was satisfied that the song was complete. He could not help but imagine Christine singing the vocal line. Though it was still without words, the song's melody was sweet and pure, and he knew Christine could bring it to life perfectly.

It was Jenna, however, who had planted the song in his heart. He took a moment to think about his houseguest, who was slumbering in the next room. In so many ways, Jenna was quite different from Christine. Where Christine was petite and delicate, Jenna was tall, and much more robust. Where Christine's skin was pale as fine porcelain, Jenna's was hued with an almost constant blush in her cheeks. Christine appeared to be almost fragile, seeming to shrink away from the unpleasantries life dealt her, while Jenna exuded an air of strength, able even to stand up to him, when he was in his blackest moods. She had brought him up short more than once, and he found himself actually smiling at the memories.

And yet, even with her strength, and air of bravado, Erik knew Jenna had her own troubles—one of which was that in some inexplicable way, she was a century and a half away from her home. "And I have been charged," he muttered glumly to himself, "with somehow helping her find a way back. Erik rose and wandered over to his bookshelf. Amid the fictional novels and architectural guides, he had many reference books that covered various folklore and beliefs of cultures around the world. He had used some of them, in fact, to look up different theories on time travel—to little avail. He pondered for a moment as to what his next move might be, realizing he had absolutely no idea how to proceed. And yet, instead of being excited by the challenge, as he so often tended to be, he found a certain agitation creep into his mind.

He began to wonder, resentfully, why in fact it was even necessary for him to be engaged in this endeavor in the first place. After all, Jenna herself had admitted that her life was not the ideal existence of which she had dreamt. Her family was dead or gone. Her suitor had left her for another. She actually had seemed to be quite content the last couple of days, spending time with the Persian and, surprisingly, himself. Why should he be expending energy trying to understand this unexplainable cosmic circumstance when he already had so much to do in order to help Christine? Was there *really* a pressing need for Jenna to get back?

He glanced over at the settee and noticed Samineh still asleep. *That's right*, he thought. *She* must *go home because her* cat *misses her.* Erik was perplexed by the sudden rise of indignation he felt at the notion that she should wish to leave his lair and return to her time where, apparently, nothing was even waiting for her except a cat. Was it really such a difficult task for her to simply forget about the time from which she had come—a time in which she, evidently, was not appreciated for whom she was and had no significant ties? After all, *he* had withdrawn from the world, shunning the light and creating his own dominion of darkness and shadows below. Was a… *friend*—as she had called him—not worth more than a cat? Could she not simply turn her face away from the world that she had known and choose instead to continue living in the dark refuge he had provided her? Surely, he could even arrange for her to have a position at the opera house, if she needed some sort of *métier* to occupy her time. He could see no reason—other than her cat—for her to go back. And now, thanks to her, he too had a cat.

Erik could not contain the scathing chuckle that rose in his throat at that thought. *Really, Erik? What are you thinking? What woman would ever choose to stay in this underground mausoleum? Why should she be expected to willingly throw her life away, and accept a sepulcher as sanctuary, just because she'd had the distinct misfortune of befriending a monster?*

He turned again to his bookshelf, having chastened himself for ever daring to believe that his acquaintance with Jenna was anything more than an affiliation thrust upon them out of necessity. After all, Jenna did not even have Christine's good fortune of believing him a figment of her imagination. Jenna was all too aware of who he was. She saw the mask that covered his accursed face every time she was in his presence. She'd felt the unkind and unjustified tempest of his wrath. *Because* she knew him to be a real, tangible being, she had all the more reason to wish to be away from him. No, she was not like Christine, who, blessed by ignorance, could think him an angel. She was all too aware that the real Erik was more akin to the Devil himself, with a black disposition and a vile, cursed face.

Having thoroughly worked himself into a temper, Erik snatched several volumes from his bookshelf and stalked over to his reading chair, trying to recall her description of the tunnel through which she had passed to emerge from the "door" she had referenced so fervently. The walls had undulated and rippled, she'd said. And the floor had crumbled beneath her. Even the door, she said, had dissolved at her touch. *Water.* It all went back to everything somehow being tied to water.

He opened one of the tomes and began to leaf through the pages, looking for anything he could find about strange occurrences that happened in or around water. Much to Erik's chagrin, these events seemed to be plentiful.

Every river, it seemed, had its own indwelling spirit, and the great and mighty sea was just brimming with fairies and mermaids and nymphs. Naturally. So many mystical inhabitants were purported to live in the sea, in fact, that he was beginning to wonder how the waters ever had room for fish. Erik let out a deep sigh and rolled his eyes. More fairy tales—more fantasies which had no element of truth. How would he ever find anything useful in these books that seemed obsessed with yarns and fables of mermaids sucking the soul out of a sailor with a seductive song or fishermen being dragged down to an empire under the sea by a magical turtle?

Finally, however, Erik came across a few stories that piqued his interest. The Welsh Mabinogion told tale of the young hero Peredur, who encounters a river in a mysterious valley. On one side of the river was a flock of black sheep and on the other side, a flock of white. Whenever a white sheep would cross the river to the other side, it would turn black and any black sheep crossing over would turn white, suggesting, that the river was some sort of means of mystic transport, which had the power to change the traveller's very essence. In Greek mythology, entrance to the otherworld was accomplished by crossing over the River Styx. Once the river had been crossed, it was very rare that the traveller could ever return. In Celtic legend, a trip upon the misty sea, often led to a sojourn into the "otherworld," where time behaved differently. When the visitors would return to their own land, after a seemingly short dalliance, they would find all their loved ones withered and gone and the world around them changed.

Erik closed his book. He was more certain than ever that water had somehow swept Jenna into his world, and he was beginning to feel that water would be her only way out. After all, so many cultures could point to myths of the waterways around them serving as entry points into other lands. But Erik was also left with more questions than answers.

Of course the question still first and foremost in his mind was *how*? The stories—should he choose to believe them—had shown that water could serve as a passage between worlds, but he still did not understand how. Surely people—even in Jenna's time—travelled in water every day. Great seafaring vessels sailed across the oceans on a daily basis, and one never heard of them being mysteriously lost—except in shipwrecks and storms, in which cases, their fates were clear. Children swam in lakes and in streams all the time, and the shrieks of laughter and glee that issued from their upturned mouths were testament that nothing evil befell them. Jenna herself had fallen into *his* very lake, Erik thought, remembering the day that he'd thought he would finally have to strangle the Daroga for the sin of trying to drown his guest. She had not been magically transported back to her time and place. *No*, Erik smiled a little at the memory, *she had still been here, filthy and dripping on the settee.* So what was it that allowed for water to sometimes just be water and other times be an entrance to another world?

Further, it did not escape Erik that while these aquatic travelers seemed to reach their new destinations relatively unscathed, the return trip rarely seemed salubrious for them. An otherworldly visit which lasted only a short amount of time seemed to span years, even centuries in the traveler's home. Even if Erik could find a way to send Jenna back, how could he be sure of the state in which her world would exist when she got there? Would she be returning home, or would she be entering yet another strange new existence, one without even himself or the insufferable Daroga to watch over her.

He glanced back over at the peaceful Samineh and wished that he too could find the peace in his heart that seemed to come so easily to the small, elegant creature. He stood and crept over to his settee, reclining next to the sleeping kitten, who stirred a bit as his weight was added to the cushion. Reaching out and stroking her silken fur, Erik murmured, "You are a good cat, Samineh. Perhaps even good enough to entice Mademoiselle Jenna to stay."

❧

When Jenna awoke, the house was quiet. Music had drifted into her room, long into the night, as she had lain dozing in her bed. In her mind, she was lifted and twirled by melodies so achingly beautiful, and hauntingly familiar, and yet she could not say she had ever heard them before. They were Erik's songs, she was certain, and they'd filled her mind with the sweet scent of roses. As she'd listened, she had the distinct sensation of floating on a song, and she'd drifted off to sleep, feeling as if she were wrapped in the soft, dark velvet of the night.

Jenna sat up in bed and reached for the long white dressing robe that Erik had snagged for her. Jenna rose and slipped the robe around herself, tying it tightly closed. She slipped out of the room, seeing only the embers of the few last candles still burning. Erik must not yet be awake, she mused, glancing over to his bedroom door. Sure enough, it was shut. He *had* been up quite late, she thought. She was content to allow him his rest. She went over to the drawer, where she had seen Erik stow his matches, and relit a few of the candles, affording herself a meager amount of light in which to move around.

She was about to take a book and read for a while, when the gurgling of the lake drew her attention. Wandering slowly over to the sluice of water which cut through the opera house, she sat down quietly at its edge. Candlelight danced lightly on tiny ripples of glistening liquid, as they journeyed through Erik's shadowy kingdom. She was overcome once again with the fragrance of roses and soft sweet strains of ethereal music. She felt her eyes flutter closed at the memory, and allowed her fingers to trail into the icy cold current of Erik's secret lake.

Suddenly, the luxurious scents and sounds in her mind were accompanied by sharp images of headlights careening toward her, the loud, shrill blare of a horn, and finally the terrifyingly dark plunge into the depths of the Hudson River. She felt herself tense as she recalled her body feeling as if it were being rushed by the water toward something, *somewhere*...and then there was the foggy, shadowy image of white light, accompanied by flashes of blue and brown. A soft, rich voice beckoned her, gently calling her name. That voice—*oh* that voice made everything right, and she knew that in the presence of those resonant, hushed tones, she would be fine. *Everything* would be fine. She relaxed, allowing the blackness to take her again until she awoke to a song. Erik's song. Erik...

She sighed. "Oh, Erik," she murmured. Had it been his voice that was calling her? Her brow wrinkled at the memory. No. No, at that point, she didn't even think he'd known her name. How could he have summoned her? But that voice... Oh, it had been so lush, so tender, so very much like *his* voice... She remembered wanting to go toward it, wanting to open her eyes, but being unable, as if she were frozen until she heard Erik's song.

"Jenna?" She heard that voice again, hushed and deep, and so very velvety soft, enveloping her senses completely. She turned slowly to see him standing there, already dressed in his usual finery, ready, it appeared, to start the day. When she simply stared at him, unable for a moment to form words, she saw him extend his hand to her, and she closed her fingers around it as he helped her up. Standing now before him, she gazed into his blue and brown eyes, aglow in the dim firelight. They stood there a silent moment, neither remembering how to speak, transfixed by the quiet, and the candles and the lake. As her attention fell upon his white covering, she was filled, once more, with the intense desire to see what lay behind the mask. Slowly her arm crept up and she grazed soft fingers across cold white porcelain. A feeling of familiarity—of recognition—assaulted her mind, but before she was able to grasp it, to fully comprehend what the feeling meant, she felt Erik's long fingers wrap around her own, halting her progress, breaking the spell.

"Jenna," he said again, his voice a bit sharper.

"Oh! Erik!" She exclaimed, pulling back from him, turning a little away, "I'm sorry. I..." she fumbled around with her words, "Hope I ...didn't wake you."

"Oh, no," Erik brushed off her concern, feeling himself a bit awkward at the moment that had just passed between them. "I should have been up before you. I'm sorry to keep you waiting for breakfast."

"Oh I, " she gave a sheepish giggle, "wasn't really hungry yet. It's no bother."

"Very well... I," he stumbled a bit over his own words, "shall go make some coffee." He turned and walked quickly toward the kitchen, stopping briefly to call over his shoulder, "We shall see how mine measures up to the Daroga's."

Jenna snickered lightly. "Can't wait!" and looked back toward the lake. Her sensual memories were gone, replaced by a distinct feeling of mortification. "Oh, God," she asked, looking, once again, into the murky green water. "What am I *doing*?"

❧

"So, Erik, what are we going to do today?" Jenna asked, as she took a deep drink of the rich black coffee Erik served her. It was delicious, absolutely able to hold its own against the flavorful brew Omid had made the day before.

"Well, Jenna," Erik began, setting his own mug down before continuing, "I have some business about the opera before meeting Christine for her lesson. You, however, are free to spend the day as you wish—perhaps playing with Samineh. I'm sure the Daroga will turn up at some point; he always does. Maybe he can take you into town again."

"Oh," Jenna said, lowering her face into her coffee cup, trying to hide her disappointment.

Erik raised an eyebrow at her and leaned his head a little in her direction before asking, "*Oh* what?"

"Well," Jenna said, staring at the spot on the floor where the little Siamese kitten was lapping up her cream, "could I perhaps come with you?"

"You wish to join me on my errands?" Erik asked her, somewhat surprised.

"Yes," she admitted, once again mesmerized by her coffee cup.

"Are you still afraid to be alone here, Jenna?" he asked, a bit confused. "You know nothing here could hurt you. As long as you stay away from the tunnels…and the lake…and…"

"Oh, I know," Jenna quickly agreed, interrupting his list of the dangers in his home. "And, no, I am not…*afraid*. It's just…I'm very likely to get lonely here without…," she finally looked up to meet his eyes, "you." Erik felt a strange stirring in his chest at her declaration. Her aqua-colored eyes were pleading with him to allow her to join him. This was the second time she had made such a plea. Before Jenna, he'd never had anyone in his life to accompany him on his excursions. And now, for the second time, she asked to come along, simply for the sake of sharing his company. It was strange, but somehow wonderful.

"Alright, Jenna," Erik agreed, with a smile, "But for this trip, you are going to have to dress the part."

The knock came on his office door, as Red sat on the corner of his desk, helping him to do some paperwork. "Come in," he called, completing the sentence he was writing. "Good afternoon, Doctor," his superior, Dr. James said, as he entered the room, closing the door behind him. "I see you have Miss Wilson's cat with you again."

"Yes, I do," he agreed, looking up to greet the Chief of Neurology. "I bring him with me every day—he seems to make a connection with Miss Wilson. When I am not in her room, working on her case, he hangs out here, in my office. He's quite helpful, as you can see," he commented, as the cat sauntered over and laid down on the paperwork the doctor had been filling out.

"Hmmmm…" Dr. James said, walking into the office and taking a seat by the desk. "And how is Miss Wilson doing with the therapy?"

"Well," he began, somewhat excited to share his small successes with his boss. "Miss Wilson is responding to the stimuli of touch and sound, and to a somewhat lesser extent, to the stimulus of smell."

Dr. James looked guardedly impressed. "What are your observations, Doctor?"

"Well, she smiles when she hears certain music. She has scrunched up her nose at certain, unpleasant smells. She shivers when touched lightly on the arm." The doctor fought to keep his face from showing a blush at that last revelation, remembering how much Jenna's shivers made him shiver in return.

"Might not some of that be involuntary, Doctor?" his superior inquired, not entirely convinced of the efficacy of the therapy. "Are there any quantifiable results?"The young doctor paused. His voice growing less animated, he said, "She squeezes my hand. Not every time I ask her to, but often enough that I am convinced that she's trying to communicate."

Dr. James observed his young charge, looking somewhat crestfallen, and a wave of sympathy came over him. It was clear to James that the resident wanted desperately for this therapy to work—and regardless of what the physician said, that his interests were more than just professional. He knew that he should probably remove the young doctor from the case, but he could see that it meant so much to him to try to help Miss Wilson regain consciousness. He felt it was necessary, though, to try and keep the young man grounded. "You know, Doctor," he began in a gentle tone, "the longer a patient is in a coma, the less chance he or she has of coming out with all faculties intact."

"I know." the young doctor merely nodded, not looking at him.

"Many patients never emerge, Doctor," he pushed further.

"I *know,*" came the response, a little louder and a little sharper than before.

Dr. James looked the young man over again, surveying his demeanor, before continuing. "I meant to tell you at the meeting today,"

"Dr. James, I'm sorry about that," he quickly cut in. "I was working with Jen—Miss Wilson, and I lost track of time…"

"It's alright, son," the kind doctor said. "We've all done that. But I did want to mention to you that Miss Wilson's aunt—Penny Wilson—called to check on her niece. Apparently, she's planning a visit out here soon, to see the progress her niece is making in person. It might be a good thing," the Chief of Neurology concluded in a pointed manner, "to be able to show that we've made significant progress with Miss Wilson's condition before the aunt gets here."

He sighed deeply, and nodded his head. "Understood, Doctor."

"OK." Dr. James rose from his chair and walked to the door. "Good day, Doctor."

Alone once again, with only Red for company, he ran his fingers through his hair and let out a long breath. "Oh, Red. What are we going to do?"

19 LADY GHOST

Jenna stepped out of her room, her black boots making a sharp tapping sound on the floor. "Well?" she asked Erik, who stood in the living room, hand over his chin, examining her from head to toe.

"You certainly *look* like a ghost," he commented, the upturned corner of his lip divulging the smile behind the mask. Jenna was dressed, top to bottom, in black. He had insisted that if she were to accompany him into the opera house, she would have to dress so that she could easily blend into the shadows. He had presented her with inky garments from his own wardrobe with which to accomplish the feat. His woolen trousers were far too big for her, but cinched at the waist and tucked into the black boots, she could manage to wear them without tripping. The button down shirt—long sleeves cuffed over several times—was a stark white, but hidden beneath the floor length black cloak he had provided her, it was barely visible. She had tied her fiery hair away from her face with a ribbon—black, of course—and tucked it beneath the hood of the cloak. She would make a convincing shadow—if only she could stop making so much noise. "But your footsteps are supposed to be silent, Jenna," Erik finished his thought.

Jenna looked at him in exasperation. "Well, how am I supposed to make these boots silent? The soles are hard, and they are far too big for me!"

"Try being a little lighter on your feet," Erik offered, as if it were the most obvious idea in the world. "You're to be a ghost, Jenna, not a pachyderm."

"Erik!" she said his name sharply, hands on her hips, outraged that he had just basically called her an elephant. "That was rude!"

He smiled at her, raising an eyebrow, "It's part of my charm."

"I guess that's one way to look at it." Jenna muttered, fixing him with an icy glare that just seemed to make his grin broader.

"Really, Jenna," he said, trying to get ahold of his mischievous streak. "If you wish to help me haunt the opera, you must learn to glide across the floor. Float, even." He approached her gracefully, in demonstration, never making a sound with his shoes.

"How do you do that?" Jenna asked, not at all certain that she could ever be *that* light on her feet.

"I just listen to the *music*, Jenna," he said, a glimmer in his eye. "I let it guide me."

"There is no music, Erik," she contended, as they stood in his sitting room, which was silent except for the sounds of their own voices. "You are hearing things!"

"I am," he agreed, the glint in his eye growing brighter as he stared off at something only he could see. "The most pure, unearthly things." He brought his gaze back to his protégé ghost, explaining, "We are in an opera house, Jenna." His arm swept out to his side in a grand gesture. "This is the seat of sweet music's throne. Just hear it. *Feel* it. It's all around you."

As Jenna stared into the intensity of Erik's gaze, she could swear she almost did hear this music of which he spoke, though whether it was really there, or the power of his suggestion was just that strong, she couldn't say. Captured by his two-tone gaze, she could only nod her acknowledgement of this ephemeral sound—this music he swore was present.

"All you have to do," he uttered softly, in tones lilting and euphonious, as he took her hands and began moving backward, pulling her along toward him, "is let your feet glide as the music glides, carried forth by power of the song, floating, falling. *Trust* the music, Jenna," he entreated, his voice becoming more hypnotic with every word. "Let it *possess* you."

Jenna felt herself moving toward him, caressed by his soft, warm tones, light as air, drifting across the echoing floor, never making a sound—until he gently let go of her hands, and immediately, bereft of his physical presence, the music was gone and she tripped.

Quickly clasping her shoulders to steady her before she hit the floor, Erik rolled his eyes. "Just...*do* try not to be so clumsy!" he admonished, turning in the direction of the boat as soon as he was certain she would not fall on her face.

"Thanks for the tip!" she called out sarcastically, before gathering the edges of her cloak with a huff and stalking after him.

❧

"So why are we here, Erik?" she whispered, as they climbed the last few steps to the heavy wall before them. The corridor they traveled was made of stone, and if it had not been for the lantern that Erik carried—mostly for her benefit, she surmised—there would be no light at all. Now, however, it appeared they had come to the end of the road, and the journey truly had not made much sense in Jenna's mind.

"We are here," he said softly, glancing at her over his shoulder as he stretched his hand toward the door, "to retrieve my salary."

"Your salary?" Jenna responded, incredulous. Erik had a job? She'd certainly seen no evidence of that since she'd come to his lair. "For what?"

"For saving the managers of this esteemed establishment," he returned dryly, "from their own incompetence." Erik pressed with gentle force on just the right spot, and the wall before them slid away. Jenna gasped in surprise and Erik held a long finger to his lips, urging her silence with his eyes. She followed him into a richly appointed opera box, with curtains of rich red velvet, tied off with braided gold cords. The chairs, which were lined in three rows of two, were covered with plush crimson cushions, and on the rightmost back seat was a thick white envelope, the letters *O.G.* written in neat script on the front. Erik floated forward and retrieved the envelope, secreting it away into one of the many folds of his cape. He turned to go but saw that Jenna was no longer standing behind him, but had made her way to the front of the box, and was now leaning over the railing, peering off into the empty auditorium. "Jenna," he called to her in a loud whisper through clenched teeth, but still she simply stood and stared at the magnificent site before her eyes. She had never before seen something quite so opulent or so extravagant. The walls around her were peppered with rows of boxes just like this one, separated by gilded columns and balustrades. Below her were more seats of red, facing a stage hung with a glorious scarlet curtain, trimmed in gold. But her eyes were drawn above, to the intricately painted ceiling from the center of which hung the most decadently beautiful chandelier she had ever beheld.

She had never been in an opera house before—her mother had always been too poor to buy tickets. The scene before her was breathtaking and brought to mind images of well-dressed couples, and the bell-like clink of champagne glasses, and the type of life she had always admired, but in which she had never taken part. Caught in her reverie, she did not notice when the stage door opened and several figures entered the auditorium, until she was pulled back and silenced by Erik's hand over her mouth. He yanked her back into the corridor behind the box and released her only when a sharp pain ran through his hand as the wall slid closed behind them.

"What are you *doing?!*" he exclaimed harshly, yanking his hand away from her, examining it closely to see bite marks on the palm.

"What are *you* doing!?" she demanded in a loud whisper, rounding on Erik once he let go of her.

"We are not supposed to be seen, Jenna," he hissed back at her, rubbing his hand, to try to relieve the discomfort. "I am the Opera Ghost! Not some adoring fan!"

"Well, *I* am *not* the Opera Ghost's victim—to be manhandled and yanked around like that," she huffed.

"Apparently," he seethed back.

"I wanted to see," she spat angrily, crossing her arms in front of her chest, fixing him with a furious glare.

"Box 5 is my private box, and it is to remain empty," he said in a temper. "If anyone had noticed you, traipsing about inside, they all would have rushed up to see who had dared infiltrate the Phantom's Box! No one is allowed inside, except for Madame Giry, to tend to the dust and to deliver my salary."

"I *still* don't even know what they're paying you for," Jenna snapped angrily. "*Floating* around behind the walls? Lurking in the shadows of empty opera boxes? Do they *all* jump when you say *'boo'*?"

"Most of them, yes." Erik replied dryly, earning him an eye roll and an annoyed sigh.

"I just wanted to watch, Erik," Jenna complained, her tone a little quieter now. "I've never been to an opera before. I always thought it would be so amazing. What good is a private box if you can't enjoy it, anyway?"

Erik looked at her quietly for a moment. She really did look disappointed and confused at his need for secrecy. "It is only a rehearsal, Jenna," he said calmly, hoping that it would help to quell her disappointment. "It is not a performance."

"It is more than *I* have ever seen, Erik," she entreated. "Please, can we stay? Don't *you* ever just sit and watch?"

Erik sighed deeply, remembering the days he *would* lurk in the shadows and enjoy the glorious music that wafted up from the stage. "Since Carlotta has taken over the Prima Donna role, there is not really much *to* watch. But very well, if it means so much to you, Jenna, to see a rehearsal, then we shall stay."

A smile broke over Jenna's face as she looked up at him, and she practically gushed, "Thank you, Erik! Thank you, thank you!" Suddenly, her excitement paled, and she looked down awkwardly, saying, "I'm uh…sorry I bit your hand."

"Really, Jenna," Erik replied sardonically. "*Don't* mention it."

Erik flashed her a warning look as he reached for the secret spot that would cause the wall to slide away. "Remember we must keep to the shadows, and we must be very quiet so as not to draw attention to ourselves."

"Erik," she asked, looking at him with true excitement in her eyes once again. "Didn't I prove myself with the frogs?"

Jenna saw that conspiratorial smile return to Erik's face, as he recalled the prank they'd played on Carlotta. "Yes," he admitted, finally, "I suppose you did prove yourself rather well during *that* excursion."

Jenna felt her heart swell at the tone of approval in his voice, remembering the laughter they had shared on their way back to the lair.

Once again, Erik led Jenna through the secret door into Box 5, showing her the exact spot where he stood when he wished to observe the debacles that passed for productions in the opera house. The dark clothing they both wore helped, and to anyone who happened to look in the direction of the Phantom's Box, all that would be visible were two indistinct shadows, somewhat murkier than the rest.

Before long, the orchestra had assembled, and the maestro gave the upsweep of his baton to start their warm-ups. They were clumsy, and they were out of sync, and as Erik listened, he mentally composed the notes he would be leaving on the managers' desks, delineating every flaw, as well as his proposed solutions, to ensure that the Garnier did not become the laughing stock of France. Erik had saved them from becoming so time and again, and now that he thought of it, an increase of his salary was long overdue.

But as Erik noted each string in need of tuning, or each woodwind in need of a new reed, he glanced over at Jenna, and saw a look of pure rapture on her face. Her lips were slightly open, and her eyes were misty with unshed tears. Her body seemed pull slightly forward, toward the music, drawn by the song, and when the winds lifted up onto that slightly flatter Bb, her lids fluttered closed and a solitary tear finally escaped. For a single moment, it was enough to take his breath away.

Without thinking, Erik used his forefinger to lift her chin, and direct her face toward his. Her eyes opened and met his gaze. "It's beautiful, Erik," she whispered, her eyes glistening with sublime joy.

In that moment in time, Erik envied Jenna her less than astute ear for music—her ability to listen without hearing every imperfection, every blemish on the complexion of the song. It was clear that Jenna was *affected* by music, but she did not demand that impeccable precision for which Erik strove. She could brush aside every impurity—every maculation—until she *felt* the spirit of the song. And she could love it, flaws and all—and think it was beautiful.

"Yes," Erik whispered back to her, eyes still locked with hers, "I suppose it is." Erik used a long finger to brush away the tear that was trailing down her cheek, and for a moment neither of them breathed.

"Ahhh—a-aaah Aaaaaa-a-aaaaaaaaaah—a-a-a-aaaaaaa-aa-aa-aa-aaaa-AAAAAAAAH!" Came a loud caterwaul from the front of the auditorium. Jenna jumped and Erik had to take a step back to avoid being jostled.

"Good Lord," Jenna exclaimed, looking at Erik in worry. "Is she injured?"

Jenna saw Erik choke back what looked like a laugh, and before answering, Erik held out his hand, asking her with his eyes for permission to grasp it. Jenna took his hand and Erik pulled her back behind the wall, where he took in a deep breath and answered, "No!" his voice thick with humor. "That is what she calls singing!"

Jenna turned from him and once again looked back in the direction of the stage. "Oh, good heavens! No wonder you don't linger here often."

Suddenly the music stopped, and a hideous shriek was heard from the stage. "Sciocchi! You once again botched my entrance! Buffoni!" Carlotta stormed off the stage, muttering the whole time, "I cannot-a work like-a this!"

"Ugh!" Jenna said, in disgust, rubbing her hands up and down her arms. "She makes my skin crawl."

"Yes," Erik said dryly, still looking in the direction in which the diva had stormed. He was getting an idea.

❧

"It is a beautiful day, Miss Wilson," he said, pushing her door open. "And you and I are going to take full advantage of it," he continued, rolling the wheelchair into the room. He walked over to the side of her bed and gave her hand a quick squeeze. "Are you feeling up to a field trip?" he smiled sweetly at her, wishing with his whole heart that she would answer him, but knowing that they were not quite at that point. "Well, whether you are or not, we're going on one."

He positioned the wheelchair next to her bed and set the brakes. Turning back to Jenna, he pulled down the covers on her bed and bent over, placing one arm around her back, the other below her knees. He lifted her from the bed, and despite his intentions to remain completely professional, he could not help but take a moment to savor how exquisite she felt within his arms. He imagined a day when he would hold her in his embrace, just like this, her own arms wrapped around his neck, their lips fused in a kiss. He would carry her over the threshold of their home, and into their room, and never breaking their kiss, he would lower them both onto the bed…

He shook his head, to clear his mind of the wildly inappropriate fantasy. "One step at a time, Jenna," he murmured out loud, as he gently lowered her into the chair. It pained him to fasten the restraints around her body, but he knew they were a necessity to keep her safe. When she was fastened in, he draped a blanket over her legs before taking his spot behind her and pushing her chair out into the hallway. They rode the elevator down to the ground floor, where he waved and smiled to other doctors and nurses, as he navigated them toward the door to the garden.

"Do you smell that, Jenna?" he asked, as he pushed her down the paved pathways which wound around bushes and flowering trees. "Fresh air! Even here in New York! It's kind of rare, as you know," he smiled as he continued pushing. As they meandered through the garden, he continued to blabber on about everything and nothing, telling her about his day, telling her how loud Red had been the night before, commenting on the weather, listening to bird song. It was a nice, calming break from the hectic afternoon for the doctor, who had no idea that he was being watched from the observation deck, several floors above.

"So that is my niece," asked the petite, slender woman with the sleek blond hair cut and clear blue eyes. "It's been so long since I've seen Rhonda's child, I barely recognize her."

"Yes, Ms. Wilson," the Neurology resident confirmed. "That is definitely your niece Jenna."

"How is she doing," she asked, not taking her eyes off the young woman in the wheelchair, nor the young doctor who seemed to be happily taking her out for an afternoon stroll.

"Well, it's difficult to say, Ms. Wilson," he spoke shrewdly. "She has yet to regain consciousness. With coma patients, the longer they stay under, the harder it is for them to recover."

"Isn't there anything that can be done?" she asked, concerned. She did not want to lose her sister's only child.

"Well," he began, "Normally, it is customary to take the patient into surgery—or at least to drill boreholes into the skull around the affected area of the brain, to relieve the pressure." He noticed her balk at the thought. "But her doctor felt that such a procedure was not necessary."

"Is that him," she inquired, gesturing toward the young man so dutifully pushing her niece around the courtyard.

"Indeed," the resident replied, disdain dripping from each syllable. "That is her doctor, if you wish to call him that. He is trying a new form of therapy. One in which he squeezes her hand and plays her songs, and, apparently, takes her for walks in the sun." He watched with contempt as the wheelchair's progress stopped for a moment. Jenna's doctor leaned over one of the rose bushes, and plucked a single rose, careful to snap the thorns off of the stem. He turned to face Jenna, and presented the rose to her. After a few moments of kneeling there in front of a coma patient, holding out the rose, as if she was actually going to take it, the young doctor leaned in and tucked it behind her ear, adjusting her curls as he did so.

"They seem close," Jenna's aunt commented, a small smile turned up her lips, as she watched the scene unfold before her.

"They barely knew each other before she became his patient," the resident snarled.

The woman started at the tone of his voice, and he quickly reminded himself to keep his demeanor professional. "Ms. Wilson," he finally said, addressing her directly, no longer watching the scene below. "Would you care to accompany me to dinner?"

The older Wilson looked shocked. "Dr. Charleson, I am nearly old enough to be your mother!"

"Beauty knows no age, Penny. May I call you Penny?" he asked, laying on the charm.

"Of course," she answered, put a little off guard by the handsome young doctor.

"Come with me to dinner, Penny," Charleson asked again, this time taking her hand. "We could discuss your dear niece's case further over a nice meal and a good Merlot."

"I'd like that," she relented with a smile, "Dr. Charleson."

20 TRICKS AND ROSES

"Really, Erik," Jenna commented, as she gathered her skirts once more to bend low and retrieve her quarry. They had slipped quietly into the wardrobe room after their visit to Box 5 so that Jenna could retrieve more suitable attire for this part of their adventure. She, Erik explained, would have to take the lead in this, since it was still daylight. He had given her privacy while she changed, slipping away briefly, he told her, so that he could make a delivery to the managers—she assumed it had something to do with the reason they were paying him. They'd hastened to the boat, when he'd returned, and once again found their way to the little marsh behind the opera, which they had visited the other night. "I should just accept that outings with you will never be simple, shouldn't I," she stated, as she reached toward the underside of a leaf and quickly captured another small brown creature. It was a good thing she wasn't squeamish.

"I don't know what you're complaining about, Jenna," Erik replied softly from the shadows in which he was concealing himself, making his voice sound as if it were directly next to her ear. "I took you to the opera just this morning."

Jenna glared at Erik in his hiding place beneath a tree, and when she heard his laughter bubbling up in her ear, she flicked her hand as if she were shooing away an insect, looking directly at him as she muttered the word "gnats!" This only made Erik's laughter louder, and Jenna stalked off in the other direction to continue gathering her prey, before Erik could see the broad smile that spread over her own features.

Jenna couldn't help but laugh, even if she *were* the good-natured butt of Erik's joke. Being with him was exhilarating. Whether they were skulking around the opera house, or working together on one of his schemes—even when they fought—there was something about spending time with him that ignited a spark in her soul. When she was with Erik, she could almost forget that she was wearing a floor length dress with petticoats, or that the glow in the sitting room came from candlelight and not a TV. When she was with Erik, it was easy to forget that she didn't belong here, that she had somehow been thrust out of time into a strange world that didn't really seem so very strange, as long as he was in it. When she was with Erik, it was easy to feel at home.

But she wasn't at home, she thought, the smile fading from her face. She knew that Erik had been hard at work trying to find some way to get her back to her time. She had complete faith that with his help she would soon find herself back in New York City, with its endless hustle and never-ending noise. And there, in the midst of over eight million other people, she would once again find herself truly and completely alone.

"Jenna," Erik called, from his spot in the shadows. "I think we have enough."

Jenna took a deep breath and composed herself before turning and joining him beneath the tree, her valuable targets in the jar in her hands.

"Let's go, Jenna," Erik said, taking her hand to steady her on the way back to the boat. "We have a delivery to make."

❧

"How is your steak?" Dr. Charleson asked from across the table, as he looked up from cutting into his own filet to catch her blue eyes.

"Oh, it's delicious," Penny answered from across the table. "Thank you again, Dr. Charleson—you didn't have to do this."

"It's my pleasure, Penny," he responded with a smile. "And please call me Blaine."

Penny smiled, a blush entering her cheeks, and said, "Alright. Blaine." She felt foolish, for she really was old enough to be this young doctor's mother, but she enjoyed the attention he was lavishing upon her. She had never married and had been without the companionship of a man for many years. This young doctor was charming and charismatic—so what if she let him buy her a meal at one of New York's finest restaurants and tell her a little about her niece's case.

After seeing him so devotedly wheeling Jenna around the hospital courtyard, she'd wanted to meet her niece's actual doctor—but Dr. Charleson, who'd been the first person to greet her when she'd arrived in the Neurology Department, advised against it. It was late, he'd said, and the young doctor had a reputation for clocking out early. Charleson had convinced her to join him for dinner that night. She could always meet with Jenna's doctor in the morning, and besides, he had some insights into her niece's case that he'd be happy to share with her over dinner.

So she sat here, savoring a perfectly grilled steak, and a fragrant glass of wine, enjoying the elegant atmosphere and the light conversation that the handsome doctor—Blaine—was making. But it really was time that she ask him about her niece since Jenna, after all, was her reason for being here.

"So, really, Blaine," she asked, sipping her merlot, "how *is* my niece?"

A dark look of concern entered the doctor's eyes as he looked at her. "Penny, it would be a lie to tell you that I have much hope for her. Coma patients," he continued, "require immediate, aggressive care in order to improve. I don't feel that Miss Wilson received that at the time of her accident."

"What do you mean, Blaine?" Penny asked, her eyes narrowed in confusion, her head swimming at the idea that Jenna might not be receiving the proper care.

"Well, Penny, Jenna was brought into the ER when the first year resident was on duty. He's well intentioned but not experienced enough, in my opinion, to handle a case of traumatic brain injury. He did not do surgery to relieve the pressure—believing it was not necessary. He basically allows her to linger in her hospital bed and keeps her company in the name of *treating* her. He reads to her in lieu of surgery. He plays her music instead of giving her medicines. I don't see anything he's doing for her that is medically legitimate, Penny. And I worry that Miss Wilson is suffering for his lack of experience."

"Well," Penny asked in outrage, her voice starting to tremble, "Why is he still on her case? Why is he being allowed to mistreat her in this way?"

"He convinced Dr. James that he was trying some new technique called Coma Arousal Therapy, in which he stimulates her senses to try to rouse her back to consciousness. He wants to be published." He took a deep breath before he continued. "Penny, I think he's essentially making her a case study, through which he can advance his career."

Penny placed her fork down on the napkin next to her plate, suddenly losing her appetite. She didn't know what to say about everything she was hearing. If it was true, she was horrified that her niece was getting such terrible care. Jenna was her departed sister's only child. Rhonda had always had such a rough life, but she'd loved her daughter immensely. Penny couldn't bear to think that Jenna wasn't receiving the best of care.

Yet, it was so hard to believe that everything Blaine was telling her *was* true. She had observed Jenna and her doctor in the courtyard. If she had not known he was her physician, she would have thought him a lover, with all of the care he had been showing her. Still, Blaine had no reason to tell her these things if they weren't true, did he? What would he gain by lying?

Penny took another sip of her wine, and looked across the table at the handsome young doctor who was her dinner date. She had a lot of thinking to do. She had to figure out what was best for the only family she had left.

Erik peered into the dressing room before opening the mirror entryway and guiding Jenna in. As before, the room was a barely controlled chaos, with cosmetics and baubles and luxurious clothing strewn about in all directions. Flowers which had apparently been tossed onto the stage by adoring, but tone-deaf admirers, crowded into vases and pots around the floor. Erik crept to the mannequins on which the diva set her headpieces. "She will be using this one today," he told Jenna, as he lifted up an intricately curled auburn wig. "It is part of the costume for La Principessa Guerriera. Carlotta loves to be in full dress when she sashays around during rehearsals."

Erik reached into his cloak to retrieve the small container of honey he had pilfered from the kitchens on the way in. He drizzled a barely noticeable amount onto the wig. He then held his hand out for Jenna's glass jar. Carefully, he unscrewed the lid, and tilted the opening over onto the false hair, positioning it to make certain that all the contents fell directly onto the hairpiece and not onto the floor, confident that the honey would keep them there for the time being. Erik then reached into his cape and pulled out a small, folded piece of paper, which he tucked among the layers of the wig. When he was done, it was completely unnoticeable, and Erik placed the headpiece back on the mannequin to await its owner's return.

As they quickly retreated back toward the mirror, Erik paused at one of the vases and plucked a single red rose. "For your part in our little adventure, my lady," he bowed low at the waist, offering Jenna the flower. Taking the rose from him, and tucking it behind her ear, she smiled brightly and gave Erik a little curtsey, saying, "Thank you, kind sir." Then they hastily flew through the mirror, because they could hear motion outside the door.

Carlotta flounced inside her dressing room, going at once to the fur covered chaise. "O, non ne posso più" she whimpered, as she collapsed dramatically onto the lounge, holding the back of one of her hands to her forehead, trailing the other one on the ground. "O, non posso andare avanti," she lamented her ability to continue with the apparently strenuous rehearsals. She lay there for a few long moments, drawn out by her sniveling and mewling, while Erik and Jenna fought to control their laughter behind the wall. "Oh, ma devo," she exclaimed at length, when even she, perhaps, had grown tired of her own whining. "They need me, so I must." She hefted herself upright and walked over to the row of gowns. Once again, Erik averted his eyes, as Carlotta changed into the colorful red, green, and gold gown that she wore in La Principessa Guerriera. Jenna nudged him when Carlotta was done, and they both watched as she reached for her auburn wig.

She set it atop her head, adjusting it until the fit was perfect. When she pulled her fingers away, she looked at them closely, and then brought them to her nose. She must have recognized the sweet smell of honey because she simply shrugged, and licked the saccharine liquid off her fingers. Erik gagged at the sight.

Carlotta sat down at her dressing table and reached for a deep red tube of lip color, pursing her lips into a pout before applying it liberally. As she sat there making kissing motions to herself in the mirror, Erik and Jenna tried not to snicker as her hand went up and scratched her brow. She reached now for the blusher powder kicking up pink clouds of dust as she patted her cheeks with the pouf. This time, her fingers went to the top of her head to scratch, as she muttered about the "Stupido wig!" giving a cluck of her tongue. She'd begun to apply her false eyelashes when she had to stop to scratch again. With a huff, she reached up to the side of her head, but her fingers flinched back with a start when she felt movement. "Che cosa?" she mumbled, as she turned to look in the mirror and saw the small brown spider climbing down her cheek. She let fly a blood-curdling scream as she jumped back from her dressing table, to fling the wig from her person. "Ragni, Ragni," she shrieked, smacking at her head, as she found that several of the spiders had wandered from the wig and now took up residence in her hair. "Spiders! HELP!"

The door to the dressing room flew open and in ran Carlotta's consort, Signore Piangi. He grasped Carlotta's upper arms in his hands. "Il mio amore," he asked in concern, "What is wrong?"

"*Spiders*!" she bellowed at him, and gestured to the wig, and to the few small brown arachnids still crawling around on her head. "O mio Dio," Piangi exclaimed, as he helped to brush the spiders out of her hair, then helped the sobbing woman to her chaise lounge. Once she was settled, Piangi knelt and examined the wig, noting the stickiness and the small brown spiders that still remained within. Something white caught his eye, peeking out of a layer of false curls. He reached out to grab it, and found that it was a folded piece of parchment. Piangi unfolded the parchment and read the note out loud. *For the sin of making the lady's skin crawl. Vigilantly yours, O.G.*

Erik and Christine were a long stretch down the secret passageway behind Carlotta's dressing room, but they could still hear her carrying on. When they were a far enough distance away, they paused to slump against the wall and let their laughter consume them. It was naughty—it was so *very* naughty—Jenna knew, to be doing these things to the aging diva. But her demeanor was truly awful. Plus, Jenna was fairly convinced she would do almost anything to share these little conspiracies with Erik, to see his eyes gleam with mischief and his lips twist upward in that rakish smile.

"Did you hear her scream!?" she asked, between giggles.

"The far better question," he responded, "is if there is anyone within Paris who did *not* hear her scream!"

They both laughed again at the ridiculous soprano.

When their mirth had quieted, Erik took a moment to glance down at his pocket watch. A look of mild horror came over his face.

"Oh no!" he exclaimed, and Jenna immediately sobered up.

"What is it, Erik?" she asked in concern.

"It is nearly time for my lesson with Christine," he stated, looking quite perturbed. "And I have not yet dropped you off beneath the opera."

"That's not a problem, Erik," she declared sweetly, trying to assuage his nerves. "I'll just come with you to the lesson. I wouldn't mind."

"No, you don't understand," he cut her off in agitation. "These lessons are very important. I cannot be distracted by small talk or questions. I must give my attentions wholly to Christine, with nothing and no one else to get in the way."

Suddenly, Jenna's mirthful mood was replaced by a stabbing pain in her chest. *Get in the way? Distraction?* Is that truly what he thought of her?

"No worries, Erik," she assured him. "I can be quiet. Remember, the frogs?" She reminded him of their first excursion for the second time that day, hoping to see that same smile spread across his face.

"See to it," he snapped. "She cannot know you're there. She barely knows *I'm* there," he added, as he began to stalk off in the direction of the chapel.

Jenna followed close behind, so as not to get lost. At times, he almost seemed to forget her presence, as he withdrew into that part of himself that he kept separate for Christine. For the first time in Erik's company, Jenna began to feel alone.

21 LESSONS LEARNED

Jenna watched Erik pace back and forth in the little passage behind the chapel. There were still a few minutes left before his scheduled lesson with Christine, but he was a bundle of nerves. In the time it took them to get from Carlotta's dressing room to the chapel, he had transformed from the smooth, confident opera ghost to a barely contained animal—almost like a zoo tiger traipsing back and forth in its cage, anticipating the keeper's arrival.

"Erik, you should try to calm down," Jenna said softly, trying to soothe him from her place in the shadows. "She will be here soon."

"And *you* said you could be silent," he snapped at her, glaring as he rounded in her direction. "Remember, I said no distractions."

"Oh yes," Jenna spat back at him, quite perturbed at being relegated to nothing more than a distraction. "I heard you loud and clear!"

Erik turned from her and resumed his circuit on the stone floor. He was being absolutely ridiculous, and Jenna could not stand to watch it.

"Erik," she began again, hoping to make him see reason. "Why are you so nervous? *You* are the teacher."

"Apparently, not a very effective one," he snarled at her, "I have not been able to teach *you* to be *silent*!"

"You are being hateful," she shot back. "And my point was that *Christine* is the one who should be nervous! *She's* the student here. *You're* the one she has to impress."

"Impress me?" Erik looked at her incredulously. "She impresses me just by existing. I am not worthy to breathe the same air as her." His eyes took on a faraway look, as his voice hushed. "*She* is truly the angel, Jenna. I am merely an imposter."

Jenna regarded him silently. It was clear Erik had strong feelings for this *Christine*. They were written all over his face when he spoke of her—such a look of reverence and awe overtaking his features. It was as if a fire suddenly glowed behind his eyes at the mere mention of her name.

She was surprised to note a sense of sadness come over her at the realization. Why should *she* care? She rolled her eyes at the ridiculousness of the notion. Just because they had shared some laughs and had some tea together, didn't mean she expected him to glow for her the way he glowed for Christine. Just because it thrilled her to watch him carry out his crazy schemes with such confidence and grace didn't mean she would contemplate abandoning her own world to stay here with him. Just because he had sung to her, and held her when she'd cried, and made her believe, even for the briefest of moments, that she was worthy of a prince…

"Angel…?" Jenna's thoughts scattered when she heard a female voice, clear as a bell, float through the opening in the wall. Erik caught a silent breath at the sound, and turned toward the small fissure. "Angel, are you here?"

"I am here, Christine." Erik's voice was deep and hushed.

"Oh, Angel," Jenna heard Christine respond, relief and excitement evident in her voice. "It is so good to hear your voice."

"Yours as well, child," Erik uttered softly, in golden tones. "Have you practiced your breathing exercises?"

"I have, Angel!" the crystalline voice responded. "They have helped greatly."

"Very good," Erik nodded, even though Christine could not see him. "I am pleased. Now then," he continued, assuming the mantle of teacher, "take a deep breath for me, Mademoiselle, and begin your scales."

As the bird like warbles of the young soprano issued through the wall, Jenna's eyes were on Erik. His lips were slightly parted, and his eyes half closed as a look of divine ecstasy washed over his face. His head was inclined slightly back, and the breath seemed to still in his chest. He was so entirely transfixed by the sweet strains coming from his pupil, that he never noticed Jenna inch closer, until she too could gaze upon this mysterious creature called Christine.

The first thing Jenna noticed was the hair. Long and curly, it was the deep, rich color of mahogany. It framed a heart shaped face of porcelain skin that betrayed the slightest hint of blush on the high cheeks, and rosebud lips that were rounded in song. Her eyes, large and blue, looked like they could hold the entire ocean in their depths. She was small in stature and delicately built, and her dainty perfection shattered Jenna's spirit like a crystal glass carelessly dropped on a stone—her heart pierced by the shards. Christine was exquisitely beautiful and her voice was flawless to match. Of course Erik was enthralled by her. What man wouldn't be?

When her scales were complete, Erik smiled and said, "Brava, Christine. Now, let's try some arpeggios and glissandos. On C."

Christine began and Jenna watched Erik once more. One thing was certain—he had not needed to worry about her presence being a distraction. She was standing rather close to him now, and still he did not notice she was there, such were all of his energies focused on the petite songbird in the next room. Likewise, the girl was wholly focused on him. She hung on his every word, and did every exercise exactly as he asked, as if her very existence depended on the sweet morsels of praise he allowed her with each successful note. An invisible thread seemed to tether one to the other, their attentions so singularly honed on their own interactions. Teacher and student, angel and ingénue—the rest of the world faded to irrelevance when compared to their mutual fascination with one another.

Jenna took a few steps away—not that Erik noticed—and sat on the floor with her back against the wall. She had wanted to see Christine. She had wanted to meet this *seamstress* about whom Erik had spoken so highly. She had wanted to share this lesson with him, to understand this part of his life. So why was she now feeling so incredibly shaken?

Because now you know you will never have him! a voice in her mind answered her unspoken question. *With Christine in his life, he will never be yours.*

Of course, that line of thinking was ridiculous! She was not even *from* here. The universe had played some kind of strange trick on her, thrusting her out of her own time, sending her back 130 years! She did not know how or why it had happened, but she had to get back to her own time. Erik was trying to find a way to send her back. There was no way they could ever have been together.

But you were beginning to want him anyway.

Jenna shut her eyes tightly against the realization that once again, she had begun to fall for the wrong man. She had such an incredible talent for finding ways to make herself miserable! Even now, when her focus should be on trying to figure out this mystery and find a way to get home, her traitorous heart was dallying with yet another ridiculous romantic notion. So what if he was dashing and talented and smarter than anyone she had ever known? So what if he made her laugh, and made her furious, and made her feel so utterly alive? One look at him with Christine, and she knew he was as unattainable as the stars in the night sky. And to think she had even briefly wished that he could be her prince! It was clear that the only royalty to which he would ever swear allegiance was standing on the other side of the wall.

Jenna covered her face with her hands and felt a velvety softness tickling her finger. She reached behind her ear and retrieved the rose Erik had taken from Carlotta's dressing room and given to her. It was the tangible reminder of a frivolous moment in time when they had felt so right together—two parts of an unbreakable team. She held the smooth, thornless stem and gazed at the lush red petals, a delicate, sweet aroma wafting up to fill her nose. She reached up and loosed her hair, taking the black ribbon, and tying it around the rose's stem. Its elegance was now entwined with darkness—the black satin a perfect symbol of Erik's own shadowy grace—and the bloom's beauty was greater for it.

"Will you be here tomorrow, Angel?" came the high-pitched voice of the girl behind the wall.

"Of course, my dear," was Erik's velvet reply.

Through the pain in her chest at hearing their sweet exchange, Jenna realized that the lesson was winding down, and she removed her cloak, hastily stashing it behind her on the floor.

"Until then, Angel," there was the hint of a giggle in her voice.

"Until then, Christine," and even though his pupil couldn't see him, Erik bowed low in the direction of the wall which shielded him from the object of his affections.

He made to linger there until Christine left the chapel but Jenna coughed loudly and startled him out of his reverie. He glared in her direction to silence her, but Jenna only placed her hand to her mouth, wheezing in a deep gulp of air, as if she were going to cough again.

"Angel," Christine called again, sounding a bit confused.

Erik made no reply. Instead, he silently moved over to where Jenna sat and dragged her up off the floor, meaning to charge off toward the boat. After they took a few steps, however, Jenna dislodged her hand and dashed back to where she had been sitting to retrieve her cloak, earning an annoyed huff from Erik. As she bent down to grab the fabric, she leaned her palm on the wall for balance, tapping it lightly with her fingers as she did. Once her cloak was in hand, she hurried back to join Erik, who was growing more and more impatient by the second.

When the dark-haired soprano heard the light rapping on the wall, she turned back from the door she had just opened. She felt a trembling in her chest as she walked back into the room, and had to take a breath to quiet herself. There, on the floor beneath the far wall of the chapel, lay a flawless red rose. She knelt down before it, extending a shaking hand to retrieve the delicate bloom, bringing it close to her face to sniff its fragrant perfume. "Angel…" she whispered as she gathered the blossom to her chest, knowing that she would always treasure this gift.

"I thought you could be silent!" Erik hissed at her as they sailed the final distance to the underground home. He was so incensed by her little distraction after the lesson, that he stood as he used the long paddle to steer them toward the shore.

"I *was* silent!" Jenna insisted, irritated by Erik's show of temper. He had no idea how hard it had been sitting there watching him make goo-goo eyes at his beloved Christine. It was all she could do not to wretch at the memory.

"Silent? Really, Mademoiselle? Because to me it you sounded like a cat trying to vomit," he seethed.

"There was something in my throat," she insisted, indignantly. So what if it was not true? She had just needed him to get moving for her idea to work. "Perhaps it was some dust. If we had not been hiding *behind a wall* it might not have happened."

"If you had any decorum it might not have happened either. Have you never learned to clear your airways properly like a lady?" he shot her an incredulous look.

"No! I guess I never before had the benefit of etiquette lessons from a man who climbs into women's dressing rooms through their *mirrors*," she snapped back. She had been so tempted to tell him what she had done on his behalf—how she had left the rose to make Christine aware of his fondness for her—but now she could barely stand to be in his presence. She longed to reach shore for no other reason than to storm away from him and slam her bedroom door in his loud, obnoxious, complaining face. Ungrateful, insufferable...*jerk* that he was!

"At least *I* can conduct myself with stealth," Erik shot back with great affectation, still fuming over her uncouth, inelegant, and graceless behavior behind the chapel. She could have ruined everything with Christine!

Jenna merely huffed in response and looked away from him, crossing her arms over her chest. She'd been rather stealthy herself, she thought spitefully, considering that he had no idea she had left her rose for Christine. *Her* rose. For *Christine*. Despite her annoyance with Erik, Jenna could not help but feel her heart ache a bit at the memory of slipping the precious bloom through the opening in the wall, so that the true object of Erik's affections could enjoy its beauty.

They traveled the rest of the way in silence, Erik too annoyed and Jenna too somber to speak. As they began to dock, however, a terrible bellowing assaulted their ears. Despite the tension between them, their eyes quickly met and Erik was out of the boat first, ushering Jenna behind him, placing his body between her and the unnamed threat.

"Let me out of this thing, *will you*," came the desperate roar once again.

Jenna gasped in surprise. Erik had warned her that there were many dangers in his lair—many traps to capture those who dared to enter with ill intent. Had someone been trying to attack him tonight? Had someone meant to threaten his home?

"Erik!" the voice shouted, "Erik, this isn't funny. Let! Me! Go!"

Jenna noticed Erik's stance relax a tiny bit, and when he glanced back at her, she saw his lips curl into a wicked grin. He sauntered arrogantly into the sitting room, Jenna following closely behind. When she saw the source of the mournful cries, she put her hands to her mouth to hold in her giggles.

Omid, stood on the tips of his toes, his arm upraised above the bookshelf, seeming to be reaching for something inside a...book? Judging by the way he was struggling with his whole body to retrieve his arm, he was, apparently, stuck.

"Good evening, Daroga," Erik drawled. "Care for a drink?"

"Get me *out* of this…contraption, Erik!" the Persian sputtered.

"Did you get my note?" Erik asked, eyebrow raised, head cocked to one side as he leaned his long body against the wall, arms crossed over his chest.

"Yes, Erik," he hissed, between clenched teeth. "I got *all* your notes. The one you placed in the liquor cabinet that said, *Not here.* The one you placed in the kitchen that said *Try again.* The one you placed inside the piano that said, *Think higher.* Really, Erik, did you think I was going to look *in* the piano?"

"You *did*," he responded dryly, stating the obvious.

"And," Omid continued, completely ignoring Erik's remark, "I got the one on the false book that said *Erik's Cognac*, right before I opened the cover and my hand got snatched by…by…*shackles*!"

Erik snickered and goaded, "You missed the one on the dining table that said "*Give up now, you foolish Persian.*"

"I saw that one," Omid spat back, "But I ignored it."

"A pity." Erik clucked his tongue in mock sympathy, "I tried to warn you, Daroga."

"You made your point, *fiend!*" Omid growled, "Now release me!"

"Gladly," Erik said with amusement. He reached behind the bookshelf and flipped a hidden switch, and the shackles that had ensnared Omid's wrist instantly opened, unceremoniously dumping him onto the floor. "That should teach you to steal my alcohol!" Erik smirked, as he watched Omid pick himself up off the floor.

"Well, it's not as if *you* ever drink it!" Omid snapped, dusting off his trousers and straightening his tie. "Why do you even keep it here?"

Erik shrugged nonchalantly. "Entrapment."

Omid huffed, his voice raising an octave in outrage. "So you admit it! I…"

"Oh, do quiet down, Persian!" Erik reproved, with a roll of his eyes. "My fingers are getting itchy!"

Jenna watched the exchange with amusement. Once again, Erik was in his element—his mischievous scheme against poor Omid having brought out his sense of fun and adventure. This was the Erik she enjoyed, and she felt her irritation with him begin to melt away as she watched him lift his arm and easily reach the bottle of amber liquid on top of the shelf. He walked over to the liquor cabinet and poured a glass, taking mercy on the hapless Persian. "Here you go, Daroga." Erik handed over the goblet of brandy to Omid, who drank deeply.

When he finished his drink, Omid made his way back over to the bottle, and poured himself a refill. "Where have you two been?" he demanded, as he threw his head back and drank.

"I just finished my lesson with Christine," Erik answered.

"Well, you weren't there *all* day!" Omid remarked, dabbing his mouth with a handkerchief. "Just what did you do to Carlotta? The opera house is all a twitter about the Phantom again."

"Let's just say," Erik responded, that wicked gleam coming back into his eyes, "she had a rather hair-raising experience." He glanced over at Jenna and she could not help but giggle. Her heart jumped a little in her chest when she saw the glint in his eye grow brighter.

Omid looked between the two and rolled his eyes. "I think you are corrupting our guest, Erik."

"No," Jenna answered Omid while looking at Erik. "I was pretty corrupt before I met him."

Erik met Jenna's eyes, and flashed her a small smile. In that moment, the previous stress between them was gone.

"Well, wherever the source of the corruption lies, Erik," Omid informed, shaking his head, "you may wish to tone it down."

Erik sighed at the silly Persian. "Whatever for, Daroga?" he asked, removing his cloak and hat and laying them on the settee until he could hang them up in his wardrobe. "Carlotta deserves far more than what I do to her. She is a wicked, hateful woman."

"Nevertheless," Omid returned. "She is the prima donna. And she has vowed not to continue as such if the *Phantom* is not stopped."

Erik rolled his eyes. "Oh please, Omid. That cow will never willingly relinquish her position on the stage." He helped Jenna remove her cloak, and laid it next to his. "Phantom or no Phantom, she cannot resist an opportunity to deafen the masses with her unconscionable caterwauling."

"Regardless, Erik," Omid swirled the brandy in his glass as he tried to make Erik see reason. "The managers may take her seriously and start…poking around down here."

"Bumbling fools!" Erik muttered under his breath. "They would never make it past the traps."

"I hear she even demanded they stop paying your salary."

"They wouldn't dare!" Erik responded, completely unaffected by what he considered Omid's hysterical warnings. He sat down on the piano bench and flexed his fingers. "They know if they did that, a disaster beyond their imagination would occur."

"Still Erik," Omid warned as he took another sip of his drink. "I wouldn't push it too far. You know Carlotta can have temper tantrums. If she refuses to go on, even temporarily, there is no one who can take her place. The opera will lose a lot of money if they had to refund all those tickets, and they might not be able to *afford* to pay your salary."

A smile crossed Erik's face as he began to play softly. He remembered the angel with whom he'd spent a portion of the afternoon. How beautiful and pure was her voice! How warm and inviting was her smile. *There will soon be someone who could take Carlotta's place,* he thought to himself. *And that someone is Christine.*

> The power of a glance has been so much abused in love stories, that it has come to be disbelieved in. Few people dare now to say that two beings have fallen in love because they have looked at each other. Yet it is in this way that love begins, and in this way only.[1]

He closed the book he had been reading her, his eyes becoming too tired to continue. The room was dark, save for the small reading lamp situated above her hospital bed. He had spent all of his free moments with Jenna today. He took her for a walk in the courtyard, so that she could get some fresh air. He'd sat with her during his break and talked to her about the mundane things that filled his day. And he'd stayed with her, long after his shift had ended, just reading to her, so that she would not have to lay here alone. Even now, when he knew he should be heading home—that he should have headed home hours ago—he lingered, watching her breathe, admiring the way her strawberry curls fell over her face.

…*It is in this way that love begins*…It was crazy, he knew. He'd barely spoken to her before the accident, but as he looked at her now, he

[1] Victor Hugo, *Les Miserables*

absolutely could no longer deny that what he had just read in the book was true. No matter how unlikely it seemed, even to himself, he knew how he felt about Jenna. It had started many months ago with just one look—a glance shared over a patient, a smile shared after a mutual task completed. He had started falling in love with Jenna from the moment he'd seen her his first day at the hospital. But he had not believed, for, truly, *…few people dare now to say that two beings have fallen in love because they have looked at each other.* So, it had proven his singular talent to let unimportant things get in the way, so that he could shove aside this burgeoning feeling that a look had led him to love—a glance had led him to devotion. He should have spoken to her, asked her to dinner, let her know he was interested. If he had, things might have been so very different now.

He took her hand in his, stroking the palm gently, thinking of all the reasons why falling in love just from a look should be impossible. Yet the words he'd just read kept coming back to him… *.It is in this way that love begins, and in this way only.*

Jenna sat on the cushioned chair in her room, reading quietly to herself. It had been a long day, both when they had been navigating the opera house, and later when Omid decided to stay for dinner, after discovering there was once again liquor in the lair. When Erik had returned to the piano, after the Persian had taken his leave, Jenna perused Erik's book shelf and chose a book whose story was familiar to her from back in her own time. Victor Hugo's *Les Misérables*—the classic tale about love and redemption set with the June Rebellion as a backdrop—would have been published just about two decades prior, she thought to herself, as she eagerly turned each page. She remembered hearing the music from the stage show that, while different from the novel, had been extremely popular while she was growing up. Jenna had always been so moved by the plight of poor Eponine. She had dearly loved the hero Marius but he had only ever thought of her as a good friend, while he gave his heart to the beautiful Cosette after only seeing her once. His love for Cosette did not sway Eponine's own heart, and she even went so far as to lay down her life for her beloved Marius so that he could be safe.

Growing up, Jenna had often wondered what it was about Cosette that was so special. Yes, she was beautiful, but what else had Marius known about her when he decided she was his true love? He had known Eponine so much longer. Why could he not return her affections? Why did he have to fall for the fair Cosette after only one glance, when he had a perfectly good woman wanting to love him all along? How was he so blind that he could only recognize her love for him when it was too late?

A gentle rapping on her door startled Jenna out of her musings. "Jenna?" Erik called softly, questioning if he could open the door.

"Come in, Erik," Jenna called out, surprised to hear his voice.

The door opened slowly, and Erik entered, carrying a cup of tea. He swallowed audibly before beginning. "I thought you might like to have some tea to soothe your throat," he said, quietly, holding the cup outward to her, his eyes slightly downcast.

"To soothe my throat?" she asked in confusion, standing up and taking the tea from him.

"Yes," he said, shyly, still not exactly meeting her eyes. "After your coughing spell this afternoon, I thought tea might do you some good."

"Oh," she said simply, feeling guilty at the way she'd manipulated his actions earlier, and how angry her coughing had made him. She took a sip of the tea, which was steaming and rich, and all at once she and Erik locked eyes.

"I'm sorry," they both said at once.

"What for?" they asked in unison.

Each looked at the other and laughed lightly at the way their minds both seemed to be set on the same things. Erik quietly led Jenna into the sitting room, where he motioned for her to sit on the settee before joining her. "I apologize for being cross with you about the coughing when I should have been concerned."

"I apologize…" Jenna began, not wanting to lie, but also not wanting to admit that she had tricked him.

"No, please," he stopped her by holding up his hand. "Hear me out. I should not have been so cross with you…"

"Erik…" Jenna interrupted him.

"Mademoiselle, please," he admonished her. "Do not interrupt me when I am trying to apologize to you. It is difficult enough to do as it is."

Jenna opened her mouth to tell him he truly did not have to

apologize—that her cough had been a ruse and that she had deceived him. But when she looked in his eyes so full of genuine penitence and sincerity, the words froze on her lips, and instead she took a sip of her tea.

"I should have showed concern for you," he finally continued, when he realized Jenna was no longer going to cut him off. "Instead I only showed ire. For that, I apologize."

"It's alright, Erik," she responded, still feeling horribly delinquent.

"It is not, alright—the way I treated you," he insisted. "But…Jenna…Christine *cannot* begin to suspect that I am not actually an angel."

Jenna looked into his eyes, and saw the desperation that lay behind his remorse for being rude to her.

"Erik," she asked him gently. "Why?"

"Why?" he asked her, in disbelief at her simple question. "Because if she knew, she would only run from me."

Jenna's eyes narrowed and she shook her head. "Why on earth would you think that, Erik? She hung on your every word as if she adored you."

"It is the *angel* she adores," Erik supplied, looking down sadly. "Not the real me."

"Well, that's because she doesn't *know* you." Jenna tried to make him see reason. "If you would *go* to her, and not hide behind a wall…"

"She would run," Erik said shortly. "She would flee in terror to find that her angel was really more demon than saint, more monster than man."

"Why…" Jenna asked, shaking her head, her heart feeling tight in her chest, "Why do you say that about yourself, Erik?"

Erik chuckled sadly, closing his eyes, "Because I know the truth," he whispered, sardonically. "I know what lies behind the mask."

Jenna only stared at him, sympathetically, as Erik rose from the settee. "You have had a long day, Jenna. Perhaps it is time you finish your tea so you can rest." He walked off, then, in the direction of his own room, leaving Jenna to ponder exactly how bad his deformity could be, that it would cause Erik to believe himself a monster.

22 AN ANGEL'S BETRAYAL

"Doctor, this is Penny Wilson, Jenna Wilson's aunt," Dr. James said, as he introduced the woman who held her hand out politely to shake his. The young doctor took her hand, shaking it firmly, and trying his best to muster a smile. He had hoped for more time before having to meet with Jenna's aunt. He had wanted to be able to tell her that he had made great strides in Jenna's treatment, but he simply needed more time.

"It's a pleasure to meet you, Ms. Wilson," he said, motioning for her to take a seat in one of the overstuffed chairs near the Chief of Neurology's desk. Once she was seated, he sat down across from her.

"The pleasure is mine, Doctor," Penny Wilson replied. "Although the pleasure would be greater," she continued, "if you could tell me my niece had opened her eyes."

"That would be a pleasure for both of us," he agreed, looking down.

"Doctor," Penny began, shifting herself in her chair so that her upper body appeared straight and strong. "Can you tell me why my niece hasn't woken up? What is going on with her case?"

"Well," he began, frustrated with the small amount of information he could give this woman, who only had her niece's best interest at heart. "Coma cases are very complicated. It's very difficult to say when a patient will come out of such a state."

"In fact," Dr. James interjected, from behind his large oak desk, "Many patients never fully regain consciousness."

"But I do not believe that is the case with Miss Wilson," the young doctor added quickly, as much to convince himself as to convince Jenna's aunt. "I fully believe that she will come back to us."

Dr. James sighed heavily, as Penny Wilson surveyed Jenna's doctor. He seemed so earnest, so sure of Jenna's recovery. Did he truly have faith that her niece would be ok, or was he, as Blaine had intimated, more concerned with advancing his career than he was with her niece's well being? "Doctor," she began, carefully. "You seem so sure that my niece will regain consciousness. But what are you doing to make it happen?"

"Well," he replied, shifting uncomfortably in his chair. "I have begun a new form of therapy on Miss Wilson, one in which we stimulate her senses to try to provoke conscious responses. The hope is that with enough sensory stimulation, the patient will *desire* consciousness and work harder to achieve it."

"Are you saying my niece *wants* to be in a coma, Doctor?" Jenna's aunt asked haughtily.

"Well, no," he corrected, getting uncomfortable and feeling sweat begin to form on his forehead. "What I am saying is that it has been difficult to find the right motivation to help pull her back into consciousness. Her most recent romantic relationship had just ended, and she has no family nearby—"

"Are you questioning my involvement in my niece's care?" Penny Wilson retorted, her guilty conscience finding accusation in his words.

"Ms. Wilson," Dr. James began, to try to smooth the situation. "I am certain that Dr.—"

"I never meant any insult, Ms. Wilson," The young doctor jumped in to defend himself. "But you simply were not here. You don't live here. It's perfectly understandable. Nevertheless, I had to try to find some way to reach her."

"And are you reaching her?" she asked, still a bit uncertain. He seemed so sincerely concerned, but Blaine had said…

He took a deep breath, and his eyes took on a guarded look, which made it clear that his progress was not all that he had hoped. "Ms. Wilson, we have had some progress…"

"Like what?" she demanded, curious to see what this doctor listed as progress.

"She occasionally squeezes my hand when I ask her to," he began quietly. "She reacts positively to certain pieces of music. Her fingers will stroke her cat's fur when I bring him to visit. She seemed to enjoy the scent of the flowers you sent her…" His voice trailed off, all too aware of how inadequate the level of progress seemed. "Look, I know it does not seem like much, but these things take time…"

"Doctor," Penny Wilson asked, incredulously. "I was informed that surgery to relieve cranial pressure is usually the first course of treatment. Why didn't you do that?"

Informed by whom, he thought to himself. But out loud, he answered, "I did not think the inter-cranial pressure was serious enough to warrant that. I still don't."

"Well, if she wasn't that badly hurt," the aunt persisted, "why isn't she waking up?"

He looked at her defeated. That certainly was the question. He knew that coma recovery was little more than a waiting game—making sure other symptoms didn't develop while the brain took its time returning to consciousness. But for family—for loved ones—the wait was long and arduous. And he was feeling the strain himself, for he wanted nothing more than to be able to look into Jenna's eyes and finally tell her of his feelings for her. But he was not having much luck making that happen.

"I don't know," he finally admitted to Jenna's aunt.

"I see," she looked away from him, obviously unhappy with his answer. "May I see my niece?"

"Of course," he began, rising from his chair. "I'd be happy to take you…"

"I think I'd like to see her alone," she said, coldly.

"Of course," he answered, casting his eyes downward and writing Jenna's room number on a piece of paper.

Penny Wilson stood and silently walked out of the room, taking many of the young doctor's hopes with her.

❧

Erik could not rest. He'd gone into his room, fully intending to sleep, after apologizing to Jenna—again! It seemed to be a daily occurrence for him to do something to upset that girl. He really ought to figure out some way to send her back to her own time so that he could save her from the continued misery of his company.

And yet, as he lay in bed, he remembered her appreciative smile in Box 5, when she listened to the out-of-tune music of the orchestra. He recalled how she agreed to capture spiders for him with nary a sidelong glance, when another woman might have fainted dead away at just the thought of touching the creepy, crawling arachnids. He chuckled at how enthusiastically she'd helped him deliver said spiders into Carlotta's wig and the mischief in her eyes when the diva had discovered their surprise.

Erik could not help but admit that he enjoyed having Jenna around. She gave him a sort of companionship that he had never had before. It was different from the grudging friendship he had with the Persian, who always seemed to hold himself at least slightly morally above Erik. It was as if the man had taken it upon himself to become Erik's conscience. But Jenna—she did not judge. She did not question. She just … accepted him, exactly how he was.

Of course, he reminded himself, as he rolled over to try once more to get comfortable in bed, *she does not really know you exactly as you are.* It was true. She knew he wore a mask, but she did not know why—and even if she'd guessed that there was some deformity, she could not imagine the extent. And she did not know about Persia. Oh…Persia. He shivered when he remembered the atrocities he'd performed there, taught to him by all those in his life who'd only shown him cruelty when he yearned for nothing more than love. How many lives had he taken? How many screams had he provoked?

No, Jenna didn't know he was a monster, and neither did Christine. The thought of the young soprano's dark chocolate curls had him up and out of bed, leaving his chamber and stalking over to the piano with unchecked energy. He stroked the keys and began to play the composition he had worked so hard to construct—the melody that had been inspired by Jenna, which he had perfected for Christine. *Oh, Christine,* he thought to himself. She was the reason he had been short with Jenna. He truly did regret his brutishness, but Jenna just could not understand what Christine meant to him. He'd felt his heart leap that first night he saw her, when she was crying in the chapel over her lost father. He'd ached to reach out to her, to hold her in his arms until her tears dissolved into laughing—the way he had yearned for someone to do the same for him all those years ago. But he knew that a creature so lovely and pure as Christine could only run screaming into the night from a monster as vile as him. No, he knew she could never know him—but then, when he heard her sing, and he found that there was a way he could reach out to her, he had been overjoyed. If it was an angel that Christine needed, then he was happy to play that role, because he certainly couldn't be a part of her life as the demon he really was.

At that moment, Samineh halted Erik's song by jumping up on the piano and greeting him with a meow. Erik chuckled at her salutation and reached forward to stroke her silken hair, being sure to scratch behind her ears, as she so seemed to enjoy. Her bright blue eyes reminded him of the sea, and once again, he was imagining watery blue orbs, set in a heart shaped face, surrounded by a cascade of deep, rich, sepia curls.

Suddenly, Erik *had* to see her. He knew the hour was late and that most likely, she would be asleep. He had discovered that she shared a room with the ballet mistress's daughter—Little Meg Giry. It would be a simple thing, to slip out and visit the dormitories. Just a glimpse at her, and he was sure his heart would find peace. A glance, and nothing more—because, after all, a glance was already more of the angel than he deserved.

Erik lifted the tiny kitten and brought her into the kitchen. He poured her a saucer of cream, and after she was lapping contentedly, he quietly slipped out, back to his chambers, to don his trousers and shirt once more. After fastening his cloak and setting his hat atop his head, he set out on his solitary journey to the living quarters of the opera house, to glance upon a sleeping dream, his beautiful angel Christine.

Christine hummed to herself softly, a needle in her hand. It was late in the evening, and she should be sleeping, but she found that memories of her dear angel kept her wide awake. So she'd gathered some sewing she had brought back with her and decided to get a head start on the next day's work.

As she re-stitched the seams in the diva's dress, loosening the waist so that it would not once again tear, sweet thoughts of a soft voice rich as velvet and downy white angel wings filled her mind. *No*, she thought to herself, as she glanced over to the red rose on her bedside table. *Not white.* Despite her angel's celestial nature, the ribbon tied around the rose made Christine think of darkness—of cool, luxurious, enveloping darkness. And while some might be afraid of the dark, Christine found the notion of dark angel wings protecting her from the cruelties she had faced by day sounded just fine to her.

"Oh, Papa," she breathed, feeling a tingle down her back, "he is here—he is truly here. He has taught me so much in such little time, and it is as if he is always with me. I…" she paused, drinking in the sensations that her angel awoke in her. "I *feel* him, Papa. I think of him constantly. I go through my days, just waiting for the moments when we will meet, and I can be in his comforting presence once more. And now, he has given me a bit of himself to take with me." She glanced, once again at the rose, as its sweet-smelling perfume wafted over on a draft and tickled her nostrils. Oh how dear to her was her angel!

Christine startled slightly, as the door to her room creaked open. "Christine," came the high-pitched voice of the young ballerina with whom she shared a room. "Why are you not sleeping?" Meg had crept in quietly, hoping not to wake her friend. But now that she saw there was no need for stealth, she eagerly went over and sat across from Christine on her own bed. "What are you doing up so late?"

"I could not sleep, Meg," Christine answered, amused by her friend's questions. "What were *you* doing *out* so late?"

Meg's face crimsoned, and she cast her eyes away before answering, "I…there was a reception, to greet the new patron. Mother managed to get me an invitation—as a serving girl, mind you. But still…" her voice took on a faraway quality. "He was dreamy."

Christine chuckled at her friend, "Oh *he* was dreamy?"

"Why yes," Meg responded in a hushed tone. "Blond hair, with waves that just made my fingers tingle…blue eyes, the color of a cloudless sky…and lips that were so full and firm that I could not help but imagine…"

"Meg Giry!" Christine exclaimed, in mock outrage at her friend. "You forget yourself."

"For a moment," she sighed, twirling one of her own golden curls around her forefinger. "As I gazed upon his face, I think I did." Her voice took on a more realistic tone then as her hands pushed her hair away from her face. The spell of the memory had been broken. "But I am merely a dancer, fit to act, on occasion, as a serving girl to nobility, but never a consort." She looked again at her dark haired friend, and her eye was drawn to the flower sitting so regally in a small glass of water. "Christine," she asked, "what is this?" Her eyes took on a suspicious twinkle, as her right eyebrow rose. "Do *you* have some suitor you are keeping from me?"

"No," Christine felt her own cheeks grow scarlet.

"Well then," Meg pressed, grateful to have the scrutiny off her own actions. "Where did you get this rose? More to the point," Meg teased, "who is he?"

"*Meg*," Christine warned, hesitation in her voice, "I promised never to tell."

"Oh, well then, you *must*," Meg insisted, shifting over to sit next to Christine on her bed, taking the dress and needle from her hands and placing them in the basket on the floor. She grasped Christine's now free hands in her own and continued, "Surely he never meant you to keep it a secret from *me*! Your dearest friend! Come, Christine, we are practically *sisters*!"

Christine contemplated for a moment. She had promised her angel never to tell. But Meg was so dear to her, and surely her best friend could keep her secret. And her heart was so filled with joy at finally meeting her angel that she did, in truth, wish to share it with somebody.

"Meg," Christine began, her eyes sharp, her voice solemn. "You must *swear* to me not to repeat anything I am about to say!"

"Upon pains of death!" Meg promised, raising her hand as if swearing an oath. "That is my vow!"

Christine took a deep breath and began. "It is not a suitor, Meg." She revealed, the excitement building in her voice, as she told her story. "He is an *angel*."

Meg looked at her quizzically. In truth, Christine was a bit of a strange girl. Lovable, to be sure, and a dear friend, but strange. She seemed a bit too attached to her dear father, who had departed this world, and now Meg was truly concerned for her well being, if the girl was talking about angels imparting her with roses. "An *angel*, Christine?" Meg asked, hoping there would be some clarification for her claim.

"*Yes*, Meg." Christine asserted, her eyes sparkling now in excitement. "And not just any angel. The Angel of Music."

Meg nodded slowly at her friend, fearing the worst. Christine had been so saddened by her father's death—so tormented by Carlotta's cruelty—that her mental faculties had finally left her. "I see," she said quietly.

"Oh Meg," Christine continued, knowing that her friend must think her mad. "I know it sounds preposterous, but father promised me. Before he died, he said that he would send me the Angel of Music to watch over me, and give me the gift of song. I clung to that dream, Meg, because it made Papa seem closer—because it gave me hope that one day, things would not be so bleak. But the other night, Meg…the Angel…he was there."

Meg studied her friend. Christine spoke in such earnest, and she truly didn't sound like she was out of her mind. But what did she mean that the angel was suddenly there? "He was there? You saw him?"

"Well, no." Christine corrected. "I did not see him. I do not think I am yet worthy to look upon his beauty. But he spoke to me, Meg."

"He *spoke* to you?" Meg asked, with narrowed eyes.

"Yes, he heard me, in the chapel, crying out for Papa, asking if the Angel of Music would ever come. And then I heard a voice—a voice like no other." She recalled that magical moment, her voice taking on a dreamy lilt. "It was shimmery and lush, and it felt as if I could fall back into it and it would catch me and cushion me against all the hardness of the world. And he said he *was* the Angel of Music. And he had come to lift my voice in song—just like Papa promised."

"I see…"

"And he has, Meg." Christine's voice was excited again. "He is teaching me to sing—just like Papa always dreamed I could sing. And when *he* sings to *me*…" her eyes narrowed slightly at the exquisite memory. "It is like the heavens themselves open their gates and the sounds of all the celestial hosts are caught up blessedly in his voice."

Meg did not know what to say to her friend's rambling. "Christine, surely it must all have been a dream. A wonderful, magnificent, splendid dream, but still a dream. Stories like this—they *can't* come true."

"It was *not* a dream, Meg!" Christine insisted, beginning to regret that she had shared the story of her angel with her friend.

"But…" Meg tried to make Christine see reason, "you're…you're not making sense. This is entirely unlike you."

Christine huffed at her friend's disbelief. She knew she should leave it alone, but she could not stand for Meg to doubt her angel. "What must I do, Meg Giry, to prove to you that I am not crazy!?"

Meg thought for a moment. "Sing, Christine. Why don't you sing for me right now, so I can see the effect this *angel* has had on your voice."

"Very well!" Christine rose, closed her eyes, and began singing the tune that had been constantly in her mind since she had met her angel days ago.

Father once spoke of an Angel…

Meg stared, dumb-founded, at her friend. Truly, she had heard her friend hum absent-mindedly to herself as she sewed. She had even heard her sing a bit under her breath at times. But this…this was magnificent. "My God, Christine! I had no idea you could sing like that!"

"I could not!" Christine replied, "But then I was visited by my Angel."

Could it be? Meg wondered to herself. There was truly a change in her friend. She had grown more confident and less mousy, and her voice—oh how it soared! This unseen Angel…

"Christine!" Meg asked out loud, a thought occurring to her.

"Yes, Meg," she asked, still basking in the song about her angel.

"If you have never seen him, then how did he give you the rose?"

"He… left it for me…" Christine answered, remembering how she had found the beautiful bloom. "As I was leaving the chapel, I heard a soft rapping on the wall, and when I turned to look, the rose was lying there, on the floor."

Meg felt a chill in her heart. Things did tend to mysteriously appear around this opera house—but not usually by the work of an angel. Could it be that this Angel of Music and the Opera Garnier's own Phantom were one and the same?

"I think," Meg said, wanting some time to quietly think things over before saying anything further on the topic to her friend, "that we should rest, Christine. It is late, and I have an early rehearsal tomorrow."

"Of course, Meg," Christine replied, as she felt a yawn coming over her. Telling her story had finally stilled her mind, and she indeed felt as if she could rest.

The girls got ready for bed in quiet, and as they crawled under the covers, Christine lay in her bed, dreaming about her dark angel. Meg lay awake awhile longer, pondering the possible connection between the angel who sang to Christine and the Phantom who tormented the rest of the opera house. Eventually though, as she felt herself drift off to sleep, she could not stop her dreams from turning toward a certain tall, blond patron by the name of Raoul Vicomte de Changy.

Behind the wall, Erik stood seething. Christine had promised! She had *vowed* that she would not speak of him to anybody else! And though she had sworn him to be an angel, he could see the Giry girl's calculation clear in her eyes. Of course, she would make the connection. Her mother was the one who delivered his salary, for heaven's sake. The Phantom would be the foremost *supernatural* being on Little Giry's mind. In revealing his existence, Christine had shown him a side of herself with which he was not very pleased. A youthful, impetuous side that could prove an impediment to a life on the stage, as well as a barrier to her training with him.

But what angered him most—what surprised him and enraged him and upset him the most—was the mark of Jenna's betrayal—the single red rose, tied with a silken black ribbon, sitting in the cup on Christine's nightstand. With a billow of his cape, Erik turned, stalking the corridors back to his home. Down once more.

23 UNMASKING A SOUL

Jenna was surrounded by red velvety roses, and by swirling, enveloping music, as a pair of eyes, both brown and blue gazed intently into hers. "Jenna," he whispered, his deep husky rumble making goose bumps appear on her flesh. Her fingers trailed up and tangled in his soft, dark hair. "I want you to know…" his voice hushed even more. "That I…" his words trailed off as he cradled her cheek in his tender hands, and his lips were but a breath away. Slowly, so achingly slowly, she saw him close his eyes and those lips—those sweet, warm, succulent lips began to close in on hers. She opened her mouth to accept him, tilting her head, as he came closer…nearer…

A sharp rapping on her door woke her with a start. She sat up in bed and wrapped her arms around herself, acclimating to the chill in the air, after the heat she'd felt in the dream just seconds ago. She had been in his arms. And his hands…his voice. *Oh*, she shuddered, *his lips…*

Another knock, and a call came from the other side of the door. "Mademoiselle! Are you awake?"

Erik! Jenna threw on her dressing gown and hurried over to the door, blushing as she tried to fully emerge from her dream. She did her best to temper the butterflies floating around in her stomach before she pulled the door open to see her host leaning lazily against the frame.

"Erik?" she asked in confusion. "What are…?"

"I just wished to check on you again, Mademoiselle." Erik's tone was cordial, but cold, a strange smile plastered across his lips. "After all, maladies of the throat are often worst late at night."

Jenna shook her head, finding it a bit strange that he would wake her from a deep sleep to ask her about her throat. "Erik, I'm fine," she said, sweetly. "I'm really feeling much better."

"Much better, Mademoiselle?" he asked, his exposed eyebrow raised in question. "That was quite an expeditious recovery."

"Yes, I…" she stuttered, "I guess it really was just the dust."

"Perhaps the dust…" Erik agreed, nodding. "Or perhaps you're allergic to roses?"

Jenna, felt her throat going dry for real this time. "Excuse me?" she croaked.

"Well, it occurred to me," he began smoothly, "you had that rose tucked in your hair. The one with which I had absconded from the diva's dressing room."

"I…um…" Jenna began, flustering her words, "yes, I did, but…I'm not allergic to roses."

"I see," he said, gazing around her room, as if in search of something. "What *did* ever happen to that rose, Mademoiselle? Did you find a vase of water for it?"

"Well, I…" Jenna cleared her throat, wishing she had some water for herself right about now. "I think I must have lost it in the tunnels. I…I don't have it."

"Ah," Erik nodded. "Perhaps it fell out of your hair by the chapel?" His mismatched orbs suddenly bore into hers. "Perhaps when you bent to pick up your cloak…"

Despite the discomfort she felt from his gaze, which seemed to delve straight into her deceptive soul, she kept her eyes trained on his. She took a deep breath and said, "You know."

"That you betrayed me?" his eyes flashed with barely disguised anger. "Yes," he hissed, "I know."

"Erik, I never betrayed you!" she claimed in defense, a little horrified that he would even suggest such a thing.

"Oh no, Mademoiselle?" he continued, taking a few slow steps closer to her. "You just proved a second ago that you are capable of politely clearing your throat. Did you, or did you not cough on purpose, just to get Christine's attention and move me into action?"

"Well yes, but I…" she began, but she was cut off as he kept on with his tirade, continuing to advance toward her.

"Did you, or did you not leave the rose in the chapel for Christine to find, while you were pretending to pick up your cloak?"

"Yes, Erik, but I …" Oh, he was taking this all wrong.

"Did you, or did you not," he asked in a clipped voice, so close now that he could practically touch her, "continue the charade into the evening, never telling me what you did, leaving it for me to find out on my own?"

Overwhelmed by his closeness and the cold fury flashing in his eyes, Jenna turned her back to him. "Erik," she said looking down, "I tried to tell you…"

Suddenly she felt his hands grip her firmly by the shoulders, his breath on her neck. Leaning in close, so that his lips were right by her ear, he rumbled deeply, "You LIE."

Jenna closed her eyes against the pain of his accusation. "Erik, I…"

"Did you think I'd never know?" he hissed in her ear through clenched teeth, his voice sibilant and deadly. "Did you think she wouldn't mention it?"

"No, I…" Jenna tried to defend herself, but once again, he cut her off.

His grip grew even tighter on her shoulders as he pulled her even closer. "And yet, you lied!"

Jenna's own anger suddenly spiked, and she tore herself from his grasp and turned on him, the hot ferocity in her own eyes the perfect countervail for the cool ire in Erik's. "I did NOT lie!" she shouted at him, pointing a finger at him, her other hand balled into a fist at her side. The sundry emotions she had felt that day had finally bubbled over, and she felt them escape in cries of barely controlled rage. "I *tried* to tell you what I did. When you came to me to apologize, I tried to explain what had happened. But you wouldn't let me talk! Just like now." She waved her hand in frustration, as if proving her point. "You won't let me talk! You ask a question, but you have no interest in the answer because you've already decided upon your own version of the truth, and who cares if it matches with reality!"

"The reality, Mademoiselle," he spat through gritted teeth, his jaw tight with his rage, "is that you knew she was never to know I was a man!"

"Of course not!" Jenna threw her hands up in the air. "She's supposed to think you're an *angel*. A celestial being who flies around behind walls giving young girls singing lessons. After all, why burden her with actual reality when she can have *your* version instead?"

"I pray that she shall *never* know the reality I have known!" he roared at her, his voice loud enough to shake the walls, startling

Jenna with its force. For a moment, neither said a word, both stunned by the vehemence of his response. Emotion was thick in his voice when he continued. "I pray that she shall never know the cruelties or the pains that reality has to offer a poor, fatherless child, with no one in the world to help her—no one in the world to care." He closed his eyes against the hot tears that threatened, as he remembered another child, long ago, so alone in the world. "I had a way to help her, Jenna," his sorrowful voice quieter now. "I had a way to care." He sank, exhausted, to rest on Jenna's bed, his body slumping forward to hide his head in his hands.

Jenna's heart shattered in a million pieces to see Erik looking so fragile, so broken. She tiptoed over to the bed and gingerly sat down next to him, putting one hand on his back, rubbing slow circles to calm him. With her other hand, she reached for his fingers, gently trying to pry them away from his face, so that she could see him. When he looked at her, his eyes were guarded and vulnerable, and she wanted nothing more in life at that moment than to be able to wrap her arms around him and hold him to her until the pain *she'd* caused had subsided. Instead, she continued to stroke his back, grasping his hand in hers, and met his gaze, whispering, "Erik, I'm so sorry. Please forgive me."

Jenna saw a rueful smirk appear on his lips. "How strange," he said. "I have gotten quite used to being the one asking for *your* forgiveness." His voice sounded tired as he tried once more to smile.

"Not this time, Erik," she shook her head, her heart still aching for him. "This time it was all my fault, for shoving my own opinion into a situation that was not my business."

Erik was quiet for a moment, just looking at her, touched by her sincerity and her genuine concern. "Why?" he asked, when he was once again moved to words. "Why did you do it?"

Jenna took a deep breath before she revealed her reasons. It pained her to say them out loud, but speak them she must. "Because it was wrong for me to keep the rose, Erik," she said, her voice just slightly tremulous. "When it is obvious that you love Christine."

Erik surprised her then by doing the last thing she would have expected him to do in that moment. He laughed. "*Love*, Jenna?" he threw his head back with a mirthless guffaw that sent more chills down Jenna's spine than if he had been screaming his displeasure at her. "I am not allowed to love. Not Christine. Not anyone."

Jenna stared at him silently for a moment, as she took in the derision in his self-mocking expression. It seemed to be such a practiced emotion with him, this loathsome self-contempt, and it made Jenna's heart break anew. "Erik, what do you mean, you are not allowed to love? Everyone is allowed to love."

"Oh, no, not I, Mademoiselle," He said, a dramatic flair entering his voice, his eyes faraway, as he began to recite an old, hateful verse he seemed to have memorized long ago. "*The Living Corpse can know no love, subsisting on hate and fear. Those who see him run from him, and screams are all he hears.*"

Jenna's breath hitched on a sob, as she realized that he spoke about himself. "Oh Erik," she whispered, mournfully. "What kind of life have you known?"

"My life?" His hollow eyes focused on her for a moment as he began his tale. "My life cemented my mother's heartache. It had begun, you see, when my father died, after having just awakened her heart to the joys of love. She had loved him like no other, and to lose him so early in their marriage…well, it was all she could do to go on living. But live she did, for she had discovered that before he so thoughtlessly left this life, he had gotten her with child. The babe became her reason for living those next long months. While she may no longer have her beloved Charles to brighten her world, she would have his child. His son would bear his name, and she would care for the babe, all the days of her life, only dreaming about that far off time when she and her dear husband would be reunited, to gaze for all eternity, at the wonder their love had created.

"Imagine her surprise when it was not a baby born, but a gargoyle—a carcass barely fit for this earth."

"No," Jenna whispered, quietly, shaking her head in horror at the way he spoke about himself.

"Oh *yes*, Jenna," he continued. "The midwife offered to throw me on the fire—said it would be an act of mercy. My mother was not so sure her mighty God would agree with that, and so she deemed that I should live, until she could ascertain what level of care was required to ensure the safety of her eternal soul. When the priest insisted that I could not simply be allowed to die, she agreed to feed me and clothe me—including my face, which she covered with a mask at the first opportunity she could find—but she refused to call me by the name that should have been my own. *Charles* was for a beautiful child, and I was anything but. She left it for the priest to name me, for as far as she was concerned, I required no name at all. After all, why-ever would a monster need a name?"

Jenna shook her head back and forth in disbelief at the coldness Erik's own mother showed her child, and she felt hot tears run down her face. But if Erik noticed, he made no mention, only continuing with the tale that inspired her to weeping.

"And so, thanks to the priest, I became Erik, a name that held no meaning for my mother, and certainly not for me. As I grew, so did my mother's lack of affection. Once I no longer needed her body for sustenance, she took to never touching me, unless she was beating me for one disobedience or another. The time I asked for a kiss on my birthday was a trouncing of particular intensity, ensuring the request would never be made again.

"I soon became petulant, and the day I refused to wear my mask, my mother lay hands on me once again. She dragged me to her room, the one with the wide dresser mirror, and shoved me in front of it. When I saw the beast peering back at me, I screamed, only to have the fiend scream with me. When I shook my head in horror at the monster that was before me, it shook its head as well, and when my tiny fists were bleeding from pounding at the mirror, trying desperately to scare the ogre away, I could see, through the shards, that the ogre's hands bled too. For days, my mother locked me in that room—with nothing but the beast and the shattered mirror to keep me company. Eventually, she let me out, and from that day forward I wasn't ever without my mask—I even slept with it, for fear of the beast finding me in the dark. But then," he let out a joyless snicker, "it was *always* dark, since my mother had boarded up my window and continually locked my door. She never engaged me in conversation or anything else to feed my mind, but she was always very good at plying me with books, tossing them in to the room to keep me quiet or perhaps pacify some latent form of guilt. So when the sun would creep in between the slats, I would read—anything and everything she left me. Architecture, philosophy, Biblical texts—I devoured them all, so desperate was I for information about a world of which I would never be a part.

"On the rare occasions when my mother would let me out of my room, I would sit at her piano and play. I never needed lessons, for my fingers just knew what to do. My mother said that was another one of the devil's marks, for it was unnatural for musical ability to be so easily displayed in a child. She forbade me from singing, claiming that when she heard my voice, she heard my sire calling her to do strange things—and by the way she said it, she was not talking about her dearly departed Charles. No, she heard the devil in my voice, and therefore my songs were silenced."

Jenna reached for him, trying to stop this story that was full of such pain, but he was up and pacing the floor as the years of sorrow and heartache came flooding out. "I left my mother's house when I was nine years old. She had begun a dalliance with a village doctor, and I overheard them discussing the prospect of sending me away. An asylum, the doctor had suggested, where I could be with others of… my kind. I was well read, Jenna. I knew the atrocities that would await me at the asylum. Besides, there really weren't *any* others of my kind.

"So I ran. I left in the dark, so sure I would be fine—so convinced I needed no one. I soon found, that while perhaps I didn't need any other person in my life, I did need the occasional loaf of bread. And one night, out of desperation, I tried to snatch one from a wandering band of gypsies who had made camp. I was captured, and a fresh form of degradation began.

"My mother's debasement had at least been private. She locked me away from the world's view because she did not want my hideousness to reflect poorly on her. The gypsies, however, saw the profit they could make if they bared my repulsiveness to all who would pay to witness it, so I became the main attraction of their traveling fair. Shackled and caged in a foul tent, with only a sack to cover my head, I was kept on display in a cesspool of my own filth. Day after day, the tent would be opened and the sack would be lifted so that the paying multitudes could view my detestable ugliness. The tent would first fill with gasps of disbelief, then screams of horror, and finally, the unavoidable heaves of those cursed with weak stomachs. Children would run, ladies would faint, and my keepers would spend night after night counting the money, praising my homeliness for the cash that it brought in.

"I was never allowed to exit my cage, unless the owner of the fair decided to whip me for one imagined transgression or another. For four years I lived there, amongst the Gypsies—in filth and squalor and humiliation. Until the one night when the master decided that whipping was not going to be enough. He had to teach me a lesson, and it had to be done not only with my pants down, but with his. He had underestimated, however, the hatred which had grown within me in those four years, and when he lay his hands on me, to begin his *instruction*, I whipped my hand around, grabbed the knife he always kept at his waist, and sunk it deep into his gut. He was incapacitated, and I could have escaped, but instead, I pushed the knife deeper, twisting it as I went, watching the life spill out of his body in a steaming flood, and finding that I enjoyed seeing it go. It was on that day, as I rose to exit the tent, on calm alert for any other attackers, that I realized I had truly become the monster I had been born to be. And it was time that I embraced it."

Jenna's hand covered her mouth at the atrocities poor young Erik had suffered, and she found that she felt no sympathy for the evil pig that he had killed. She regretted only that she had not been with him, so that she could have slayed that bastard herself.

"For years after that," he continued, always pacing, running a circular path on the rug in her room, "I wandered. I had learned how to be cunning; I had learned how to be stealthy; and so eating did not usually pose a problem.

"I traveled through Europe studying architecture, which had been a particular interest of mine when I was yet in my mother's house. I roamed on foot mostly, stowing away in wagons when I wished to visit some new exciting land. I made it to Italy, and managed to work awhile with a master mason, learning the trade of building, honing my skills, and becoming quite adept. But that alliance was dissolved after an unfortunate incident with the master mason's daughter, and once again, I found myself on my own, wandering the towns, performing magic tricks at traveling fairs, occasionally even singing for money. I became known as the Masked Magician, and since I kept that cursed covering on my face always, I experienced trepidation from other people—a certain *wariness*—but never screams. It was at one of those traveling fairs that the Daroga found me.

"Omid?" Jenna asked, when she heard Erik mention the Persian that was still his friend today.

"Yes." Erik looked at her momentarily, nodding before he continued his story. "He was the Chief of Police for the Shah of Persia, who had heard tales of the mysterious masked magician and ordered the Daroga to find me and bring me back. The Shah's mother, you see, was always in need of some new form of *entertainment,* and the Shah thought that I would do…for a time.

"When I arrived in Persia, I did, indeed, entertain the Shah and his mother for a while. I was praised, and plied with gifts and treasures and drugs in gratitude for their enjoyment. I am not proud to say it, but I enjoyed the sense of power that the drugs gave me, and I found that the strange dark world of Persia suited me well. But before long it became clear the novelty of my presence had begun to wane. It seemed necessary to prove myself useful to the Shah in ways other than sleights of hand and acts of illusion.

"At this time, the Shah had commissioned a torture chamber, by which to punish criminals. It was to be the greatest source of entertainment yet for the Shah and his mother, who reveled greatly in the suffering of others. I had found a way to prove my worth, for none of the architects of Persia had had my invaluable experience with the Italian mason, and when my plans were put forth for the bidding, the Shah began to see me in a different light. The torture chamber was built, and the Shah was so well pleased with his new toy, that he put me in charge of its operation. I became the lead executioner for the Shah, and truly, I *enjoyed* the power that the job brought with it. I was looked upon, not with derision, but with respect—not with ridicule, but with fear. No longer the Masked Magician, I became known as the Angel of Mercy, for my role in ending their torment, delivering the hapless miscreants swiftly with my lasso, when the tortures had done their worst. But my true title should have been the Angel of Death, since it was I who initiated their agony as well.

"My favor with the Shah began to fade, however, when I insulted him by refusing his most precious gift. The riches, the treasures, the drugs—oh, *those* I took, and indulged in them greatly. But the night the Shah presented me with a nubile young slave girl to do with as I pleased, was the night that I said no. She stood before me, trembling with lowered lashes. I spoke to her in dulcet tones, promising her I would be gentle, swearing she would have her freedom with the morning light. But as I approached her, she screamed, and cowered away from my touch. In my frustration, I asked her if she would rather die than lay with me. All the drugs in the world could not numb the humiliation I felt when she said yes.

"And so I turned her out, complaining to the Shah that she was not of my liking, and that I did not desire any more gifts of weak willed Persian girls as payment for my efforts on his behalf. The Shah did not appreciate my insolence, and without my knowledge the little slave girl was, in fact, sentenced to die. And yet, the Shah, in his cunning, sought to punish *me* more greatly than her. It was to *my* torture chamber that the slave girl was sent, and when I looked down and saw who it was that would now suffer in my manmade hell, something inside me just snapped. It was as if the cloud of drugs was lifted, and I looked at the Shah, and at his mother, and for the first time, I said to them, "No." I was not going to torture and then kill this slave girl for a sin no greater than shrinking away from a monster. I told them if they wanted her dead, they could do it themselves. And then I did the unthinkable. I walked out.

"I had sealed my fate that night," Erik said, looking off into the distance, "No longer was I the Shah's favorite pet. I was defiant and branded a troublemaker, and I knew that if I did not find some way to get out of Persia, in short time I would find myself on the other side of that torture chamber door. So I turned to the Daroga.

"I had helped him, you see, when his dear little Aziz had fallen ill, so he felt it was his obligation to do the same for me. I stopped taking the Shah's drugs, to clear my head, and we made a plan, he and I, of how to get out of Persia. When the time came to go, he had to come with me—for to stay behind was to ensure his own death for treason.

"So I came back to Paris, with the Daroga in tow. I learned of the chance to build this very opera house, so I ingratiated myself to the head architect, and made myself indispensable to him. I helped him rework his original plans, solve problems he encountered, and I even did much of the masonry work myself, alongside the other laborers. At night I would return, and I would build in the parts of the opera house that were not for everyone to see. *Fourteen years* it took to build this place, Jenna. *Fourteen years* I planned and toiled—to build a fitting palace for the one true beauty I had encountered in my life of misery. Music. And I have been here ever since, alone with my music, apart from the world, save for when I am forced to consult with the buffoons above who think they know something about running my opera."

He turned to her, finally, meeting her eyes as he said, "So that was my life, Jenna. It has always been my lot to be alone, to hide in the shadows, lest the light reveal what I truly am. *That* is why I am not allowed to love. For who could ever love a monster?"

Jenna held his gaze, tears in her own eyes, her mind swimming from all that he had said. "You are *not* a monster," she spoke with conviction, her voice thick with her tears.

"Have you been listening to a word I have said, Mademoiselle?" He asked, his voice rife with derision. "I have killed. I have *murdered.* Countless times over."

Jenna rose from the bed and approached him. "You killed in self-defense, Erik, after four years of unthinkable torment. In Persia, you were drugged and used by sadists and fiends to do their dirty work while they sat back and watched."

"But…I *enjoyed* it, Jenna," Erik railed, raking his hands through his hair. "I *reveled* in the power of taking a life—in the fearful respect it earned me in place of derision and subjugation."

Jenna walked even closer to where he stood. "The gypsy master deserved his fate and more, for the abuse he doled upon a child. The Shah and his mother surely knew exactly how much of that drug to give you to be certain you would continue to do their bidding. And yet, when faced with committing a truly heinous act upon an innocent, even the drugs were not enough. *You* are not a monster."

"Are you sure, Mademoiselle?" Erik's voice was once again a rolling whisper, heavy laden with threat, as he began to circle her just slightly. "Are you *so* sure? I have been off the drugs for years now, and yet my Punjab lasso is always by my side. Death always waiting, Mademoiselle, *lurking* patiently at my fingertips."

"And how often have you used it, since you came to Paris, Erik?" she asked him, challenging him with her eyes.

"I have not been given cause," he answered, "but that does not mean that I *would* not use it, Mademoiselle."

"I gave you cause," she countered, moving closer, raising her head to keep his gaze. "That first night when I appeared out of nowhere, you had no reason to believe I was not a threat. If you were the monster you claim yourself to be, you could have strangled me without question, and this whole crazy mess we're in would not have even started."

"No…" Erik said, a little flustered, shaking his head.

"A monster would have just let that carriage run me over on the square. After all, I would have received what I deserved for running from you—like *all* the others who ran." She continued to advance on him, getting closer, ever closer. "You could have let the horse's hooves and the carriage wheels grind me into the ground, crushing the life from out of my broken form."

"No," Erik said, this time with a bit more force, the horror of her words beginning to break through the walls of his self-reproach.

"Yes, Erik," she insisted, moving closer still, until they were a hair's breadth from touching. "You could kill me now and be done with me. No mystery to solve. No meddling girl to get in the way of your music lessons." She saw him shaking his head, but still she continued. "You wouldn't even have to use your lasso. It would be so easy," she whispered, taking his hands in hers and bringing them to rest on either side of her throat, "to use your hands just to snap. My. Neck."

Erik's hands dropped to grasp her tightly by the shoulders once more. "No, Jenna!" he shouted, with eyes desperate to be believed. "I could never hurt you!"

"And that is because you are a *man*—not a monster!" Jenna declared triumphantly, seeing the last of Erik's shell shatter before her. He crumbled into her then, a wretched sob escaping his lips. Jenna caught him with her arms around him and held him tightly as he wept. All the years of bleak desolation, the decades of loneliness and pain, left his body in choking gasps and hot, searing tears. She slowly steered him over to the bed, helping him sit so that his exhausted body could rest as it rid itself of the vestiges of abuse he had suffered his whole life. She continued to cradle him in her arms, stroking his hair and whispering soft words to soothe him, her own heart breaking with each trail of sorrow that left his eyes. When at last his sobbing quieted, he lifted his head from where it had been resting on her shoulder. His eyes were red and puffy, and he looked completely exhausted.

Jenna reached forward and cupped his unmasked cheek with her hand, and as he closed his eyes and leaned into her touch, it seemed as if his tears would start anew. But he somehow managed to gather his emotions and when he lifted his lids, his gaze was full of gratitude. "Jenna," he said her name, in a hoarse whisper, as he continued to find comfort in her touch, his hand grasping hers and holding on for dear life. "I never thought myself a man. I was always an abomination—a fright to all who knew me."

"Oh Erik," she answered, sure that her heart would burst out of her chest from the sadness in his tone. "I have never thought of you as someone to be afraid of."

"I know…" he gave a small smile, and Jenna saw a tenderness in his eyes that made her tummy flutter. "And you should, for all of the boorish, uncouth, ungentlemanly ways in which I've treated you. But you've never vilified me, or ridiculed me like the others. You've always just accepted me as I am, and for that, I want you to know…" he paused briefly, uncertain how to continue. "That I…"

Jenna recalled the words from her dream as she gazed into the brown and blue eyes that never failed to captivate her. She couldn't help but lean in closer to him, wishing desperately to feel the kiss of which he had deprived her earlier. His lids fluttered closed, and Jenna waited, her lips slightly parted, each moment taking a century to elapse. Just when she thought her body would scream from the tension of the moment, his eyes opened once more and he met her gaze and said, "Thank you."

Jenna was slightly taken aback by his words, as she realized that she had not been breathing. She took a deep breath and nodded, smiling at him sweetly, before she heard him sigh and say, "But, Jenna, it changes nothing."

"What?" she blinked at him, not certain she was really hearing what he had just said.

"Jenna," he began, looking down at their hands still joined together. "You say I killed in self-defense. You say I murdered because of the influence of the drugs. I am still not wholly convinced that either is true, but even if it *were* true, the world would still view me as a monster." He lifted his eyes to meet her gaze. "You know now why I wear the mask, Jenna. I was born with a face so hideous, so deformed, that it looks as if it were crafted by the devil himself. My own mother could not look at me without horror."

"Your mother," Jenna interjected, anger once again filling her tone, "sounds like a disgusting, sick, and abhorrent woman. *She* was at fault for the way she treated you, Erik, *not* you. It is in a mother's nature to love her child."

"And she did love me, Jenna," he countered, "until she had to look at me. And then her love turned to fear and hatred for the monster she had borne. *That* is why Christine can never know I am anything other than an angel."

Christine. Jenna thought. Of course. They were back to Christine. "But Erik," Jenna argued, her mind sobering a bit at the mention of the ingénue. It made sense that, in his mind, this was still all about Christine. She had been a fool to ever hope otherwise. And though Jenna longed to tell him how *she* was beginning to feel about *him*, she knew that was preposterous. If she wanted to help him, she needed to help him get what he wanted, not what *her* heart desired. "If you give her a chance…"

"She would *run* from me, and I would lose even the opportunity to shape her voice and mold her for the greatness she deserves. Don't you yet understand, Jenna?" Erik gave her an incredulous stare. "*No one* can look at me and see anything other than a malformed, horrific freak of nature."

"I can," she said simply, eyes burning with conviction. "And I *do*."

Erik looked away from her. "You have not seen the real me," he scoffed.

"So show me." Her words were once again direct and without drama. She gazed at him calmly with certainty in her eyes.

"Jenna…" he began to shake his head.

"You said yourself, Erik," she pressed, sure that this was what he needed if he was ever going to get past his self-doubt, "that I have always accepted you, never ridiculing you or vilifying you like the others."

"Yes, but in this…" he continued to shake his head, not able to meet her eyes.

"I would be no different than I've always been," she promised him. "You told me that you murdered, that you killed, and I did not reject you."

"But my face…"

"What makes you think a face is so important? I have seen your eyes, Erik—and through them, I can see your soul. Your face could not possibly be ugly enough to mar the greatness I have glimpsed inside you."

Erik looked at her then, uncertainty still obvious in his gaze. "You do not know what you ask," he said, softly.

"I *want* to know," she asserted.

"Please," he implored simply, once again on the verge of tears, "do not run."

Jenna let loose a little chuckle at that. "Erik, where would I go?"

Erik closed his eyes and swallowed hard. Perhaps, after all this time thinking differently, she truly *was* insane. Or if she had not been when she'd first arrived, his presence had driven her to such a state. She wanted to see his face. She had to be mad! But if she was mad, then so was he, because he was going to show her! He *needed* to show her—he needed to know if it were possible that he could be looked upon with anything other than revulsion. So he felt his fingers, as if of their own accord, reach up and find the ties that secured the covering to his face. Slowly he undid the knots loosening the disguise to which he was constantly confined.

He lowered the article of equal protection and torment slowly from his face, thinking to himself that perhaps the Persian would continue to look after Jenna until he found a way to send her home. Surely, despite what she said, despite what she professed, his face would drive her from him, bereaving him of the only *friend* he'd ever had. For as much as she swore she would not run, no friendship could be strong enough to withstand the hideousness of his unholy visage.

When his mask was completely separated from his face, he was certain he would hear a gasp, and a scramble for the door. Instead, the unthinkable happened. Starting with the impossibly sunken section of his forehead, tentative fingers began to trace the channels of his ruined flesh, grazing the ridges of his malformed nose, probing each crevice of his folded skin, until they rested on his puffy, bloated lips. Erik's eyes popped open at the contact, to see tears welling in Jenna's eyes. He opened his mouth to talk, but before he could say anything, he heard Jenna whisper, "Thank you. Thank you for showing yourself to me."

The sentiment in her words—her gratitude toward *him*, when she had in fact just gifted him the greatest treasure anyone had ever bestowed on him—completely overwhelmed Erik, and without further thought, he threw his arms around her and hugged her to him, burying his head in her shoulder.

Jenna held Erik tight, whispering to him again and again, "I'm here, Erik. I'm still here." And she knew, without a doubt, that despite his feelings for Christine, if he but said the word, she would never, ever let him go.

24 WARMTH

Erik's head remained buried in Jenna's shoulder, her arms wrapped tightly around him. Her fingers were trailing lazily in his hair, and her soft, honeyed words did much to calm his tempestuous spirit. He had battled an army of his greatest fears this night, exposing both the blackness of his soul and depravity of his face. He had been so sure he would hear her screams, her cries of terror as she fled from the room. It would not matter that she could not go far; she would run regardless, as far as she could, to be away from his accursed visage. He had been certain, as he'd loosed the ties that secured the mask that she would tremble and quake, as he made plain his shame to her eyes.

But once again, Jenna had bought him up short. She had shocked him by staying. She did not flinch from his hideousness; rather she continued to accept him with open arms—quite literally, in fact, since he was still enclosed within them. It was a new feeling for Erik—one that was both strange and wonderful. He had never known the tenderness of a caress or the shelter of an embrace, yet now Jenna gave him both, and it stirred...*something*...deep inside. She was just a girl with so many problems of her own—and she looked to him to help her solve them. And yet somehow, here she was, *saving* him—helping him feel more secure than he ever had. He knew if he lived another hundred years, he would never be able to fully express his gratitude for her kindness in that moment—when he'd removed his mask and revealed his sorrow.

When at last he felt strong enough to raise his head from her shoulder, he lifted his gaze to hers. He looked at her face which he had seen express so many varied emotions—confusion, elation, mischief, fear—it seemed as if in their short time together, he had witnessed every one. But this night, as he gazed into her crystalline aqua eyes, he saw something there that he had never seen before. There was compassion, to be sure—and happiness. Yes, she did seem to be happy. But there was something other, something new, and despite his genius, despite his learned nature, he could not, for the life of him, give that emotion a name. It seemed to light her eyes and warm her smile and he thought to himself in amazement that he could stare at her like this for the rest of his days, never tiring of that sweet new expression he had found on her face. Urged on by this new feeling that was radiating inside him, Erik raised his hand and trailed his fingers down her cheek, a smile washing over his features.

He felt Jenna shiver then, and asked, "Are you cold?"

No, Erik, she thought to herself as she continued to gaze at the man before her. *No, I'm not cold at all.* In fact, she desperately hoped he had not noticed the flush in her cheeks, or the heat that radiated throughout her body. Hearing his story had broken her heart, but holding him so close, feeling his soft hair under her fingers, his whispered breath on her neck—that had ignited a flame, and right now, her insides were smoldering. His smile. She had finally seen him smile—without the mask to block the view.

He was not a handsome man—that she could not deny. He was malformed and grotesquely disfigured, just as he had warned. His paper-thin skin was all wrinkles and scars, translucent in some places so that she could clearly see the veins that ran underneath. His skull was sunken in, forming a wide depression on the right side of his forehead. His eye, the blue one, sat in a dark, recessed hollow, and the nasal cavity was devoid of structure, appearing more like a hole than a nose. His lips were bloated, swollen, distending unnaturally toward both the nostril and the chin. No, Erik was not a handsome man—and yet the beauty of his soul lit his features from within, and with that smile—that full, beautiful smile—Jenna found he took her breath away.

She almost told him how she felt—that her shiver was not from cold, but from desire; that the only thing that could soothe her now was his touch…his arms…his kiss. But then she remembered how this whole thing began. Christine. Erik wanted Christine. And so, desiring to help—not to hinder—she simply nodded, and said, "A little."

Erik rose from the bed, extending his hand to her. "Come, Jenna," he said, with another little smile, and she had no choice but to heed his command. He led her to the settee, bidding her rest, as he stoked the fires in the hearth. "There," he said, when the flames had risen brightly, "that should help." He excused himself to the kitchen, and set on a kettle for tea.

Once deprived of her presence, Erik realized how cold it really was. Funny, even frigid temperatures had never seemed to bother him before, yet after the warmth of Jenna's arms, the cold seemed biting, and he longed for the comfort the contact had provided. Had he so quickly grown accustomed to her embrace, that he grieved now at its absence? *How ridiculous*, he scoffed, as he willed the kettle to boil faster, eager to present her with the warming liquid that should dispel the chills that plagued them both.

Jenna stared at the flames, flickering in the hearth in an impassioned tarantella, and imagined herself spinning, dancing in his arms. With a twist and a whirl, he would lead her in a melodious rhythm, a dizzying waltz that would intoxicate them both. And then, only then, he would gaze into her eyes, and their lips would entangle and their souls would kiss.

Oh Jenna! She scolded as she heard the logs pop and the fire hiss. *What have you gotten yourself into*? For she knew that despite her burgeoning desires and her fiery dreams, Erik wanted Christine. Jenna knew he cared for her—that much was clear. But she had seen the way he looked at the young soprano—the adoration and the reverence in his eyes. He had never looked at *her* in quite that way.

Despite the heat from the fire and the flames that had just moments ago been in her heart, Jenna did feel suddenly cold. She wrapped her arms around herself, trying to stave off the chill, but it did not work, for this iciness was on the inside, and her attempts to warm herself were only locking its bitterness in more. It would take the arms of another to drive out the cold.

"Your tea, My Lady." Erik emerged from the kitchen, tea service in hand. He set down the tray on the end table and bowed low as he offered her a cup. Jenna could not help but chuckle at the absurdity of his dramatic display, and she took the cup he offered. Erik took his own cup then, and sat next to her on the settee. They sipped their tea in a comfortable silence, feeling no need to talk, because earlier actions had said all there was to say. Eventually, Erik's fingers reached tentatively for Jenna's hand, and Jenna rested her head on his shoulder. And long into the night, they sat there together and watched the flames.

❧

It had been at least an hour since Penny Wilson had gone to visit her niece *alone,* as she had requested. He had spent much of that time in Dr. James' office, having a heart-to-heart with the Chief of Neurology.

"I think it's time to face the fact," the older doctor began, "That Miss Wilson might not be coming back."

"Doctor," he replied, not able to look his superior in the eye, "with all due respect, there is nothing on the test results to indicate that she is so badly injured that her damage would be permanent."

"How about the simple fact that she is in a coma and she hasn't woken up?" Dr. James answered. "You know that the longer a patient stays in a coma, the lower the odds—"

"I know," he said quietly, still not looking up.

"Few people recover consciousness fully after being in a prolonged coma," he pressed, trying to make his young charge see reason.

"I know," his voice was a bit louder than necessary, his hand raking through his hair.

"Then why did you tell her aunt that you were sure she'd regain consciousness?" A little exasperation started to enter Dr. James' voice.

"Because I believe she will," he insisted, finally meeting his boss's eyes. "I am not ready to give up on her yet, Doctor."

His eyes were full of such earnestness, such fervor. It was clear that, to him, Jenna Wilson's recovery was an absolute imperative, as if his own life depended on it. A stark realization came over Dr. James then, and he covered his face in his hands, groaning out loud, in exasperation. "Oh damn it all to hell! You're in love with her!"

His felt his face turn bright red and cast his eyes down once more, slumping back in his chair. "I only want to help her."

"Her? Or *you*?" The Chief sighed deeply and shook his head, "You're playing a dangerous game, Doctor. Why have you never told me that you and Miss Wilson were *involved*?"

"Because we weren't!" he insisted. His spirit deflated, he added, "I never had the courage to let her know how I felt."

Dr. James shook his head back and forth, a look of absolute vexation on his face. "Ethically, I am bound to take you off the case."

"Please," the young doctor implored, his eyes desperate. "Please. I am making progress! She squeezed my hand!"

"Reflexes, and you know it," Dr. James countered.

"Just give me a little more time," he beseeched him. "Please, Dr. James. I beg you."

The Chief of Neurology stared at him in extreme frustration. "Look! I will keep my mouth shut about your feelings for your patient, *for now*, but you must conduct yourself with the utmost professionalism."

"Of course, Doctor," he agreed, grateful to be given another chance. "Thank you." He rose to exit the room.

"Doctor," James said to him, as his hand hovered over the door handle. "False hope is a horrible thing. For the sake of Jenna's aunt, *and* for your own sake, do *not* engage in it."

"I understand, Doctor," he said, his eyes looking down.

"There is a reason why we normally do not allow doctors to care for their loved ones. Don't make me regret my decision to let you remain on the case."

"I promise, I won't," he asserted, as he turned the handle and exited the office.

He made his way quickly to Jenna's room. He had not seen her all day, and it was beginning to drive him to distraction. He was certain Jenna's aunt would have departed by now. When he got there, however, Penny Wilson's petite figure was still clearly sitting in the chair next to the bed. She had wanted her privacy, so he remained outside the room, watching through the window, the interactions between aunt and niece.

Penny appeared to be trying to talk to Jenna, holding her palm gently in one hand while stroking her niece's wrist with her fingers. Jenna made no reaction at all, and eventually, he could see Penny's head fall forward and her shoulders slump. A wave of sympathy for the older woman washed over him, and he began to move toward Jenna's room to offer Ms. Wilson comfort, when suddenly, a hand appeared on Penny's shoulder and he realized she was not alone.

He shifted slightly to get a better view into her room, as Penny stood and a familiar head of blond hair came into view. Charleson! He watched, horrified, as Charleson opened his arms and pulled

Penny Wilson into an embrace! Charleson stroked her hair and seemed to whisper words of comfort into her ear. Well. That would certainly explain Ms. Wilson's attitude during the meeting with Dr. James. It was suddenly clear who was acting as her informant.

After a moment, Penny Wilson moved out of Charleson's embrace, only to take his hand as they walked from the room. He was certain to stay out of sight in the shadows, so as not to be seen. Once they were down the hall, he strode forward into Jenna's room, closing the door behind him.

"Good evening, Jenna!" he said, forcing a bit of good humor into his voice. "Red couldn't come today—quite the busy schedule, that cat! He had a full evening planned of grooming, napping, eating, then sleeping. Sends his best, but he simply couldn't get away."

"I see you've been socializing with your aunt. I hope you quite enjoyed her visit." He walked over to her bed, pulling the privacy screen, so that they could not be viewed from the hall. Taking a seat in the chair beside her, he took her hand in his, stroking lazy circles on her palm. "I'm not sure," he said quietly, for some reason not able to look at her face, "that your aunt thinks very much of me. She seems to believe I'm not doing enough to help you. She thinks I'm just working with you to advance my career. Nonsense fed to her by Charleson, no doubt—the doctor who was just in here with her." His voice became tense at the thought of that arrogant idiot Charleson having been able to win the trust of Jenna's only family when he could not.

"Nothing could be further from the truth, Jenna, I promise you," he continued with his thought. "I care nothing about advancing my career—I only said I'd publish a study to get Dr. James to agree to allow me to do the therapy on you. The only thing that matters to me—the only thing that has *ever* mattered to me this whole time—was to get you well."

He looked up at her then, leaning in close. "Jenna," he whispered, his voice hitching in his throat, "I want you to know that I…care for you very much. I'm…never going to stop trying to get you to come back to me. I…" his voice trailed off at a loss for how to continue his sentence. He shook his head in frustration, and laid his forehead on the bed, next to hers. "Jenna, I'm *trying*," he murmured more to the pillow than to her.

He kept his head there for a moment, just drinking in her

closeness, when, suddenly he felt her head shift slightly, and her cheek was pressed against his. He felt a gentle flutter in the fingers of the hand he held as well, signifying that she was squeezing his hand. *Inappropriate* Charleson would bellow, even though if there was any damage being done here, it was to his own vulnerable heart. *Reflex* James would call it. *Wishful thinking. False hope. Not enough*, Jenna's aunt would say, expecting a miracle overnight. They might all be right, but he didn't think so. No matter what they told him, he knew that these little gestures, these little reactions were somehow for him, somehow her way of saying to hold on—that she was coming. He lifted his head and looked at the perfectly serene expression on her face. Once again, he reached forward and smoothed the curls on her forehead, and whispered, "I will be right here, Jenna. Waiting."

Erik was warm. Yes, as he drifted on the edge of a dream, he felt blessed, radiating heat circulating all around him. Something soft and sweet smelling was tickling his cheek, and a pliable, yielding weight was draped across his chest. Instead of being an encumbrance, however, this burden was welcome, comforting, soothing, and he actually felt himself nestle deeper into the cushioned warmth and draw the form more tightly against him. Somewhere there was a breath, a tender sigh, which made the darkness that much more inviting, and Erik felt that if he never again opened his eyes, surrounded by that warmth, that scent, that …*sigh*, he would be quite happy to surrender to endless night.

He felt the weight shift, and suddenly, there were gentle flutters, mere whispers of touch, stroking, caressing his cheek. Both cheeks. Still half clinging to his blissful slumber, Erik slowly lifted his lids to find that Jenna was the source of the sweet sensations he had been experiencing in his sleep. She was lying with him on the settee, draped comfortably over his chest. Her gaze followed the trail that her delicate fingers made across his face, so she did not immediately notice that he was looking at her. He saw her lips turned up in a sweet smile, as she beheld the sight that had heretofore only inspired terror and disgust.

"How do you do this, Jenna?" he asked her in a hoarse whisper, still awed by the tenderness in her fingertips.

Jenna's fingers froze, and she met his gaze. "What?" she asked, in a sweet whisper.

"How do you look upon me—how do you touch me—as if I were no different than anyone else?" he asked, still in disbelief as he gazed into her eyes.

"Oh Erik," she corrected him, softly, still gently stroking his cheek. "You *are* different from *everyone* else." Jenna noticed a shift in Erik's gaze and suddenly her cheeks went hot. Oh God, she had said too much. She had allowed herself to get caught up in this moment of sweet and blessed peace and now she had revealed feelings that she knew Erik could never share. With a slight sickly burn in her stomach, she began to pull away, only to feel Erik immediately tighten his arms around her.

"No, don't go, Jenna," he whispered imploringly. "Finally, I am warm."

Jenna gazed into his eyes a few seconds longer, silently adoring him. Hands still placed gently on his cheeks, she smiled at him. Without even knowing what she was doing, her face began to lower, and her eyes began to close, as she moved to place a gentle kiss upon his lips.

"Sweet Allah!" came the Persian's cry out of nowhere. "Erik!"

Erik startled to an upright position, and Jenna, landed with a *humph* on the floor. "Daroga," Erik hissed, glaring at the Persian, who was looking at him with a mixture of horror and shock. "You always have such impeccable timing," as he leaned toward Jenna and extended his hand.

"Well, it's not as if I could have had the doorman announce me," Omid protested. "If you *had* a doorman, you likely would have killed him by now."

"Ahh, Daroga," Erik seethed crossly. "You so easily steer my mind toward murder." Jenna gazed up at him from the floor, stunned, and reached for his hand, whispering, "Erik, your mask." His free hand self consciously covered his cheek, and as soon as Jenna was upright, she muttered, "I'll get it."

When Omid saw Jenna race off to her bedroom, he faced Erik again, and mouthed the words, "Her *bedroom*?" with wide eyes. Erik fixed on him the stare of death as he spat, "You disgust me, Persian," disdain dripping from every syllable. He continued to glare at him, even after Jenna returned with his mask, which he immediately fastened to his face.

Jenna's gaze darted between Erik and Omid, and found that she could look neither in the eye. Feeling embarrassed and awkward, she excused herself back to her chambers.

"So you're going to keep her?" Omid asked, as soon as Jenna was out of earshot.

Erik scowled at him. "She is *not* a *pet*, you fool!"

"Ahhh, but it looks like she could be *your* pet," Omid answered, with a mischievous twinkle in his eye.

"Oh, good God, man, *what* are you saying?" Erik asked in exasperation, still slightly flustered from the rude way in which he was awakened.

"She was *laying* across your chest, Erik," Omid explained, enjoying the rosy tint that crept to his friend's impossibly pale cheek. "And you were holding her in your arms—rather tightly, it appeared. And you were smiling…"

Erik listened to what the Daroga was saying and the sensation of luxurious warmth he'd felt in his dream came back to him. That comforting presence on his chest…had been Jenna. It was all coming back to him. They'd shared a kettle of tea last night after…well, after he'd told her everything, and she had seen his face. They'd been quietly watching the dancing flames, and he had not been able to stop himself from reaching for her hand—the only hand that had ever shown him any measure of kindness in his whole miserable existence. Then he had felt her rest her head upon his shoulder, and too overcome by all that had happened that night to speak, they had both simply remained silent.

The fire had been very relaxing. They must have drifted off to sleep while gazing at the hearth, shifting in their slumber. Had she really found comfort lying in his arms? Her hair had tickled his cheek, her breathing had entranced him so that he never wanted to awaken, but her gentle, tender touches had coaxed him to open his eyes.

Had he really been brazen enough to hold her, begging her not to go, when she made to disentangle from his arms? Where had he found the temerity? How could he have been so bold?

"And your mask, Erik…" Omid continued, a devilish smirk playing at the corner of his lips, a roguish glint in his eyes. "In her bedroom? Whatever could you have been doing there?" has asked, eyebrow raised.

Laying bare my soul, he thought to himself. "Nothing that you would understand, Persian!"

Omid guffawed loudly, throwing his head back in amusement. "Oh, I assure you, Erik. I *well* understand what happens in a woman's bedroom!"

Erik's eyes narrowed. "Jenna is a *lady*, Omid. Not the type of female with whom *you* would be used to passing time."

"But still, Erik," Omid commented, "you showed her your *face*. That must mean something."

It means everything, was his first thought. He remembered that moment when he was sure she would run but instead she stayed. Her sweet acceptance. The warmth…*her* warmth.

"Surely, you're not still looking for a way to send her home," he heard Omid mutter, breaking him out of his pondering.

Suddenly, Erik felt a pounding in his head that soured his stomach, and he knew he *had* to get away. "I must go upstairs and check on rehearsals," he blurted, and without another look in Omid's direction, he rose and stormed in the direction of his boat.

25 A DOOMED REHEARSAL

Rehearsals were in full swing by the time Erik reached the stage. *How late had we lingered in slumber*, he wondered, but the memory of reclining there, on his settee with Jenna wrapped in his arms once again made his stomach feel strange and he pushed the image from his mind.

Erik slinked above the stage in the rafters, wishing to get a closer view at how the scenery and props for the opera were coming along. Joseph Buquet, the stagehand, was slumped in a heap in the corner. Erik crept over to him soundlessly, and the smell wafting off his pathetic form was enough to make Erik's head spin. Buquet was passed out, stinking drunk, when he should have been working the flies. He would become the subject of Erik's next note to the management. Competency was required in the rigging, where inattention or carelessness could not only prove disastrous for the production, but dangerous for the actors as well. Buquet's slovenliness, coupled with his consistent lecherous behavior with the ballet rats, should be more than enough fodder for his immediate dismissal. Moving away from him in disgust, Erik peered over onto the stage.

They were practicing for La Principessa Guerriera and the large prop elephants were being dragged across the stage by the men in slave costumes. Carlotta was shrieking on about a trophy while brandishing a severed head in her left hand. *Poor bastard*, Erik thought to himself, a wry smile appearing on his lips. *Probably decapitated himself just to make the screeching stop.* The diva lifted both arms above her head on a high C and the bloodcurdling racket was mingled with the sound of tearing fabric.

"Oh, non ancora!" she bellowed. "NOT again!" She placed her

hand on the side of her bodice where a large hole had torn along the seam. Erik could not help but snicker softly to himself. *Cows should not wear dresses*, he thought. "Where is that seamstress?!" she screamed. "Seamstress! *SEAMSTRESS!*"

Erik saw the mane of mahogany curls bob into view as Christine hurried to the distressed diva's side, her sewing basket on her arm. "Yes, Signora?" she said, keeping her eyes cast down in a submissive demeanor. Erik longed to reach out and tip her chin up and make her look the unpleasant soprano in the eye. Christine was inferior to no one, especially not this heifer who continued to split her seams because her vanity forced her into dresses that were at least a size too small.

"I told you to do your job *right*! These seams…they rip—*again*!"

"I…I…I'm sorry, Signora." Christine stumbled over her words. "If you will just change into something else, I…"

"No!" she spat, sticking her nose in the air. "I will not be further *inconvenienced* for a *little girl* who cannot do her job right! You will mend the tear right-a now." The prima donna removed her hand from the busted seam, raising her arm above her head, and jutting her hefty torso toward Christine. Erik saw Christine take in a deep breath and move closer in to the diva's side. As she pushed her hair behind her head before she began her work, so unpleasantly close to Carlotta's distasteful form, Erik caught a flash of red behind her ear, and peered more closely to see the rose Jenna had left behind in his name, now tucked behind Christine's ear.

His breath caught in his chest. Why would she carry his rose with her? She did not seem to be the type of girl who walked around with flowers in her hair. In fact, there had never been even the hint of such vanity any of the other times he had seen her—she was always so modest and meek, almost trying to detract attention from herself. But today, she wore his rose. Could it be that it…*meant* something to her?

Carlotta gave a little flinch and a yowl of pain when her fidgeting caused Christine's needle to miss and nick her skin. "Be careful, you fumbling fool!" she bellowed, rounding on her, raising her hand as if to strike. Erik's eyes narrowed and he felt his fingers curl into fists. If that sow dared to lay her hands on his Christine once more… His own thoughts hit him hard in the chest, momentarily distracting him. *His Christine?* Jenna's words echoed in his ears, "…*It is obvious that you love Christine."* Was she right?

Christine's own trembling voice brought him back to the present. "Signora," she pleaded, "just be still and my needle will not touch you."

"Your needle had *better* not touch me, *impertinent brat*, if you know what's good for…" Carlotta's disdain laden tirade stopped short as she too noticed the delicate bloom tucked into Christine's tresses. "What is this?" she demanded, as she inelegantly pulled the rose from behind the girl's ear.

A look of pure distress washed over Christine's features. "Please Signora," she begged, reaching her hand out toward the diva, "give it back."

"Where would *you* have gotten a rose, little wench?" she asked, moving away, holding the flower just out of Christine's grasp, her voice dripping with scorn. "Are you a trollop as well as a dolt?"

Erik felt a low growl rumbling in his chest. The diva was playing with fire, and so help him, if she continued this abuse of Christine, she *would* be burned.

"Signora, no," Christine implored, continuing to reach for the bloom that was still tied with the black ribbon. "It was no gentleman caller."

"Then where?" Carlotta again insisted haughtily, holding the rose even farther away from the desperate seamstress.

The other actors and the conductor had all taken a step away from the pair, watching the scene with curiosity. They had seen La Carlotta dispatch underlings before, with her wicked temper and her unholy tantrums. Erik held his breath. Once again, Christine was in an impossible position because of him. He waited to hear if she would tell—if she would reveal her Angel of Music to this bullying diva, as she had to her ballerina friend.

Christine lowered her gaze and stared at the floor. "I cannot say, Signora."

Carlotta's eyes began to darken and she tilted her head, as if in realization. "You have been in my dressing room."

Christine looked up at the diva and her eyes flashed in horror, "No!"

"Of course you have! You need to go there to collect the mending—not that you do any of it right!" she spat at Christine, moving a bit closer to her.

Christine backed away, "Yes, Signora, but—"

"Carlotta," the tenor Piangi approached, placing his hands on her shoulders in an effort to calm her down.

"No, Ubaldo!" she declared, shrugging him off of her easily, and continuing her advance on Christine. "You stole from me!"

"No!" Christine shook her head back and forth.

"This is *my* flower—I earned it with my hard work on the stage," she bellowed at her. "And you, in your jealousy, and your knowledge that you will never amount to anything, decide to take it for yourself!?"

"No! Signora, please…" Christine stumbled back in her efforts to get away from the incensed soprano, and fell, a quivering mass, onto the stage.

"Well, nobody steals from La Carlotta and gets away with it!" She lifted her hand to strike the cowering girl, when a large, heavy backdrop and its batten suddenly fell from its suspension in the gridiron, and landed right on the diva's back, sending her sprawling on the floor.

The unintelligible shriek that ripped from the soprano's lips was almost enough to bring down the chandelier, as Piangi and the rest of the cast hurried to Carlotta's aid. The tenor lifted her in his arms, as she continued her rant in hysterical Italian, and carried her off the stage. The managers called irately for Buquet as they began to ascend the ladder to the fly tower. The cast deteriorated into a cacophony of gasps and cries. "He's here! He's here," came the chorus from the Corps du Ballet. "He is with us! It's the *ghost*!" Madame Giry tapped her cane against the stage, in an effort to quell the madness. "Silence!" the ballet mistress roared, and girls' cries immediately quieted to whispers. Meg rushed over to comfort Christine, who was shaking and sobbing on the floor, holding the now mangled red rose in her trembling fingers. And as Meg took Christine into her arms, she glanced up toward the flies to see a billow of a black disappear into the dark.

It was quiet outside her room. For a while, Jenna had heard Omid and Erik yelling at each other. She had not been able to make out their words, but she could imagine what they had been yelling about.

Omid had found them, wrapped in each other's embrace, curled up tightly together on the settee. Jenna recalled how she had felt in the seconds before Omid's discovery had caused her to be so unceremoniously dumped her on the floor. She'd been warm, she'd been cozy, and she'd felt Erik's arms tighten around her, pulling her nearer, as he curled closer to her in his sleep. Jenna had never before floated so close to heaven or clung so dearly to a dream. And when she reluctantly opened her eyes, it was impossible for her not to touch him—to caress his face with her fingertips.

She sighed deeply, remembering how much had happened last night. When Erik had come to her room, shattering her first blissful dream, he'd been angry enough to strangle her. Accusations, and condemnations had flown from both their lips. But then he had shared with her the sorrow of the life he had lived—had revealed to her the horrors of his face. And she had held him as he cried and dried his tears with her words of comfort. And they had ended the night wrapped in each other's arms. She knew it had not been intentional—that they had simply dozed off watching the fire, and their bodies had repositioned themselves in their sleep. But still, nothing had ever before felt so…*right*…to Jenna than to be cradled in Erik's embrace.

She brought her own fingers to the spot where he had touched her cheek. His fingers had been so perfect, as he'd gazed into her eyes, unmasked, exposed—just Erik, just for her. She shuddered again at the memory. How she had wanted to kiss him! She had longed to tangle her hands in his soft black hair and pull his face toward hers and just press her lips to his—feather soft kisses at first, leading to deep, searing ones later. She was not an innocent—she had been around. And still, never in her life had she longed so greatly for a kiss, yearned so deeply for a pair of arms to encircle her, to crush her in their passion. And this morning, when he had begged her not to go, she had almost done just that, her senses leaving her as she had leaned in for a kiss.

But it could never be. She closed her eyes tightly and shook her head back and forth. *Christine.* She knew his heart belonged to Christine. And though she knew she could have seduced him in that raw, vulnerable moment, she would never be Christine. What good would it do to feel his desire, if she could never have his love?

Jenna rose from her bed and paced the floor, running her fingers through her hair. *This was ridiculous*, she told herself. There was so much about this situation that was impossible—starting with the fact that she was here in the first place! How could she even consider being in love with Erik when she did not even belong here? She had to find a way back to her time—to her job, to her…cat. She *had* to somehow get back. She *had* to… right? *Oh,* his arms…

Stop it! she scolded herself. Of course she had to go back—and that was just…that. In fact, Erik said he had been looking for a way to get her home. It was quiet out there now—that had to mean Omid had gone because those two could never stay quiet for long. She would go out now and ask him about the progress he'd made. She would not gaze deeply into his eyes or get so close that he took her breath away. She would simply ask him how she was going to get home.

Jenna straightened her gown and smoothed her hair before determinedly turning the door handle and entering the sitting room. It was empty, except for Samineh who immediately started slinking around her ankles. Erik was nowhere to be seen. There were no glorious, intoxicating sounds from the piano, no gentle whisper of a page being turned at his reading chair. She walked over to the small dock by the lake, but she could see, halfway there, that the boat was gone. Had Erik left her here alone?

"Erik," she called, although she knew it was futile. If the boat wasn't here, he wasn't here. "Erik!"

"Oh, he's out," Omid said, as he emerged from the kitchen, giving Jenna a start for the second time that morning. "Something about a rehearsal he had to go foul up. Or some such nonsense like that." Omid waved one hand in the air while sipping the brandy he held in his other hand. "I found his new hiding spot for the brandy!" he smiled, raising his glass in the air. "Kitchen cabinet this time. I honestly just don't think he's trying anymore."

"Oh," Jenna responded simply, slowly walking over to the settee and sitting down. Samineh immediately jumped up on her lap, and Jenna absently stroked her fur, her mind so many miles away.

"So, Jenna," Omid made himself comfortable on Erik's chair, "I'm sorry if my entrance this morning interrupted something…"

"Oh, no!" Jenna was quick to refute. "It was…" she swallowed a lump in her throat before she could whisper, "nothing."

Omid looked at her quietly for a moment before continuing.

Judging by the way she couldn't look at him and the sadness in her eyes, the girl certainly seemed extremely affected by *nothing*. "I see," he said quietly, taking another sip of his drink. "So I noticed his mask was off."

"Yes," she nodded, still not looking at him, still petting Samineh.

"Well, considering that you're still *breathing*, he must have agreed to removing it?" he asked, with an eyebrow raised, realizing that getting information out of her was almost as hard as getting it out of Erik himself.

"He did," she nodded again, not adding any more.

"Oh, for heaven's sake, Jenna," Omid finally lost his patience, throwing up his free hand. "You two are both so somber. Did somebody die here last night?" Omid paused, as if remembering something. "No…can't be… That wouldn't make Erik somber at all."

"Omid!" Jenna gave him a scolding look.

"Well, what is it then, Jenna?" he asked her point blank, in exasperation. "What happened here last night?"

Jenna sighed, and saw no real reason for keeping Omid in the dark any longer. "He told me everything, Omid," she finally admitted. "All about his *mother*," she said the word with disdain dripping from her lips. "All about the horrible gypsy camp, all about Persia…"

"He told you about Persia?" Omid questioned in surprise.

"Yes. He told me about Persia," she nodded.

"He told you …what he *did* in Persia?" Omid clarified.

"Yes, he told me about the drugs, and the torture, and the killings, and how he had to escape because of losing favor with the Shah over a slave girl."

"I am amazed, Jenna," Omid looked at her in awe. "He *never* talks about Persia."

"Well, like I said, he told me everything." She took a deep breath. "And then, he showed me his face."

"He just…showed you his face? After telling you his life story?"

"Yes."

"Oh, come on! He would never just do that! How did you manage to persuade him?"

"Well," Jenna looked thoughtful, as if she were remembering details of the evening that had just passed. "I tried to get him to strangle me…"

"Oh Allah save us!" he swallowed down the rest of his drink in one swift gulp, slamming the glass on the side table so hard that Jenna was surprised it didn't shatter. "Are you insane, Mademoiselle?"

"Omid…" she tried to continue her tale, but Omid just continued on his diatribe.

"Oh you are definitely going back to the asylum—"

"*Omid*—"

"For your own safety's sake. I told Erik you were a mental patient and that it didn't matter *how* pretty you were—"

"*Daroga*!" she shouted, finally halting Omid's tirade, as he looked at her in shock. No one but Erik ever referred to him by his former Persian title, and it was a bit unsettling, coming from her. "I only did it to prove to him that he was *not* the monster he thought he was. I *knew* I had nothing to fear."

"You have such faith in him, but, oh, Jenna," he began in a worried tone of voice. "That was very dangerous. You don't know Erik. His past—"

"I *know*," she interjected, cutting him off, "That he could *never* hurt me. And I proved it to him last night," she continued, her eyes getting a faraway look. "I placed his hands on either side of my neck, and listed all the reasons his life would be better if he just killed me right then—if he just snapped my neck. But of course, he didn't."

"You are a brave woman, Mademoiselle." Omid's look of shock turned to one of awe and respect.

"No," she shook her head. "I just knew he wouldn't hurt me. And I knew *he* needed to know he wasn't a monster. And when he protested that his face still made him one, I swore to him that he was wrong, and if he would just *show* me, I would prove it. It took a little convincing, but he finally did."

Omid was on the edge of his seat, by now, intrigued by her tale revealing a different side of the man he had known for years. "And what did you have to do to prove it to him, Mademoiselle?"

"I stayed," she said looking in his eyes intently. "All I had to do was stay, and not run from him like so many other people had done before me. That's *all* he needed." Jenna swallowed and looked away, "And after that, we had some tea in front of the fire. It was late, and we must have fallen asleep."

Omid looked at this woman before him who possessed the

strength of a mountain to be able to confront so many demons with his maddening friend and come out triumphant on the other side. Of course, he knew the pain that Erik had faced. He'd even mentioned some of it to Jenna himself. But he had gleaned bits and pieces of the information from Erik over the trials and tribulations of many years. Never had he expected his friend to be so open with another. Never would he expect Erik to agree to show his face or to be so comfortable with another human being that he could fall asleep in her arms. "You are truly amazing, Jenna," Omid declared in a voice filled with soft reverence. "To have done what you did for him. You are like no other."

"Oh, Omid," Jenna shook her head, suddenly bashful when recalling the position in which the Persian had found them. "I didn't really do anything but listen."

"You did *everything* he needed, Jenna," Omid refuted her dismissal. "You listened, and you cared, and I daresay, you showed him the first affection he has known in his entire life." Jenna took a deep breath, but remained quiet, because she knew that what Omid said was true. "Oh, I am just so happy that he will no longer be alone!"

Jenna looked up at him with a start. What exactly did he mean by *that*? "Um, excuse me?" she asked. "What are you talking about?"

"You just told me that all he needed was for you to stay with him. I agree. You stay, and he can forget this nonsense about trying to somehow send you forward in time. You'll be happy together, and I might finally be able to stop worrying about when he's going to next kill somebody. Although, I will say, you haven't been able to convince him to leave the diva alone. Hmm…maybe I *will* still have to worry about his murderous tendencies—"

"Omid, I can't stay," she said plainly, stopping his excitement in its tracks.

"What? What do you mean? You just said Erik needed you."

Jenna felt as if a knife was slicing through her heart, at Omid's misinterpretation of her words. "No, Omid," she sighed, "he needed me last night. Not forever."

"After what you told me about last night," Omid countered, "I'd say he wouldn't mind having you around forever."

"No…" she shook her head sadly, "He doesn't want me."

"Jenna, don't forget, I *saw* you," he replied, reminding her once again of how he walked in on them. "I saw *both* of you—in each other's arms."

"I told you, that was not intentional."

"Intentional or not, it looked pretty comfortable to me. Jenna, I have known Erik for many years, and I had never seen him look so...*happy*."

The knife in Jenna's heart twisted at his words, for she knew where Erik's true happiness lay. "Omid, he was sleeping. He probably didn't even know it was me."

"Well, who else could he have thought it was?" he asked in exasperation. "Certainly not me!"

"Christine," she said, through melancholy eyes. "I am sure he was dreaming about Christine."

Omid looked at her through narrowed eyes. "The seamstress? Really?"

"His ...*angel*." She closed her eyes and shook her head. "He's in love with her, Omid."

"He...he *told* you this?" he looked at her very intently, having a very difficult time believing that his friend would admit to loving anyone.

"He did not have to," she shook her head. "I was there for their lesson yesterday. I saw the way he looked at her."

"It cannot have been very different from the way he looks at you, Mademoiselle," he said in all seriousness, for truly, he had seen the way Erik's eyes lit up in Jenna's presence—the way the two of them seemed to spur each other on to one mischief or another, the way she stood up to him, and the way he seemed to relish it. The blush on his friend's cheek this morning, when Omid was good-naturedly teasing him, said much to his inner feelings, and he just could not believe that Erik felt nothing for this lovely visitor who had happened upon his home through some miracle of fate. His comment seemed to render Jenna speechless, and when she made no reply, he asked, "And what of your feelings, for him, Jenna? Do you not *wish* to stay?"

With all my heart, she screamed in her mind. With everything she had, she wanted to stay—she wanted to *love* him. But it did not matter if he did not love her.

"Jenna?" Omid's question weighed on her, making her head spin and her stomach churn. Suddenly, she realized she had to get out of the room. "I've got to go feed Samineh," she announced, as she quickly rose off the settee, tucking the kitten into the crook of her arm, and hurried into the kitchen.

As Omid watched her go, a sudden realization dawned on him. He guffawed loudly, shaking his head at the epiphany. "Allah above," he exclaimed. "Now I know why, out of all the places in time and space you could have chosen, you dropped her in Erik's home. She is *just* like him."

❧

"Penny, I think there may be other methods of treating her." Charleson said, as he drove her to her hotel. It had been a difficult visit with her niece, and she had declined his second dinner invitation, preferring, instead, to call in for room service. He had insisted upon giving her a ride, however, so here she sat, in his car, discussing Jenna's case with the only person she had come to trust since arriving in New York. Jenna's own doctor seemed so hopeful, but he could not point her to any concrete sign of any progress she had made, beyond squeezing his hand and smiling at some music. Blaine had explained to her that both of those movements could be considered reflexive, and not in response to any type of therapy at all. And in truth, the therapy being provided seemed nebulous at best.

"What ways, Blaine?" she asked, exhausted, rubbing her forehead. "You said yourself, it was probably too late for surgery to do any good at this point."

"That is true, Penny," he said, as he turned the corner into the well-lit driveway of her hotel. "But I have been doing some research into some drugs—drugs that have been shown to have great effects on coma patients, sometimes even waking them up. But it's late, and it's probably not my place anyway to suggest this. After all, she is under another doctor's care and…"

"No, Blaine," Penny said, suddenly feeling more invigorated. "It's not too late to talk about this."

"But Penny, we're here, and you said you were tired and just wanted to go upstairs and relax with some room service… in bed." He turned the car off and opened his door.

Penny watched Charleson get out of the car and walk around to open her door for her. She had to do some quick thinking. It would probably send the wrong message, but she wanted to hear what he had to say about these drugs—Jenna's doctor be damned.

Charleson opened her door, and Penny took the hand he offered to help her out of the car. “Blaine,” she asked, laying her hand on his forearm, “Would you care to join me for some room service?”

A smile flashed across Charleson's features as he tossed his keys to the waiting valet. Pulling Penny's arm more snugly around his he answered, “I'd love to.”

26 CHRISTINE DA'AE CAN SING IT SIR

"I am telling you, Ubaldo," Carlotta insisted, her voice still bordering on hysterical, "it was the ghost."

"Hush," Piangi whispered in his lover's ear, as he guided her down the hall toward her dressing room to collect her things. "*Hush*, il mio amore. It was that buffoon Buquet. Moncharmin and Robert' found him passed out in the fly tower—obviously too drunk to do his job." He tightened his arm around her shoulders, and continued to speak to her in soothing tones. "He will no longer be a problem, cara. He has been dismissed."

"Well, *I* do not believe it was Buquet, Ubaldo," Carlotta responded, haughtily, shaking her head. "Why would-a the backdrop fall if he was simply passed out drunk?"

"Who knows how sober he was when he hung it in the first place, mio caro?" They had finally reached her dressing room. "Come, my love. We get your things, and I take-a you home." He smiled at her, and pressed a gentle kiss to her forehead. It had taken quite some time for the physician to settle Carlotta's nerves enough so that he could examine her. Aside from some bad bruises, and soreness, she would be fine, but Piangi still wanted to get her home so she could rest. "I will make you feel better, eh? A foot rub, perhaps? A nice warm bath?"

"I still say it was the Phantom," she insisted, hand on the door handle to her room, reluctant to let go of her suspicions. "There is something between him and that seamstress. He always seems to be there to rescue her when…"

"Well, perhaps you have been a bit harsh on her, cara?" Piangi interrupted, in a gentle tone, trying to make his mistress see reason.

"Harsh on her?" Carlotta asked incredulously, rounding on him. "*Harsh* on her? She is nothing but a little idiota! She cannot even sew my dresses correctly!"

"She is a child, cara. Thin as a rail," he spoke, in mollifying tones, putting an arm around her waist and pulling her close. "What does she know of a woman's curves, eh?"

Carlotta allowed the tenor's caress to soothe her somewhat, and her voice was more relaxed when she next spoke, holding only a grudging annoyance for the inexperienced costume girl. "Well, she better learn quickly."

"She has *much* to learn, my dear," he murmured, brushing a wisp of hair away from his paramour's forehead.

Smiling into his touch, Carlotta finally sighed and asked, "Can it be a bubble bath, Ubaldo?"

"Of course, mio amore," he whispered, pressing gentle kisses to her forehead.

"*And* a foot rub?" she purred now, allowing Ubaldo's attentions to thoroughly carry her away from her troubles.

"At *least*, my darling," his kisses trailed down her neck, sending little tingles throughout her body.

"Let's go!" Eager now to collect her things and leave, she reached behind her, and turned the handle to her dressing room door, pushing it open while still enclosed in Piangi's embrace. "O mio Dio!" the tenor exclaimed in dismay as he took in the scene that revealed before them.

Carlotta's dressing room was in a shambles. Her gowns were heaped on the floor, tattered and torn. Her cosmetics and accessories had been emptied from their drawers, strewn wildly over every surface. But most pointedly, the heads of all the roses Carlotta had collected for her performances from patrons and admirers had been snipped off and were lying, crushed on the floor. Horrified, Carlotta moved into her dressing room, Ubaldo right behind her. As she knelt by her ravaged dresses, gathering remains of rose petals into her hands, Piangi noticed a folded piece of parchment, shoved into the frame of her dressing mirror. Slowly, he walked over and retrieved the thick paper, unfolding it and smoothing out its crease. Carlotta, who had noticed her lover's actions and had followed him to her mirror, peered over his shoulder, reading the short, simple message on the inside.

You will be replaced.
O.G.

She fainted dead away.

❧

After laying waste to the bovine's dressing room, Erik made haste to the dormitories to check on Christine. He had seen the little Giry girl go to comfort her, and he'd assumed the young ballerina would usher her friend back to their room to rest after the harrowing incident at rehearsals. Erik fumed once again, when he thought of how cruel the diva had been to Christine. *Trollop* and *dolt* were the words that she had used to describe Christine, telling the girl that she would never amount to anything—when in truth, Christine's ability as a singer was already far superior to that of the aging prima donna. When that cow, that absolute *pig*, raised her hands to strike Christine, Erik had seen red. He had lashed out with the first thing on which he could lay his hands—the large backdrop which had landed soundly on her back. If it led to Buquet's dismissal, all the better. He did not belong at the opera—and neither did Carlotta.

When he reached the room shared by Christine and Meg, he found it empty. Surprised, he wandered behind the walls of the dormitories a bit longer, overhearing a few of the ballet rats tittering about being late for afternoon practice. He should not have been surprised that rehearsals were once again underway for the corps du ballet. Madame Giry was a harsh taskmaster and would accept no wasted time, regardless of how traumatized her girls must have been by the strange events on the stage. He smiled a little to himself in appreciation of the ballet mistress's tough attitude, making a mental note that he would have to leave her a special token of gratitude in Box 5 for the utmost professionalism with which she ran her portion of his opera house. But still, he had not found Christine.

He crept back to the auditorium, where he did, in fact, see Meg and the rest of the ballerinas pirouetting across the stage, with Madame Giry keeping pace with her staff. Still, Christine was nowhere in sight. A quick peek into the costumery revealed that she was not there either. He wandered the hidden pathways of the opera house in search of his gentle hearted prodigy, until he heard soft crying coming from the direction of the Chapel.

His heart clenched when he found her there, curled in a crying mess on the floor. Once more, *he* was responsible for her tears. If

Carlotta had not seen Christine with the rose left behind in his name, the situation on the stage would likely not have escalated to the heights that it had. He knew it was actually Jenna who had left the rose, but he could no longer be angry with her. It had been his actions, his emotions that had inspired her to do it, and truthfully, in that moment, she had known his heart better than he had known it himself.

"Papa," his angel sobbed. "Oh, Papa what am I going to do? Carlotta! She is a wicked woman! She accused me of stealing a rose from her—of taking one from her dressing room. You know I would never do any such thing. But what *could* I have done, Papa? I could not tell her where I really got it. I promised my angel. I promised…"

Her crying intensified, and Erik's heart broke at the memory that he had judged her as impetuous and untrue for mentioning his existence to the young Giry girl. Obviously, she had seen the young ballerina as no threat, for when she might have saved herself from Carlotta's wrath, she did not choose to betray him.

"Oh, my angel. Papa, I wish he would come to me now and take me away from here. Far away into his kingdom where music reigns supreme." Her crying quieted now, as she closed her eyes and seemed to be imagining something glorious. She began to hum that sweet, haunting melody that Erik had come to associate with her, and he was entranced by the words that next left her lips.

I once heard the song of an angel
Oh how I wish he'd appear
And with his wings, strong and gentle,
Lift me far from here…
High on the wings of that dark angel
Melodies float freely
Music and beauty interwoven
Tangled in sweet rapture.
Maybe in dreams I shall meet him
See his mysterious face
There shall his symphonic spirit
And my voice embrace
Angel of Music
Song in my heart
Majesty unrivaled
Angel of Music

Inspiration
Sing with me
Dear Angel

Christine was breathless as she ended her song, and there was silence in the chapel once more. Erik could not speak, for the beauty he had just heard. She had sung with such clarity, such purity of tone, yet such strong, all-encompassing emotion. It humbled him that her words had been about him—that she sang of him with such admiration and even affection…

But no, he reminded himself. It was not of *him* she sang, but of her "dear angel." She sang of dark wings, and of sweet rapture, a celestial embrace between his spirit and her voice. Such an entanglement seemed so…ethereal—glorious, but untouchable. Would it feel as soft and comforting, he wondered, fleetingly, as the blessed warmth he had found in Jenna's arms? Christine sang of seeing his face in her dreams. Surely his actual face would turn her dreams to nightmares—for how could she gaze upon this face without fear? *Jenna looked upon you*, the traitorous voice in his head reminded him. *And then she spent the night in your arms.*

Jenna is not Christine! Erik shook his head. No matter what Jenna thinks, Christine did not need *him*. She needed her angel.

"Oh, Angel," she whispered again, in pleading tones. "*Angel*."

"I am here, Christine," Erik's soothing, silvery voice seemed to come from everywhere at once, as he could no longer hold himself back from the innocent waif before him. "Are you alright, child?"

Her eyes flashed open, and Erik saw the curve of a smile begin to play on her lips. "I am now, Angel. Now that you are here, I will be fine."

Erik's heart jumped at the faith which she had in him—no, in her *angel*. The mere presence of her celestial guardian was enough to make all her sorrows melt away—something else Erik's true presence would never be able to do. "My dear, you shall be more than fine," he assured her in the mellifluous tones of the Angel of Music. "We shall continue our lessons, and when you are ready, you will soar to the heights of the opera stage, and no one, Christine, *no one* shall treat you unkindly again."

"You were there…" Christine remarked at his words. "You were in the auditorium this afternoon. You know what she did."

"Carlotta?" he answered, and even the Angel's voice bristled with contempt. "Yes, my dear. I know. I am *always* watching, and I saw what she did to you—and what she *almost* did."

Christine wrapped her arms around herself. "She is just so *cruel*, Angel."

"And her cruelty will be repaid, my dear," he vowed, trying to assure Christine that the Diva would never get away with hurting her again.

"It already was, Angel. The scenery just mysteriously fell from the sky, as if…" she paused, seeming to consider her next words. "Well, as if to stop her from touching me."

"The stagehand's incompetence certainly proved convenient this day." Erik said in a non-committal tone. It *was* true. If Jospeh Buquet had not been passed out drunk, Erik's reprisals might have become more…unpleasant.

"She ruined your rose, Angel," she said, softly, looking down. "I don't know why I brought it with me—why I wore it in my hair. I just…" she blushed a bit before continuing. "I suppose I wanted to feel like you were with me—close to me…" She trailed off, the redness in her cheek revealing the embarrassment she felt.

Erik could not help but feel tenderly for this lovely girl who had clung so sweetly to the rose that had been left by *her angel*. "My dear," he whispered, in hushed, honeyed tones, "I am *always* with you. Watching over you. I am never far."

"I am so sorry she crushed your gift. I didn't even have the chance to thank you—" she continued to apologize until she was interrupted.

"Christine, turn around," he commanded her in shimmery tones.

She, turned, and there, on the floor was another red rose that Erik had slipped through the crack in the wall, thankful that his gift of ventriloquism had caused Christine to look the other way. Like the first, this one was tied with a black ribbon, and was in perfect bloom. Erik saw new tears—joyful tears—well in her azure eyes.

"Oh, Angel," she exclaimed, "It is so beautiful. Thank you so much!" She leaned over and picked it up, holding it to her nose. "I promise I will keep this one safe. It will not be destroyed like the first."

Erik couldn't help but let loose a melodic chuckle. "There will be more roses, Christine. Once you take the stage, they will be heaped at your feet, on a nightly basis."

"But this one is from you," she said, closing her eyes and smiling dreamily as she sniffed it again.

Erik thrilled at the thought that a rose from him would somehow be sweeter, more beautiful than any other rose. The thought that she could think so highly of him—for a brief moment it did not matter that her affections were directed toward an incorporeal, celestial being. He *was* her angel, and he whispered back, "There will be more from me as well." The smile that lit up her features at his declaration took his breath away. "Sing for me, Christine," he muttered, more a plea than a command.

"Sing *with* me, my Angel!" she begged right back. And so the two, together, lifted their voices, which mingled and merged as they rose to the heavens.

❧

"We're ruined!" Claude Moncharmin declared, burying his face in his hands while slumping in his chair. "Absolutely ruined!"

"I wouldn't go *that* far," Jacques Robert' replied, trying desperately to keep a somewhat more level head. "But the situation is not good."

"The situation is appalling!" The conductor, Giles Herriot inserted! "Two weeks before the show, and the Prima Donna quits! What am I supposed to do with that?"

"Can you not teach another girl a few new songs in that amount of time?" Robert' inquired, seriously, which made the conductor's face turn red, as he began to sputter about how great singing took time, which caused Robert' to interject that Carlotta had had years and time obviously hadn't been working. Moncharmin's head was still rocking back and forth in his hands, muttering about the fall of his opera house, when a sharp crack of wood on wood echoed through the room, ending the multitudinous tirades and drawing everyone's faces to the ballet mistress and her daughter who had just entered the room. "Messieurs," Madame Giry addressed the small gathering of men as would a scolding school marm. "The clamor spilling from this office is deafening. We could hear the shouting halfway from the auditorium. What, might I ask, is the matter?"

"It is Carlotta," Moncharmin informed in a pathetic voice. "She has refused to sing in La Principessa Guerriera."

For a moment, Madame Giry looked taken aback, but she

recovered quickly enough to ask, “Over a fallen backdrop?”

“There is more, Madame.” Robert' took over for Moncharmin, who had resumed cradling his head in his hands. “Her dressing room was tampered with.”

“Completely ransacked, is more like it!” Herriot chimed in. “The Phantom wrote her a note, telling her she would be replaced! So she quit!”

“Ruined,” Moncharmin groaned once more, as Giry's eyebrow rose at the mention of the Phantom. “We just finished securing full patronage for the coming season, and now we are without a leading lady. What will the Vicomte think? He will probably withdraw his funds…”

At mention of the Vicomte, the ballet mistress's young daughter made her voice heard for the first time, blurting out the name that popped into her mind. “Christine Da'ae could sing it.”

All eyes turned to her, including her mother's exceedingly disapproving ones. “Marguerite Giry! You will keep silent.”

“Christine Da'ae?” Moncharmin asked.

“Who is that?” inquired Herriot.

“Let her speak!” Robert' insisted, since obviously no one but Little Giry knew anything about who this Da'ae girl was. Turning to her, he asked. “Madamoiselle Giry, who is this Christine Da'ae of whom you speak?”

Meg took in a deep breath, and let it out once again. “Christine is…currently…” She twirled an errant curl around her finger. “Working as a …seamstress.” Audible grumbles began to fill the room, as the three men, along with her mother, were now expressing their discontent that they had ever even hoped to believe that the impish girl could have had an idea that would save them. “But wait!” Meg insisted, raising her voice above the din. “She has been taking voice lessons, and she sings beautifully! I have heard her myself!”

“Voice lessons?”

“To a *seamstress*?”

“Who would ever…?”

“Please, Messieurs!” Meg cried above the noise of the room. “She has a secret instructor. But you must believe me when I say she has the voice of an angel.”

“I would have to hear this…*angel*…to be the judge of that!” Herriot asserted, haughtily, sticking his nose, pretentiously, in the air.

"Perhaps you should let her sing for you, Messieurs," Madame Giry suggested, giving her daughter a suspicious look.

"It is decided!" Robert' announced. "Bring her to the auditorium, Mademoiselle Giry," he ordered, rising from his seat. "We shall meet you there."

27 A NEW PRIMA DONNA

The otherworldly sounds emanating from the chapel told Meg she had finally found her friend. "Christine," she called, immediately silencing the divine refrains that had been issuing from the room. She opened the door to see a somewhat bewildered looking Christine staring at her. "Christine! I've finally found you!"

"I did not know that you were looking," she stated, still somewhat confounded.

"You must come with me at once!" Meg demanded, reaching for Christine's hand.

"Come with you?" Christine questioned, not wanting to leave the chapel, where she had just been communing with her angel. They had been making such glorious music, and now he had gone silent. "Where?"

"To the auditorium!" Meg answered in a huff. "The managers want to hear you sing."

"*What!?*" Christine asked in horror—as stunned lips silently mouthed the same question behind the wall.

"They want to hear you sing!" she repeated, impatiently. "Christine, Carlotta is refusing to perform La Principessa Guerriera! The Phantom pillaged her dressing room after the events of this morning, and she quit!"

"The Phantom?" Christine's eyes grew wide with trepidation. "But why would he—"

"Who cares?" Meg stalled her question. "Maybe she gave him a headache!" she shrugged, as Erik chuckled silently to himself in the tunnel. He could see that Little Giry had much of the same pluck that her mother possessed. They would both deserve a special thank you. "At least there will be no more temper tantrums or split seams to deal with! But you must come *now*, Christine," Meg pulled on her friend's hands. "I know she will come crawling back, and if they do not have someone to take over her role, they will have no choice but to reinstate her!"

"I cannot do it!" Christine protested, shrinking back from her friend. "I am not ready!"

"Of *course* you are!" The ballerina countered. "I've *heard* you sing, Christine!"

"But, Meg, I..." her objection was cut short when a ghostly whisper, urged in her ear, "*Go*, Christine. I will be with you." The young soprano suddenly stood up a little straighter and composed herself. Taking a deep breath, and tucking her rose behind her ear, she looked at her friend and said, "Let's go."

❧

"Ahhh, Mademoiselle Giry," Robert' exclaimed when he saw Meg enter the auditorium, dragging a shy, reluctant Christine behind her. He was waiting on the stage, next to a fretful Moncharmin, and a pacing Herriot. "I was beginning to wonder if you had gotten lost."

"No, sir," Meg answered, a bit breathlessly, "It took me a little bit to find Christine."

"Ahhhh," Herriot exclaimed, appraising the mousy looking young girl. "*This* is the little songbird?"

"Monsieur Herriot," Meg said, by way of introduction, pulling Christine forward to stand in front of him, just as she had been trying to slink back into the shadows. "This is Mademoiselle Christine Da'ae."

Feeling a sudden wave of terror, Christine whispered to her friend, "Meg, I cannot do this," while plastering a fake smile on her face for the managers.

"Ruined," Moncharmin muttered, wringing his hands, when he saw her trembling form, and heard her slightly too loud whisper.

"Of course you can, Christine," Meg whispered back in reply, smiling a bit too brightly herself. "Just think of your angel."

"*Christine*, *Christine*..." came the soft, gentle song in her ear, and suddenly, an air of confidence surrounded her. She reached up gently to stroke the rose behind her ear, and turned to Herriot. "What shall I sing for you, Monsieur?"

"Are you familiar with the aria from Act III of La Principessa

Guerriera?" he asked her haughtily.

"I am, sir," Christine nodded, respectfully.

"Well then," he looked at her, cynically. "Let's not waste anymore time, shall we? Maestro," he called to his pianist, "the first two bars of the aria, please." Leaning over to Robert', he muttered, "This should tell us right off if she is capable or not."

As Christine heard the piano begin, fear seized her heart. The first few notes she sang were thready and frail, and Erik could see her trembling ever so slightly in the spotlight, as he watched from Box 5. He saw Robert' and Herriot regard her with a distinct lack of enthusiasm, and he knew that her nerves were getting the better of her. Erik sent soft, soothing words of support and encouragement to whisper in her ear, and when Christine again opened her mouth, her voice swelled in a sublime melody that no one could deny was perfection. The managers reacted in exactly the way he'd known they'd react when they heard those first golden strains of song—they gasped in sheer and utter amazement that a voice like hers could be found this side of heaven.

"Amazing, Mademoiselle!" Robert' exclaimed as soon as Christine had completed her song. "Wouldn't you say so, Giles?"

"Quite astonishing!" agreed the shocked conductor. "Mademoiselle Da'ae, you will do quite nicely!"

"Oh!" Moncharmin clasped his hands together in glee. "Where have *you* been hiding, little lark?"

Christine's eyes darted back and forth between the three men who immediately began insisting she perform the lead in La Principessa Guerriera, replacing Carlotta in the role. Meg hugged her stunned friend as the conductor explained to her the rehearsal schedule she would be expected to follow. "Brava!" Erik threw his voice to murmur gently in her ear, and he was gratified when he saw that familiar smile wash over her features, as her fingers absently brushed the rose behind her ear.

❧

Erik arrived at the dock beneath the opera and continued floating even after he'd tied the boat to its post. The events of this afternoon had lifted his spirits after the disastrous scene in the auditorium. Comforting Christine—singing with her and hearing her vocals so intricately entwined with his, had been an exquisite pleasure. Music had always been at the core of his soul, but her singing lifted his music to heights he had never before imagined. She was the heart of his song. And he could hardly have believed his luck when the Giry girl had interrupted them to announce that Carlotta had quit the performance. He was a bit surprised that the cow had scared so easily. He had thought he would have had more time to groom Christine into her full potential as a singer. But it had not mattered, for when the conductor and the managers had heard her sing, there had been no further question.

It was all coming together. His subterfuge as Angel of Music had worked. Carlotta was out—at least from the La Principessa Guerriera production—and Christine would rise to the status she deserved. She would become the star her talent dictated her to be, and soon she would be the darling of the Paris stage. Droves of roses would fall, nightly, at her feet! And he would be there to secretly encourage, to quietly promote—her Angel of Music always watching, always guiding.

"Erik," he heard his name on the lips of another sweet female voice. He looked up to see Jenna, hair pulled away from her face, cheeks a ruddy pink, smiling at him from the kitchen. "You're home just in time for dinner."

"Jenna!" He said, speeding his step to reach her, and throwing his arms around her in excited greeting when he met her. Surprised, Jenna's arms slowly wrapped around Erik's back, returning his hug, enjoying the closeness despite her earlier resolve that she had to go. If he asked—if he'd *only* ask—she'd be his. She could gladly forget the time from which she'd come and stay here with him, if it meant spending the rest of her life folded in his arms. "You're not going to believe what just happened!"

You've decided you love me? she allowed herself a second to dream. "What, Erik?" she asked out loud, with a chuckle.

"Christine has replaced the bovine in the starring role of La Principessa Guerriera!" His eyes glistened with the proclamation.

"What?" Jenna asked in confusion. "I thought she was working as a seamstress."

"She was, but there has been a change of plans..." He released her from his embrace, as he took her hands and pulled her to the settee, beginning the tale of his busy day. Any recollection of the last moments they'd spent together on the settee was lost to Erik in his haste to inform Jenna about his adventures. But Jenna remembered.

She watched the glittering in his eyes as he explained Carlotta's cruelty, his own revenge, and the resulting exaltation of his seamstress-turned-soprano. His voice was tremulous with elation as he extolled Christine's rise to success, knowing that he would be a part of it, even if from afar. Jenna listened patiently, smiling at his joy, never interrupting his narrative. When he was finally finished, Jenna smiled and squeezed the hands that were still holding hers, saying "I'm happy for her, Erik!"

"Thank you, Jenna," Erik smiled, warmly. "I am pleased for her as well. And you had a part in this too, you know."

She looked at him quizzically. "What do you mean?"

"The rose you left behind precipitated so much of what transpired today. If it had not been for that, Christine might still be just a lowly seamstress instead of a rising star!"

Jenna's smile was tight as she answered, "I imagine you're going to be very busy getting Christine ready for the show."

"Well, yes, there will be additional rehearsals, and she will likely need some extra encouragement. She is very nervous, as you can imagine."

Jenna took a deep breath and smiled at Erik once again. "Well then maybe it's time for me to go."

Erik looked at her with a start. "Go, Jenna?" he asked her incredulously. "Whatever are you talking about?"

"Well, I've been thinking about it," she looked down and began. "You have a busy life—so much important work—so much to do now to get Christine ready for her debut on the stage. We knew from the beginning that I did not belong here. Perhaps," she took in another deep breath and closed her eyes. When she opened them again, they were focused on his. "I should find another place to stay until I find a way to get home. Or…maybe I should even think about what to do if I *can't* get back home."

Erik stared at her with crestfallen eyes, and his voice was hollow when he asked, "You wish to leave, Jenna?"

NO! Her traitorous mind screamed at her. But she knew it was no use to stay. She had no desire to watch him go on and on and on about Christine, when secretly she wished he was dreaming about her. "Erik, I just…" she took a deep breath to compose herself. "I should go. And now that Christine needs you, I don't want to be a burden, or…"

"You've never been a burden, Jenna," he answered, his deep voice serious and plain.

"Well, thank you, but—"

"Where could you stay?" Erik asked, a little irritation mixing in with the sadness that had pervaded his voice. "This isn't your world, Jenna. You don't know anyone or—"

"I know Omid!" she interjected quickly.

"Never!" Erik hissed, glaring at her sharply, effectively putting an end to that possibility.

Jenna huffed in exasperation. "Why are you making this so *hard*?" she threw up her hands, questioningly. "Don't you *want* to be rid of me? Don't you *want* to go back to the way life was before I just… *appeared*… on your lakeshore?"

"What have I done to give you that impression, Jenna?" he asked her, shaking his head incredulously. How could she think he'd want that lonely, dismal existence back?

"*Christine* could be your sole focus if I were gone. If you just help me find a place to stay, you won't have to worry about me anymore. You'll never even have to think of me again."

"Not even *think* of you?" he repeated, a sudden chill replacing the warmth that had surrounded his heart since he'd woken that morning in her arms. "Do you honestly think that I wouldn't? That I could forget? Jenna…last night…" his voice trailed off with a hush, as he once again reached out and traced his knuckles down her cheek.

Jenna's heart pounded so wildly in her chest, that she was certain it would break free. She felt her own fingers reach up to graze the hand that caressed her face. "Last night…" she repeated, on a breath. They gazed at each other a moment longer, unspeaking. Erik slowly began to feel the cold melt away, and was beginning to wonder what that meant—that the thought of her leaving could turn his heart to ice, yet the look in her eyes radiated heat throughout his being. He did not understand these new emotions that Jenna made him feel—but he was not ready yet for her to go. If that was selfish of him, so be it. But he had only just begun to feel the warmth. He was not yet ready to be out again in the cold.

Erik inhaled deeply, and Jenna was surprised to see a certain pleading lodged in his eyes. "I have not yet found a way, Mademoiselle, of sending you back in time—though I do have my theories. As you have stated, this is to be a very busy time for me, getting Christine ready for the opening of La Principessa Guerriera. That must be my priority. And…" Erik looked down bashfully, willing his traitorous body to stop shaking, "I had hoped you might accompany me in Box 5 on opening night. If this arrangement is agreeable to you, I shall do my best to find your way home after that. I would feel much more comfortable if you remained here in my abode until that time, so that I can ensure your safety. Can you stand to be here just a little longer? It is only two more weeks."

Jenna saw the sincere entreaty in his eyes, and her heart twisted. Two weeks. She could truly stand to be here a lifetime, if it meant sharing her days with this fascinating, frustrating, amazing man. Two weeks could never be enough time to be with him. And yet it would be far too long to watch him pine over Christine. But what choice did she have? "All right, Erik," she nodded her agreement.

She saw him smile—a half smile once again, since his mask hid the rest of what Jenna knew to be a beautiful expression. "Thank you, Jenna." His voice was soft and sweet, and she felt her heart melt with its tone.

"Come on, Erik," She said, rising from the settee starting to make her way toward the kitchen. "It sounds like you caused a lot of trouble today. You must have worked up quite the appetite."

Erik followed her with a chuckle. "Now see, who's going to remember my meals when you go back to your own time?"

"Omid," she threw the name over her shoulder without missing a step. She giggled softly to herself when she heard him gag and insist that he was losing his appetite already.

28 BLINDSIDED

Erik sat at his piano, the flickering of the candle beside him providing just enough light for him to make note of the keys his fingers were touching. He was playing his latest composition again—the song that Jenna had hummed for him, the aria that he built up in hopes of gifting it to Christine to sing at her debut. Well, the debut was now in two weeks, and the lyric line on the score was still empty.

Dinner had been pleasant. Jenna did not broach the topic of departing his home again, and for that Erik was grateful. He was not proud to admit how distressing he had found the idea of her leaving to be. Jenna baffled him. Jenna *infuriated* him. But most of all, Jenna had brought him more comfort, more companionship than he had ever known. She had shown him the blissful warmth of an embrace, the luxury of waking up in another's arms. She'd taught him how easy it could be to smile, or how genuinely good it felt to laugh. He recalled how she touched his face after he exposed his deformity, and he felt the shivers of tenderness and wonder brush his cheek anew. Jenna had changed his life so much—*so much*—in just the short time she'd been here with him, and while he knew that he had promised to find a way to send her back to her time, he had been beginning to feel as if she would always be there—and he would never really have to let her go.

Until tonight. She had told him she wanted to leave, so that she wouldn't be a burden—and that once she had gone, he'd never have to think of her again.

Never think of her. Those words stayed with him and cut him to the core. As if it were possible to push her from his mind. He would think of her always. With fondness and … something *more*. He didn't quite know what that *more* was, but he knew he'd never forget the way her eyes rolled at his sharp tongue, or the tear that had trailed down her cheek at the imperfect strains of the orchestra. He'd remember how hard she'd tried to hold in her laughter when he fell into the pond while frog hunting, and how lovely the sound was when she'd finally lost the battle. He could never forget the terror that gripped his heart when he thought she would be hurt by the carriage, or how he didn't even have to think twice about putting himself in mortal danger to protect her. *"You'll never even have to think of me again,"* were her words. But truly, Erik knew, there would never again come a day when he wouldn't.

She'd made it clear tonight, however, that there *would* come a day when they would say goodbye. Erik felt a dark mood building up in him. When that day came, would *she* remember him? Oh, he knew there were things she would wish to forget. The way he bellowed at her that night after the near accident with the carriage. The way he'd derided her for simply not knowing how to make tea. Dear God, even last night, before she had shown him the greatest act of acceptance he had ever known in his life, he'd been so rough with her, so angry. Surely she would wish to forget his temper, and his hot headedness and his horrible thoughtlessness. Were those the very things that drove her away? If he could somehow get his horrible temper under control, would she think instead on their shared excitement as they executed a plan? The evenings spent conversing over tea? The night she lay asleep in his arms? Would she no longer wish to leave?

Erik sighed, because he knew it was no use. Jenna wished to go back to her home, which was not plagued by ill-tempered masked men or howling divas who needed discipline. A few cups of tea and a night spent dozing in front of the fire wouldn't change that. He let his fingers tiptoe across the piano keys once more, quietly, because he didn't want to wake her. He played the first few measures through, and this time, when the melody danced beneath his fingers, a bittersweet plea poured out from his lips—a tender petition that she not forget the good times they had shared, that she try to remember them even after they'd said goodbye. And this time when his fingers stilled, his music had words. His aria was complete.

❧

"What do you think, Jenna?" the doctor asked, as the last strains from his acoustic guitar faded into oblivion. "Did you like that one?" Jenna made no answer, but he did earn a loud "Mreeeoooww" from her feline companion. Chuckling, he commented, "Well, I'm glad you liked it, Red, but I was hoping to gain the lady's opinion."

He let his fingers absently strum the strings of his guitar. He was off rotation, which meant he could while away the day in jeans and a T-shirt, relaxing and spending as much time with Jenna as he wished. He'd decided to bring the guitar with him to see if Jenna would enjoy a little concert. Music had always been a very relaxing hobby for him. It had helped him ease the stress of medical school, and was a favorite way to pass the time. Since he knew Jenna was a music lover, he'd hoped that a live serenade might reach her in some way that recorded music didn't. "So Jenna, any requests?" he asked jovially, always wanting her to hear joy in his voice—always hoping to convey that there was something worth coming back for.

"Mrrrreeeeeeeoooooooow." was the only response.

"Red!" he scolded good-naturedly. "You've made the last two requests! Give Jenna a chance!"

"Mreh!" the cat retorted as he continued to circle his owner's head. The doctor just laughed and rolled his eyes.

"So what do you want to hear, Jenna? Hmmm?" he asked again sweetly, his fingers forming the shape of a chord on the neck of the instrument. "What would you like?" He looked down and very gently began to play a few quiet chords. "Anything I like, you say? Well, ok," he whispered, "I know what *I* want." After a few measures of the rhythmic strumming, he began to sing a song of deep, conflicting emotions, of promises made and broken. His voice started out as a hushed murmur, but as the tension in the song rose and became feverish appeal, his voice grew stronger and more pleading, desperate for the all-consuming desire to be fulfilled. "You," he crooned soulfully on a raw high note, gazing upon her face. "All I want is you."

Penny stayed just outside the door until his song was over. She could not deny that her heart was moved by hearing the young doctor's musical confession. The emotion in his voice had been almost overwhelming, and as he sat there now, silently just staring at her niece, while his breathing quieted from the song, she could tell that his greatest desire was for Jenna to open her eyes just then and reach out to him. If things were different, she would be a champion for a relationship between her niece and this sweet, passionate young man.

But things were not different, and Jenna was not reaching out to him, she was lying motionless in a hospital bed. It was not his job to *woo* her back to consciousness—although if anyone could, she was certain this doctor would be able. It was his job to administer effective treatments. And thus far, he hadn't been very successful at doing that. It was entirely inappropriate for him to be entertaining feelings for his patient, for those feelings were obviously obscuring his thinking.

Her mind wandered back to several nights before, when she herself had been locked in a passionate embrace with Blaine. She knew that inviting him up to her room for dinner had been a mistake, but she had been so intent on hearing what he had to say about the medications that had promise to help Jenna. He had told her about the drug which had been known to help coma patients regain consciousness—both for short stretches of time and for longer periods—and she had been so excited that she had not thought twice about throwing her arms around him in a grateful hug. When his lips had found hers moments after, in a searing kiss, she had found it impossible to resist his advances, even though she knew she should. It was not proper for her to be carrying on a romantic affair with a doctor who would be working on her niece's case, but it had been so long since a man had kissed her like that. When he'd led her to the bed, she'd been powerless to resist. Relief was immediate when his beeper went off, rousing him from their embrace before they could do something she had absolutely no business doing—something which she knew would cloud her judgment even more.

She knocked quietly as she pushed open the door and entered the room. "Good afternoon, Doctor."

The young man reluctantly looked away from Jenna, and up into her eyes. "Oh, hello, Ms. Wilson."

"I…I'm surprised to see you here, Doctor," she stumbled a bit on her words, trying to make conversation. "I was told it was your day off."

"It is," he smiled. "I'm just visiting."

Penny smiled back. Despite what Blaine said, and despite her dissatisfaction with Jenna's progress, she could not help but feel sorry for what she was about to do. This doctor truly seemed to have

Jenna's best interest at heart. It was because of her guilt that Penny informed him of the plans for the afternoon. "If you are free, Blaine and I are having a meeting with Dr. James in about an hour and a half, to discuss Jenna's treatment options."

"Blaine?" he asked, a bit taken aback. "I…I wasn't aware of any meeting."

"I apologize," she said sheepishly. "It was the only time Blaine had free, and since it was your day off, we didn't want to disturb you."

"Oh, I understand," he said with a tight smile. And truly, he *did* understand exactly why the meeting had been planned for this afternoon—because *Blaine* didn't want him in attendance. But Dr. Charleson would just have to get accustomed to not getting what he wanted, because of course he would be attending the meeting. "I am free all afternoon, Ms. Wilson," he said out loud. "Just let me know the time and the place, and I will be there. Your niece's health is of the utmost concern to me."

It had been a busy morning for a day off. After Jenna's aunt had informed him about the meeting, he had gathered Red and his guitar, and left Penny to visit with her niece. The drive across town was slow with traffic, and he barely had enough time to deposit the hungry feline, feed him, and change into more professional attire before he had to be back at the hospital for the meeting. He dashed down the hall much faster than he should have and opened Dr. James's door after knocking first to announce his arrival. "I'm here," he said somewhat breathlessly, as he entered the room.

Blaine glanced quickly over at Penny who would not meet his gaze before setting his eyes back on his colleague and saying, "So you are."

"Welcome, Doctor," his supervisor said by way of greeting, waving toward an empty chair at his small conference table. "Pleased you could join us after all. Dr. Charleson told me yesterday that you would not be able to make it."

"That is only because I had not been informed until this morning," he said, meeting Blaine's smug blue eyes with a glare.

"Well," said Dr. James, a bit surprised by the revelation. "We shall have to make sure that type of oversight doesn't happen again. Dr.

Charleson," he began, clearing his throat in obvious irritation. "You initiated this meeting. Would you care to tell me *why*, since you are not Miss Wilson's doctor?"

"Actually, Dr. James," Charleson responded, his voice smooth and calm. If he was at all taken aback by the younger doctor's presence, he did not show it. "It was Penny, who initiated the meeting on behalf of her niece," he said, placing a hand on the blonde woman's back, creating an image of intimacy between the two.

All eyes turned to her as Penny swallowed once and began to speak, obviously a bit intimidated to be speaking to this group of doctors. "Well…I…that is, Blaine told me…"

"What Miss Wilson is trying to say," Dr. Charleson took over for her quickly, acting as self-appointed spokesperson for the flustered family member, "is that she is dissatisfied with the level of care Jenna Wilson has received to date."

"Oh, really?" the younger doctor stared daggers at him from across the table.

"Yes," was all the answer Blaine made as he continued. "Young Miss Wilson has shown no real improvement to date—other than occasionally *squeezing* her doctor's *hand*—and her aunt is ready to explore more aggressive treatments."

"Is that so?" Jenna's doctor asked, surprised, since Jenna's aunt hadn't mentioned anything about this when he had seen her at her niece's bedside.

"Yes, I…" she once again stumbled over her words, "Blaine…"

"We would like to start a course of Zolpidem with Miss Wilson." Charleson informed them, matter-of-factly.

"Excuse me," Jenna's doctor interrupted in annoyance. "*Who* would like to start a course of Zolpidem, because as her doctor, *I* certainly would *not!*"

"Well, that's another thing we need to discuss, Doctor," Charleson smiled cunningly at him. "Penny?"

"Well," she began shakily, as all eyes were once again on her. "I would like for Blaine," she cleared her throat as Blaine seemed to pat her on the back, "I mean Dr. Charleson, to take over Jenna's case."

The young doctor felt anger and embarrassment course through his veins, and he worked hard at keeping the hurt out of his eyes. "Ms. Wilson, I beg you reconsider," he said, calmly to Jenna's aunt, trying with all his might to keep the desperation he was feeling at the moment out of his voice. He knew that Jenna's aunt had been railroaded by lies fed to her by Charleson.

"Doctor," she said, meeting his wary eyes with kindness in her own. "You've tried your methods of treatment on Jenna, and they are not working."

"They take *time* to work, Miss Wilson," he implored, hoping that she would see reason and let him continue a little longer. "I have seem some modest improvements…"

"No disrespect intended, Doctor," her voice gaining a bit in strength, "but the improvements have been too modest—and, apparently, only seen by you. This drug…it has brought people *out* of comas. How can I not want to try that on Jenna?"

"But Ms. Wilson, please," he beseeched her. "Listen to me. Zolpidem is not the wondrous answer that Dr. Charleson may have made it out to be."

"Are you saying I would lie?" Blaine interjected.

"In a heartbeat," he answered, not once looking away from Jenna's aunt. "It has been successful in a small number of cases in restoring consciousness—but only for short periods of time and—I must *stress—only* in a handful of cases. The majority of patients who undergo Zolpidem treatment gain no beneficial effects. And then there are the side effects. Zolpidem can be a dangerous drug, Miss Wilson, causing chest pain, back pain, anxiety, tremors…the list goes on and on. And if Jenna is unconscious, and experiences these symptoms, how is she going to tell us she hurts?"

Penny looked quite uncertain at this point and turned to Blaine as if to ask if all of this was true. Before she could, however, he interjected, "What if she hurts now, Doctor? How can she tell us beyond the occasional *hand squeeze* and a shiver in the cold?"

He turned to Blaine, eyes blazing. "You are so quick to dismiss the small measures of success I have had with her, but tell me, Doctor, when have you ever exhibited a greater results with a coma patient? How many have you treated successfully?"

Dr. Charleson was unflappable. "I look forward to counting Jenna as my first."

"Oh, so you have no problem using her as a guinea pig, then," he retorted, anger now clear in his voice, "using treatments you, yourself have never used before."

"And *you* are so accomplished in Coma *Arousal* Therapy?" he snickered as he named the younger doctor's choice of treatment out loud, emphasizing the most untoward part of the name.

"*First do no harm*, Charleson," he spat out, absolutely irate. "Do you remember that tenet from Med School? It is one of the first things they teach you in ethics class. Or were you sick that day?"

"I was there the day they cautioned against falling in love with your patients, Doctor, for fear it would *cloud your objectivity*," he looked pointedly at the young man whose cheeks reddened in embarrassment. "Were *you* there then?"

"What if you send her deeper?" he asked desperately, his desire to argue with Charleson taking a back seat to his worries about Jenna's well being. "Zolpidem is hypnotic in nature! So many coma patients who take it never gain any benefit and never wake up."

"That is true of coma patients in general," he stated, dismissing the concern with a wave of his hand.

"Granted. But what if the Zolpidem doesn't work to rouse her from her coma, but instead puts her into a deeper state? She is reacting some now. Why can we not remain patient and see if she can come out of this on her own?"

Penny took that moment to speak up, "I can no longer be patient with my niece's health, Doctor. I'm sorry," she said, looking the younger doctor in the eye. "I know you mean well and care deeply about Jenna. But I care about her too, and I want to give her every chance."

"So do I, Ms. Wilson," he begged her with his eyes to change her mind—to just let things continue as they were for a while longer. He was certain he could reach Jenna—that he *was* reaching Jenna. He just needed more time.

She reached out and clasped one of his hands in hers. "Then will *you* continue on as her doctor and try the Zolpidem?"

For the first time, Blaine seemed to bristle a bit at her words. This was not a part of the equation. He wanted to perform the Zolpidem treatments on Jenna. He was not about to let this pathetic excuse for a neurology resident take that away from him. He turned to tell Penny so, but heard his rival answer, meekly, "Ms. Wilson, I *can't*. In good conscience, I cannot administer that drug to Jenna. There are too many unknowns."

What a fool, Blaine thought. He had the chance to retain full control over Jenna's case, and just threw it away over his ridiculous feelings for a girl who hadn't even noticed he existed before she'd had her accident. She'd been screwing a physical therapist, for God's sake. And who knows whom else. She wasn't some innocent angel that was just waiting for him to come and sweep her off her feet. This idiot had created these feelings entirely in his head—and now he was passing up a career goldmine because of them.

"Well, then, will you at least continue with your therapy?" she asked, gently. "I want Blaine to try the drug, but perhaps it would work best in conjunction with what you are already doing?"

He closed his eyes and nodded his head. This was *not* what he wanted. He wanted to continue his treatments without the interference of Charleson and this drug. But he had no claim over Jenna. He was not her family. He could not make these calls—he could only advise against them. And since he'd tried that already and it didn't work, there was nothing left for him to do. But he'd promised that he would not give up on Jenna. He swore that he would do everything he could to help her, so he would have to accept this compromise. If it was the only way he could remain close to her, then he would do it. He still had to try.

"I can do that, Ms. Wilson," he told her aunt, refusing to look in Charleson's direction.

"Thank you, Doctor," she smiled. "I think your involvement would mean a lot to Jenna. It means a lot to me."

"Well," said Dr. James, pushing away from the table and looking his two charges in the eye with an expression that was both worried and firm. "That's settled then. The two of you will be in charge of Jenna's case from here on out. I expect cooperation and collaboration, is that clear, Doctors?"

"Yes, sir," the younger doctor answered.

"Crystal," was Charleson's smug response.

"Very well," James adjourned the meeting, still looking at the younger physician with concern. "You may go."

"Thank you," he murmured as he rose from James' table, intent on going to visit Jenna once more.

"Hey, Doctor," Charleson met him at the door, as he exited the room, his hand on the small of Penny's back, an oily smile on his face. "Why don't you go enjoy the rest of your day off? I've got things covered here."

29 WICKED GAME

He heaved a heavy sigh and tried once more. “Alright, Jenna. I know you're probably a little tired from the medication, but if you can hear me, please try to squeeze my hand. It would make Red and me feel so much better if you did.” He held her hand gently in his and waited—as he had been waiting for a while now, and still nothing. It had been about a week since Dr. Charleson had begun administering the Zolpidem, and since the start of drug therapy, the sensory therapy had been completely ineffective. Gone were the little moments when her smile would brighten, or her fingers would close around his. Before the drugs, he had been so sure that Jenna was in there, trying to let him know that she heard him, but now…he wasn't sure *where* she was.

He had had his misgivings about the new course of treatment, but his concerns had fallen on deaf ears. No, he thought to himself, remembering how Jenna's aunt had been so clearly manipulated by Charleson. Maybe not deaf ears, but ears that were simply clogged with the noise of another.

Now he was really beginning to wonder if his fears were being realized. Had Jenna slipped further into the coma?

He was still there, holding Jenna's hand, his thumb rubbing slow circles on her palm. He held his head low, praying for something, anything to let him know she was still with them. When the door to her room opened, he did not bother to look up. He knew who it would be, and he had no desire to see him ever again.

“Still here?” Charleson asked, a bit of smug humor in his voice. “How many squeezes did you get today, Doctor?”

“Since you began your miracle treatment,” he spat with rigid jaw, “she has been entirely non-responsive, and you know that.”

“Hmmm,” Charleson murmured, as he flipped open her chart.

"Seems to me she's been unresponsive since she had her accident. It was only your wishful thinking that allowed you to think otherwise."

He gritted his teeth together and told himself not to engage on that matter. Charleson wanted to get the better of him, and he refused to allow it. "How long are you going to continue your charade, Charleson?"

"And what charade would that be?" he asked, with a pompous grin.

"The one where you pretend to actually care about Jenna's well being," he looked up then and met Charleson's gaze. "The one where you keep pretending your treatment is going to work?"

"Oh! I'm sorry," Charleson retorted. "Did you *not* want me to play *your* game, Doctor? That's not very friendly of you. You really should be better about sharing your toys."

"You know as well as I do," he began, not allowing himself to be swayed by the act Charleson was putting on, "that when Zolpidem has been effective, results were seen much more quickly than this—starting with the first dose. Jenna has been receiving the drug three times a day for a week now. There has been no therapeutic effect. So when are you going to admit it isn't working?"

"Oh," Charleson responded nonchalantly, checking Jenna's pupils with his penlight, and writing something on the chart. "It probably isn't working."

The younger colleague could not believe his ears. "What?"

Charleson looked him directly in the eye. "It probably isn't working."

"Then stop the treatment," he retorted, surprised to even be having this conversation with Charleson if he admitted the medication was having no effect. "Start weaning her off the drug."

"Maybe I will," he answered.

"What do you mean, *maybe* you will?" he asked incredulously. "Why would you continue to medicate her when you know it isn't working?"

"Well, basically, because the ball's in *my* court now, Doctor," he said, with an egotistical expression. "Go ahead and tell James we had this conversation. Let's see if he believes you for one minute. Go ahead and pester Penny about it. I have *ways* of persuading *her*." He let out a self-assured laugh as he closed the cover to Jenna's chart.

"You're disgusting," the doctor noted, disdain dripping from his words.

“Your point?” Charleson asked, looking right at him.

“Don't you care that you could be harming her?” he asked, outrage coloring his tone.

“No,” he answered, matter-of-factly. “I care about winning, Doctor. And from my vantage point, I win.”

“You *pig*!” he spat, rising as if to advance on him.

“Careful, Doctor,” Charleson warned, in a condescending tone of voice. “You wouldn't want me to mention this little tête-à-tête to Penny now, would you?”

The younger man backed off, breathing heavily, knowing that he could not afford to do anything that would get him tossed off Jenna's case.

“That's what I thought, Doctor,” Charleson said, making his way toward the door. With his hand on the door handle, he turned back and said, “Good luck getting a squeeze out of her tonight. I hear she's not that kind of girl.” He turned the handle and left the room, chuckling as he went.

It seemed somehow strange to be walking these quiet corridors alone. For the past week, Jenna had been his almost constant companion. The night they had discussed Jenna's eventual leaving had made Erik realize that she would not be with him forever, and he wanted to make every moment she *was* there count. So, on a whim, he had invited her to join him for rehearsals the following day, and even though *Erik* had been busy making a long list of issues that needed to be resolved, Jenna had watched with rapt attention, a look of pure joy on her face. He'd found her expression so captivating, that he'd asked her to accompany him again the next day, and when she did, he actually found himself joining her in one of the seats in the back row, and just listening. When she would look up at him from time to time and smile, he'd found that he could not keep the corners of his mouth from curling up as well while watching her.

Christine, of course, sang beautifully. While she was still learning her blocking around the stage, her *voice* was flawless. It filled him with such delight to hear her sing, and, he found even greater pleasure when Jenna complimented him on his teaching techniques. Truly, he knew that Christine had a star quality voice even before he started teaching her. Yet, strangely, he found that when Jenna gave him the credit for her success, he felt his chest expand with pride.

This morning, however, when Erik knocked on Jenna's door to wake her for their morning meal, she was not feeling well. She met him at the door with one hand held to her forehead, and the other out against the frame, as if supporting her weight. Immediately alarmed, Erik asked, "Jenna, what is wrong?"

"I'm fine, Erik, I just…" a wave of dizziness washed over her and she felt her legs buckle a bit beneath her. In a flash, Erik's arms were about her, catching her before she could fall, and guiding her over to the settee, where Samineh jumped up to join her.

"You are obviously not *fine*, Mademoiselle," he said, using her formal title instead of her name, exposing his nervousness at the state of her health.

"Erik, I have a headache, and it made me dizzy," she argued, waving off his concern, and looking over to the purring kitten, giving her some scratches behind the ear.

"You complained about a headache yesterday as well, Jenna," he looked at her with worry, while checking her forehead for fever. "Do you need to see a physician?"

"Erik, no," she said calmly, touched by his concern, but feeling that he was greatly overreacting. "This is probably just a touch of the flu. I just need to sleep it off," she asserted, still petting the preening cat.

Erik sighed deeply, "But Jenna, the Daroga could easily…"

"There is no need to trouble him!" she insisted, finally meeting his gaze. "I will be fine! I'm a *nurse*, remember?"

"So you have said, Mademoiselle," he relented, using his hand, which was still on her forehead, to smooth the hair away from her brow. "I will go bring you something to eat."

"No, Erik," she shook her head. "I'm not hungry right now. Besides, you have to get off to rehearsals."

"I am not going to rehearsals today, Jenna," he answered, as if the fact should be obvious. "You're not feeling well, so I will stay here and look after you."

Jenna stared at him with horrified eyes. "Absolutely not!" she exclaimed, at what he was suggesting. "I told you I am going back to sleep. You would only keep me awake with your incessant piano playing."

Erik looked offended, "Who said I would be playing piano?"

"You would," she insisted. "You always do, eventually!" Erik huffed, and Jenna added, a bit more gently, "Erik, I can take care of myself. And besides, what about Christine?"

Erik did feel a bit torn at the mention of Christine, but countered, "Christine is not currently lying on my settee, too dizzy to stand. And I will see her tonight at our lesson."

"But she will miss you if you are not at rehearsals," she argued. "She'll *know*. Go, Erik. I will be fine."

Erik looked at her a moment longer in uncertainty. "Can you make it back to your room?"

"Sure, I can," she said as she rose from the settee, causing Samineh to jump to the floor. All of a sudden, the world began to spin, and she was grateful, once again, to have Erik's arms reach out and catch her.

"Allow me to help you back to your room, Jenna," he said, steadying her step with an arm around her back. Once back in her room, he helped her into her bed, pulling the covers up around her shoulders. "I am still not sure I should leave you, Jenna," he said, looking ill at ease.

"Erik," she smiled, wearily. "Get out of here! I'll be fine."

Erik found, once again, that when Jenna smiled, he could not help but smile too. "Sleep well, Jenna," he'd whispered, and gave her hand a little squeeze, before leaving her room and closing the door, so the little kitten would not disturb her rest.

But now, as he arrived at his secret entrance to Box 5, he was having second thoughts. It suddenly did not seem right to be here without her. What a strange notion, he thought, as he gazed over to the chair where it had become customary for her to sit. He had been coming here for years on his own, and after a week of having her here with him, he missed her presence so much that the box seemed rather empty without her. *Get a hold of yourself, Erik,* admonished the voice inside his head. *She will not be here forever, and when she leaves, you will be required to go back to being what you have always been. Alone.*

Erik took his seat in the back row and compelled himself to watch the rehearsal. Christine was taking the stage, and once again, she was exquisite—as he knew she would be. Every word, every note that spilled from her lips was a pure, crystalline jewel of perfect pitch and resonance—a honeyed timbre more divine than earthly. He expected nothing less from his protégé' and he was gratified at her success, and yet he found himself distracted. The third time he found his eyes had wandered to the seat that was usually occupied by his tag along houseguest, he realized he had to go. He could not sit here any longer and pretend that his mind was even remotely engaged by the melodrama being rehearsed on stage. Erik stood, and with a swirl of his cape, exited the box through his secret passage.

He began to make his way back home, but then remembered that Jenna didn't want him there, for fear he would disturb her rest. *This is ridiculous!* he thought, with a huff. *Am I really allowing her to keep me out of my own home?* He'd had years of experience slinking around places unnoticed. He was fairly certain he could manage to be at home and still allow Jenna to sleep. *But what if you wake her?* His inner voice asked. He knew that upon arriving in his lair, he would never be able to simply go about his business. He would have to creep into her room and check that she was ok—and he most likely would not be able to stop himself from brushing the hair away from her forehead, just to check that there was no fever, of course. And once his fingers were on her skin, he might be tempted to trace the curve of her cheek, which would be so soft and smooth…

Erik shook his head. No, he took too much of a risk of waking her if he returned home now—and he knew she really needed her sleep. The headaches had been troubling—perhaps more so to him than to her. If he had to forego the comforts of his home for a few more hours, he would, on the chance that rest would, in fact, alleviate her pain.

Erik took a detour down one of the side corridors that led to the forgotten storage rooms in the Opera. Here was where the props and costumes of productions past went to languish and fade, in hopes that they might one day be used again. Erik knew from experience that it was entirely unlikely that such a day might ever come—due to the management's complete inability to keep inventory of what they had in stock—so he found the storage rooms to be one of his favorite places to search and plunder for supplies.

Today, his goal was to find more black velvet ribbon. He had taken to leaving a ribbon-tied rose for Christine each night before her lessons—which now took place in her own private dressing room, rather than the chapel—and as such, his supply was running low. As he rummaged the boxes and shelves of discarded treasures, a delicate bauble caught his eye. There in the midst of fake pearls and glass diamonds, a cameo pendant hung from an old bronze chain. While the chain was obviously trash, the shell of the pendant retained a beautiful coral glow, and the intricacy of the white carving indicated the great skill that had gone into its crafting. It was set amidst a tangle of intricate filigree fashioned out of antique gold. What truly made it stand out, however, was the subject of the sculpting itself. Unlike most cameos he had seen, this one did not illustrate the bust of a noble woman with impeccably coifed hair. On the contrary, this trinket captured the essence of nature's most delicate of beauties—a single rosebud, just about to burst into bloom.

Erik lifted the cameo away from its drab companions, a smile beginning to form on his misshapen lips. He had come in search of ribbon, but instead had found a treasure that he would put to much better use.

30 TERROR IN THE DARK

It was not fair! Eight years he had been with the Garnier—since the day it had opened. Eight years he had toiled, lifting heavy scenery, navigating the treacherous scaffolding which comprised the fly space. Eight years of aches in his back and tears in his chest that had turned him to take the bottle to numb the ever-present pain. Eight years of constant temptation from the scantily clad little tarts that called themselves ballerinas. So what if he succumbed on occasion to their enticing seductions? Should that really have caused his wife to abandon him, leaving him flat? After all, it was because of *her* grand tastes that he had to slave away at the Garnier, working his fingers to the bone, while the whole time the rats flaunted their wares in front of his face.

He had given his life to the Garnier, but that had not been enough. It had taken his family, his health, and now his home. After having been unceremoniously dumped by the muttonhead managers, he had nowhere to go any longer to rest his weary bones. Sacked! Fired! Canned! And all for something he didn't do.

Buquet tossed back another swig of whiskey. How blind were those managers that they couldn't see it was the ghost? *He* was the one who had been causing mischief around the opera house for years—demanding cast changes and extorting money. *He* was the one who could snap his spectral fingers and make the entire cast go boo. And *he* was the one who'd had a long-standing feud with La Carlotta. Why wasn't *he* the prime suspect when a bolt of scenery had fallen on the diva's back? Buquet had done nothing worse than report for work. He'd set up everything the clowns on the stage needed for their bloody rehearsals. Why shouldn't he have taken a few minutes to sleep off the previous evening's bender in the corner of the flies?

The thought of sleep made Buquet take another long guzzle from his bottle. He would need the warmth of the whiskey to get him through the cold, now that he was out on the mean Parisian streets. Winter had hit with a vengeance, the blustery winds biting right through the threadbare overcoat he had won in a card game years ago. As he lowered the bottle from his lips, he felt the first plump raindrop splash down on his forehead, and soon he was bespattered with a dozen more of its kind. Wonderful! Cold, windy and now, wet. These Parisian winter days kept getting better and better.

He reached into the holey pocket of his coat to find that he was out of coins. He would not be able to buy his way into any bar or drinking establishment without money to pay for libations, no matter how starved he was for their warmth. Until he was able to earn more cash—doing God knows what—it was the bleak city streets for him—and all because of the one sin he *didn't* commit! Thoughts of the true culprit responsible for the debacle with the diva plagued his mind once more. *He* would be warm and dry tonight in his demon's lair so many stories below the opera house.

A besotted snarl crossed Buquet's leathery lips. He rose from his spot against the stone wall and began to teeter down the familiar paths that would lead him to his recent home. After all, if the Phantom could haunt the Palais Garnier, then so could he.

❧

Jenna opened her eyes and blinked against the soft fire glow of the lantern near her bedside. She stretched her arms up above her and rolled languidly onto her side. She felt like she had slept for hours—days. It was time for her to get up and out of bed.

Pushing herself up with her hands, she hung her legs over the side of the bed and gingerly, rose to a standing position. After a few steps around the bedroom, she was happy to discover that the pain had passed and there was no trace of the dizziness she felt earlier that morning.

"Erik," she called as she threw open her door, expecting to find him reading or composing, as was his wont in the afternoons between rehearsals and lessons with Christine. "Erik…" she said again, not seeing him anywhere, but instead being greeted by a squeaky *meow*, as little Samineh discovered she was awake. She checked the small kitchen, grabbing an apple out of the bowl to stave off her hunger, and putting out some fresh chicken for the cat, but Erik was not there either. When she walked over to the little dock and saw that the boat was still gone, she realized that he must still be at rehearsals. "Maybe I didn't sleep as long as I thought," she muttered to herself in disappointment.

She wandered about Erik's home a bit, trying to figure out what to do with herself. She walked over to the piano and plinked a few of the keys, smiling at the thought that Erik would be irate with her if he knew she was tampering with his beloved instrument. It made her want to sit down and play a concerto. But truth be told, Jenna did not really know *how* to play piano, so she tired quickly of her illicit game, and wandered over to the bookshelf.

There were so many titles on Erik's shelf, and so many subjects covered. She searched among the well-worn tomes on architecture, medicine, art, and of course, music until she came to his collection of novels. She selected one she had not yet read and wandered over to curl up in Erik's reading chair. She snuggled deep into the overstuffed leather, drinking in his lingering scent and tucking her feet up beneath her. She opened the ornate cover and began to read. After scanning the same page several times, and still having no idea what she had read, she realized she was not really in the mood for a novel. She felt a nervous energy, and she knew that it would not be calmed until she saw Erik. She still did not really enjoy being in Erik's home alone—not because there was anything uncomfortable about it, per-se, but more because she enjoyed *his* company so much. She did not want to spend her time without him. *You better get used to it, Jenna,* chimed that voice inside her head, that she had begun to loathe. *Christine's debut is in a week, and after that Erik will be working full time on finding you a way home!*

Jenna sighed heavily at the thought. She looked around the lair that had seemed so strange when she had first arrived. Now as she took in the majestic grand piano, the bursting bookshelf, and the myriad glowing candles, she wondered how she would ever find it within herself to leave this place. She did not have much choice, however. She knew that, being the genius he was, Erik would find a way for her to get back home in no time. Soon, her days here would be over.

Suddenly, her eyes fell on the little corridor off the kitchen through which Omid always entered and a smile lit on her lips. *Soon* her days here would be over, she thought. *But not yet!* She scrambled out of Erik's chair and dashed back into her room. She donned the extra cloak Erik always had her wear for their travels in the opera house and pulled the hood over her hair. When she was satisfied that she looked every bit the ghost that Erik did, she made her way to the passage that she had traveled with Omid the day she accompanied him to the market.

She recalled the winding route that they had taken through back ways of the opera house and was confident that she could find the offshoot that would lead her to Box 5. There she was certain she would find Erik enjoying the morning's practice. Oh, he would be angry with her—she was sure—but she could also imagine the glimmer of respect in his eyes when he realized she'd navigated the treacherous tunnels alone, always mindful to sidestep the traps and hazards he set for intruders. Most importantly, she would be *with* him, and not wasting a moment of their precious two weeks alone.

The tunnel was dark, and steep, and with its rough stone walls and uneven, earthen floor, it was certainly a harsher way to travel than crossing the lake in his boat. Jenna snickered to herself when she thought that perhaps that was why Erik had taught this particular route to Omid! It did require some extra care to avoid the pitfalls that could befall a less observant traveler, but she was cautious to hold to the left side of the tunnel and lift her skirts a bit with her fingers, so that they would not be snagged on the snares Erik had planted.

She had just ascended into the first cellar passages, still so wholly focused on evading Erik's perils, that she was entirely taken by surprise when a slurred voice uttered, “So, Ghost, we are finally face to face.”

With a gasp, she looked up in horror to find a dirty, middle-aged man jeering at her. He was shorter than Erik, but still taller than her, with a round, paunchy middle and stubble covered jowl. His head was mostly bald, with the thin wisps of hair he still possessed floating around his head in a mousy gray cloud. He stank of whiskey and filth, and Jenna found herself naturally backing away. “Who are you?” she asked.

“Me?” he let out a disturbing chortle. “I'm no one. Just good ol', *good for nothing,* Buquet.” He beamed a toothless grin at her as he took a step closer. “And you're not a ghost,” he said in something akin to wonder. “You're a *girl*.”

"Stay away," she said, putting her hands out in front of her and taking a few more steps back. "I may not be the ghost, but I *know* him, and he would not want you here."

"But he wants *you* here?" A wolfish gleam entered Buquet's eyes as he continued to advance on her. Though his steps were unsteady with drink, his gaze was determined. He enjoyed having the upper hand on the ghost, and was looking forward to taking something from the specter that had already taken so much from him. "I didn't know the Phantom had himself a *woman*."

"It's not like that," she blurted, continuing her retreat.

"'Course it is. The Opera Ghost would never let a girl stay with him if he didn't *want* her." Buquet reached out to touch a grimy, gnarled finger to her flinching cheek. "And how could he not want such a *pretty* girl?"

Jenna recoiled from his touch as she spat, "Don't touch me!"

With more speed than she would have expected, Buquet leaned forward and grabbed both her arms with his thick, fleshy hands. "I bet you let the ghost touch you," he leered over her. "I bet you let him touch you *real* good."

"*No*," she whimpered, as she pulled away from his grasp, and setting him momentarily off balance. She turned to run back down the tunnel. Blinded by fear, and twisting to peer over her shoulder, it was much more difficult to be mindful of Erik's traps, and she soon found herself tumbling to the unforgiving ground after a wire caught her ankle. She landed hard on her knees, her hands splayed out before her.

"Oh, this is going to be *real* fun," purred Buquet, who had caught up to her. He began to loosen the belt that held up his filthy trousers. "A spirited wench who's already on her knees."

She tried to scramble away on her pulverized knees, but his hands were on her hips too fast. Never before had she wished so fervently for the little can of pepper spray she would carry on her key chain at home. One squirt of that, and a good swift kick to a very strategic spot, and it would be lights out for this brute. *Oh God*, she thought to herself *why didn't I just wait for Erik to come home?* She'd thought herself so careful, so clever, and yet, she had fallen prey to an attacker. The cold realization hit her that nobody knew where she was, and nobody would hear her scream. Help wasn't coming. She was going to have to take care of herself.

She shifted her weight to one arm, thinking to elbow him in the gut and take his breath away, but before she did, she suddenly felt his nauseating form being lifted from her. At the sound of a gurgling scream, she turned, to see Buquet struggling against the catgut lasso around his neck, as Erik loomed menacingly behind him. "You *scream*, Buquet?" Erik seethed through clenched teeth. "You were about to abuse an innocent woman and *you* scream when you are caught?" He twisted the noose in his hand, tightening its hold on Buquet's neck even more. "I should have done this long ago, you pig," Erik spat as Buquet strained and twisted in his efforts against the lasso. But it was no use. "Your lifeless carcass will be a boon to the opera house," Erik growled as Jenna saw him begin to pull his hand upwards, yanking on the lasso, intent on extinguishing Buquet's miserable life.

"*STOP*!" she shouted, clambering to her feet, ignoring her screaming knees and ankle so she could stand closer to Erik's great height.

Erik paused, looking at her. "Why? He was about to *violate* you, Jenna!" he bellowed. "*Why* does he deserve to live?"

"He doesn't!" she implored him, "But *you* do." She saw Erik's expression become quizzical as she continued to explain herself. "He is a piece of subhuman excrement that doesn't deserve the life that still runs through his veins. But *you* are no longer the type of man who would take it from him." She reached out and put a hand on his forearm that was taught with the desire to squeeze the breath out of Buquet's lungs. "You've come so far," she continued, in a softer tone. "I don't care about him. But please, don't do this to *yourself*."

He looked into her pleading eyes a moment longer before gently nudging her hold loose. Without warning, he dropped Buquet hard to the floor. Bending over him menacingly, he seethed. "You should thank the lady for your miserable life, because I would have gladly relieved you of it. But know this, Joseph Buquet. If you *ever* lay a hand on her again, if you ever look at her, or so much as dare to allow her memory to play across your mind, there will be *nothing* and no one that can save you from me. Go now, Joseph Buquet. Go now and leave this place."

The terrified former stagehand scrambled to his feet, scurrying away from them as fast as his inebriated legs would carry him. Once he was entirely out of view, Erik turned to her with wounded eyes and uttered a single, heart wrenchingly confused word. "Why?"

At that moment, the passageway began to swim around her, as the pain shot through her head once again. Her last coherent thought, before the world went black, was that she was grateful to feel Erik's arms closing around her before she could hit the ground.

31 MISSING YOU

"Erik, *stop* it!" Jenna protested, as she felt him lift her out of the boat. She remembered blacking out in the tunnel, and waking up, some time later, to steady rocking beneath her as they glided across the lake to Erik's home. Erik was, of course, steering the boat, but he would not answer her when she called out to him. "You can put me down now. I'm *FINE!*"

"I seem to remember hearing those words before, Mademoiselle." Erik made his first response to her in a clipped tone, slinging her over his shoulder. "I regret believing them then. I will not repeat that mistake."

"Erik!" she yelled, outraged at the indignity of being treated like a sack of potatoes. "Put me down this instant!"

Erik quickly closed the distance to the sitting room and dumped her unceremoniously on the floor, the Persian rug softening the worst of her fall. "As you wish, Mademoiselle," he seethed, stalking off in the direction of the piano.

"Oh great," she called after him as she rose to a standing position, smoothing her skirts and blowing an errant strand of hair away from her eyes. "Are we back to Mademoiselle?"

She heard the beginnings of a wild concerto in answer to her question.

"Of course we are!" she spat, storming over to him, her voice rising with her annoyance, "You *always* call me Mademoiselle when you're angry with me! It's your favorite trick for pushing me away!"

"Should I *not* be angry with you, *Mademoiselle*?" he questioned, his fingers never stopping their furious dance on the ivories. "After what you did?"

Even though she knew to what he was referring, she was angry enough to want to hear him say it. "What are you talking about, Erik?

The sin of taking a walk? I was not under the impression that I was a *prisoner* here."

For the first time, Jenna thought she heard him play a sour note, and she noticed the look of frustration on his face grow darker. "Have I never told you, Jenna, that the tunnels are dangerous? That there are scores of traps and perils laid specifically by me for the purpose of ensnaring intruders who happen to wander in?"

"I didn't realize you still thought of me as an intruder!" she snapped purposely being obtuse in her annoyance with him.

"I *do not*!" he retorted, "but if you wander the tunnels alone, you are just as vulnerable as if you *were*."

"But I *wasn't* vulnerable!" she insisted, trying to plead her case. "I made it all the way to the first cellar, traveling the passages myself, keeping a watchful eye for your pitfalls and hazards, veering to the left always—as *you* taught me. I wore the black cloak and pulled the hood over my hair, so as to blend into the shadows, and I moved quietly, so as not to draw attention."

"And yet," he snapped, at last abandoning the piano to glare at the true target of his ire. "You *did* draw attention, didn't you? Of the worst kind!"

Jenna balked as she remembered Buquet. "*That* I did not expect," she admitted, her voice faltering a bit as she recalled how close she had come to real harm.

"But still, the danger found you," Erik reminded her, as if she could forget. "Why is it that you were in the tunnels anyway, Jenna?" he demanded, with a tone of great frustration.

"Erik, I just…" She paused and took a deep breath. "When I woke up, I wanted to see you. But you weren't here."

"Well, of course not," he answered incredulously. "You *told* me to go! You basically said you could not rest with me here, and you wanted me gone."

"Oh Erik," she shook her head, "I didn't mean it that way."

"But, that's what you said!" he shouted in exasperation. Raking his fingers through his hair, he asked, "*Why* did you need to see me so urgently, that you elected to risk your life by traversing booby trapped tunnels unaided?"

"I *missed* you!" she blurted out, before thinking. When she saw the shock that lit his features, she added, in a smaller voice, "I woke up feeling much better, but I found that I was lonely without you." She looked down sheepishly before telling him, "I decided to make my own way to Box 5 to surprise you."

After a moment of tense quiet, Erik responded in a dark tone, "It is never a good idea to surprise the opera ghost, Mademoiselle."

Jenna looked up, surprised that his tone remained so icy. "Erik, I don't understand why you are still so angry with me. I told you, I only went out on my own because I *missed* you. I wanted to be *with* you."

"Well you have an interesting way of showing it!" He shot back at her, feeling his fury rise once more.

"Erik?" she asked in confusion.

"You push me out of my own house, refusing my offer to stay and care for you, but then you want to *be* with me?" he ranted, beginning to feel his hands tremble.

"But Erik, you had to get to rehearsals…"

"You cause me to feel as if I should not even consider venturing back to my own home, for fear of disturbing you," He rose from the piano to a standing position, "but *you* go traipsing around places I had *warned* you about because you wanted to surprise me?"

"Erik, I told you…"

"That you *missed* me," he hissed, his eyes glowing in their rage. "Last week, you were ready to leave here and forget all about me, bidding *me* to forget all about *you.* But this afternoon, after being alone for just a short time," his voice grew to a roar, "you put your life at risk because you *MISSED* me?"

"Yes!" she cried, too alarmed by his anger to say anything else.

"*Why*?" he demanded in painful confusion. "Why ever would you *miss* me?"

"Because, Erik I…" she trailed off, unable to give voice to the feelings in her heart, knowing they would simply complicate the situation in which they found themselves.

"Oh, please don't stop on account of me!" they both heard, from the corridor off the kitchen, as Omid walked in with a cheery smile on his face, munching on one of Erik's apples. "I know I'm interrupting *something.* From all the yelling echoing about in the tunnels, it sounded like it was something really good, and I would hate to miss it!"

"Ah, Daroga!" Erik called, turning his face from Jenna. "For once I find your arrival rather fortuitous!"

Omid's brow knotted as he looked at his masked friend in

concern. "Are you quite alright, Erik?"

"Yes. But I have somewhere I need to go, and it appears my houseguest needs some *minding*." Jenna opened her mouth to protest but before she could, Erik added. "Do *not* let her step one foot out of this house, Daroga. If she tries, tie her up." He threw the shocked Persian the length of rope that he always carried in a pocket in his cloak. "And if she says anything about *missing* me and needing to *see* me," he added, glaring straight into Jenna's eyes, "don't believe her!" With that, Erik grabbed a stack of papers from the piano bench and stalked back over to his boat, heading to his lesson with Christine, trying to put the afternoon, and his infuriating houseguest, behind him!

❧

As the new prima donna, Christine now found herself in possession of Carlotta's former dressing room. She was slowly transforming it from the pigsty Carlotta had maintained into a respectable respite from the grueling schedule of the stage. As such, Erik had decided to move her lessons to this room, as it afforded more comfort and privacy than the small, cold chapel.

Erik stalked back and forth behind her wall. His hasty departure from his home had placed him at the mirror about a quarter of an hour before their lessons were to begin—which worked to his advantage, when he slipped inside to deposit the new sheet music onto her dressing table. He'd returned to his hiding spot, expecting Christine to arrive posthaste. However, now it was about fifteen minutes past when their lessons were to begin, and the irritation Erik had tried so hard to quell on his journey from his lair was now coursing through his veins with renewed vengeance. Was his time so undervalued by his youthful student that she saw fit to waste it?

The door to the dressing room opened and Christine burst in, a bundle of energy. "Angel, are you here?" she called, looking up and around the room before closing the door behind her.

"I have *been* here, Christine." he answered, his celestial tones somewhat cold. "Where have *you* been?"

Christine smiled and said, "Oh, forgive me for being late, Angel. The managers kept us past the hour. They had a grand announcement to make," she informed him excitedly.

Erik rolled his eyes, wondering what bumbling managerial decision he was going to have to clean up this time. "Oh *what*, pray tell, was their announcement?" he asked, his angel's voice still sounding somewhat perturbed.

Christine practically gushed. "They are holding a grand masquerade ball after the first performance, to celebrate opening night!"

"I see," Erik commented shortly, expecting that that would be the end of the topic. But to his great annoyance, Christine continued to prattle on.

"Oh, Angel, it is going to be such fun. There will be a grand banquet and champagne! And everyone will be in a mask! And there will be dancing!" Christine began sashaying across the floor, as if in an imaginary waltz. "I may not even know who I will be dancing with!" Christine seemed to realize something, and as if in surprise, she added, "Perhaps the Vicomte! Meg says he is very handsome indeed."

Erik felt his lip snarl. He had had quite enough of her drivel about this dance! "Christine," he began, cutting in and trying to redirect the lesson to singing.

"Or perhaps," she continued, her voice softening a bit in shyness, "you?"

"Christine!" Erik responded to her unexpected comment curtly. "I am an angel. You know I cannot dance with you."

Christine cast her eyes down in equal parts embarrassment and disappointment. "I understand, my Angel. I just… there is no one I would wish to dance with more…"

"Oh, but you *did* say the Vicomte was very handsome indeed," he interjected in irritation. "I am sure you would *most* prefer to dance with him. Of course," he continued scathingly, once again trying to focus her wandering mind to the task at hand, "as a future prima donna, all of your energies should be directed toward song—not dance."

"Yes, Angel." she hung her head in shame.

"Now then," he began fresh, "On your vanity, you will find a new aria. I shall inform the managers that you will be singing it on opening night. I would like to work on it with you now."

Christine crossed over to her dressing table, where indeed, she found the score. She read it over quickly, the disappointment over her Angel's scolding beginning to fade as she heard the resplendent melody in her mind. "Angel, this is glorious."

"Thank you Christine." Erik dismissed her praise quickly. "Now, shall we begin? I will count two measures and you come in on one."

Christine listened as her Angel set the beat, and, at the appointed time, came in with the lilting melody, sweet and pure. She sang the first verse through, the joy of the tune pouring from her lips, before Erik stopped her, saying, "Expression, Christine. Sing with more emotion."

Surprised, Christine simply said, "I'm sorry, Angel. Shall I begin again?"

"Yes, please."

When Christine began the song with the same amount of *joie de vivre* as she had the last time, Erik stopped her immediately. "Christine, *think* about the words," he commanded, impatience beginning to color his tone. "Make the song come alive."

"I had hoped I was, Angel," she said, a bit dejected. "I am singing of the sweet love affair that the singer is remembering—of the joy and happiness she felt during the time spent in her lover's presence."

"You are looking at it all wrong, Christine," he admonished in exasperation. "This song is not about the joyful carefree feelings of a love affair. It is about the desperate wish that the lover has that he be remembered when love is lost."

"But Angel," Christine responded, confused. "The music is so light—so airy…"

"It is irony, Mademoiselle," Erik insisted, in a huff. "It belies the absolute despair the lover feels at the apparently doomed relationship. He knows they must part, and yet he knows he will never forget her. He is begging her to promise she will not forget him either, so that they can at least be united in their memories, together in their hearts."

"Angel," Christine began quietly, a bit unnerved by the frantic way in which her angel was speaking. His voice was not its usual rich, booming baritone, but rather a desperate, frenzied jumble of syllables, that for a celestial being, did not make any sense. She did not understand the change in him, and she was about to tell him. "I don't understand…"

"Have you *never* lost someone, Christine," Erik blurted out, his voice now a hoarse bark, "who meant the entire world to you?"

The raw emotion in his voice caught them both by surprise, and each stood breathless, motionless for a moment, until Christine made her simple, quiet reply. "My Papa."

Erik felt a thousand blades pierce his heart at the recognition of his complete idiocy. "Christine, forgive me," he implored. "Please forgive me. I am so sorry. I was uncouth, and rude, and I apologize."

Christine looked down at the floor, "Angel, you do not seem quite yourself today."

Erik closed his eyes and shook his head. "No, I suppose I am not quite *feeling* myself today, my dear."

"But…" she looked up in confusion, to the spirit she believed was with her in the room. "You are an angel…"

"Even angels can sometimes bruise their wings," Erik sighed. "Christine, you sang beautifully. You always do. I may have brought this music to you, but as the prima donna, *you* have to bring it to life—in whichever way *you* see fit. We shall work on it more tomorrow, when I promise, I shall be my usual, angelic self. But for now, I think it best I should take my leave."

"Alright, Angel." Christine said again, still sounding so unsure.

Erik's heart hurt at the sadness he now saw in Christine's eyes. It reminded him of another pair of sad eyes that were also his doing. "Christine," he whispered, his voice taking on that supernatural, shimmery tone for the first time that night, "I will be with you at the ball. I will be watching over you. I am always watching over you."

Once again, he saw Christine's eyes glimmer, for the first time since his insensitivity had doused her inner flame. "Thank you my Angel!" she said, with a smile.

"Goodnight, my dear," Erik whispered, as he soundlessly closed the panel behind the mirror, and began his journey back home. He had more amends to make and another pair of eyes to brighten.

❧

The hour was late, and there was no light on in Jenna's room, except for the soft glow of the bedside reading lamp that made her niece's hair glisten like copper. Penny gazed into the window and watched as the young doctor held her hand between both of his. She knew his shift had ended long ago, but still he sat here, keeping Jenna company, making sure she was not alone. Blaine had taken her out hours ago for a movie and a quick dinner. They had then spent some time in her hotel room, she was not proud to admit, before he left for his apartment, claiming an early shift at the hospital the next morning. That was when she had gotten the urge to go visit Jenna. She had spent hours being entertained and romanced, and all that time, *he* had been here, with her niece, holding her hand.

She knew he did not agree with the treatment she had insisted upon for her Jenna. She knew he felt it was actually holding her back. He was getting nothing from Jenna any longer—no squeezes, no smiles. And yet, his resolve never faltered. His heart remained true. She was humbled that her niece inspired such devotion in the young physician. She quietly opened the door to tell him so, when she realized he was speaking. Silently, she stood by the door, listening as the young man poured out his heart to a love who was not listening.

"Jenna forgive me, please forgive me," he whispered, with red rimmed eyes. "I did everything I could for you, but it seems to all be for nothing. Charleson has won—he got what he wanted. I don't even know why he wanted it, but he got it, and *I*—" he paused, taking a deep breath "—and *you*—got nothing."

He bowed his head low and shook it back and forth a few times before continuing. "God, I wish I had told you, Jenna, how my head turned every time you walked in a room—how my heart leapt whenever I would catch you smile. You were so beautiful, so vibrant. And I was so socially backward that I couldn't talk to you. I just didn't know what to say. But now, if I had the chance, I would tell you, Jenna. I would tell you how beautifully your hair shines in the lamplight, and how the fire in your eyes drives me wild. I would tell you that your laugh sounds like music, and that the skin on your hand feels like the softest silk. I would not be like the other guys, Jenna. I would proudly take you out to plays, or fancy dinners. I would feed your cat," he chuckled softly, "I *do* feed your cat."

He reached one hand forward and smoothed the hair on her brow. "And at night, I would hold you. And whisper sweet promises in your ear that I'd have every intention of keeping when the daylight came. I would kiss you and caress you and never let you go.

"And I know if you are hearing this, it is not what you are used to hearing from me. I like to keep it light, keep it funny, to make you feel like you have something to come back to. But Jenna, tonight I want to *tell* you exactly what you have to come back to. Me. Please come back for me, Jenna. I love you. And I just want you to give me a chance to *show* you how much. Please come back to me, Jenna. *Please*, come back."

Penny saw the doctor lean forward and place his forehead against Jenna's, his back trembling slightly in what she assumed were quiet tears. She shut the door soundlessly and leaned back against it for support. She pulled a handkerchief out of her purse, using it to wipe away the tears that had sprung up in her own eyes. Oh that poor man!

When she had come here, she had not seen her niece for so many years that she had barely recognized her. But she had immediately started making decisions for her, as if she had any real right. For so long, she had been an aunt to her niece in name only, and even now, when her deceased sister's only daughter lay motionless in a hospital bed, she had allowed herself to be wined and dined into having a meaningless affair with one of her *doctors*, while the other one had kept a sad, lonely vigil at her bedside. What was she *doing* to this poor man? What was she doing to her niece?

Penny dabbed at her eyes again with the cloth. She had had enough. Tomorrow she was telling Blaine that it all had to stop. The medication had to stop. Their relationship had to stop. And she needed to start focusing her attention on her niece and this poor, sweet doctor who was so selflessly in love with her.

Omid witnessed Jenna stare in the direction that Erik's boat had gone. Long after it was out of view, still she stared, almost as if she thought somehow that her unbroken gaze would magically bring the vessel home, and turn back time to before whatever had happened between them to make Erik so irate. Finally, she crossed the room, and slumped down despondently on Erik's reading chair—and Omid could have sworn he'd seen her take a deep sniff of the leather, before tears began to well in her eyes.

"Jenna," Omid asked gently, closing the distance between them and kneeling down on the floor in front of her. "What's wrong?"

"This is not the way this day was supposed to have gone, Omid." Jenna told him sadly, shaking her head and holding her hands up in a gesture of defeat. "I just don't understand him."

"Erik?" He asked, as if to clarify. "Nobody understands Erik. You just have to learn to survive him. Your best bet is to smile and nod and drink lots of whiskey," he quipped, trying to lighten the mood. And though a thin smile played upon her lips, the tears that had gathered in her eyes began to fall, and Omid found himself at a loss for ways to help this sweet young girl who was now crying for his friend. "Tell me, Jenna," he'd urged, taking one of her hands in his. "What happened?"

"I only wanted to *be* with him, Omid," she sniffed, shaking her head back and forth. "I only wanted to *be* with him." When the Persian still gazed up at her, confusion coloring his face, Jenna heaved a deep sigh and launched into her tale, recounting her sickness in the morning, and her misguided decision that led to the disaster of the afternoon.

As Omid listened to her describe the frustrating, and at times horrifying, events of the day, he was struck by the bond that had developed between this surprise visitor and his extremely antisocial friend. Erik had allowed her to become a part of his daily routine and Omid marveled at the actual *partnership* that seemed to have been forged between the two. Though Erik *had* taught him the way down to the lair, it had only come after years of acquaintance and shared adversity—*and* grudgingly at that. Erik had never allowed Omid to accompany him on any of his jaunts in the opera house, and yet, Jenna had become his constant companion—so much so that he had even been willing to forego hearing Christine in rehearsals in favor of staying back and caring for Jenna. Did *neither* of them recognize the significance of that fact? Were they *both* really so blind to what was right in front of them? While each of them, in their own way, had been so focused on Erik's relationship with Christine, their own relationship had blossomed into something strange and new—something that could be wonderful if they would only let it.

When Jenna's story had drawn to a close, she gazed off into the fire, and tears wet her lashes anew. "He didn't believe me, Omid," she whimpered in a soft voice, her eyes still locked on the fire, which held memories of such tenderness between them. "When I told him I missed him. Why didn't he believe me?"

Again, Omid was wonderstruck that, after all the events of her harrowing day, including the near brutalization by Buquet, the fact that Erik didn't believe her was the thing that upset her the most. He squeezed the hand he still held in his own and very gently asked, "Jenna, why did you make him leave to go to rehearsal?"

"Because, Omid," she sighed, as if the reason was the most obvious one in the world, "he would not have been very pleased with me if he had missed Christine sing."

"Jenna," Omid corrected her kindly, "he was *choosing* to forgo hearing Christine sing, because he wanted to stay and care for *you*. You were not preventing him from going. He was putting you first."

Jenna stared at Omid in silence for a few moments. "He chose me…" she whispered finally, comprehension slowly lighting her eyes. When Omid simply smiled and nodded, Jenna continued, "And I pushed him away. That's why he was so angry when I told him I missed him."

"Those words would be hard for him to believe under the best of circumstances, my dear," Omid confirmed. "But after the tensions of the morning and afternoon, I believe he just snapped. He was trying to do what you wanted, by leaving, but if I know Erik, he probably feels as if he was somehow to blame for the danger that befell you *because* he was not there."

The sorrow that now contorted the young girl's face was almost too much for Omid to bear. "Now, now, Jenna," Omid patted the hand he was holding with his other hand. "Just give him time. He will come around."

It was at that moment that a shadow fell over the room, and Jenna and Omid both looked up to see Erik standing tall at the edge of the rug, taking in the scene before him. His gaze was locked on Jenna's from the moment their eyes met, and Omid was barely an afterthought as he commanded, "Daroga, leave us."

Omid turned back to Jenna, squeezing her hand once more and asking "Are you alright?"

"I am, Omid," she nodded, never shifting her gaze from Erik's as she murmured, "Thank you. You should go."

Omid rose from the floor, and with a gentle pat to Jenna's back, he crossed to the passage by the kitchen from which he could take his leave.

Jenna stood, when they were alone, and they stared into each other's eyes for a silent moment more. Then, all at once, they closed the distance between them, and with hands clasped, each in the other's, they both spilled apologies for their thoughtless actions and begged each other's forgiveness.

"I'm sorry—"

"I'm so sorry—"

"Forgive me for my rudeness—"

"Forgive me for my stupidity—"

"Jenna…" he whispered, and her heart flopped in her chest. His eyes said so much more as he guided her over to the settee and sat down beside her, never letting go of her hands. "Jenna I was wrong for being so angry."

"No, Erik," she interrupted. "I understand. I never should have traversed the tunnels without you. It was thoughtless. It was stupid…"

"It was *dangerous,* Jenna. *So* dangerous, and I…" Erik paused, realizing that with his next words he would be exposing a part of himself that he had never before revealed to another person. But just as with his past—just as with his face—he *trusted* her to understand. With a deep breath, and a shaky voice, he admitted, "I was so afraid."

"Afraid, Erik?" she looked at him quizzically.

"*Afraid,*" he said again, admitting a vulnerability he himself had only recently realized he possessed. "When I saw Buquet, with his filthy hands all over you, I wanted blood, Jenna. I was *going* to kill him—I was going to return to my murderous ways."

"But you didn't," Jenna was quick to point out.

"But I *would* have, Jenna. Because at that moment, through the rage, through the bloodlust, I was so *afraid.*" He paused slightly, his eyes entreating her to understand before he continued. "Of losing *you.*"

Jenna just stared at him, dumbstruck, at that declaration. "Oh, Erik," she whispered when she once again found the breath to speak.

"Jenna, if anything had happened…" he continued, and to her horror, Jenna saw that he was shaking. "I would never have forgiven myself."

So it *was* as Omid said. Erik blamed himself for her carelessness. "Shhhhh, Erik," she whispered, as she freed one of her hands from his and used it to cup his cheek. "I'm here. I'm still here."

"I am not ready, Jenna," he looked at her, his eyes dark with emotions that he could not yet articulate. "I'm not ready to let you go."

"You don't have to, Erik," she murmured, pulling him close as he rested his head on her shoulder. “I'm here,” she assured him, stroking her fingers through his hair. “I'm still here.”

Neither knew how long they sat there, the comforts of each other’s arms chasing away the demons of the day. They had not lost each other, as they each had feared. But in the back of both of their minds was the knowledge that one day—one day soon—they would. And that made their mutual *need* to be together seem so much more urgent.

After a time, when she felt Erik's heartbeat calm and his breathing return to normal, Jenna asked him, “So, how did your lesson go?”Erik sighed and pulled a bit away from her, but his eyes looked much more relaxed as he said, “In truth, it was not the most productive lesson, Jenna. I was not in the best of spirits, and I argued with Christine about the interpretation of a new aria I wrote.”

Jenna chuckled at him and teased, “Well it's nice to see you are a ray of sunshine wherever you go today, Erik.”

He rolled his eyes at her and smirked. “It hardly mattered, *Mademoiselle!*” he said, using the formal title in jest this time, instead of in anger. “Christine was far too distracted by the ball that the managers are holding in honor of opening night.”

“A ball?” she asked.

“Yes, a masquerade ball,” he informed, as if the matter bored him. “To be held immediately following the first performance. She actually asked me if I would attend.”

“And what did you say?” Jenna asked in excitement.

“I told her that Angels did not dance!” He huffed.

“Oh Erik!” Jenna sighed. “Angels may not dance, but men do. You *should* go. It would be the perfect opportunity to introduce yourself to Christine as a man. And since you wear a mask all the time, you would be in your element.”

Erik groaned, “Can we please not discuss this tonight, Jenna? I just want us to enjoy a quiet evening. Maybe reading by the fire? Perhaps later I could make us some tea.”

Jenna smiled and remembered Omid's words from earlier, about Erik having wanted to put her first. For now, she would let him. “I guess I should go make dinner,” she said, as she rose from the settee and began to make her way to the kitchen. When she was almost there, she turned to him and called, “Erik I really *did* miss you this morning.”

He looked up at her with a shy smile. “I missed you too Jenna. I missed you too.”

❧

Omid moved quickly from his hiding place behind the wall when he saw Jenna approach the kitchen. Oh these two fools! They were so in love with each other that their feelings were almost a palpable thing. And yet, he was beginning to believe they would truly never figure it out. They hemmed and hawed, and actually looked for obstacles to set in the way of their love instead of trying to find ways to be together. They would forever be lonely and pining for one another at this rate!

Without *his* help, that was. As he traversed the tunnels of the opera house to the streets that would lead him to his home, Omid was hatching a plan. It might just light a fire under the feet of those two nincompoops who were both so smart about many things, but so blind when it came to the one thing that truly mattered: their love for one another.

32 A DANCE WITH AN ANGEL

"Ahh, good morning, beautiful," Charleson said, rising from his café table when he saw Penny walk into the room. He had been enjoying a cup of coffee while waiting for her to join him. She'd called late last night and said she had some things she'd wanted to discuss. He'd offered to come by her hotel room, knowing that their discussions could be so much more productive—at least for him—in bed. But she had declined, saying she'd rather meet for breakfast. So here he stood, in the hospital coffee shop, kissing her cheek as he ushered her into her seat. She did not display the blush that usually appeared whenever he showed her some affection, and he noted that with a bit of concern.

His time with Penny was certainly not a love connection. The somewhat pleasant dalliance had, however, led to great advances to his cause of being named as Jenna Wilson's primary physician, which allowed him to try the drug therapy on her. If she had responded positively, his name would have been published in the leading medical journals, since treating coma cases with drugs was still new therapeutic ground. Of course, she had shown no improvement, and perhaps—if he were honest—*did* back-pedal a little. Still the experiment had been worth it, if for no other reason than the sheer pleasure he derived from watching that fool first year resident squirm.

He remembered him from Med School—always so quiet, always so studious; rarely with his nose out of a book. He had been completely oblivious to the attentions the female students showered on him, always preferring to spend Saturday night with his studies, never participating in the parties or other social occasions that were a natural part of dorm life. Blaine had been in a few seminars with him, and though he was brilliant, Blaine had never understood his backwardness and considered him to be a waste of his time. That was, until Cynthia took note of him.

Blaine had had his share of women during his Med School tenure. He was often with another girl every Friday or Saturday night. He did the work required, and he made the grades, but he also intended to have a little fun—because you're only young once, right?

But that was before he met Cynthia. Long raven hair, and stunning gray eyes, Cynthia was a beauty like he had never seen before. He was immediately smitten and tried to get to know her, thinking it might finally be time to settle down with one girl for a while. They had a few dates—movies, lunch—but Cynthia never seemed as smitten with him as he was with her. When he finally realized the reason why, he couldn't believe it. While he was crazy over Cynthia, Cynthia was falling head over heels for the bookworm! And apparently, she was enough to finally make *him* take note that he was a guy, because they started dating.

After that, Blaine had not stopped trying to woo her away from him. He insinuated himself into her study group, and made sure to be named as her lab partner. He would sometimes meet her after class, or walk her back to her dorm after late lectures. He pulled out all the "friend" stops with her, but he had not been able to sway her away from the lame underclassman. One night, Blaine even got drunk, and went over to her dorm room with the excuse of having a research question, and forced a kiss on her lips. Of course, that was when Dr. Loser had shown up and pulled him off of her punching him in the nose. Cynthia and Dr. Loser lasted until graduation—when she left the country after being recruited by Doctors Without Borders. Funny, Blaine had always pegged *him* to be the one who would run off and join a philanthropist cause. But no, lucky for Blaine, a year after he had started his own residency with the hospital, Dr. Loser had shown up. And it had only recently begun to get interesting.

With Jenna Wilson's case, even if the treatment had not worked, he had still won. He had seen something his colleague had wanted so desperately—as much as he himself had wanted Cynthia—and had taken it for himself. And if he had ruined it a little along the way, at this point, he honestly didn't care. Most coma patients never woke up anyway.

"Good morning, Blaine," Penny responded, calling him back from his memories. He had to make a point to be attentive to her because it was only by keeping her clueless that this arrangement could possibly work.

"And how are you this morning?" he asked with an alluring smile. "After our *very* good night?" he reached out across the table and stroked the palm of her hand.

Penny looked down at the table and pulled her hand away, using it to smooth out the cloth napkin that was in front of her. "Quite frankly, Blaine, I'm not that good."

"Oh?" he plastered a look of concern on his face. "And why is that, my sweet?"

She cleared her throat and looked up at him. "Because of Jenna. Last night, after you left, I went over to the hospital to see her."

Blaine let out a husky chuckle, "Really darling? I thought for sure I had tired you out!"

"When I got there," she continued, not letting his innuendos sway her purpose. "It struck me that she has made no more progress on the drugs than she had before you started giving them to her."

"Well, Penny," he said, trying to keep his tone soothing. "These things take time."

"You said they wouldn't take this much time," she countered. "Blaine, I think I would like you to take her off the drugs. I think I'd like to go back and try the sensory therapy her other doctor was trying on her. At least he seemed to be having some small measure of success."

Blaine looked at her, his eyes growing cold. *Again!* That thorn in his side was doing it again! Interfering with his plans—getting in the way. "I see," he said simply to Penny's statement. "Is there any way I could persuade you to keep trying the medication?"

"No," Penny said, looking him square in the eye.

"Well," he said, removing the napkin from his lap and tossing some money down on the table, "I suppose I need to go write some orders." He pushed back his chair and rose from the table.

"Blaine," Penny called out to him.

"What is it?" he asked, looking very put out.

"This means we're finished as well."

As if there would be any reason for him to continue banging a middle-aged woman now! "I understand, Ms. Wilson," he responded, moving away to take his leave. "Enjoy your breakfast."

❧

Erik reached out his hand to help Jenna from the boat. It had been a long morning and afternoon of rehearsals, with only a quick jaunt to the pantries around lunchtime for a bite to eat. Though Jenna had awoken again with one of her headaches, she had not felt dizzy, and nothing would have caused her to leave Erik's side today. Her need for rest had proven disastrous yesterday, and she truly felt the best thing for her was to stay close to Erik at all times. Conveniently, he agreed with her diagnosis, having begun her treatment the night before with a quick dinner and a quiet night of reading and tea drinking in the parlor. He had not occupied his usual reading chair, but had joined her on the settee, and they had each enjoyed that arrangement just fine.

Today, he seemed to stick closer to her in the tunnels, even lifting her over a few of the obstacles she could easily have side stepped on her own, and he moved his seat a little nearer to hers in Box 5. Every now and then she had felt his fingers brush her hand, and they would glance at each other and smile, and blush, and go back to watching the rehearsals, contact broken. But the last time it happened, his fingers actually curled around her hand and lingered. She looked up at him, but his eyes remained steadfast on the stage. She did detect the hint of a blush in his cheek, though, so she followed his lead and looked back at the players. But her fingers circled his palm as well.

So now, when she grasped his hand to step out of the vessel, she did not immediately release it, and as he made no move to take it back, they walked hand in hand into the lair, two specters all in black, their capes billowing and swishing behind them.

"What in the bloody hell?" Erik blurted as the sitting room came into view.

His expertly appointed sitting room, in which the furnishings had arranged placed exactly as Erik wanted them, had been ransacked! Raided! Utterly destroyed. His beloved reading chair had been pushed to the far side of the room and now resided practically in the bookshelf. The settee remained, but it was much farther back from the fire, and cushions and blankets had been set out on the floor before it. The Persian rug had been rolled up and was stowed in a corner, out of the way, so that the floor between the settee and the hearth was laid bare. Myriad blooms were scattered about, some in vases placed on the floor, others woven into the arms of the candelabras. At the forefront of the room was his small dining table, elegantly set for two with a pair of silver plate covers arranged across from one another, and a lit candelabra in the center, red rose petals strewn about the cloth. Next to the table was an ice bucket on a stand, and in it were two bottles of the finest Parisian wine, one red, one white. Affixed to the side of it, was a note written on heavy parchment.

Enjoy this elegant feast and dance floor in preparation for the upcoming masquerade ball. (I cooked, I cleaned, but I assumed Erik would have the masks covered.) – Omid

P.S.: Don't ruin it, Erik.

"I really *am* going to have to kill him now," Erik growled as he read the note a second time.

Jenna smiled, amused by Erik's grumpy reaction to Omid's efforts. She had been planning all along to try and discuss the masquerade ball over dinner with Erik tonight, and it's almost as if Omid somehow *knew*.

"Well before you do," Jenna joked, "let's eat. After all, murder requires strength."

Erik looked at the plates laid out on the table with disgust. "If he cooked, he probably poisoned it."

"No, Erik," she teased. "That's *you* you're thinking of."

"Great idea!" he retorted. "Let's invite him over for dinner."

"Oh, if you were to willingly invite him into your home, he would *suspect* that some scheme was afoot."

"You're right," he admitted, lost in thought. "Better idea," he said, holding one finger up. "I'm going to poison the Cognac!"

"Erik!" Jenna laughed despite herself at what she hoped was simply his dark humor. "I'm hungry." She removed her cloak, laying it across the back of his reading chair and moved over to the table. "Let's eat."

Erik looked up at her and saw her, for the first time that day, without the cloak obscuring her figure. What he saw took his breath away. Jenna had chosen a coral and black ruffled frock that he vaguely remembered snagging from the costumery. However, though he had seen the dress before, he had *not* seen it on her.

The hue of the gown enhanced the natural peachy glow of her skin, making her eyes seem to glisten a little brighter. The bodice fit her better than most of the dresses he had chosen, and it needed no belt to expertly hug her curves—which Erik was noticing, for perhaps the first time, were rather pleasingly ample. The neckline on this dress fell a bit lower than the others too, and Erik was embarrassed to admit his eyes were lingering a bit overlong on the trim of delicate lace that skillfully framed the gentle rise of her bosom. *She's beautiful*, he thought to himself and he marveled at the fact that he had not really noticed it before. As she stood there, gazing at him, an absolute vision of sweetness, he was reminded of something he'd wanted to give her.

"I'll be right back!" he said, and quickly ran off to his bedroom to retrieve the mysterious item. When he returned, his hands were behind his back. Jenna looked at him quizzically, as he swallowed hard and said, "Since tonight's dinner is apparently going to be an elegant affair, I thought it fitting to give you this." He held his hand out to her.

Jenna gasped at the gift proffered and she covered her mouth slowly with her hand. In Erik's grasp was a stunning cameo, depicting a rosebud whose beauty would never fade. It was surrounded by a setting of rich antique gold, and hung gracefully from a black velvet ribbon. Of all the roses he had ever given Christine, including the one she herself had left behind, *this* one was the sweetest, and Jenna knew she would cherish it all the days of her life. "My rose…" she said, with a hushed gasp.

"Hopefully you won't leave this one behind in the tunnels," he responded drolly, to cover up his delight at her reaction, "since it shall be tied around your neck."

"Oh, Erik," Jenna said in a tearful whisper.

"Oh, don't cry, Jenna!" Erik cajoled awkwardly, not quite sure what to do with this moment.

"It's just so beautiful, Erik," she murmured by way of explanation for her tears.

"Then it is fitting it should grace your neck, *Mademoiselle*," he answered in a husky voice, which in no way conveyed any desire to push her away.

Jenna stared at him, transfixed. Something had changed in Erik in the last few moments, and the fire in his eyes set her heart aglow. It was almost as if…as if… No, she would *not* even let herself think like that! It could only lead to her getting hurt, for though Jenna knew Erik cared for her deeply, she'd always known his heart truly belonged to Christine.

"Will you help me put it on?" she asked in a shaky voice, pulling her hair away from her neck and turning around.

"Gladly," Erik answered, as he lifted the necklace over her head with trembling hands. The scent of her hair tickled his nose, and he found himself intoxicated by the smell of soap and candles. Good lord, what was happening to him? Everything about Jenna tonight, her smile, her scent, her voice—it was as if it was all magnified a thousand times, and he had the strangest sensation that he was drowning. Stranger still, he *wanted* to.

Though his fingers were most uncooperative, he managed to tie a knot in the ribbon. "There," he said, and his voice was deep and warm. "All finished."

Jenna turned once again toward him, her hair loosed once more to rest on her collarbone.

"Thank you, Erik," Jenna said, a smile lighting her eyes.

"Lovely," he whispered, gazing at the woman before him who he was seeing in such a different light tonight.

"Yes," she nodded, placing her fingers to the cameo, where it rested on her chest. "It is."

Not quite ready to correct her mistaken assumption, Erik gracefully pulled out Jenna's chair. "My lady," he said, making a gallant gesture with his hand.

He caught the blush on her cheeks as she nodded at him with lowered lashes and took her seat at the table. "Let's see what the Persian cooked up for dinner, now, shall we?" With one arm tucked around his back, Erik leaned over and removed the cover from her dish.

Delicious aromas and spices wafted up around her, but Jenna barely noticed because Erik was standing so close. It was a little easier to breathe when he crossed over and took his seat on the other side of the table, but not by much, because then she had the view of his smoldering eyes and the gentle upward curve of the exposed side of his lips, and the last thing on her mind was eating. The way he was staring at her almost made her wish she were the meal laid out before him. *Or* the dessert.

Jenna! She scolded herself, and realized that if she did not start some kind of conversation she was going to embarrass herself by drooling into her dinner. "So," she said, clearing her throat to try to dislodge the dryness that had gathered there. "Would you care for some wine? Personally, I'm parched."

"Red or white, Jenna?" Erik asked, reaching toward the bottles that Omid had so thoughtfully uncorked, allowing them a chance to breathe.

"Oh, white," Jenna responded, and Erik deftly filled her glass. After he placed the bottle back in the bucket without pouring himself a glass, Jenna asked him, "Aren't you going to have some?"

Erik paused. "I don't *usually* indulge in spirits, Jenna," he stated. "After Persia, I have been rather wary of ever letting my guard down again." Reaching for the bottle of red wine this time, he smiled and added, "But in present company, I believe it wouldn't hurt to indulge—*just* a bit." He poured himself a glass of the dark liquid and raised his glass to hers. "To what shall we toast?"

"How about," Jenna said, seizing an opportunity to broach Erik's favorite topic, "the masquerade ball?" She quickly clinked his glass and took a sip of her Chardonnay.

Erik sighed, "Jenna, I told you, I am not going." He took a long drink from his glass himself. "I will be there to observe. But I shall not go as a guest. Besides, I cannot go. I was not invited."

"When has that ever stopped you?" Jenna countered, adding, "Besides, you *were* invited by Christine."

Erik sighed, "Christine invited her *angel*! Not me. And her *angel* shall be there, watching." He took another drink from his glass, as if in punctuation.

"She invited her angel, because she does not know you as a man." Jenna replied in exasperation. "I swear we've had this conversation before."

"We have," he swallowed holding his somewhat empty glass up to her. "And as such, you should remember that I have said she shall *never* know me as a man. Jenna," he said, seriously, without sorrow, but as a matter of fact. "You've *seen* my face. It is an abomination. A curse." He sipped long from his wine glass until he reached the bottom. Absently he reached over to pour himself another serving.

"Oh, Erik," she admonished, "I've *seen* much worse. Back at the hospital, I saw patients come in with the majority of their skin burned off in fires. I saw accident victims arrive with their skulls collapsed inward, or their jaws hanging unhinged. I've seen kids born missing limbs. Your face, Erik, is not the worst deformity there is."

Erik was truly touched by Jenna's attempt to downplay the

disfigurement that had plagued him his entire life. "Though by some miracle it does not bother you, Jenna," he began, topping her own glass off with more wine. "It *would* bother her. Perhaps it is a peculiarity of your time that people are able to look upon the deformed and not think of them as unholy monsters, but *here-now*-there is no hope. Christine could never look upon me as a man, Jenna. For her, I would always be the stuff of nightmares."

"Oh Erik, you haven't even given her a chance!"

"I do not intend to."

"Well then," she grasped for another angle to try to make him see reason. "Go in your mask. Everybody will be wearing one. It will seem only part of a costume. Then at least you can dance with her."

Erik rolled his eyes. "I cannot dance, Jenna!"

Jenna stared at him in shock, "*Of course* you can dance, Erik. Every move you make is a dance. You are the epitome of grace. You *are* music."

Erik brushed off her praise, and looked away bitterly. "She will be too busy dancing with the Vicomte."

"Erik," she said, getting serious now, "You defeat yourself before you even try." She stood up suddenly from her chair, and crossed over to his side of the table. Extending her hand, she commanded, "Dance with me, Angel."

Erik looked in surprise from her offered palm to her smiling face. With raised eyebrows, he asked, "What on earth are you doing, Jenna, and why are you calling me Angel?"

"I," she said with a smug smile, raising her voice about an octave in pitch, "do not know who this *Jenna* is. I am *Christine*, and *I* would like to dance with you."

"Jenna," he said, rolling his eyes.

"*Christine*, Angel," she corrected him with a bat of her eyelashes.

"We cannot dance, *Mademoiselle.*" Erik said, refusing to use the name Christine for his ridiculous houseguest. "There is not even any music."

"Ah, but I was under the impression that this was the seat of sweet music's throne. That there is music all around you." She gestured again for him to take her hand as she gazed, piercingly into his eyes and whispered, "Can you not you hear it?"

Erik mocked annoyance but was secretly amused that she was using his own words against him. She truly knew how to get to him like no other he had met before. Without breaking her gaze, he took her hand in his and slowly rose to his full height. "I do not have any idea, *Mademoiselle*, what it is you wish me to do."

Jenna smiled a satisfied grin, realizing that she had gotten her way. She pulled him out onto the makeshift dance floor that Omid had provided and guided his free hand to the middle of her back. She, in turn, rested her free hand on his upper arm and taking a deep breath, said, "Just follow my lead, *Angel*."

Jenna had intended to lead them in a circular waltz, but she had forgotten the fact that she herself was no great dancer. Her movements were jerky and a ungraceful, and the wine she and Erik had consumed was not really helping. Though he tried to follow her lead, Erik found himself being thrown a bit off balance, stumbling with the extra effort of keeping them both upright. Playing into her game, Erik muttered, "It is a good thing I am teaching you to *sing* and not to dance, *Mademoiselle*. I am not certain ballet would be the safest profession for you."

"Oh *Angel*," she smiled tightly, barely resisting the urge to step on his toes. "The things you say certainly sweep a lady off her feet."

"No my dear," he replied with a smile, trying desperately to hold in a chuckle, as she bumbled them around a bit more. "I am afraid *that* is your dancing."

She tried to sweep them into another arc on the dance floor, but the ankle she had twisted in her flight from Buquet suddenly buckled and she tripped almost taking them *both* down in the process. Erik caught her fall, of course, pulling her tightly to himself in the process, and finding, once he had, that he had no great desire to let her go.

Gazing into her slightly mortified eyes, he said, "Perhaps I *should* lead this dance after all, Mademoiselle."

Jenna merely nodded as she felt Erik begin to move them slowly from side to side. His movements were fluid, graceful, and she felt suddenly, like she was floating on air. "Angel," she murmured as he turned them in gentle circles around the dance floor, holding her so close that their bodies were barely a breath away from touching.

"Mmmm?" he responded, taking a deep sniff of her hair.

"It appears as if the music has slowed," her voice was trembling because of his nearness, wishing that this moment would never have to end.

"The music of the night has *many* tempos, Mademoiselle." His voice was thick and rich, eyes half closed, as if drunk on the sensations he too was now feeling. "Sometimes a wild, frenzied allegro, other times, it is andante with a strong, pulsing rhythm. Still other times," he whispered, as he lowered her into a dip, and slowly, fluidly guided her up again, brushing the entire length of her body against his, "A sweet adagio, languorous and slow, floating," he breathed, the hand on her back reaching up to tangle in her hair, "*flying* on the wings of the song."

"And you said angels couldn't dance," she whispered, gazing up at him, falling deeply under his hypnotic spell.

"*Angels* cannot dance." He reiterated, his voice hushed and low. "But *men* can."

In that moment, that blessed moment that seemed to last for hours but was spent in a heartbeat, Jenna saw Erik's eyes flutter completely closed as he leaned forward and allowed his lips to brush against hers. Soft as a feather, but electric like lightning, the gesture was over almost before it had begun, and Jenna's eyes shot open to see Erik's gaze hazy with desire. Oh how she had dreamed of this moment, when their lips would meet and he would finally claim her as his own. But now as she saw his head once again slowly descend to steal another kiss, she suddenly heard that voice inside her head. *It's not you he's kissing,* it admonished. *You started this game! You know he's dreaming of Christine. How can you accept his kisses when you know they're not for you?*

It took every ounce of strength she had, but Jenna pulled slightly away from his embrace, and looked up at him, shaking him a little as she did so. "Erik, I'm not really Christine," she began, intending to break the spell of the game she had been playing. "I'm…"

But then he opened his eyes, that brown and blue gaze penetrating directly into her soul, and whispered, with a smile, "*Jenna…*"

Jenna. *Jenna!* She felt her heart give a leap and she let out a quiet whimper because in the heat of his desire, in his impassioned state, Erik knew her, and had called *her* name.

She reached her arms up slowly, holding his face in her hands, and pulled him to her for another precious kiss. This time, when their lips met, there was exquisite pressure, Erik's mouth at once both firm and pliant against hers. She felt his arms tighten around her waist and she sighed as she felt him pull her even closer to him, her lips slowly beginning to dance against his. Jenna felt him shudder at first, but soon he began to match her movements with a sensuous shifting of his own.

Slow and unhurried, long and languorous, it was the first moment of pure, unadulterated bliss Erik had ever experienced in his life. When they had parted, for the imperative of breathing, Erik studied Jenna, eyes glazed in wonder, caressing her cheek with his thumb. "Is this real, Jenna? Are *you* real?"

With a loving smile, she shifted her head so that she could lightly press her lips to the hand that was stroking her face. "I promise, Erik. I *am* real."

"Never before," he told her, his voice a thready whisper, "has there been *anyone* in this world who could see fit to kiss me."

Jenna's heart clenched at the reminder of how lost and alone this remarkable man had been his entire life. She looked him directly in his eyes, tangling her fingers in his thick black hair, and said, "Then we have a *lot* of time to make up for, don't we?" When she pulled him back to her mouth, it was with an abandon that had not been there before. Her tongue traced the line of his lips, and when they parted for her tentatively, she nipped and nibbled at them, causing him to groan low in his throat at the tightening sensation he began to feel deep in his stomach. When she felt his arms hold her even closer, almost crushing her against him, she went to deepen the kiss, only to find that the mask got in the way. Gently she pulled back from the kiss and her fingers began to loosen the ties of his mask.

Instinctively, Erik stilled her hand, looking, for a moment, panicked. "Please, Erik," she implored him. "I want there to be *nothing* between us."

Though his hand still held hers, he allowed her fingers to continue their work, and when they were finished and the mask fell away, he was amazed to feel her lips grace the crevices and folds that her fingers once traced. Slowly, so deliciously slowly, Jenna's mouth traveled every inch of that papery skin, that had only once before felt the kindness of her sweet hands. She placed delicate kisses on his eyelids and forehead, and nuzzled his cheek with her own, grazing her lips gently against his jawline on her way back to his mouth. When she looked up at him, with the intention of kissing his lips once more, she noticed that there were now tears in his eyes.

"Jenna…I…" He struggled for words to express the raw emotion he felt at what she had just done. "You…" at a loss, he settled for something far less profound than what he wanted to express, "are so beautiful."

Eyes shining with tears of her own, she reached up and kissed him firmly on the lips before saying, "So are you, my Erik."

With a whimper, he crushed her to him and his lips crashed down desperately on hers. Even his mother had refused to show him the slightest modicum of affection, but this woman, this beautiful, magnificent woman kissed his lips, kissed his *face,* and then claimed him as hers. The sweetness in his heart was almost too much to bear.

When Jenna parted her lips to deepen their kiss, he was right there with her, melting into her, almost forgetting where his lips ended and her lips began. He felt his legs begin to sway, and before he lost his balance entirely, he lifted her into his arms and carried her over to the settee, never once abandoning their kiss.

Firmly nestled on his lap, no longer having to put forth any frivolous effort to stand, Jenna was free to marvel at the magic of his kiss. His lips, so misshapen and deformed, proved themselves quite capable of creating the most exquisite sensations. Firm on one side of his mouth, yet soft on the other, his kiss was both commanding and yielding, vulnerable and strong, and so uniquely Erik. Jenna felt the kiss growing deeper and deeper, as their tongues sought one another in an impassioned, fervent dance.

When the intensity of the kiss had threatened to overwhelm, Erik broke away, panting heavily. "Oh, my Jenna," he whispered, grasping a handful of her precious hair and bringing it forward, burying his face in it and breathing it in, letting the scent intoxicate him once more. "You are exquisite."

"And *you*, my Erik," Jenna purred, as she craned her neck for the kisses he was now trailing down her throat, "are sublime."

Though she was still seated on his lap, entirely ensconced in his arms, with their next kiss, Jenna could not help but feel that she needed to be closer to him—so much closer. She let her hands trail across his back, adoring the feel of the taut muscles beneath the fabric of his clothing. When her hands reached his chest, her fingers began to work the buttons on his shirt. Erik broke the kiss and looked at her questioningly.

"Jenna?" he rasped.

"I *need* to feel you Erik," she explained the burning desire she felt in her chest. "I *need* to touch you."

Erik groaned in response, as she continued to fiddle with the buttons, unable to utter more than a breathy "Jenna," when she began trailing hot kisses down his throat. When at last the buttons were done, she temporarily stopped her ministrations to push open the front of his shirt, and gaze at her prize. She winced at what she saw.

His entire chest was crisscrossed with scars, obviously not designed by nature. Some were raised and almost white. Others were still pink, almost red in hue. There was not a region of his chest that was untouched by the evidence of past cruelties, and Jenna blinked to hold back tears.

"Still beautiful, Jenna?" Erik asked darkly, a bit of bitterness entering his voice. "Still sublime?" Jenna felt him emit a mirthless snort as he cast down his eyes and looked away from her.

"Let me show you how much," Jenna responded, as she leaned forward and brought her lips to his battered chest. First she placed a tender kiss over his heart, which she knew was the most beautiful, yet most tortured part of his body. She allowed her lips to journey from there and soon they had traveled the path of every wound, her tongue tracing every scar. Her hands kneaded and soothed the oft-abused flesh, teaching pleasure in a place that had heretofore only known pain. By the sounds of the little gasps and moans that escaped Erik's lips and the way his fingers tangled in her hair to pull her closer, she got the impression that he was enjoying the lesson, which only urged her to kiss him and touch him more. If she could erase every lash of cruelty with each fevered kiss she would gladly do so. Instead she prayed that her touches, her kisses would replace the remembrances of cruelty with the expression of her love, for that is what she wanted Erik to know in his heart at this moment—that he was loved.

When she wrapped her arms around his back and lifted her lips to adore the tender skin of his neck, she felt that he was trembling. "Erik," she asked, knowing that she had to check in with him—she had to be gentle. "Are you alright?"

"Oh Jenna…" he sighed, looking in her eyes with absolute awe and adoration. "I am more than all right. I just don't know what to do with…these feelings…" his voice faltered as a wave of emotion washed over him. "Jenna, I just don't know what to say."

"Shhhh," she whispered, hugging him tighter and kissing his lips gently to quiet him. "You don't have to say anything. Just *trust* the feelings, Erik. And know that they are real," she kissed him fully once more on the mouth, breaking away only to say, "And know that they are *shared.*"

Erik's moans grew stronger and more frequent as his body responded to Jenna's continued kisses and touches. He hissed in a ragged breath when she flicked her fingers across his nipples and he groaned deeply in his throat as she pressed her body tightly against his. As she ran her fingers through his hair, to pull his mouth even deeper into their kiss, he felt a burning ache join the sweetness that was filling his soul. Long-repressed desire was re-awakening in his body, and as she shifted slightly in his lap, moving against his ready manhood, he had to pull away and bite his lips together to stifle a shout that threatened to break loose.

"Erik?" she questioned, her eyes enjoying the look of absolute rapture on his face.

"I *want,* Jenna," he gasped, breathlessly, as he shifted his own hips to try to recreate the sensation. "I *need.*"

A sensual smile curled on her lips as she asked, "What do you want, Erik? What do you need?"

"I want…" he panted, looking in her eyes, his hand cupping her flushed cheek, "I *need* to touch you," he implored, asking her permission. "As you have touched me."

"Then touch me, Erik," she murmured, reaching for his hand and slowly bringing it down to rest just above the neckline of her dress. "I am yours."

Erik gazed at her reverently, as he watched his hand carefully trace the outline of her bosom, which had, just heartbeats before, been pressed so exquisitely against his bare chest. With agonizing slowness, he allowed his fingers to trail along the gentle curves of her breasts, pausing briefly at her gasp when his thumb brushed her nipple through her dress. "Do you like that, Jenna?" he asked in a hushed whisper, remembering how good it felt when she had touched him similarly.

"It is heavenly," she answered, eyes closed, her head falling back as she drank in the sensation of his hands on her, loving each feeling, but aching for more.

Encouraged by the blissful expression on her face, he cupped her breasts in his hands, applying more pressure this time, as his face fell forward and he trailed hot, but gentle kisses to where her breasts swelled above her neckline. When she arched forward, effectively burying his head in the sweet valley of her cleavage, Erik soon felt he too desired more, and gazing in her eyes to gauge her acceptance, he slowly began to unfasten the buttons on the back of her dress. "*Please,* Erik," she nodded, her eyes glazed with need. "Yes, *please.*"

Erik had often wondered why women's fashions required so many complicated layers, but in that moment he discovered the true reason. It was to forestall the sweet Elysium, that earthly paradise that occurs when a man first gazes upon his woman's breasts. Though deft at many things, Erik's trembling fingers stumbled and erred as he tried to free her sweet flesh from the confines of its clothing. When Jenna noticed a look of despair cross his face, she removed her hands briefly from his person so that she could help him achieve his goal. Bodice unbuttoned and pushed away, Erik muttered a brief prayer of thanks that Jenna had never taken to wearing a corset. He gazed at her body, so beautiful to behold, and slowly, gently, he pulled her shift away.

When she was bare to him, Erik swallowed hard, feeling a shudder run through his entire body at her sheer loveliness. He looked up into her eyes, as if to beg the privilege to touch her, but when Jenna gently smiled and whispered, "Please, Erik. Touch me," he found all the encouragement he needed. Almost reverently, Erik reached forth a shaking hand to touch the now unfettered treasure that was presented before him, luxuriating in her breast's silken texture, delighting in its warmth. "Jenna," he marveled in wonder as his hands continued to knead and explore, "You are so *soft.* And yet," he added, as he delicately pinched the nibs in the center of each breast, "*here* you are so hard."

"It is because of *you,* Erik," she told him, her voice a ragged and harsh whisper. "Because of the desire you inspire in me."

Erik moaned and lowered his lashes as he bent to take one of her pink pearls between his lips. As he sucked her into his mouth, Jenna could not hold back a cry of sheer abandon as she threw her head back and clutched him closer to her. "Erik," she whimpered, "*Oh,* Erik."

"My Jenna," he moaned against her breast at the sound of longing in her voice, "you make such sweet music." Too far gone to make any reply, she simply shifted her body so that she was straddling his hips. With her skirts hiked up, so that there were only his trousers and her pantalets between them, she pulled his head up so she could once again claim him with her lips. Pressing her breasts firmly against his bare chest, she wrapped him tightly in her arms as she ground herself against him. "Oh, Jenna," he whimpered, his body raging for release from this exquisite torture. "You have truly shown me the magic of an embrace."

"Erik," she moaned, pressing his head against her throat as his lips once again began a fevered journey down her neck. "I could *die* in your arms."

Erik took a moment to look deeply into her eyes. When her lashes lifted and she stared right back at him, he said to her in an imploring tone, "I would rather you live in them."

Jenna whimpered at the implication of those words and pulled him desperately back to her lips. When they were each heaving and gasping for air, she trailed her finger down to the closure of his trousers, now stretched and tight with his need. "Make love to me Erik," she entreated when she met with the proof of his undeniable desire.

"Truly, Jenna?" Erik murmured, sure that he was dying due to the heaven of her touch.

"Truly, my Erik," Jenna whispered, gazing adoringly into his eyes, bringing her hand to once again cup his misshapen cheek. "Make us one."

If Erik had been capable of rational thought, in that moment he would have realized that indeed, he was acting under the influence of some elusive emotion—the same one that had been tugging at his soul every time Jenna looked at him, smiled at him, touched him. In that moment before the two were to become one, logical consideration would have proven, without a doubt, that this woman had become a partner to him, a confidant, a *mate*. This was the woman who took the curse of his face and somehow made him judge it a blessing, just in the way she *looked* at him. This was the woman who took the pain in his heart and turned it into laughter. With the proper analysis, it would have been obvious that if this was to be the culmination of his lifetime of sorrows, he would gladly go through each one again, a thousand times over, if it meant he would one day reach this moment with this extraordinary woman. But with Jenna astride him, touching his face, holding him so blessedly close to her nearly naked body, Erik was not capable of thought. He could only feel. And everything he felt in his heart told him he loved her.

Before uniting them, Erik reached up and cupped her face in his hands, whispering, "Jenna. *My* Jenna," and brought her forward for a kiss. He felt Jenna begin to fumble with the fasteners of his trousers, until she suddenly began to tremble. At first he thought it was in reaction to their passion, but then he realized that her lips had gone slack and the tremors had become violent. "Jenna?" he called, all vestiges of his desire being replaced with concern, as her head lolled to the side, and the shaking consistently got worse. He pulled her face to him to look into her eyes, and noticed, with horror, that they had rolled back into her head.

"Jenna," Erik was now frantic trying to get through to her. He lifted her gently in his arms and laid her down on the settee, kneeling beside her and stroking her face as her body continued to convulse. "Jenna, please," he implored her to answer him, taking one of her hands in his and squeezing it firmly, tears flooding his eyes. "Jenna, please don't leave me. Please come back," he begged.

When the tremors had finally subsided, Jenna lay unconscious on the settee. Covering her to her neck with a blanket that Omid had placed nearby, Erik pushed her hair away from her eyes, and gently stroked her cheek. "Oh, my Jenna," he cried, as he lowered his head to her chest and sobbed. "What have I done?

The nurse ran into him, out of breath, in the hall. "Doctor, come quick!" she panted, grabbing him by the arm. "It's Miss Wilson. We have an emergency." He began to run, reaching Jenna's room far before she did. Throwing open the door, he found another nurse observing Jenna, who was thrashing wildly in the bed, her body bucking violently off the mattress. Her skin was blue, her jaw was tight, and her breathing came in shallow, labored breaths.

"My God, Jenna!" He exclaimed, as he rushed to her bedside, checking the blood pressure monitor, which indicated that her level was through the roof. "How long has she been like this?" he demanded, reaching for the oxygen mask stowed above her bed and turning up the level to 100.

"It's been going on for the last five minutes or so, Doctor," she responded, as she watched him frantically place it on her face, his hands trembling.

“We're going to need to medicate her to stop it. Get a push of Midazolam ready, stat! And we're going to need some Sodium Nitro for her BP,” he ordered. “And a crash cart in case of—”

“Yes, Doctor,” she said, as she rushed from the room to ready the medication.

Once alone with her, he battled his urge to take her into his arms, to hold her and whisper sweet words to calm the spasms, knowing as a doctor, that he could not touch her, for fear of injuring her overly laboring muscles. He raked his fingers through his hair as he felt the panic course through his veins. *Dear God, what had happened?* When he last saw her, she had been resting comfortably, not responding, but not showing any signs of distress. What on earth had changed to cause this reaction in her?

As the nurses rushed in, pushing the crash cart and brandishing syringes, he felt the tears spring to his eyes. He was a doctor—a neurologist! Yet he felt so useless in this moment, as he waited to see if the drugs would have their desired effect and ease her body's turbulent state. He had dealt with convulsing patients before, but seeing Jenna like this, her body so fragile and unstable, was killing him.

“Jenna,” he whispered, knowing that she could not hear him, in the flurry of activity happening all around her, and even if she could, it would be no use. “Jenna, please don't leave me. Please come back!” And his tears began to fall.

33 BROKEN

He walked down the stairs from his room—well, bounded, really, might be a better word, considering the exuberance of youth and the novelty of being allowed into the main part of the home. His mother's friend Miss Devereaux had come for dinner, and he had been warned that he was to be on his best behavior. "No fussing with your mask, Erik," his mother had warned him in her sternest tones that morning when delivering his breakfast. "If you are to be allowed out of your room, it is to remain on your face at all times. Is that clear?"

"Yes, Mother," he said noticing the customary way her pretty mouth sneered and her shoulders shivered a bit when he used that word.

"Yes, Ma'am, *Child!" she snapped at him. "You shall refer to me as* ma'am.*"*

"Yes, Ma'am," he responded, too delighted about the evening to come to drop his head as was his habit when his mother snapped at him.

As she had turned to exit his room, he called out to her, "Ma'am?"

Once again, he saw her shoulders tighten as she stopped, and, not turning back to him asked, "What, Erik?"

"Why will I be eating dinner downstairs tonight with you and Miss Devereaux," he asked in his childish wonder, "instead of here in my room as I usually do?"

Still not turning to look at him, his mother answered, "Because today marks five years since the day that you were born. Miss Devereaux thinks that is something to be celebrated," she added as she walked out of the room and closed the door.

Five years since the day he was born! That meant it was his birthday! Erik had read about birthdays in some of the books his mother had left with him. Birthdays were days of treats and of presents—of songs and of candles and smothering hugs. Is that what would be awaiting him tonight when he went down to the dining room and ate with his mother and Miss Devereaux? Would this be a birthday party? Would his mother agree to a gift?

"Erik!" his mother had called through the door when it was time for their

dinner. It had only taken him a moment to reach the door, since he had been pacing back and forth, imagining birthday cake and fancy paper and presents, but she had not waited, preferring to turn the latch and continue on her way, allowing him to find his own way down stairs.

Miss Devereaux was there and held a brightly wrapped package in her hand. His mother said he should open it later, but Miss Devereaux said he could have it now, earning an eye roll from his mother, as she left the room to bring out the meal. His present—his first one ever—was a book on magic tricks with a special section dedicated to ventriloquism. He remembered to thank Miss Devereaux without his Mother even having to threaten him, and he immediately sat down and began to turn the pages. When his Mother emerged from the kitchen with a tray full of food, he was forced to put the book away so that they could eat, and Miss Devereaux was scolded for spoiling him.

Dinner had been delicious, and there was a sweet torte afterward—of which his mother allowed him a few bites—but there were no candles for him to blow out, no songs sung for him, and he had begun to notice that the book from Miss Devereaux had been the only thing in the room wrapped with pretty paper. "Ma'am," he asked, in anticipation of her *gift, "do you have a birthday present for me?"*

His mother bristled and looked at him in anger. "You ungrateful brat!" she spat, as she glared at him with flashing eyes. "I slave all day making a nice dinner, I let you have a bite of torte, and I even let you eat here in the dining room, instead of on the floor upstairs in your usual spot, and you have the nerve to ask me for a present?"

He noticed Miss Devereaux gawk at his mother in horror, and he felt angry. His mother's friend, who was barely more than a stranger to him, had seen fit to give him a gift, but not his mother. Not his own mother.

In the books which she so regularly shoved under his door—to keep him occupied, she explained—there were always scenes of families who spent time together, who did things together, who celebrated birthdays and gave their children presents. In the books, there were mothers who loved their children—and who showed *them they did. All mothers loved their children, did they not?*

"Mother," he asked, finding the courage to look into her angry eyes.

"Ma'am!" *she barked at him, raising her hand.*

"Mother," *he insisted, not feeling inclined to be obedient if she would not grant his wish. "Will you give me something for my birthday?"*

He could tell that she was about to snap—about to yell at him again, or perhaps even hit him. But Miss Devereaux cajoled, in a gentle voice, "It is his birthday, *Bernadette. Do not be so cross."*

His mother took a deep breath, and closed her eyes for a moment before looking at him and asking through clenched teeth, "What is it that you want, Erik?"

He looked at her, his mismatched gaze wide, as if assessing if it was true—if his mother would truly be willing to indulge him, just this once. "Mother," he said in a pleading tone, beseeching her with his eyes to grant his birthday wish—a wish he had secretly harbored for the whole of his little life. "I would like a kiss."

His punishment was swift as her hand flew across his face and knocked him off the chair on which he had been sitting. "Insolent boy!" she shrieked, as Miss Devereaux scrambled from her seat to try to get to him. She was too late, however, because before she could reach him, his mother was at his side in a rage, her arms squeezing his shoulders tightly, shaking him violently as she screamed. "How dare you ask for the one thing you know I can never give? Do you wish to taunt me, devil child? Do you wish to prove to me how inferior I am to other mothers? I was aware of that on the day you were born, when I spawned a demon instead of a babe! I cannot kiss you Erik! Nobody will ever *kiss you! You are a* monster*!* YOUR TOUCH IS POISON!" *Miss Devereaux was finally able to pull his mother off of him, and by the time she turned to comfort the boy, he had already scrambled up the stairs toward his room, the slam of the door a moment later not nearly as loud as the endless refrain that played and replayed in his head. You are a monster, Erik.* YOUR TOUCH IS POISON.

When Jenna's tremors had finally died down and the nurses had left her room to start setting the chaos on the floor aright, he sat there a few quiet moments more, simply staring at her and stroking her hair. He thanked God that the medicines had worked and that Jenna had stabilized and was merely unconscious once more. Yet, as he gazed at her, the oxygen mask still covering her nose and mouth, making her breathing come easier, he got the distinct impression that something had changed. "Jenna," he whispered, "Why do you suddenly feel so much farther away?"Eventually, he rose from his vigil beside her bed and made his way to the nurse's station, taking her chart with him. He flipped to the most recent entries and scanned the notes on the page, his eyes crinkling, as he flipped the pages in a backwards direction. Looking up, he saw Jenna's nurse, and called her over. "Maureen," he asked in a quizzical tone. "When did Miss Wilson receive her last dose of Zolpidem?"

"Oh, that was discontinued yesterday," she told him matter-of-factly. "Dr. Charleson wrote the order." She turned the page and pointed to the uneven scrawl that indeed stopped the medication.

"Alright," he said nodding, still scanning the page, "but when was she given her taper down dose?"

"Taper down dose?" The nurse asked.

"Yes," the doctor said, "you cannot stop Zolpidem cold turkey. You have to taper the dose over several weeks."

The nurse began to look confused. "I spoke with Dr. Charleson myself yesterday. He said the family was demanding that she immediately be taken off of the drug, stating that it has been ineffective and detrimental to her recovery. Oh wait," she said, suddenly, looking behind him. He turned and followed her gaze to see Charleson and a colleague laughing and walking down the hall. Charleson moved right past Jenna's room, never even stopping to check in on his patient who had just had a severe acute neurological episode. "There he is now," the nurse said. "You can ask him about this yourself."

"I see. Thank you Maureen," he said, and the nurse smiled and went on her way.

He rose from his chair and placed Jenna's chart on the desk. He made his way to the elevator where Charleson and his colleague were waiting, apparently discussing something more important than his patient's life, since they did not see him walk up.

"Charleson, I need to talk to you," he interrupted, his voice cold as ice.

Dr. Charleson momentarily looked confused, but upon turning and seeing who it was, he rolled his eyes and a bored expression came over his face. "Oh. It's you. Look I really don't have time for—"

"Could we talk in private, Doctor?" he said tightly.

"I don't really have anything to say to you, Doctor."

"Well, I have plenty to say to you!"

"Look," he began, looking at his watch, "send it in an email, because—"

Suddenly, Charleson felt himself picked up by the lapels of his lab coat and shoved up against the wall. "I suggest you *make* the time to listen to me, Charleson! Just like it would have been nice for you to take the time to check on your patient who could have *died* this afternoon."

Charleson looked at him in confusion, "What are you talking about?"

"Miss Wilson—"

"You can have your little pet back, Doctor," Charleson sneered. "I recused myself from Miss Wilson's case."

"I wish you had done that before you discontinued the Zolpidem," he seethed through clenched teeth, shaking Charleson a bit by the collar.

Charleson rolled his eyes. "I did exactly what you and Penny wanted. I thought you'd be glad. Now get your hands off of me before I—"

"You know you can't discontinue Zolpidem cold turkey! It has to be tapered or else it can cause withdrawal symptoms."

Charleson shook his head, "That type of reaction is very rare."

The younger doctor brought his face very close to Charleson's and through clenched teeth, he spat, "Well, I just spent a half hour in Miss Wilson's room because she was convulsing uncontrollably. She was cyanotic and her blood pressure was dangerously high. She needed medication just to stop the seizing and to prevent her from going into cardiac arrest, and she is currently hooked up to an oxygen machine to help her breathe. I do not care that the reaction is rare, Doctor. It *happened* to her!"

By this point, a large group of staff members had gathered around the two, to check on the commotion, but that didn't stop Charleson from looking the younger doctor directly in the eyes and, sneering, "Oops!"

The first swing sent Charleson hurtling to the floor, his jaw dislocated, his teeth rattled. The younger doctor landed on top of him, and the second swing broke his nose. "How could you, you bastard?!" he shouted, as he let his fists fly again and again. "Does she mean *nothing* to you? You could have *killed* her!"

Charleson's face was a bloody mess before security was able to separate the two. "I'll have your license!" he screamed, spitting out a tooth as the younger doctor was carted off the Dr. James's office.

"What in the hell is wrong with you, son?" James bellowed at him, when the door was closed.

"Charleson could have killed her!" he spat. "He took her off Zolpidem cold-turkey and caused her to have a severe Grand Mal seizure. He could have *killed* her! And he doesn't even care!"

"So file a grievance!" he shouted. "Report him to the ethics committee. But you do not throw punches in the hospital."

"I couldn't help myself, Dr. James," the young man answered. "He did all of this because of *me*—just to get the better of *me* in some imagined rivalry. And Jenna …" he paused a minute to catch his breath. "Jenna paid the price." He slumped into the chair across from Dr. James' desk, raking a hand through his disheveled hair.

"He could sue you, you know!" Dr. James said nervously, taking his own seat behind his desk, and huffing loudly. "He could sue me!"

"I *love* her," the young man said. "I don't care about lawsuits."

"And that's exactly why I am going to have to take you off of this case," he said, trying to make his younger charge understand. "You've lost all objectivity. You are not thinking rationally."

"Dr. James, please," he said panicking at his superior's words. "You have to let me continue to help her. After we get her weaned properly from the Zolpidem, I'll be in a better position to continue the sensory therapy and—"

"Doctor, when are you going to face the fact that it's over?" Dr. James asked, interrupting his rambling. "You have tried the sensory stimulation, and it didn't work. We've tried the drugs, and nothing. Sooner or later, Doctor, you have to accept that Miss Wilson simply is not coming back!

❧

Monster, he heard the long ago echo, the sibilant, crackling hiss still thrumming loudly in his ears. *Your touch is poison.* He sat alone on the settee, staring at the fire. Reverberations from his past, flared and popped, taunting and jeering at him with the same fervor, the same wicked lack of mercy as they had years ago. But there was a difference this time. This was no nebulous future of which they warned—some unnamed horror that may or may not come to pass. This nightmare had already happened, and he knew now that those voices spoke the truth. *Did you really think you could love her, Erik?* asked the mocking specters, whose laughter dripped with derision. *That she could love you? Did you actually believe that she* wanted *you to touch her—that she would allow the monster inside her? She told you she could die in your arms. She would* rather *DIE Erik, than to have you love her.*

Still Erik stared, unseeing, at the flames. The drama of the night before played and replayed in his head. He had carried Jenna to her bed after his cowardly tears had stopped falling. He was careful only to touch the blanket, never allowing his malignant fingers to graze any more of her skin, not wishing to contaminate her with any more of his peculiar toxin. *He* had done this, he knew. *HE* had poisoned her—when he dared to kiss her, to touch her, to… *love* her. He had not believed the truth. He had foolishly dared to hope, dared to dream, but reality was that his touch *was* poison…and Jenna had paid the price.

This was *his* fault. *He* was the one who had allowed himself to get so absorbed in his lessons with Christine that he had not searched hard enough for a way to send Jenna home. *He* had then used those same lessons with Christine as an excuse to beg Jenna selfishly for two more weeks because he was too cowardly to go back to living without her. *He* was the one who made her a part of his life, allowing her to travel with him through the opera house, causing her to feel enough a part of his world that she had endangered herself by setting out in the tunnels alone and meeting with Joseph Buquet. And when he had successfully defended her, and protected her virtue from the drunken fiend, *he* himself had damaged her—*soiled* her—with his demonic kiss. His mother had *warned* him. But he had not listened to his mother.

And now he did not know if she would ever wake up.

The sound of footsteps near the kitchen vaguely registered within his mind, but Erik didn't care. He continued to sit there, staring without seeing, hearing without listening, breathing without living. He wondered, *what would it feel like to be consumed by the flames.*

"Erik?" The Persian called, almost afraid to enter his friend's sitting room for what he might see. If things had gone according to plan, last night could have been a *very* pleasant evening for his stubborn friends, and perhaps even a better night, and there were certain things that he did not *want* to see. Of course, if *that* sort of thing was still happening this morning, he'd imagine there would be more noise. They weren't exactly *quiet* types when they were alone together. Sigh…he should have been a little more emphatic when he had told Erik not to ruin things. Perhaps he should have *underlined* his command?

Omid walked in expecting to find Erik irate at his apparently unsuccessful attempt to make a match. What he did find, however, took him by surprise. Erik was sitting alone in the dark, practically catatonic, staring into the hearth. His normally impeccable hair was wildly disheveled, his shirt open and un-tucked. The right side of his face was as exposed as the left, while his mask, his most consistent article of clothing, lay, discarded, beside him on the floor. Omid called his name again, but Erik still did not answer, and a cold chill began to run down his spine. He walked slowly over to his friend, who was still staring, transfixed, at the flames. He knelt down and retrieved the mask, holding it out toward Erik's hand.

Without looking away from the fire, Erik's hand closed around the mask, and he asked in a faraway voice, "*Shall I wear the mask for you, old friend, with my wickedness already laid bare? For I am a demon, evil my soul; it matters not what clothes I wear.*"

"Oh dear," Omid sighed to himself. "He is speaking in verse again."

"Why have you come here, Daroga?" Erik asked, still staring straight ahead of him.

"Well, I had hoped to see something that would make me blush, like the other morning when the two of you were cuddling so sweetly on the couch," he said sarcastically. "But it appears I am destined to be disappointed." When Erik made no answer, no snide remark, Omid asked him directly, "Erik, where is Jenna? Why is she not with you?"

"She is in her bed," Erik responded in a monotone voice.

With a huff, Omid decided he needed to try the direct approach. "And why are you not with her?"

"Because, Daroga," Erik smiled a mirthless grin, "*My* touch is poison."

Omid's blood ran cold at Erik's comment, so much so that he dashed into Jenna's room, prepared for the worst, only to find her sleeping peacefully in her bed. When he returned to the sitting room, he had had enough of his friend's cryptic game. "What happened, Erik?" Omid asked directly, pulling a chair over from the dining table and placing it directly in Erik's line of view, so his friend had no choice but to look at him. "What did you do?"

Erik finally looked up and met Omid's gaze, and Omid noted that his friends eyes were red rimmed and puffy—almost as if he'd been…*crying*? "I *touched* her, Daroga," Erik said plainly. "And *my* touch is poison."

"Erik," Omid shook his head, "stop being ridiculous!"

"Ridiculous, Daroga?" Erik asked, raising an eyebrow. "As I said, I *touched* her. *And* I finally got the kisses I had been waiting for my entire life."

"So what's the problem, Erik?" Omid asked, confused. These were things to be happy about. Surely even his blind friend could see that.

"Because *while* I was kissing her, Daroga," Erik's voice darkened with emotion, "she began to have convulsions. She has been unconscious ever since." Erik buried his face in his hands, groaning once again, "What have I done?"

Omid was pained to see Erik so upset. He knew his friend was in love with Jenna, and he knew that this medical episode must have been terrible for him to behold. He could still remember the agony he felt at watching his own beloved wife slip away from this life. But Erik, in his emotional state, was forgetting the big picture. "Erik," he said, keeping his voice gentle, "all you did was fall in love."

"It is not for me to be in love, Daroga," Erik said sadly.

"By Allah, that is nonsense, my friend!" Omid exclaimed. "Have you *seen* the way Jenna looks at you? She loves you too, Erik."

Scenes from the previous evening replayed in Erik's mind. He recalled Jenna's smiles, her kisses, her touch. He remembered her sighs and moans of pleasure, and the way she kept pulling him closer, when the immediate reaction of almost every other person he'd encountered in his life had been to push him away. *Make love to me, Erik,* she had purred, with fire in her eyes. *Make us one.* She *had* wanted him as much as he had wanted her. But before he could join them, one body, one soul, she had been taken from him by the violent convulsions that seized her—her body rebelling against his touch, even if her beautiful spirit had not.

Erik shook his head sadly at the memory. "My love is poison, Omid. And because of it, I have lost her."

"Erik," Omid began gently, trying very hard to be patient with his friend. He knew all about the abuse that Erik had suffered in his life, beginning at the hands of that witch who was his mother. "Your touch did not harm her."

"Are you sure, Daroga?" He retorted miserably. "Are you so sure?"

"Are you so sure that it did?" Omid asked, somewhat exasperated.

"Have you forgotten that when she arrived here—by whatever means she did—she had a *head* injury? You sewed it closed yourself."

Erik's head shot up, suddenly looking very alert. It was true, he had forgotten about the gaping wound that marred Jenna's forehead on the night she first arrived. That seemed so long ago, and so much had happened between them. But he recalled now, that while he had stitched closed Jenna's wound, he had not removed the stitches. And yet, one morning, they were simply gone.

Erik suddenly rose from the settee, and if Omid had not quickly leaned back, he would have been knocked off his chair by Erik's haste. Erik began pacing the floor, one hand covering over his mouth, the other arm crossed over his chest. "I did sew her wounds, Daroga," he stated as he paced, "but I did *not* remove the stitches."

Omid now remembered the morning Erik had been so distraught about her stitches being gone. His irritability had led to Jenna accompanying Omid on an outing in Paris. It had been shortly after Erik had given up on the outrageous idea of Jenna being a mental patient, replacing it with the much more sound notion of her being a time traveller. The disappearance of her stitches had spooked him, because it was one more thing that he could not explain.

"Erik," Omid began, "I did not mean to imply anything about her stitches, simply that her seizure was more likely related to her head injury than to your…romantic ministrations."

"But what if it's all connected?" Erik responded, and it was clear to Omid that his mind was rapidly making connections between the many and varied strange events that had occurred since Jenna first appeared. "What if her being here is somehow *directly* related to her head injury? After all, Jenna herself said she received that injury in a terrible accident that happened in her *own* time. What if her stitches disappeared due to something that had also happened in her own time? And what if her convulsions…" Erik's voice trailed off suddenly as he felt a chill run down his spine.

"Erik," Omid began, finally finding a moment to get a word in edgewise. "The only problem in your theory is that Jenna is no longer *in* her own time. She is here."

Erik looked back at the Persian, and his usual pale face had taken on an even more ghostly pallor. "What if she somehow exists in both?"

34 WHISPERS THAT SCREAM

Christine quietly turned the handle to her bedroom door and carefully pushed it open. The hour was early, and she desperately hoped Meg was still asleep. She did not wish for anybody to see her right now—she did not wish to talk; she did not wish to explain why she was returning to her bedroom in the wee hours of the morning. She had spent the night in her dressing room, waiting for her dear angel to arrive—but he had not come. At some point, her eyes had drifted closed, and she had given in to sleep. But her slumber had not been restful, and she woke this morning with tired red eyes and a spirit crushed by disappointment. To have anyone see her stealthily returning to her room after a night not spent in her own bed was more than Christine could bear. The opera house was already talking about her sudden rise to the status of prima donna. She did not need to add to the gossip by providing reasons to question her reputation.

"Christine, where have you been?" came the concerned voice of the blond dancer. Meg was standing in the center of their dark room with her arms folded across her chest. "I was worried sick when you did not come back last night after your lesson. Are you alright?"

So much for not having to see anyone, Christine sighed as she answered, "I'm fine, Meg. I just fell asleep in my dressing room, is all." She went to her small wardrobe and began to search for a new dress to wear to rehearsal that day.

Meg eyed her friend closely. Christine was acting suspiciously. She looked drawn and depressed, and Meg knew that there was absolutely no way that her friend could have simply fallen asleep after a visit from her angel. It generally took her hours to come down from the ceiling after a lesson with him. Something had happened to Christine during the night, and Meg was not going to let the matter rest until she found out what.

"Christine," she asked. "What happened?"

"I told you," she asserted a bit irritably. "I am fine. I simply did not rest as well in my dressing room as I would have here, and now I have to hurry to get ready for rehearsals…"

"We have plenty of time before rehearsals!" Meg insisted, as she walked over and grasped her friend's hand. Christine looked at her, and Meg could see the exhaustion and sadness in the singer's eyes. "Come," she said, pulling Christine toward the beds where they could sit. "Tell your best friend what's wrong."

Christine heaved another deep sigh. So much for not having to talk. She allowed herself to be dragged over to her little bed, where she obediently sat down. Meg sat across from her, expectantly, and said, "Well?"

Christine looked down at her hands which were wringing in her lap. "My angel, Meg." she finally admitted. "He did not come for our lesson last night." When her friend made no reply, she continued. "I waited and I waited, but still, he never arrived. He promised me that he would be there, Meg. And he wasn't."

"Oh, Christine, I'm sorry," Meg answered sympathetically, seeing the distress in her friend's eyes.

Now that Christine had begun her tale, it was as if floodgates had opened, and she could not stop unburdening her soul. "That's not all, Meg," she continued, her voice sounding sad and forlorn. "The night before, he was upset with me. He said I was not interpreting his music properly—not *feeling* it the right way. He was cross with me. He has never been that way before." Sad tears began to well in Christine's eyes, as she stated, "I have angered my angel, Meg, and now I fear that I have lost him. And none of *this*—*none* of it—matters without my angel."

"Oh, Christine," Meg began, trying to sound soothing and handing her friend a tissue. "Don't say that. It will be all right. Perhaps he was just…detained…last night."

"What could detain him?" Christine blurted. "He is an *angel*, Meg!"

"Is that why you wore your best dress to meet with him?" Meg inquired, an eyebrow raised.

Christine looked up at her friend in confusion. It was true that she had returned to her room yesterday after rehearsals to change into her rose colored frock—the one that hugged her figure just a little tighter, and brought out the pink tones of her cheeks—but she failed to see what that had to do with her angel being upset with her. "What does that have to do with anything, Meg?"

"Well," her friend began gently, "I would think it would not matter *what* one wore for a meeting with an angel. And yet," she smiled sweetly at her friend, "you always strive to look your best, sometimes even skipping dinner to give yourself enough time to get ready for your lessons."

Christine felt her cheeks redden at her friend's implication. "He is a *heavenly being*, Meg!" Christine asserted. "It is out of respect, that I strive to look my best. Do you not wear your very best to Church?"

"Alright," Meg conceded, holding her hands out and nodding a bit, "I see your point. But why," she continued to probe gently, "do you need to meet him in your dressing room, and before that the chapel? And why at a set time?"

"It is so we can have privacy to focus on the lesson," Christine answered, looking a bit confused. "Is that so strange?"

"I would think that an Angel could meet with you anywhere, at any time," Meg mused. "He would know when you were not busy. He would know when you were alone. Why could he not simply *appear* when it was convenient? Hasn't he said he was always watching over you?"

"He did…" Christine agreed warily, wondering what point the dancer was trying to make.

"Then he would have seen you waiting in the dressing room," Meg answered. "Would not a celestial being at least have whispered for you to go back to your room? He knows rest is important for good singing, and that is his goal. Is it *not*?" Meg asked her last question while looking Christine pointedly in the face.

Christine felt her mind begin to swirl. The questions Meg asked were ones for which Christine had no answer, but now that she thought of it, her friend made a good point. Her angel was not acting overmuch like…an angel.

"What are you saying, Meg?" she finally asked her friend point blank.

Meg took her friend's hand in hers before continuing gently. "This opera house is inhabited by another being who is always watching over every move we make. He knows what happens on the stage, he knows what happens behind it, and he has a very pivotal role in making sure the opera runs smoothly."

Christine shook her head, and looked down. "You speak of The Phantom, Meg. Not my Angel of Music."

"Are they so very different, Christine?" Meg asked quietly.

"Of *course* they are!" Christine insisted, standing up and beginning to pace back and forth. "The Phantom threatens and cajoles…"

"He warns those who are not doing their part to make the opera the best that it can be."

"He extorts money and steals—"

"If not for his guidance, the opera house would have failed long ago. He is only taking what is his due."

"He causes great catastrophes—"

"Mostly harmless pranks that help get his point across." She paused briefly before adding, "And some *have* had…*personal* benefits." Meg looked at her friend in a pointed way.

"Carlotta…" Christine breathed, as realization struck her and she sunk limply back down onto her bed.

Meg merely nodded.

"But I thought it was Buquet's incompetence that was responsible for that backdrop."

"Perhaps," Meg allowed, "but Buquet did not ransack the diva's dressing room, which is what ultimately caused her to quit."

"But the managers *fired* Buquet."

"Well, Christine," Meg retorted, "They could not exactly *fire* the ghost."

"Ghosts do not exist, Meg," Christine made one last feeble attempt to assert her position.

"Do angels?" Meg asked.

Christine looked beaten and worn down, and Meg's question stung because, truly, Christine didn't know the answer. She wanted to believe her father had told her the truth. She wanted to cling to the idea that the Angel of Music had finally found her because her beloved father had sent him for her. But then what did she do with the feelings inside her that wished he were more? How could she account for the dreams she had when his soft dark wings transformed into strong arms that he could wrap around her? Did her angel truly exist? Did the ghost? Who was the voice that called to her and taught her to sing and made promises of protection? The one who left her roses?

"But, *why*, Meg?" Christine asked in confusion. "Why would the ghost decide to personally *help* me, when he has never done so before? Why would he say he was an *Angel*?"

Meg inhaled deeply and took Christine's hands in hers. "I don't know anything for sure, Christine, but as you know, my mother has been delivering the ghost's salary for years. She is the only one of the opera staff who is allowed to set foot in Box 5. Over the years, she has…sensed …certain things about him."

"What *things*, Meg?" Christine asked.

"Well, he has a great love for and understanding of music, for one. His demands have done much to improve the quality of the musical program here at the Opera House. He cannot abide cruelty, which was probably the main reason for his long-standing feud with Carlotta. And…" Meg paused, as if not sure to go on.

"What is it, Meg?" Christine urged, intrigued now by what her friend had shared. "Come on, you must tell me."

"Well, there *have* been sighting over the years—mostly by the younger, more hysterical ballerinas—and they all agree on one thing. That he has a hideous, terrifyingly ugly face. They say it's as if his face isn't even there!"

"Oh dear!" Christine shrunk back in horror. "How is that even possible?" Could it be that the ghost was real? An actual spectre living in the shadows?

"My mother tells the story," Meg began, "of a time from her childhood, when she and her family attended a gypsy fair. There was an exhibit—The Living Corpse, they called it. When my mother went into the tent to view it, she saw that this "corpse" was merely a boy, younger even than herself, who had a dirty sack covering his head. When the gypsy master stepped forward and removed the sack, he exposed the horrible deformity in place of the boy's face.

"Most of the other patrons fled in terror, but my mother was moved with pity. She stayed and she watched for a time. The boy hung his head, and did not look up, but after a while, the gypsy master demanded a song. The boy hesitated at first, but when the master threatened with his whip, the boy did, in fact, begin to sing.

"My mother called his voice unearthly, as exquisitely beautiful as his face was ugly. In that voice, she heard the call of the angels—the soft, sweet whisper of their wings, the powerful strength blazing in their eyes. And after his song, as she stood there, transfixed, he finally looked up, and directly at her. She said that his eyes seemed to hold the glow of intelligence and the fire of determination, and all the sadness of the world. It was a moment she has never forgotten.

"Later that year, she'd heard tell that the gypsy fair's "living corpse" had disappeared. He had escaped his confines after killing the cruel master. It was just a passing piece of news, but my mother never forgot it, and she often wondered what had become of that poor young boy. When she started to hear tales so many years later, of the Opera Ghost and his hideous face, there were many times when she was reminded of that poor child, and the intelligence burning in his eyes. And she wondered…"

"Meg, why are you telling me all of this?" Christine asked, shaking her head. For some reason, she found herself trembling.

Meg took another deep breath before saying, "What if the Phantom was not a ghost, nor an angel? What if he was simply a man?"

"No," Christine shook her head.

"A man who hid because his face was too horrible to behold? A man who hid because the world had always thought him a monster?"

"NO!" Christine's voice was a little louder, tears of frustration springing to her eyes.

"No more than a carnival attraction? What if he hid, Christine, because the world had always hidden from *him*?"

"I would *not* hide from him," she answered, springing to her feet with conviction. "I could not hide from my Angel. He has shown me a kind and tender soul. He is brilliant, and musical, and encouraging, and sweet, and—"

"What if he were a man?" Meg interrupted.

"If he were a man he could love me!" Christine blurted, before she could stop herself. She gasped and brought her hand to cover her mouth.

"You love him," Meg supplied simply.

Christine looked at her friend and sighed. "I think I do, Meg." She looked down at her hands, which were clasped in her lap. "And I do admit, I had dared to dream that he might…" Christine stopped and shook her head. "But I have angered him, and now…he is gone."

"Christine, he is not gone!" Meg encouraged. "If my belief is indeed correct, he is still here somewhere. I do not know if it is true that you have angered him, or if he was absent for some other reason, but you must not let him think his work with you has been in vain. You must hold your head high and continue to practice confidently—whether he is with you or not. For on opening night, I *know* he will be there, watching you from Box 5. The Ghost is *always* there."

Christine listened to her friend and recognized the wisdom of her words. She hugged her tightly, saying, "Meg thank you. You have given me so much to think about."

"Hold it close to your heart, Christine," Meg warned. "Do not speak of it to anyone, but remember, he *will* be watching."

She nodded her head and took a deep breath, "Meg, you are right. As always. But now I really do have to dress for rehearsal."

Meg smiled and leaned forward to give Christine another hug. "You will be flawless, Christine. And mark my words, *he* will know. He *always* knows."

❧

"Brain injuries…" he muttered to himself, as he used his index finger to travel down the page. He had checked on Jenna a little while ago, and she was still resting after the traumatic events of the previous night. The Daroga had taken his leave after much…convincing, and Erik was now using the quiet to pore through his medical texts to try to find some type of supporting information for the revelation that he had had earlier. Everything happening right now *had* to somehow be related to the injury Jenna had suffered before arriving here—he was just sure of it. And somehow, she was existing in two different worlds at once. He knew the idea was absolutely insane, but regardless, it was the only thing that made sense in Erik's mind. Somehow, the stitches that he himself had placed in Jenna's head had vanished. Someone *had* to do that for the sutures could not have simply disappeared on their own. Was that same *someone* somehow still interacting with her now, creating the health problems that had recently beleaguered her? The headaches, the dizziness, the seizure—they *had* to be related. *Or are you grasping for straws, Erik, trying to find some way—any way—that your touch was NOT to blame for the horror that befell her?*

Erik took a deep breath as the traitorous voice filled his mind once more. He had heard that voice his entire existence—that voice which was so much like his mother's. It had reminded him time and again throughout his life that love would never find him, that it *could* never find him, for if it touched him in any way, it would die. *The Living Corpse can know no love…*

But now, by some miracle, after a lifetime of believing love had no interest in him, somehow, it had seized him in its grasp, holding tight to him, consuming his entire being. Jenna had woken in him, joy and laughter, excitement and desire. They had been about to make love—her touches, and kisses, a sweet succor that he had never before imagined, healing wounds that long had festered, making the broken whole. And *he* had kissed *her* and had *touched* her as well, all at once the discovery that he had a heart making him eager to give it away. They were just about to join their bodies as their time together had already joined their hearts, when her tremors had begun.

But did that mean one had caused the other? He had spent a torturous night, staring at the fireplace, certain that he was somehow responsible for her suffering. He had wallowed in the dark, pondering on how he had stained her, tainted her with his wicked desires. But one thought rebelled against the voice in his head preventing him from diving head first into his own personal pit of despair. It was the knowledge that he would *never* hurt Jenna. He could never bring himself to harm a single precious hair on her head. He loved her, and he only wanted to protect her. And it was for that reason that he *had* to discover some way to help her. He had to find out, once and for all, how Jenna had come to him, and how it was all connected to the ailments that had been plaguing her. *But your touch is poison, Erik,* The voice still whispered. *Everybody knows that.*

Her body ached all over. Her muscles screamed, and her head throbbed, and it was as if her lungs had been set on fire. She felt awful. She felt confused. She felt lost.

Jenna's eyes fluttered open to survey her surroundings. The soft glow of the candlelight revealed that despite her disorientation, she was still in her small bedroom in Erik's home, her covers drawn to her chin. She pushed the blankets down a bit to discover that she still wore the peach colored gown she had on when she and Erik had…

Jenna shot up in bed and tried to ignore the way the room began to spin, as shards of memory swirled around her foggy brain. His body against her as they danced in the candlelight; that first feathery brush of their lips; his arms tightening around her; his hands tangling in her hair, stroking her face, cupping her breast. Jenna felt a heat begin to enter her body as she recalled their night of passion. Christine—she had been so sure he was in love with Christine. But he had been kissing *her*, touching *her*, moaning *her* name. *My Jenna*, he had whispered as he pulled her closer. She smiled at the memory, because she could finally admit she *was* his. There was no going back now.

But then it had all gone blank. She remembered kissing him, knowing that they were about to make love. One moment her lips were on his, and the next, an inky black nothingness had washed over her. For a moment she felt herself shaking, and she'd thought she heard Erik call her name. But she couldn't answer him, though she tried, and then the darkness took over and she was out.

Erik. Oh, he must have been so frightened. She had to get to him. She had to show him she was all right. She swung her legs around and off the bed. The room still spun, but she managed to get to her feet, coughing harshly with the effort. She put aside the pain in her head and the screaming in her chest, and she walked over and opened her door.

"Erik?" he heard her small voice call his name, and Erik looked up from the tome he had been perusing. Jenna leaned in the doorway to her room. She was still wrapped in her now wrinkled peach gown, her hair a wild, coppery cloud around her head, her skin pale and drawn. He saw her shoulders shake as she held her hand to her mouth and covered a cough, giving the impression that she was weaker and much more frail than he had ever seen her look before.

In a heartbeat, he was across the room. "How are you feeling, Jenna?" he asked quietly, reaching out as if to grasp her hands, but never quite touching her. His voice was full of concern, taking in every detail of her appearance, watching her for any signs of distress. "Are you alright?"

Despite the pounding in her head, and the ache in her chest, she smiled at him and said, "I'm a little sore, but I'm alright now." She *was* all right—for she was with him.

When Jenna smiled at him, Erik felt his heart leap in his chest, and he had the unmistakable urge to take her in his arms and hold her close. He had been so worried about her, and to see her standing and talking to him—it was all he had been hoping for! His Jenna was all right. He reached out his arm to touch her cheek when he heard it. *Your touch, Erik.*

Jenna smiled and she saw Erik's hand reach out to touch her. Yes, this was what they both needed—that connection—that touch. But before his fingers could reach her face, she saw a darkening in his eyes. It was as if he remembered something, and his hand fluttered, trembling, back to his side.

"Erik?" Jenna looked at him, questioningly, wondering why he had held back, why he hadn't touched her. When she reached for his hand and she saw him pull away, she felt a pit begin to form in her stomach. "Erik what's wrong? What happened?"

"You had a seizure, Mademoiselle," Erik told her guardedly, and the term he always used to distance himself from her was like a blow to Jenna's gut. "You've been unconscious ever since."

A seizure! She thought she had merely passed out again. No wonder Erik was so distant. It must have been terrifying for him. "Erik…I'm sorry, I…"

Erik interrupted, "No, Mademoiselle. You have nothing for which to apologize. I am the one who should…"

Jenna reached out and touched a finger to his lips to stop him from saying what she was sure was about to spill from his lips. "Erik, no. You did *nothing* wrong."

She was so close, her finger on his lips to quiet his fears. Even though *she* was the one who had suffered the horrific convulsions and had been unconscious for the better part of a day, *she* was still comforting *him.* He wanted so badly to fold her in his arm, to hold her close to him and stroke her hair, and just *feel* that she was all right. He longed to kiss her lips, to feel that connection he had been so sure he'd never again feel. He knew she would welcome him. Nothing had changed in her eyes that had always looked at him with so much acceptance, so much longing, so much…love.

And yet, he *couldn't.* The voice in his head was stronger. *Poison, Erik,* it screamed in his ear. *Your touch is poison.* And though his logical side warred with the voice—tried to drown it out, tried to identify it as the remembered ravings of a heartless woman who could not overlook her own son's imperfections long enough to love him—the voice still won. He might claim to never be able to harm a hair on

Jenna's head, but he could not take the chance.

Moving away, and out of her reach, Jenna heard him ask, "Can I get you something to eat, Mademoiselle?" She noticed that he did not meet her eyes.

All of a sudden, all semblances of an appetite left her, and she shook her head. "No, Erik," she muttered. "I think I should just go lie down and rest a bit more before dinner."

She saw him nod, still not looking at her, as he uttered, "Very well." He turned and walked back over to his reading chair in the sitting room that had, at some point, been set to rights.

Jenna retreated to her own room, shutting the door. As she made her way back toward her bed, she surmised that the benefit of Erik not being able to look at her was that he would not get to see her cry.

"I am sorry to have to tell you this, Ms. Wilson," Dr. James, Jenna's new neurologist said from across his desk. The last few days had been a whirlwind for Penny. She had finally done what she felt was the right thing and dismissed Blaine from Jenna's case. Seeing how much Jenna's original doctor cared for her made Penny realize, once and for all, that he really should be the lead physician on the case, since he seemed to have a vested interest in her well being. No sooner had she made that decision, however, than Jenna had suffered a massive seizure, and the sweet young doctor had attacked Blaine and gotten himself suspended. So now, Dr. James, the Chief of Neurology, had taken over Jenna's case, and from the ominous look on his face, he was not optimistic about her prognosis.

"I do not foresee Jenna getting any better." The look on his face was sad, but calm. Delivered with cool professionalism softened by genuine compassion, Dr. James' declaration seemed to cut straight to Penny's heart. Gone was the passion with which she had seen Jenna's previous doctor fight for her niece; gone too was the arrogance with which Blaine had held fast to his own view. Dr. James told her the news as if he was simply stating a fact, and the finality of his statement sent a chill down her spine. Jenna was not going to get better. Jenna was…gone?

"Dr. James," Penny asked, her voice thin and small. "What does that mean?"

He took in a deep breath and released a heavy sigh. “Ms. Wilson, of course every coma patient is unique, and we do not have any evidence that says your niece's brain was severely damaged in the accident. However, there is still much we don't know about the brain's function, and the fact that Jenna has not responded more than she has, or regained consciousness yet is not a good sign.”

Penny merely nodded grimly. “What's next for her, Doctor?”

“While it is still possible for her to regain consciousness, I will stress that it is unlikely. Most coma patients who have not regained consciousness at this point move into what we call a vegetative state. They tend never to regain any kind of cognitive awareness. She may, at some point, be able to open her eyes, but even still, it is my opinion that she will never regain awareness.”

Penny covered her face with her hand, and fought back tears. *Her sister's only child.* “What can I *do* for her?” she asked, in a shaky voice.

“Well,” he told her, in a gentle tone. “It might be time to consider moving her from here into a long term care facility.”

Penny let out a long sigh, still holding her head in her hand, and nodded. “I had a feeling you were going to say that, Doctor” With a heavy heart, she said, “I will look into making arrangements.”

35 A WORTHY OPPONENT

He stepped out of the elevator with a defiant set to his jaw. Being on suspension meant that he couldn't practice at the hospital, but it did not mean that he couldn't visit. He would just love to see anyone try to stop him from seeing Jenna. Dr. James had taken over her case, he knew, and was in the process of stabilizing her system, which had been thrown into the shock of withdrawal by Blaine's cruel handling of her case. He knew Jenna was in good hands with Dr. James, but he had to see her for himself—he had to *see* that she was all right.

He entered her room and was glad to see that the oxygen mask had been removed and that she appeared to be breathing comfortably on her own. He took his customary seat beside her bed and took her hand in his. It felt so cold.

"I'm back, Jenna," he said, with a crooked smile as he rubbed her hand in his, trying to warm it up. "You didn't think I'd let a little suspension keep me away, did you?" He let out a little chuckle. "Never! I may not be your doctor anymore, but I still…" he allowed his words to trail off, shaking his head to clear his thoughts. "You should have seen the fight, Jenna," he continued his conversation in another direction. "I got Charleson real good. Broke his nose, and I think I knocked out a tooth or two! Pretty boy will probably just have them replaced with gold crowns." He commented, rolling his eyes at the thought of Blaine with gold teeth in his mouth. "They'll make his smile sparkle even more." He shook his head a little before redirecting his attention on her. "Would you have been proud of me, Jenna?" he asked, quietly, stroking her palm with his thumb. "Or would you have told me violence wasn't the answer?" He thought a moment, remembering the spunk that he had always observed in her. Smiling, he said, "If I were to guess, you probably would have wanted to get a punch or two in yourself." He nodded again, continuing, "It was all worth it, Jenna. What he did to you…" He shook his head, his mouth forming a tight line against his teeth. "And

I prefer to think of a suspension as a little more free time I can spend with you. So what would you like to do today? Would you like me to read to you? Would you prefer music? Music *while* I'm reading, so you can multi-task?" He grinned, as he reached into his jacket pocket to pull out a paperback he had brought with him. "I brought this new novel with me." He turned the book to look at the title. "Siren of the Sea…It's an adventure novel about a masked pirate. I don't know how good it is, but it was the only book in the gift shop that did not have a sexy half naked man on the front cover, put there for the express purpose of making me feel inadequate."

"Doctor!" the nurse exclaimed in surprise, as she entered to check Jenna's vital signs—a routine task, performed several times a day. "I did not expect to see you in here."

"Not to worry," he assured the nurse, who he was sure had been updated to his situation. "I am only here visiting. See," he gestured with his hands to his attire, "No lab coat."

"Well," she said, as she reached over to wrap the blood pressure cuff around Jenna's arm. "It's a good thing that you're visiting her now."

He looked up at her questioningly. "What do you mean?"

"You know I'm not supposed to tell you this, Doctor," she said sheepishly, catching herself before she went on. "You're not her doctor anymore, and HIPPA…"

"Maureen," he looked at her with pleading eyes. "You know the only reason I was taken off Miss Wilson's case was because I lost my temper with Dr. Charleson. Can you blame me for that? He could have *killed* her."

The nurse looked torn. "No, Doctor, I cannot blame you at all. You've tried to take very good care of Jenna."

"Well then, please," he implored her. "Tell me what's going on."

She took a deep breath before delivering the news. "Dr. James told her aunt that she was entering a vegetative state. They are in the process of making plans to transfer her to a long term care facility."

This news came to him as a shock to him. How could Dr. James give up so quickly? "When?"

"Probably before the end of the week, Doctor," the nurse answered.

"Which one?" He wanted to work on getting visiting privileges at whatever care facility they chose for her as soon as possible.

The nurse's face look pained as she said, "They're moving her to Maine, to be closer to her aunt."

❧

Erik tossed the book he had been reading on the floor. It landed among the dozen or so others with which he had busied himself since Omid had gone, having halted his research only briefly when Jenna had emerged from her room for a few moments that afternoon. He was completely frustrated. He knew it was unreasonable to expect an answer to Jenna's dilemma to be clearly defined in any of his books—to his knowledge, a case such as hers had never happened before. But the urgency he felt to figure out how to help her had only increased when he'd witnessed her frail condition earlier. Following an afternoon of research, he was not certain he had made any real progress.

He'd read all he could about brain injuries—but the writings were sparse. Most seemed to center around the case of Phineas Gage who'd managed to survive a iron bar shooting straight through his skull in a railway accident. As there had never been any metal pipes sticking out of Jenna's head—that he'd noticed, anyway—Erik did not think Gage's case had any relevance to hers. There were some mentions of seizures, but usually recurring ones that were a part of epilepsy—not much on the one time phenomenon that Erik sincerely hoped Jenna had suffered. There were also mentions of patients who had been left in a stupor for extended periods of time due to some trauma to the head. Except for the period right after her seizure, however, Jenna had always been quite aware.

Not quite able to come up with an answer on the medical front, Erik had begun looking up the idea of existing in two worlds at the same time. If he thought the medical evidence was sparse, then the evidence for this more esoteric idea was almost non-existent. How did one research the concept of living in two planes of existence at once? The best he had come up with was a concept sometimes seen in folklore and fairytales in which some alternative *other* world existed in conjunction with the physical world. The belief was that at certain *liminal* times—or times of transition that were *in between* other times—the thresholds into these other worlds could open, and entry could be achieved. Interestingly, one phenomenon that often acted as a liminal threshold was water—an element that Erik had suspected being involved in Jenna's case from the very beginning. He had to admit, this concept of liminality, or "time in flux," was perhaps the most compelling evidence he had found so far, and the idea of crossing a threshold definitely brought to mind Jenna's claim of a secret door that had somehow allowed entry into his home. It all sounded quite interesting, except for the fact that Jenna's life was not a fairy tale. *How* could it have been possible for a threshold to open to allow Jenna into his world? And if she *had* crossed over some threshold, why did there seem to be some case to be made that her *own* world still held some hold over her? He kept coming back to the stitches. Where had they gone?

Erik rose irritably and walked over to his piano. He sat down and began to stroke the ivories that had for so long been his most faithful friends. He begged the music to help him think, because so far, even with all the reading he had done, Erik was at a loss. He closed his eyes and allowed his fingers free reign over the keys. But he soon found that they had no interest the dominion that was offered them. Even music was not coming freely to him tonight.

Jenna had cried away all her tears, and she lay there in bed staring at the ceiling. What had happened to change Erik's mind? They had come so far together. She remembered the bashful way he had reached for her hand in Box 5, the same hand he had retained possession of throughout rehearsal and again later as they walked back from the boat. She remembered the beautiful cameo he had given her, and the playful little dance that had led to…

Well. Their dance had led to more. *Much* more.

Jenna turned on her side, and wondered if *that* was the problem. Once again, she had let her feelings get away from her and things had gotten out of control. Erik had been through so much hell in his life. He had been physically and emotionally abused, and had almost been the victim of rape. They had started out their morning holding hands—*really* holding hands—for the first time. How could she have let things go from holding hands to making love all in one day?

She had always had a habit of letting things happen too fast, of falling for the wrong guys, and giving them what they wanted in hopes that they would love her back. But it had not been that way with Erik. The idea of making him love her had been the farthest thing from her mind. Even the idea of kissing him had not seriously entered her thoughts as a possibility. She had been so sure his mind was set on Christine, she had resigned herself to giving up her own wishes and desires.

But when he first kissed *her*, it was like a dam had burst. All of her feelings for him came flooding out of her in wave after wave of kisses and touches—all of which endeavored to show him the love and acceptance he had never known before. Their passion had been beautiful and unselfish. She'd had no thoughts in her mind other than to love him—*just* to love him. To show him the tenderness he should have lived his whole life knowing. And when he touched her, it felt like he just wanted to love her back. *My Jenna* he had called her. And truly, she *wanted* to be his. Forever. She knew this was not her home, but she felt like she belonged more here than she ever had elsewhere in her life. She felt valued here. She felt important. And last night, she'd felt so loved. All because of Erik.

But she knew she could not rush him. He had lived a life full of abuse and full of pain. Love would not be easy for him, and she had to wait for him to be ready. But for Erik, she was prepared to wait a lifetime.

Feeling much better about things between them, and more certain about a course of action, Jenna rose from the bed. She still felt a little dizziness, but it was much less than before. She changed from the peach dress to a much simpler one made of dark blue. She managed to wrestle her nest of curls into a ribbon and tied them away from her face. Before she opened her door, she reached down and placed her hand on the cameo that Erik had bestowed on her the evening before, giving her cherished rose a squeeze for luck, hoping she could dispel the awkwardness that had arisen between them.

She emerged from the bedroom to find books strewn all over the floor. Erik, however, had moved to the piano. Instead of the usual full, lush chords she was used to hearing from him, however, his fingers were halting, uncertain as they ghosted over the keys. His eyes betrayed a feeling of frustration. She walked over to him, and when she was right behind him and he still had not looked up from whatever irritation had claimed him, she reached out and touched his shoulder.

He flinched when he felt her touch and whirled around to look at her. When their eyes met, it was an electric moment, and Jenna felt the almost irresistible urge to lean over and touch his lips with hers. She pulled back a bit, instead, however, remembering her vow to go slowly, and wait for Erik to set the pace of their relationship. "Hi," was her only word.

Erik took a breath, as if needing to calm himself, and said, "Good evening, Mademoiselle. Are you feeling quite rested now?"

Though the title of Mademoiselle still stung, Jenna realized it was a coping mechanism that for some reason he needed right now. "I'm feeling much better, Erik," she assured him with a smile. "Thank you for asking."

He made to get up from the piano, "I should make you some dinner…"

"Erik, I'm not really hungry yet," she informed him. "I…" she began, feeling a little sheepish. "I'd love to hear you play."

The exposed side of Erik's face reddened a little and he shook his head, "I'm sorry, Mademoiselle. The music…seems to have abandoned me tonight."

Jenna gave him a sympathetic smile, and began to scan the room for something they could do. She had had enough of wasting away alone in her room, and though she had vowed not to push things too fast with Erik, she still craved his presence. Jenna thought she noticed something poking out of the bottom shelf of his overburdened bookcase. Walking over to take a closer look, she found an old, weathered chessboard. "Erik, do you play chess?" she asked, in surprise, having never noticed the board before.

"I *played* chess, Mademoiselle," Erik corrected her, the corner of his lips turning up just slightly. "The Daroga finally got tired of losing, so we haven't played in a few years."

Jenna smiled slyly at him, and commented, "*I'd* play with you."

"Oh, please, Mademoiselle." he rolled his eyes. "As I just said, the Daroga *never* won against me. Why would you wish to play?"

"Because you also said that you haven't played in a few years." A mischievous gleam sparked in her eyes. "I bet you're pretty rusty."

Erik rolled his eyes. "I am *not* rusty, Mademoiselle. Chess is merely child's play for me. It's hardly a challenge."

"Oh, child's play, huh?" Jenna asked, eyebrows raised. "Then you should enjoy watching me lose!"

Erik made a loud sigh, and stood from the piano bench to retrieve the chessboard. "Do not say I didn't warn you, Mademoiselle," he commented, opening a drawer on his side table and removing the playing pieces.

"Oh, never," she insisted, shaking her head back and forth, biting back a grin. "You have been very clear about your intentions to wipe the floor with me!"

Erik looked at her again with raised eyebrows. "Another one of your futuristic saying, I presume?"

Jenna giggled a little bit and nodded. "It means you plan to win."

"Well, then," he nodded. "It's true."

"We'll see." She giggled with a smile.

Erik placed the board on the dining table and he and Jenna began to arrange the pieces to start the game.

"White or black, Erik?" Jenna asked.

"Black, of course, Mademoiselle," Erik said in a silky smooth tone. "It is my preferred color, and it allows you the privilege of moving first." Then, under his breath, he added, "You're going to need all the help you can get."

Jenna heard his little remark, but only raised an eyebrow and smiled, deciding not to comment. She was truly enjoying the return of Erik's mischievous side, *and* she had a surprise for him.

Just as Erik had offered, Jenna made the first move, staking her claim for the center of the board. Erik just smiled and made a move counter to hers and the game was afoot.

"When did you learn to play chess, Erik?" Jenna asked Erik as he studied the board.

"It was a favorite way to pass the time at court in Persia," he answered, positioning his pieces according to his favorite strategy. "The Daroga and I spent many a night engaged in fierce battles of wits. As I said earlier, he never beat me. Considering his level of wit, it should not be hard to understand why."

Jenna rolled her eyes at Erik's insult to the man she knew he actually regarded quite highly. "Did *anyone* ever beat you at court?" she asked coyly as she continued to arrange her own pieces.

"No, Mademoiselle," Erik answered simply. "Chess is a very cerebral past time—a thinker's game—and no one at court ever thought quite the way I did."

"Oh I believe that," Jenna smiled at him, building up his sense of self-confidence. "Musical genius, architect, master ventriloquist—I don't think there are too many people who *could* think like you, Erik."

Erik snickered, as he moved another pawn. "And the world is better for it, I am sure."

"Oh I don't know about that," Jenna said, capturing Erik's pawn, taking him by surprise. "I think the humanity could benefit very much from your unbounded genius. Even just your music alone is so beautiful, it would enrich the world greatly."

"Is that so, Mademoiselle?" he asked, a little irritation entering his voice, as he realized that there were not very many safe spaces on the board where he could move his pieces. Jenna had spread out her players rather strategically, and to Erik's surprise, he had not noticed, since she had kept him talking. "Wasn't it just the other day you were complaining about my incessant piano playing?"

"I had a headache, Erik," Jenna brushed him off, nonchalantly capturing another of Erik's pieces. "I cannot be held responsible for what I said."

And so the game went, the two battling on the chessboard, the whole while engaging in easy conversation. Though Erik knew the talk was distracting, he could not help but answer Jenna's questions, especially when she posed them so sweetly, and was so complimentary to him in her own responses. They passed at least an hour in this fashion, which was odd for Erik, since he was used to beating the Daroga in a matter of minutes.

"Mademoiselle," Erik asked finally, looking directly at her, eyes narrowed questioningly. "When did *you* learn to play Chess?"

"Chess is a very popular game in my time. We had a chess club at my grade school," Jenna said, a grin spreading across her face as she moved another piece into Erik's territory. "I was a member as soon as I was old enough to join. I stayed with the game through high school and college, eventually entering tournaments." She continued, removing another of Erik's players. "And winning. The game always appealed to me. The intellectual challenge. The strategy of battle. Finding ways to distract a worthy opponent, leading them into defeat when they were so sure of victory." She looked up into his eyes. "I won a couple of championship games back in my day. *And* I just put you in check."

Erik glanced away from her eyes, which were holding him so captive, and glanced at the board. Sure enough, his king was at the complete disposal of her queen, powerless to her every whim. He glanced back at Jenna, her eyes blazing with excitement and pride at her accomplishment. It was all he could do not to kiss her—she looked so tantalizing at that moment. His own gaze full of wonder, he said, breathlessly, "You are amazing, Mademoiselle."

"Can I ask a prize?" she questioned, reaching out and taking his hand in hers. "Can you please go back to calling me Jenna?" Her eyes implored him, and she continued, "When you call me Mademoiselle, you seem so far away. And I want you to be closer."

Erik looked at her, her expression so sincere. He wanted nothing more at that moment than to wrap her in his arms. Oh how he loved this woman, and her endless efforts to draw him close. He relished the feel of his hand in hers, even though he knew he shouldn't. He *had* to concentrate on finding an answer to the problems that had been threatening her health, so that maybe they could fix them and … move on. He knew he had to fight this wave of desire that was currently washing over him, for this intriguing, intelligent, and *beautiful* woman, but, maybe, it wouldn't hurt to just let her continue to hold his hand?

"Jenna," he asked her, his voice strained with the battle he was waging to control his desires. "Can you tell me more about your accident?"

She was surprised at his question, but he was not flinching away from her touch, and he had used her name, so she simply stated, "I've already told you everything I can remember, Erik. What more would you like to know?"

Erik wondered himself what useful information he was trying to glean from the question. He already knew that the accident was a horrendous event when his dear Jenna was plunged into a river and somehow found herself walking in a tunnel that led to his home. But was that all? "What happened," he began, grasping to find the words that would give voice to the thoughts in his mind, "between the time you landed in the river and the time you were in the tunnel? How did you get out of this…*car*…of yours? Do you remember?"

Jenna thought for a moment, trying to find an answer to his question, but honestly not remembering. "I…I don't know, Erik." she paused, trying to recall those moments once more. "I don't remember getting out of my car at all. I think I must have passed out. I remember blackness and then the darkness of the tunnel."

Erik continued to probe, needing to know more about this mystery surrounding her accident. "What would have happened, Jenna, if people from your own time had found your car and…you were still in it?"

Jenna looked at him in confusion, shaking her head a little. "What are you talking about, Erik? You know they didn't. I'm here…with *you.*"

"I know you're here," Erik said, and despite himself, he gave her hand a little squeeze, so grateful that he could, at least in this small measure, still feel her. "But what if you hadn't found yourself in that tunnel? What if you hadn't come here?"

Jenna looked away, considering, for the first time, a different outcome to that terrifying night. With a dry throat, she began, "I don't… I don't really know. I…I suppose the police would have come. And they would have sent a rescue team into the river. If I hadn't…" she took a deep breath as she contemplated what could very well have been her fate. "If I was still alive…"

Erik felt a shiver run through his body, and he looked down and away from her. "Oh, Jenna, don't even speak of that."

"Well, it is a strong possibility that I *could* have died in that accident, Erik," she squeezed his hand even tighter, seeing how hard that seemed to be for him to hear. "But if I *hadn't*, I would have been rushed to a hospital, where the doctors and nurses would have tended my wounds." She thought for a moment. "I might have even been brought to my *own* hospital, where I worked."

"And then?" Erik probed, trying to understand what might be happening to her, since he was still certain that somehow events in her world held sway over what was happening to her in his. "What then, Jenna?"

"It's really hard to tell." She shrugged her shoulders. "Judging by the injuries I had when I first arrived here, I could have just been stitched up and sent on my way—maybe kept in the hospital overnight for observation."

"And what if the injuries were worse?" He asked, grasping at any bits of information he could get from her. "You say you blacked out before you found yourself in that tunnel. What if they had found you unconscious in your car before you made it to the tunnel?"

"Well, that could have been an indicator of a more serious brain injury," Jenna postulated, uncertain why he was asking these questions, but sensing that it was important to him that she answer.

"How soon would you have awakened?"

"I have no idea, Erik. Sometimes people who lose consciousness in accidents like that *don't* wake up. They enter a coma and remain unresponsive until they eventually die."

Erik felt his blood run cold at her answer. "How long can these comas last? Weeks? Months?"

"Sometimes they can last years..." Jenna's voice trailed off as she remembered the coma patients she had tended in the hospital, as well as the cases she had studied in school. "They sometimes speculate that coma patients can hear everything that is going on around them—they know what's going on, but they cannot communicate. Others say that coma victims have very lucid dreams, where their brains create an alternate reality in which they can go on living, since they can no longer interact with the world around them. Eventually though," Jenna added, "whether they have been aware of their surroundings the whole time, or whether they have been living in some alternate dream world, most coma patients simply die, never having been in touch with the world around them ever again."

Jenna's words were like a vice around Erik's heart. He could not point to exactly why, but her words about the fates of coma patients somehow rang true in his mind. It made sense, Erik thought. If by chance Jenna *had* entered a coma—as she called it—in her own time, perhaps that had freed her soul, on some level, to somehow enter into his. And though Jenna had mentioned the concept of this alternate life being a dream world, were not dreams sometimes so distinct, so *graspable,* that they themselves could often seem real—as if they were lived, and not simply imagined?

Of course, he knew that this could not simply be a dream. Who would dream about his world of solitude that was so depressing and so heartbreaking in its cruelty? And he knew it was not merely her soul that had traveled into his realm, because of the beautiful, blessed, warmth of her touch.

What if it were merely a lack of understanding about their experiences that lead the medical profession to guess that coma patients were dreaming? After all, few would believe Jenna's current situation if they had not been living it themselves. Did he himself not assume at first that Jenna was a mental patient deprived of her faculties, when she mentioned what her life was supposed to be?

Would a cold, detached doctor who prided himself on objectivity, have even lingered with a patient so afflicted long enough to realize that there was more to their ravings than a very vivid dream?

He recalled his own research about the circumstances of patients who lay in a stupor, lingering and languishing in their hospital beds—sometimes moving, sometimes even opening their eyes—but never again having any meaningful interaction with the outside world. Were *they* also living in a universe created inside their heads? Were they *dreaming* of other lives to replace the lives they had effectively lost when their brains were injured? When they were being tended to by physicians, did those ministrations enter into their experiences in the new existence they were living? And most importantly, did that substitute life also end when the doctors lost the fight and their battered bodies stopped breathing?

Jenna saw the look of abject horror on Erik's face, as she described these hypothetical scenarios to him. "I feel I was very lucky, Erik."

He looked at her with narrowed eyes, emerging from his pondering at the quiet sound of her voice. "You suffered a life-threatening accident which thrust you away from everything and everyone that you knew, and you consider yourself fortunate?"

"I do," she said, looking down before once again making eye contact with him. "Because I found you."

Her eyes were so sincere, so honest when she spoke that she took Erik's breath away. A lifetime of people viewing him as a curse, as a nightmare—and Jenna looked at him as a stroke of good luck. Mesmerized by the sweetness of her words and the look in her eyes, Erik could not stop his free hand from reaching out and stroking her cheek, at which point, Jenna closed her eyes and turned her face into his touch. "*Erik*," she whispered, and he felt himself leaning closer to her soft, slightly parted lips.

You cannot touch her, Erik. That venomous whisper once again screamed in his mind. *Your touch is poison.* With a visible shudder, Erik pulled away. "It really *is* time I go make dinner, Jenna," he said, rising from the table, causing Jenna's eyes to blink open in surprise. "It is past Samineh's feeding time, and you're going to need sustenance if you hope to regain your strength." And with that, he turned and swiftly left the room.

36 HER CHOICE

Penny heard the knock at her hotel room door and placed the sweater she had been folding in the suitcase before walking over and looking through the peephole. *Oh dear,* she thought, as she unchained the lock. This was going to be difficult.

As she pulled open the door, she looked at the face of Jenna's doctor, and her heart broke. His hair was disheveled, his shoulders slumped. He was looking down at his feet, but she could see the expression on his face was tense. "Doctor," she said in greeting, and he glanced up at her, and when he did, his eyes held such sorrow, such defeat.

"You're taking her away, Ms. Wilson," he stated, his voice breaking on the last word.

"Please come in," Penny said, ushering him into her room and closing the door, so that they were not talking in the hallway of a New York hotel. She drew him to one of the overstuffed chairs by the window. "Would you care for a drink, Doctor?" she asked, as she poured herself some water.

She saw him shake his head quietly, still looking too stricken to talk. She took her glass and sat down in the other chair, facing him. When their eyes met once more, he asked her simply, "When?"

She took a drink from her glass. "They are coming to pick her up tomorrow."

"Tomorrow?" his eyes widened and his voice was hollow. "That's…that's too…" he trailed off as the enormity of her words hit him.

"Too soon?" she asked sympathetically, hating the vacant, lost look he wore on his face.

"Yes," he whispered looking down again. "Far too soon."

They were quiet for a few moments, him staring at the floor,

Penny staring at him. When at last he broke the silence, he asked, "*Why* so soon? And why so *far*?"

Penny reached out and took his hand. "I live in Maine, Doctor. I found an excellent facility that will give her the very best of care. And I will be able to visit her often. I can finally be real family to her—not simply caring for her from afar. They were able to arrange for transport tomorrow, so I had to agree." When he simply stayed quiet, staring at the floor in front of him, she added, "Dr. James told me that there was very little chance of her ever waking up. He said she was moving into a vegetative state."

"That's debatable," he argued.

"Are you questioning Dr. James' judgment?" she asked gently. "He's the Chief of Neurology. Your *boss*."

He heaved a heavy sigh. "No, I know Dr. James is an excellent doctor," he conceded. He glanced imploringly in her eyes. "But there is *always* hope."

"But how much?" Penny challenged, quietly. "Can you honestly tell me you think she is going to wake up?"

"I *wish* it," he answered. "I wish it with all my heart."

"But that is not the same," she said gently, "as believing it." When she saw his head hang again, she continued. "Doctor, I know that you would do *anything* to make Jenna wake up. You've tried so hard and you've shown such care."

"And it has all come to nothing." He sighed heavily.

"You don't know that, Doctor," Penny disagreed. "You have no way of knowing how you may have helped her."

"If I had been successful, she would have opened her eyes." He raked his fingers through his hair. "And you would not be taking her away to Maine."

"Doctor," Penny said, sadly. "I know that you love her, and if love could work miracles, I *know* you would have brought her back. "

"But love was not enough."

It pained Penny to hear him so distraught. "Maybe not this time," she said, sadly. "But you have to promise me that you are not going to give up on love." When she saw him begin to shake his head, she added, "I have never seen someone give such unselfish love as you gave to my niece. It would be a horrible shame if you were to waste that on someone who could never give it back."

"It was not *wasted* on Jenna, Ms. Wilson. She is special to me." His eyes took on a faraway look as he recalled the days before she was confined to a hospital bed. "Before the accident, she dazzled me. She was so beautiful, and confident, and full of life. I was so drawn to her, but so shy. I curse that shyness, because I never talked to her, aside from a few quick words about patients. And now…" His voice trailed off as he rose to his feet and began to pace the floor. "Ms. Wilson, I should have told her. I should have introduced myself as a man, not just a doctor. I should have asked her to dinner, I should have told her she was beautiful. I should not have held myself back for fear of being rejected. And now…now I'm never going to have the chance."

Penny swallowed and struggled to hold back the tears that had sprung to her eyes. Oh, what she wouldn't give for her niece to know the devotion of this wonderful man. He could have been the answer to all of her prayers—the final destination on her thus far disappointing journey into romance. The look in his eyes when he spoke of her…any woman would be fortunate to find that level of adoration in her mate. It seemed so consummately unfair that Jenna could not experience this type of love. But Penny knew that *he* could.

"Doctor, listen to me," she stood and took his hand in hers once more. "You are young. Your whole life is ahead of you. I would want nothing more for my niece than to know your love for her. But that cannot happen." She looked deeply into his eyes, begging him to accept the gravity of the situation. "She is *gone*."

"I promised her I would never stop trying. " He shook his head, his eyes watering with unshed tears. "I promised her I would never give up on her."

"Then don't give up," she squeezed his hand in hers tightly, "on *yourself*, Doctor. The next time you find a woman who catches your eye, who *dazzles* you, as you put it, don't be shy. You will make some lucky woman out there so *very* happy."

He closed his eyes at her complimentary words. He was touched by her kindness and her desire for him to move on, but she didn't understand. He loved *Jenna*. There could not be another.

"I found it, Jenna! The door. It's here," he declared, in shock as, in fact, the small wooden door appeared by the lake. True to Jenna's description, it was made

of boards that undulated and pulsed, held together by heavy rope. There was light glistening through the slats, engendering hope that there was, indeed, something new and wonderful on the other side. He looked away from the shimmering door, with a mixture of excitement at finally solving this confounding mystery and sadness at what he knew would be his impending loss. "Jenna," he said again, "It's the way back to your world. We've found it! You can finally go home."

Jenna smiled lovingly at him, her eyes shining, as she took his hand in hers. "I am *home, Erik."*

Erik stared at her, unbelieving. "What are you saying, Jenna?"

"I'm not leaving," she answered.

In confusion, he pressed, "But your life *is there, Jenna. Your home."*

*She pulled him closer to her and gazed deeply into his eyes as she whispered, "*You *are my life.* You *are my home. Erik, I love you." She reached up and cupped his cheek in her hand adoringly, as she added, "I* choose *you, Erik."*

He felt her pull his head down toward hers, to join their lips in a tender kiss. When she pulled away, joy was in her eyes as she said again, "I choose you, *Erik. I won't leave you."*

He cupped her face in his hands, gazing at her adoringly, completely humbled by the auspicious turn of fortune that landed this woman in his arms. "Jenna, I…" he began to declare his love for her when a breeze rustled through their hair and they heard a creak behind them. Erik pulled Jenna fully into the protection of his arms as they noticed that the door, under its own power, was beginning to swing open.

The light shining through the slats once again proved deceptive, as a long tunnel suddenly surged and rippled before them. Without moving, their eyes traversed the length of the passage, enclosed by its rough-hewn walls, and ceiling. Standing still, they navigated the path that the earthen floor laid out before them, until at last the shaft opened unto a small room, with walls of white and a single bed. Surrounding the bed were women in the long white dresses and small white caps that signified the medical profession. Within the bed, the still, prone form of a figure with closed eyes and hair of golden flame lay motionless under a cover of white. Her skin was pale, as if she were made of the finest porcelain, her lips barely pink. She looked so cold and breakable—nothing at all like the strong and exquisitely fiery young woman he had come to know.

Erik felt his breath come faster at the vision of Jenna reposing in the hospital bed, and he hugged her to him a little tighter to reassure himself that she was still with him, still breathing, still whole. He felt her nuzzle her head against his chest as she whispered once again, "I'm still here, Erik. I won't leave you."

In the vision before him, the nurses who were tending her suddenly stopped and moved away from her bed, a look of sorrow on their faces. A doctor came forward into the room, pressing a stethoscope to her chest, and once again, in another position before moving back from her and removing the instrument from his ears. He reached forward and took the sheet in his hands, and slowly, gently pulled it to cover Jenna's face, looking sadly at the nurses and shaking his head. With downcast eyes and defeated expressions, the doctor and the nurses filed out of the room, leaving it empty except for the lifeless body of the woman that he loved, lying covered by a sheet.

Erik knew he was trembling, shaking at the horror that had just played out before his eyes. He clutched his love closer, tighter to his pounding heart, hoping that somehow, her nearness would stop his soul from shivering. Lowering his head to drink in the scent of her hair, he found himself unable to look away from the tragedy before him. Again, of its own volition, the door slowly closed, yet still Erik stared, lost in a world of his own terrifying visions.

Then he felt Jenna's arms loose their hold around him and fall limply to her sides. He looked down to see that while her head still rested on his chest, it lay there listlessly, and suddenly, her body felt heavy in his arms. "Jenna," he called, but she did not answer. "Jenna," he said louder, but still, she made no reply. He lifted her chin up so she would face him, and he saw that her eyes were closed.

He lowered the two of them down to the ground, and cradled her in his arms, thinking she had passed out yet again. But this time was different, for her breathing was shallow, and her skin was growing cold. "Jenna," he whispered over and over again, placing whisper soft kisses on her forehead, her eyelids, her cheeks. "Jenna, wake up. Wake up." And then, finally, struggling, she opened her eyes and looked straight into his, her lips curving into a slight, tired smile as she rasped, "I chose you, *Erik," as the life left her body and her head lolled awkwardly to one side.*

"No, Jenna," he moaned as he shook her, tears spilling out of his eyes. "No!" his voice continued booming to a deafening roar as she made no reply, save for the cooling of her skin. "Jenna, come back!" He demanded with a harsh shout. "You swore you wouldn't leave me! Jenna, please, come back…"

Erik felt the hands on his shoulders, shaking him awake. With a start, he lifted his head from where it rested in the center of a large book that was laid out on his dining table. His fear stricken eyes attempted to focus on the force that had woken him from his nightmare, as he struggled to regulate his breathing. "Daroga," he panted. "What are you doing here?"

"Hello, Omid," the Persian began, sardonically. "Thank you for coming in and waking me from what was a horrible nightmare! I am so grateful to you and—"

"Jenna!" Erik exclaimed, cutting Omid off, as he sprang to his feet and instantly crossed the distance to Jenna's room. Quietly, he pushed her door open and stealthily glided to where she lay sleeping peacefully in her bed. He stood there silently for a moment simply watching her breathing. It seemed to him the most precious of sights, as the terror of his dream washed over him in renewed tremors of trepidation. When he felt calm enough to leave her, he exited her room, closing the door silently behind him. With a deep breath, he slowly walked back to the sitting room where the Persian awaited him with concerned eyes.

"Erik," he asked, shedding all artifice of humor. "Are you quite alright?"

"I am fine, Daroga," he nodded, sinking into his reading chair in exhaustion.

"What were you doing sleeping at the table, Erik?" Omid questioned his friend.

"Must I justify my every action to you?" he asked, with eyebrow raised. Sighing, he acquiesced and said, "I must have dozed off while reading."

Omid glanced over at the book laid out on the table. *The Treatment of Patients Afflicted with a Long Standing Stupor* was the title at the top of the page Erik had been reading. "Are you considering a career change, Erik, or were you having trouble falling asleep?" he asked, a bit of sarcasm finding its way back into his tone. "If the latter is true, it looks like you found a solution."

"I have to send her back, Daroga," Erik stated, his eyes looking stricken, his expression haggard.

Omid looked at him in annoyance. "Erik, what is wrong with you? It is obvious how much you and Jenna love one another. Are you truly so terrified of the happiness that you could find with her, that you are renewing your efforts to send her over a century into the future?"

"Daroga, her head injury—" Erik began to explain, but stopped short when Omid flew into a diatribe.

"—was *not* your fault, Erik!" he interrupted in aggravation, finally snapping at what he perceived as his friend's eagerness to hold fast only to sorrow. Slapping his hands on the table, he demanded, "When are you going to let that damnable witch of a woman die? She was never fit to have a child, Erik! She was a depraved, embittered woman. Her child was *healthy*—her child was a *genius*—and yet she cut him down because of the misfortune of his appearance—a deformity over which *he* had no control, but to which *she* surely contributed. She had no concept of the blessing she could have held in her arms and nurtured into greatness—while others in this world desperately cling to their own precious, *sick* children that the world takes from them too young. Do not let that termagant, that… *harpy* … destroy your chance at happiness with her sick, deluded ravings. She is *dead*, Erik. When will you let her be buried?"

Erik looked at his friend with surprise, jaw slightly agape at the vehemence of his declaration. "Daroga," he began quietly, the weight of the Persian's words still hanging heavily in his mind. "This has nothing to do with my mother. It is Jenna's health—"

"Have you taken her to a doctor, Erik? If her health is a concern, then let's find her a physician who can examine her and tell us—"

"Daroga," Erik interjected, "I do not believe one of the doctors from *our* time will find anything wrong with her."

"Oh for Allah's sake, Erik," Omid blurted in exasperation. "What on earth could be so wrong with her that only doctors from a hundred years in the future can treat her?"

"She is in a coma, Daroga," Erik stated plainly, keeping the emotion that was roiling in his heart from coming to the surface. "A stupor. A somnolence. She has been in one the whole time she has been here."

Omid stared at him in confusion. "How can that be, Erik? She has been awake and aware—"

"Not here, Daroga," Erik corrected him. "In her own time. I believe that she entered a coma at the time of her accident, and that somehow, because of her altered state of consciousness, she was able to travel to my domain and exist here, in this alternate universe, while her brain convalesced and healed in her own world."

Omid shook his head, "Erik you're speaking insanity! How is it that something like that could even happen?"

"The concept of liminality, Daroga. Her existence was in flux. A traumatic event deprived her of consciousness, leaving her in a state *between* life and death. At times like this, Daroga, doors can open, allowing passage between the worlds—forcing her to make a choice."

"The secret door…" Omid murmured, as he recalled this illusory door through which Jenna claimed she had entered Erik's lair. Erik nodded his head, but made no further answer. Omid tried hard to make sense of what his friend was saying, but he was not having much luck. "So are you saying that she chose *here?* She chose *you?*"

Omid's words once again pierced through his heart. Taking a deep breath, he attempted to explain. "Not exactly, Daroga. You see, I am more certain now than ever that she is somehow existing in two places at once—she is both here *and* there. Here she interacts with us, living this strange new life in the best way that she knows how. But in her own world, Daroga, she exists only to heal—to strengthen her body, to mend her spirit, so that she can once again go back to living the life she always knew. She has not yet made her ultimate choice, Daroga, but soon, I believe, she will have to."

"She will have to choose between going back to her life as a nurse, and living the rest of her life here with you?" Omid asked, to make certain he understood what Erik was saying.

"I believe so, yes," Erik nodded, a look of fear once again darkening his eyes.

"Then what are you afraid of, Erik?" Omid asked with a chuckle. "She is in *love* with you. You must realize she is going to choose you." He gave his friend a congratulatory pat on the back, already wondering if Erik would choose to continue his life beneath the opera house once he was a husband, or if he would instead choose to move with his wife out into the light—perhaps somewhere out in the country, to raise a family.

Erik shook his head back and forth. "I must do everything I can, Daroga, to make certain that she does not."

Omid once again looked at his friend in confusion. "But, Erik…*why?*"

"Because, if she chooses me, Daroga," Erik began, his voice tremulous with dismay, "she rejects her own life. Once she finally, irrevocably chooses to close the door on her own world, there will no longer be any reason for her to heal. Her body will fail, Daroga. Her breathing will slow and her heart will stop beating. We have seen that what happens to her in her world happens to her here. So if that happens, Daroga—if she rejects her former life, and chooses to remain in this pseudo existence," Erik's breathing was heavy with the enormity of what he was about to say, "she will *die.*" He swallowed hard, before adding, "And she will be lost to *both* worlds."

37 HIS HEART'S RESPONSE

"Let's go, Red," he said as he reached for the cat who was curled up in a ball on his couch. As he gathered him in his arms, the feline let out a lazy *Mreeeeoooow*, in protest. "I know, big guy," the doctor said, cuddling the cat close as he walked him over to the carrier. "I'm interrupting your nap. Bet you'll forget all about it by the time we get to the car, though. You'll sing to me all the way to the hospital, won't you? But we've got to get going," he said, his voice becoming quieter. "We can't be late today, Red." He lowered him into the crate to which the cat had become quite accustomed in the past few weeks. "We've got to say goodbye to Jenna," he said, with a hollow voice, trying to fight back the emotions that were warring in his soul. "She's leaving for Maine today." *Mreeeow*! was the cat's only comment. "I agree, Red. I don't want her to go either," he said sadly, as he zipped up the carrier. "But it's not our call, Buddy. Even though we both love her."

He lifted the carrier by the handle and looked around his home once more before turning toward the door. Empty. It suddenly struck him that his home was so empty. No family pictures on the wall. No clutter on the coffee table. In the kitchen, only one mug was stained with that morning's coffee, only one cereal bowl lay in the sink. There was nothing to show any real warmth here—any real love. It was proof that, aside from Red, he was so totally and utterly alone in the world. Without Jenna, that's how he knew he was going to stay.

"Come on, Buddy," he said, as he opened the door with a sigh, "Let's go say goodbye to the woman we love." He closed the door behind them, knowing that after this morning, he would return, along with Jenna's cat—just the two of them, alone with the emptiness.

Perhaps she should have given this a little more thought before deciding it was a good idea. Her arms were on *fire,* her clothes filthy, and she was sure that at any minute Erik was going to walk in and find her, ruining her surprise. But then again, considering how wrapped up he was in other things these days, probably not.

She sighed deeply, and continued to whisk the dark mixture, begging it with all her heart to thicken already. She had done this before, plenty of times, but always with the aid of an electric mixer. This hand-whisking thing was more difficult than she had expected, but if this is what life was like living in the 1800s, then so be it. For Erik, she could give up electricity. For Erik, she could give up everything. She would do anything, just to see his smile.

The treat was to be a gift to celebrate opening night. Tonight was the night that Christine was to make her debut, singing the lead role that had once been claimed by Carlotta. All thoughts were on the young diva. Omid informed them she was the talk of all of Paris. Would she shine? Would she falter? Would the spotlight prove too much for her? Would she thrive under the public's adoring gaze?

Of course, she would succeed! Of that, Jenna had no doubt. She was Erik's pupil—his finest creation—and she would prove his genius to the world with her voice. She had improved so much, in fact, that Erik no longer felt the evening lessons necessary, as he had not given her one in about a week. Even without her lessons, though, when Jenna had *insisted* the other day that Erik take her to see how rehearsals were coming along, she sounded exquisite. But Jenna's greatest concern was *not* Christine.

Erik had been a bundle of nerves for the past week. Since the night they'd almost made love, he'd been so distant. He was polite to her, he was kind, but he always seemed at least partially preoccupied—never fully with her. She knew that things had moved too fast that night, and that her seizure had truly frightened him, but ever since the evening they had passed playing chess, he had not touched her—not even to help her in and out of the boat, on their journey to Box 5. She had begun to wonder if the desire he had so beautifully expressed in her arms had, for some reason, faded.

But then she would catch him glancing at her over dinner, or from across the sitting room while they would have tea, and she would catch the passion—recognize the longing in his eyes. If they found themselves a bit too close to each other when passing in a room, she could hear him catch his breath, and see the struggle he waged inside himself *not* to touch her. She reminded herself about his past over and over, and renewed her resolve to stay strong—to not push him too far too fast. But it was so hard when he had *that* look in his eyes, and Jenna began to wonder if he held back because he was afraid that she would somehow reject him.

So tonight she meant to make her feelings plain. With the clandestine help of her ally Omid, she had procured all the ingredients needed to make Erik a lovely dinner before they left to enjoy the opening in Box 5. And though she knew The Palais Garnier would be focused on the fresh young ingénue, it would be Erik's night of triumph too. Hopefully, the chocolate mousse—which had finally begun to thicken—would be just the special treat to show him how proud she was of him. And after the show, when he was relaxed and content with his pupil's success, while the cast and guests cavorted above, with the masks on their faces concealing their identities, her own heart would be laid bare, her own secrets made known. She would tell him, finally, that she loved him. And she would loose him from the bonds of the promise he made to help her find a way home after the gala night had passed. It was no longer wanted, nor was it necessary. Jenna no longer needed to find a way home. She had found all she desired in Erik's arms.

"Thank you, Jenna," Erik said politely, placing his napkin back on the table. "Dinner was lovely." And, certainly, it had been. While he had spent the day absorbed in his research, she had spent the day in the kitchen. Her results had been delicious—coq au vin, and freshly baked bread. His results had not been so savory, and he only wished they had not weighed so heavily on his mind, so that he might have been able to relish more in the flavors of the culinary delight Jenna had prepared for him. Instead, he had been too busy trying to take in what he feared would most likely be one of their last evenings together. Though it would kill him, he knew it would soon be time to let her go.

He'd done all the research, analyzing his theory from every point, and he was certain he knew how to force a liminal threshold to open and allow her to return to her own time. The hard part was actually making himself do it. He had been trying for the last couple of days to make her *want* to leave. He had been withdrawn, distant—almost cold. But it was difficult to keep pushing her away when all he wanted to do was draw her closer. Surely, she must have read the desire that smoldered in his eyes when he would see her smile. She must have noticed the strained effort it took for him not to grasp her hand as they entered and exited the boat. When they sat and sipped their tea in the evenings, could she sense how badly he wanted to taste the sweetness of her lips? Did she guess at the fantasies that played out in his mind about what might have happened that night had the seizure not taken hold? If they had not been interrupted, would she have trembled and quaked for another reason entirely, as she lay entangled in his arms? Dear God, having this woman so near and not being able to touch her—to *love* her—was maddening, and surely, it would prove his undoing.

Erik took a deep breath to try to calm his spirit, as he made to push away from the table.

"Wait!" Jenna commanded him before he could stand. "There's one more thing." She stood and began to scurry off to the kitchen.

"Jenna, I couldn't possibly eat one more bite…" he protested, his stomach full and his appetite dampened by his sour spirits.

"Oh, please, Erik," she begged. "Just…" she held out her hands in front of her, "don't move! I'll be right back!" She turned and dashed into the kitchen.

Erik rolled his eyes and sighed, "Fine!" and sat back down at the table. He knew, however, that despite his outward bluster, he was going to miss her and her ways of caring for him so much. God, was there any other way to ensure her safety? Did he truly *have* to send her back?

True to her word, Jenna reemerged from the kitchen within minutes—carrying a tea service with two extra teacups that appeared to be full of …*something*…topped with what looked like freshly whipped cream.

"What's this?" he asked, with narrowed eyes.

"Homemade chocolate mousse," she beamed proudly.

Erik's eyes widened with surprise. "Chocolate Mousse, Jenna?" He asked with delight. "You made it yourself?"

"Yes, I did," she nodded. "It's a favorite recipe of mine." She set down the tray and handed one of the cups to him along with a spoon. "But let me tell you, it's a lot easier to whip up in the twenty first century. If you need a project for your spare time, *Monsieur Genius*," she continued, pouring them each a cup of tea, "You should consider inventing the electric mixer. Lifesaving device."

Erik chuckled a little at her sage guidance, and loved the way she could coax good humor out of him so easily. "I shall take it under advisement, *Mademoiselle Chef!*" he responded, wondering if it had ever been so natural to tease before she came into his life? Would he ever laugh again after he made her leave?

Jenna moved her own seat to be closer to Erik's and looked at him with excitement. "Well…*taste* it," she urged, gesturing with her hand for him to take a bite.

Erik glanced at her a moment more before dipping his spoon into the dessert and bringing it to his mouth. The smooth richness of creamy chocolate exploded on his tongue, and he was certain he had never tasted anything quite so sweet. "Oh my," he said, mouth partway full. "Jenna, this is delicious! You've come a long way in my kitchen from the night you didn't even know how to make tea!"

Jenna laughed at that somewhat embarrassing memory as she enjoyed her own bite of mousse. "Well, thank you, Erik. I've quite gotten used to things in the 19th century since then. I think I've gotten rather proficient."

"You truly have!" he agreed, enjoying another mouthful of the delectable dessert.

"There's more in the ice chest. Maybe Omid would like to try some the next time he—"

"I am *not* sharing my mousse with the Persian!" Erik declared, a look of horror on his face. "He already drinks all my alcohol!"

Jenna laughed at Erik's reluctance to part with any of his special treat. "You don't have to share with anyone, Erik. Well," she added with a giggle, reaching for another spoonful, "except me."

"I have *no* problem sharing with you, Jenna." He looked up from his dessert and smiled at her.

Jenna's smile grew even brighter at Erik's obvious enjoyment of her efforts. "This is all for you, Erik. To celebrate."

"To celebrate what?" he asked in confusion.

"Well, opening night, of course!" she told him. "Christine may be singing tonight, but *you're* the reason why."

Jenna was sure she saw Erik's exposed cheek redden a bit self-consciously. "Christine already possessed a beautiful voice, Jenna. I only made her realize its potential."

"But if it were not for *you*," she insisted, "she would still be working as a seamstress. Your talent will shine through in her voice tonight, Erik. And all of Paris will owe you a debt that it is not Carlotta on stage, strangling the music instead of singing it."

Erik cocked his head to look at her, enjoyment in his eyes, "You sound just like me, Jenna."

"No," she quipped back. "If I truly sounded like you, I would have referred to her as a cow, or a bovine, or some other type of farm animal."

Erik actually snorted in amusement at her comment, knowing it to be true. When he was joined a second later by her own bell like giggles, he could only look at her and smile. "Oh Jenna," he sighed without thinking, "I have never before found it so *easy* to simply be myself."

"Well, I'm glad you do now, Erik," Jenna answered him sweetly, "Because I think your *self* is pretty wonderful."

Erik's eyes locked with Jenna's and he simply gazed at this incredibly beautiful woman before him, taking in the way the candlelight danced in her hair, and glimmered in her eyes. How in heaven had he been fortunate enough to earn her love? How on *earth* was he ever going to let her go?

"Erik," Jenna whispered, leaning forward slightly and reaching a finger toward the corner of his mouth. "You've got a little whipped cream…" her voice trailed off as she wiped the offending confection from his from his face.

Time stopped as they each inched forward, as if compelled by the force of their shared gaze. "Do I?" Erik murmured as his eyes began to close.

"Mmmm-hmmmm," she purred as her lids fluttered shut too.

Their lips met as if of their own accord, teasing, tasting, becoming reacquainted after too long a separation. Jenna felt Erik's hand move to the back of her head, fingers tangling in her hair, clasping her to him tenderly, reverently. She snaked one arm around his neck, the other wrapping around his waist pulling him closer, never wanting to let him go. She drank in his essence, as their lips mingled, letting it fill her soul. When the kiss ended, she felt him nuzzle his face against her cheek, before finally resting his forehead against hers, eyes still closed. Their breaths were coming in quick gasps, and she could feel the heat of his desire rising up and blending with hers. "Erik," she moaned, a breathy sigh.

Suddenly, she felt him stiffen in her arms. She opened her eyes only to find him gently disengaging himself from their embrace. He rose from his chair and began to pace the floor. "As you know, Jenna," he began, and his voice sounded thready, strained. "I have not been meeting with Christine in the evenings for our customary voice lessons. That has allowed me the time," he continued, "to resume my investigation into how to send you back earlier than we'd anticipated."

"Erik, it's not—" Jenna began, rising from her seat.

"I think that I have found the way, Jenna," Erik continued on.

"Erik stop—"

"—but it's going to require that you make a choice—"

"Erik!" Jenna said, loud enough to break through his rantings. She stood in the path of his pacing, putting her hands gently on his arms to stop him. Jenna looked directly into his eyes, which, though guarded, displayed such sorrow—such pain. It was time to end this ridiculous charade. It was time to tell him she had already made her choice. "I don't want to go home. I want to stay with *you*, Erik," she said, her gaze never faltering. "I love you."

Three words. Three simple syllables that had never before been uttered for him. He had guessed at her feelings. He had sensed them in her smiles, her actions, her embrace. But to hear them! To hear the words he longed for—words he knew no one would ever say—he was struck breathless by the sound. "Jenna," he whispered, his own voice tremulous and low. "I love…" He saw her move forward, wrapping her arms around him. Of their own accord, his arms folded around her back, and he held her tightly against him. Oh, she felt so right there—as if she were born to fill his embrace.

It would be so easy at this moment, to tell her of his love, to ask her to be his, to take her for his own. She had taught him what it was to truly live for the first time. She had shown him, indeed, that he was not a monster. He was no angel either. He was a man—no more, no less. And as a man, he was free to take her as his woman—his *wife*.

They would live a glorious life…*together*—laughing, loving, arguing, then making up. She would inspire within him new heights of passion. They could discover new joys together that were impossible for them each to know alone. She even made him long to live in the light, once more, for he could imagine nothing more beautiful than waking up to the morning sunbeams dancing brightly in her hair, except, perhaps for the serenity of her smile as she fell asleep at night, tucked into his arms. They could have that, Jenna and him. There *had* to be some way they could have that.

Jenna moved even closer and leaned her head against his chest, murmuring, as she did, "Oh, Erik, I could die in your arms."

Erik heard her breathless sigh, and his heart made the only response it knew how to make. *I would rather you live in them, Jenna. I would rather you live.*

Erik pulled back, and lifted her chin so that she would face him. "...*Christine*, Jenna," he finished his sentence, into her widening gaze. "I love Christine."

Jenna felt the world fall out from under her as a wave of nausea washed over her. She took a few small steps back. Cheeks red in embarrassment, she asked, "*What*?" smiling a little in disbelief.

Erik swallowed the lump that had formed in his throat. "It has always been Christine, Jenna. Her voice," he paused, his own voice cracking and faltering as he saw the look of betrayal enter her eyes. "Her music. She is the only one, Jenna, who would ever be able to make my song take flight."

Jenna closed her eyes against the confusion, and shook her head. She felt her hands shaking, "But you said," she began, her voice thin and trembling. "You said..." *nothing* she realized. They had laughed, and they had danced, and they had almost made love—yet he'd made no declarations, given her no promises. She'd read so much into his actions—so much, she realized, that hadn't been there. It had never been about her. She'd been right all along. His heart had always belonged to Christine. She had just been...*available*. She swallowed hard, her throat suddenly dry and sore. It was the same thing yet again. She hadn't learned a thing! She made herself available. She made herself too easy. She fell in love too fast.

"I'm sorry, Jenna," he told her, hating himself for what he was doing to her, dying inside from bearing witness to her pain. "But it will *always* be Christine."

Jenna felt herself sink to her knees, not able to look at him. Her world was crumbling around her, and she felt like she could not breathe. Erik was supposed to have been the one. She had been so *sure* he was her prince.

Erik's heart ached in sorrow as he watched Jenna so hurt, so broken—knowing *he* was the cause. He crouched down next to her, reaching out a hand to comfort her, but he was reminded of another night—one that now seemed so long ago—when his boorish behavior had caused her to cry. Just like then, he let his hand hover over her back, not able to make contact. Once again, he knew he had already done enough to hurt her.

"I must go, Mademoiselle," he said softly, rising to his full height. "I do not wish to be late for Christine." And slowly, quietly, Erik walked away.

❧

There was a great deal of hustle and bustle in Jenna's hospital room. Ironically, he thought, it was more crowded than it had ever been since she had been there. Nurses were milling about, gathering her belongings, disconnecting I.V.s. Penny was there, sitting on a chair in the corner, staying out of their way. Dr. James was giving her a final examination, to make sure that nothing had changed with her condition. It was strange, he thought to himself. All of this commotion when they were finally giving up. Maybe if she had had this level of attention from everybody around her earlier, she would have been coaxed out of the coma—if for no other reason than to insist everybody leave her alone so she could rest.

He walked in the room, joining in the fray. He went over to Penny, who rose from her seat to give him a warm, welcoming hug. "I'm so glad you're here."

"Did you think I could let her go without saying goodbye?" he asked, his voice cracking on the final word. He was barely holding his emotions in check, and this morning was not going to be easy on him.

"You brought Red…" she began, smiling down at the carrier.

"He loves her too," was his only answer.

Dr. James approached him after he finished his exam. Putting a hand on his shoulder, he asked, "How are you holding up?"

He gave a mirthless chuckle, "How do you *think*?" The agony was clear in his voice. "I really don't agree with this, Doctor."

The elder doctor gave a deep sigh. "I know. But I hope one day you'll understand. No matter what we do, we cannot *make* her wake up." His only response was to close his eyes and shake his head in silence. "You tried everything, son," James added, reassuringly.

"It wasn't enough," he muttered, not looking up to meet his superior's eyes.

With a final squeeze to the shoulder, James let him be. He assured Penny that there was no difference in Jenna's condition, and that he was certain she would be fine for the long journey to her new facility. After Penny thanked him, he gave his young charge one last glance before quietly leaving the room. The nurses had finished their ministrations and exited as well, leaving Penny as the only other person in the room.

"The transporters are going to be here soon," Penny told him, taking his hand in hers and giving it a squeeze. "I'll give you two some time alone with her."

He nodded his thanks silently, as Penny walked out into the hall, closing the door behind her.

Finally alone with her, he felt his heart pounding in his chest. He walked over to the side of her bed, and with trembling hands, he unzipped Red's carrier, and let Jenna's feline companion free. The cat immediately made his way to her face, rubbing her cheek with his, purring so hard at her presence that he was emitting little squeaks. When a few moments passed without a touch from Jenna, Red let out a long *Mreeeeeeow*, that at once sounded mournful and pleading, and it was just about all the young doctor could take. "Come here, boy," he said, tears gathering in his eyes, cradling the cat in his arms. "I'm going to miss her too." He gave the cat a long, firm squeeze before letting him loose again to snuggle up against his beloved owner's side.

He turned to Jenna, taking her hand in his. He gazed lovingly at her face, studying her delicate bone structure, memorizing the luminescence of her skin, the fiery blaze of her hair. There were so many beautiful things about Jenna that he longed to commit to memory, because he knew after today, memories were all he'd have. Memories and dreams. Dreams of her walking with him hand in hand in Central Park, or gazing at him across a candlelit table. Dreams of her laughing at one of his corny jokes, or resting her head on his shoulder as they watched TV. Dreams of her falling asleep in his arms after a long night of making love and waking the next morning with a devilish glint in her eyes that told him she was ready for another round. These were all dreams he knew would never come true, dreams at which he'd never had a chance. But he would need them now to sustain him through the devastating blow of losing her.

"Jenna," he whispered, his voice hushed and low. "I'm so sorry. I tried so hard—but I failed. I promised you I'd never give up—and I *will* never give up hoping you awaken—praying that you will one day open your eyes. But…" He swallowed hard before continuing. "They're taking you away, Jenna."

"I promise I'll come visit. First chance I get, I'll pack up Red and drive up to Maine to see you. Your boys will not forget you." He leaned forward and touched his forehead to hers, eyes closed tight against his tears. "I will never forget you, Jenna. Not even for a day. Not even for a heartbeat."

"I'm not ready for this," his voice shook with the effort of holding in the sobs that threatened to overtake him. "I'm not ready to lose you." His free hand came up to gently cup her cheek. "I love you," he whispered, and he placed a soft, gentle kiss on her lips as the tears rolled down his face.

❧

Jenna still stared straight ahead of her, feeling empty, seeing nothing. She had no idea how long ago Erik had gone—was it an hour already? A heartbeat? All she knew was that he *had* gone. He had left her, once again, alone in his home. He had left her for Christine.

She had known. She had always known that he had loved Christine. Looking back, *she* was the one who had been trying to convince *him* of that. So why had she let herself believe—even for one moment—that he could possibly love her?

She was nothing, when compared to Christine. She was not talented—she was not beautiful. She would not be the one singing tonight on the Paris Opera stage, bringing him joy, and pride and elation. She couldn't give him any of those things.

But she had loved him. For the first time, she thought, she had *truly* been in love with another human being. She had wanted him imperfections and all. She had strived to show him he was beautiful in her eyes. She had held him close to her heart, and given him acceptance, and trust, and friendship. She adored the man that he was. But it was not enough. Erik did not want to be with her as a man. He wanted someone who believed in angels—especially an angel who would place her high on a pedestal and worship the very air that she breathed. He wanted Christine. And *she* had always known that.

But she had loved him anyway.

And it *hurt.*

Jenna somehow found the strength in her legs to stand. They were a bit wobbly, but they somehow still worked. The pounding in her head was absolutely excruciating, and it reminded her of that night—that seemed a lifetime ago—when she left work early, only to find her life forever changed. She had run that night, away from the horror of another broken relationship, and her flight had landed her here. Where could she run this time, she wondered. How could she escape the pain?

One thing she knew for sure, she could not stay here. If Erik wanted Christine then he should have her, but she could not stay here and watch. Her heart was not strong enough for that abuse. She had to find somewhere else to stay, until Erik could explain to her what he'd found out about getting her home. Maybe Omid *would* take her in.

Jenna felt something furry at her feet, and looked down to see Samineh curling around her ankles. "Hey, Sweetie," she whispered, as she picked the little kitten up for a cuddle. Suddenly an image of her own dear Red entered her mind, and she could almost hear his purrs—the squeaky little rumbles he would sound when he was perfectly content. Would she ever get to see him again, she wondered, and she ached to touch him, as she set down Samineh on the settee—another cat she would have to leave behind.

Jenna found herself walking down by the lake, gazing into the greenish waters that were forever shrouded in mystery. Drawn on by the rippling current, she continued to wander until the terrain once again became rough. Remembering her last jaunt to this part of the cavern, which had ended with her falling *into* the lake, Jenna thought she should head back. With the gala performance happening upstairs, chances were slim that Omid would come to save her from drowning.

But just as she began to turn, she noticed a light glowing from deep in the cavern ahead of her. Strange, she thought. It had not been there before. She ventured a few more steps down the twisting path before she saw it—a wooden door, curved at the top, light spilling through the slats. Her heart stopped beating in her chest, and she stood there mouth agape, staring at it. She felt her knees begin to go weak as she realized that this was it—the secret door, that she had begun to believe did not exist. Erik had been right. Somehow, he *had* found a way to send her home. She didn't know how he did it, but she did not feel she should wait around for him to explain. There was nothing to hold her here any longer—Erik had made his feelings quite clear. She began to take a few more steps toward the door, and she saw it open, quite on its own, revealing a long, familiar tunnel before her.

She thought briefly of Omid, and a melancholy smile crossed her lips. Oh, she would miss him and his silly ways. She wished that she had had a chance to say goodbye to him—maybe give him a hint as to where Erik had hidden the Cognac. "I will miss you, Daroga," she whispered, as a few burning tears sprung to her eyes.

When she had reached the entrance to the door, she took in a deep breath and placed her hand on her chest to steady her fluttering heart. It was then that she felt it—the cameo that Erik had given her, was still hanging from her neck. She reached behind and loosed the ties, taking one last, longing look at the exquisite rosebud that had never quite fully burst into bloom. The tears overtook her and she sobbed as she leaned down and laid the treasure on the rocky shore. "For Christine," she said, as she once again left one of Erik's roses behind. And then, with a shattered heart, she stepped one foot through the door.

38 HOME

Christine. He heard the deception pounding in his head as he stormed through the tunnel toward Box 5. *It will always be Christine.* Those words were sickening to his ears—the pierce of a dagger every time they echoed. He closed his lids against the torment, but still he could see Jenna's eyes—so haunted by pain and disbelief. Her voice had sounded so brittle, so hollow. The betrayal had been an almost physical thing between them—one he wished he could shake and strangle and crush to pieces with his bare hands. But the damage had been done. One look at Jenna's face had told him that her heart was broken—and he cursed himself that he should have been the cause.

Erik slammed a fist into the stone wall of the tunnel. Then, with a guttural growl, he slammed it three times more, finally hanging his head as he used his battered hands to brace himself against the wall. Why did he have to hurt her—Jenna, the one woman in the world who had seen his shame and still looked at him with love and not revulsion? He had wanted nothing more than to hold her and love her for the rest of his life, and amazingly, she had wanted the same. He had somehow found his miracle—but *because* he loved her, he had been forced to let her go.

He knew he had had no choice. He knew it was for Jenna's well being. Still he feared that he had managed to *break* them both beyond repair—for now he found that he could not breathe with the pressure of guilt and loss and pain weighing so heavily on his chest. He had seen so much agony in his life. He had known the loss of his dignity, his pride, his hope. How was it that losing Jenna's love could *hurt* so much? "I'm still not ready, Jenna," he groaned in the darkness. "I'm still not ready to lose you."

A spark ignited in his mind. He didn't *have* to lose her, he realized, slowly lifting his head. He had to let her go, but he didn't have to let her go alone. He could go to her, he thought, starting to move away from the wall. He could tell her that he lied, and beg for her forgiveness, groveling at her feet. And then he could explain to her how to open the door and he could go through *with* her! *After all*, he thought, as he turned and began to walk back the way he had come, *she had come here, to this place out of her time. What was to prevent him from joining her in her world?*

Erik's footsteps increased in speed and soon he was running, *sprinting* away from the gala night. He could not cross the lake fast enough, to right the wrong he had committed and tell Jenna how sorry he was and how much he really did love her. "Jenna!" he shouted as he tied the boat to the dock. "Jenna, I'm sorry." He charged into the sitting room, rushing into the kitchen when he could not find her. "Jenna!" He called as he knocked on her bedroom door. "Jenna, please listen to me." When she did not answer, he pounded harder. "Jenna, talk to me, I beg of you. I lied, Jenna. It's not Christine I love—it's you." The door creaked open at his insistent banging, and he realized that she was not inside. "Jenna?" he whispered in his confusion.

In the silence of his home, the rush of water suddenly caught his attention, and icy fingers of dread began to inch across his stomach. He was compelled toward the lake. The murky water lapped and receded along the rocky shore and, grabbing a lantern, Erik found himself following a path he rarely took—a path that had once before led him to a surprise visitor that had become his salvation. Panic obligated him to follow the call of the water, and Erik found himself deep in the back cavern. He remembered mentioning he had found the way to get her back home. Had she decided to come down this way to look for the door once again? Had she found it?

"Jenna," he called, more quietly now, in the darkness of the cave. "Jenna, where are you?" he asked as he found no trace of her. He was still walking slowly when his foot hit on something, causing it to skitter along the ground. Kneeling down, and holding the light in the direction of the sound, Erik felt the breath leave his body at the sight before him. There, on the rocks of the lakeshore, was Jenna's cameo. Once again, she had left his rose behind.

He gingerly lifted the cameo in his hand, turning it over to examine it from all angles. Suddenly he felt it. With Jenna, there had always been an energy about his home—as if her spirit somehow brought his world alive. But now as he gazed at the cameo she had loved resting sadly in his hand, a sense of emptiness surrounded him. And he knew, without a doubt, that Jenna had gone. It had worked. His wretched lie had caused her mind to open the door, and quite possibly, saved her life. Yet that did not stop him from feeling hollow inside.

He closed his fingers around the cameo and clutched it to his heart. "Oh, my Jenna," he sobbed quietly, tears flowing freely from his eyes. "How am I going to live without you?"

❧

She had taken a few small, tentative steps in the tunnel, when the door slammed shut behind her. Jenna turned back at the sound, and saw that there was no longer any light shining through the cracks in the slats, and the door handle, which had seemed to turn so easily for her before, was not even there. The door was no longer an entryway to anywhere, but instead, a barricade designed to keep intruders out—a dark sentinel to guard against the unwanted. The ache intensified in Jenna's chest, as she thought of Erik, now forever lost to her behind that unmovable, unyielding obstacle. Would she ever stop hurting without him?

Head hanging low, she turned away from the door that had once lead her to the wonder of Erik's world, and set her eyes on the path ahead of her. The walls on each side of the tunnel seemed malleable, undulating a bit back and forth. When she placed a hand on one, however, she felt nothing but cold, solid stone, trapping her inside. She felt her breath begin to come in rapid puffs, as the fear of being trapped in the tunnel began to play at her mind. She looked around frantically for some escape and finally saw a soft glow emanating from the far end of the passage in front of her, promising some source of light and possibly, some way out if she just traveled on.

The frigid air in the tunnel made Jenna wrap her arms around her shoulders and wish that she had thought to put on a cloak before leaving Erik's home. But would it be comforting to be wrapped in the soft black cape she always wore when she and Erik haunted the opera together? Would it remind her too much of the warmth of his arms, the musky, masculine scent that was all his own? No, it was better to be cold, she decided, than to be reminded of the sweetness she would never again experience.

But she found as she walked, that the air gradually grew warmer, and eventually, she was able to drop her arms to her side. The ground too was changing as she slowly drew across it. It had started out like sand that fell away at her feet, but as she trudged forward, the sand became more and more packed until she was walking on firm, solid ground. The darkness surrounding her began to fade into the gray of a new dawn, as she began to walk steadily nearer to the light, coming closer and closer to its source.

Suddenly, she looked up and he was with her, stopping her progress, taking her hand in his. "I'm not ready for this," he sobbed, his blue/brown gaze shimmering with tears. "I'm not ready to lose you." His other hand came up gently to cup her cheek, his forehead resting on hers. "I love you," he whispered, and he pressed his mouth forward to place his lips on hers.

She should pull back, she knew. She should slap him and tell him to go to Christine and demand that he never touch her again. But she didn't. She *couldn't.* Because she loved him so much.

She found herself dissolving into his embrace, returning the gentle pressure of his lips on hers, her own hot tears mingling with his. He was the warmth that had overtaken her, the light that had guided her, the steady ground beneath her feet. He was the breath of air now filling her lungs, her heart beating faster. In that moment, when she could not tell where he ended and she began, he was life itself to her. He was home.

As their lips parted, she opened her eyes. She was a bit blinded by the light surrounding her, so stark, so white for the first time since her accident. The edges of her vision were blurry, and everything around her seemed to exist as if in a cloud. All except, that is, for those same, beloved blue/brown eyes at the very center of her gaze. They peered at her now from behind a mask of shock and disbelief, which was quickly dissolving to reveal an unguarded expression of complete and unmistakable joy. "Jenna?" the voice was hushed and low, colored with tears of astonishment and delight.

"You're here," she cried in relief, reaching out a hand to touch his cheek, never registering that he did not wear a mask.

"Oh Jenna," he sobbed, his body shaking. "You came back to me." He wrapped his arms around her and crushed her to him, relishing the feeling of her arms holding him too. It was a moment he had dreamed about, a moment he had hoped for. He had begun to believe this moment would never come, but he was wrong. Oh, thank God, he was wrong!

When at last he pulled back, he stroked her cheek lovingly, his mismatched eyes shining with tears. “I knew you'd wake up,” he muttered, “I knew you'd come back! Oh Jenna, I have so much to tell you.”

Realization began to slowly dawn upon her, as a loud *Mreeeeeeeeeow*! broke into her thoughts. “Red!” She exclaimed, turning her head toward the yellow tabby who had sprung to life at the sound of his owner's voice, bumping his soft furry head into her hand. She gathered the cat closer to her, and rubbed her head against his, his strong, rumbly purr the most welcome sound in the world. “I never thought I'd see you again,” she murmured

“I took care of him for you, Jenna.”

She looked back in his direction, her vision beginning to clear now. His light brown hair was tousled, a few locks hanging over his forehead in a way that recalled clandestine frog hunts in a dark bog. His chiseled cheeks were both plain to her, and not a mark of deformity marred them in any way, yet the face was so familiar, so well known. His disarming smile took her breath away, as it had so many times before. And his eyes. One was a striking, icy blue, the other so rich a brown, she felt as if she could see forever in its depths. “Erik?” she asked, her voice coming out a thready whisper.

If possible, his smile grew brighter in surprise. “You know me?” he asked, amazed that she had even noticed his presence before, since she'd always shone so much more brightly than him.

“I…” she began to mutter in confusion, “I…”

“It's okay,” he said sweetly, thrilled at just the flicker of recognition he saw behind her eyes. “My name is Christopher Eriksson—but you can call me Chris.” He took her hand in his again, and squeezed it tightly. “I'm a doctor here. We worked together a few times before your accident. I guess maybe you remember me from that. I definitely remember you.”

Dr. Christopher Eriksson. Yes. Brief, fleeting memories of a new resident working alongside her at the bedside of a patient, mingled with vague flashes of blue and brown amid a sea of white. She *did* remember him. But how was it that he …

When Jenna made no comment, only stared at him in disbelief, he continued, "Do you remember your car accident, Jenna?" She nodded quietly, so he went on. "You hurt your head—pretty badly." She reached up to touch the spot on her forehead where Erik had stitched her wound, almost able to feel the gentle care his fingers had administered. The man nodded, saying, "You've been in a coma Jenna—since the accident. I've been taking care of you." He reached up to smooth her hair away from her head.

Jenna simply stared in disbelief at the face she loved so much that now belonged to a stranger. A head injury? A *coma?* Could that be true? *Oh God*, what did that mean?

The door opened and in walked a small woman, slouched forward, looking troubled. "Doctor," she said, barely lifting her eyes. "Transport is here."

"Well, tell them," he declared breathlessly, "They are not needed! Jenna just woke up."

The woman's head shot up and stared in her direction.

"Aunt Penny?" Jenna asked in confusion. "What…what are you doing here?"

The woman let out a shriek of joy as she rushed to Jenna's other side, kneeling by the bed, and taking her other hand. "Oh, Jenna, honey. We've been so worried!" she said, tears filling her eyes. "We were afraid you were never going to wake up!"

Never going to wake up! Coma! The words echoed and bounced around in Jenna's head. It was impossible! Insanity! She hadn't been in a coma! She was with Erik. How could she have been lying unconscious in a bed when she had never felt so alive in her life? How could she have been unresponsive, uncommunicative, and unaware when she had been so actively falling in love?

…Others say that coma victims have very lucid dreams, where their brains create an alternate reality in which they can go on living, since they can no longer interact with the world around them. The words she spoke to Erik came back at her with a vengeance. *No,* she thought. *Oh God, no!*

Suddenly the moments just before her accident replayed in her mind—the extreme exhaustion, the pounding in her head. The radio had been playing that seductively soothing song from the musical—the melody that lulls the frightened heroine to sleep. She remembered wishing that she herself could just give into a dream so that, for at least a little while, she could forget the mess her life had become.

Had she gotten her wish? Had it all been a construct of her desperate mind? The lair? The Opera House? The underground lake? Had Samineh simply been a replacement for her beloved Red? And what about Omid? How had she ever dreamed up Omid?

There had been so many times when she had first arrived at the lair, that it all had seemed surreal. The secret door that didn't exist, a different country a century ago, the ridiculous assertion that she was speaking French! She had almost convinced *herself* that it was all a crazy dream—if not for Erik. For through it all, she had always known that Erik was real. Erik. Was. Real.

But had she been wrong? Had her time with Erik just been a dream? Had her *love* for him just been imagined?

The feeling of despair that clutched her heart must have been evident on her face, because Dr. Eriksson suddenly asked with concern, "Jenna, are you alright?"

"I don't know…" she began to tear up, "…I don't even know what's *real* anymore."

The doctor squeezed her hand firmly, and stroking her cheek, assured her, "I know Jenna. It's a lot to take in. It must all be overwhelming for you. But it's alright," he smiled at her, locking his eyes with hers. "It's all going to be alright. I'm here, and *I'm* real" he said, in a familiar, rich, golden voice. "I promise you, I will help you work all of this out. I won't give up on you."

She did not yet understand what had happened to her—she still wasn't sure if she had spent the time since her accident living a dream, or if, somehow, it had all been real. But one thing was clear—she had heard those words before, and gazed into these eyes that were so lovingly gazing back at her right now. She did not know this man before her—but she wanted to. Why did he so strongly resemble Erik? Why did he share the same voice, the same features, the very same eyes as the man who had captured her heart.

She reached up her hand to gently touch his cheek, and told him, "I like your smile." And she felt her heart leap a little when he placed his own hand over hers, and whispered back, with a familiar glimmer in his eyes, "I like yours too."

39 OPENING NIGHT

Omid had come to collect his friend. The gala night was about to start, and Erik and Jenna had not yet arrived. It worried Omid, since Erik had been responsible for Christine's rise to prominence on the stage, having personally seen to it that his little angel had gotten her wings. It was entirely unlike him to miss her performance, so it seemed worth a trip to Erik's home, to make certain everything was all right.

It was quiet in the lair, but Omid knew it was not empty. The boat was in dock, even if haphazardly tied. A black cloak was strewn carelessly over the settee. Dinner dishes still littered the table. Omid bent over and took a closer look at the remains of what appeared to be a very fine feast, including what looked like chocolate dessert of some kind. It seemed Erik and Jenna had had a lovely dinner indeed.

A wicked smile spread across his mouth. Perhaps Erik had abandoned his insane notion that Jenna had to go back across time. Perhaps the dinner had been just so delectable, the dessert so sinful, that a moment of passion had once again ignited between them. Maybe this time, they had made it to the bedroom where Erik was making Jenna sing instead.

Omid chuckled to himself a little, happy for his friend, when he realized that the lair was too quiet. He glanced toward Jenna's room and noticed that the door was slightly ajar. *Hmmm*, he thought. *They're not in there*. He rapped gently on Erik's bedroom door, but there was no answer.

Still convinced that Erik would never leave his house in such a state of disarray, Omid once again walked down by the lake. It was then that he heard it—the sound of someone…weeping. Quickly, he followed the path before him, eager to find the source of the distressing sound. When he reached the far end of the cavern, the sight before him gave him pause. There was Erik, the Great Phantom of the Opera, down on his knees, heaving quiet, heart wrenching sobs, clutching his hands to his heart, a black ribbon trailing between his fingers.

"Erik?" he asked, in alarm, "What the devil is going on?"

"She's gone," Erik answered, his voice thick with tears. "She's gone." He dropped his head to his chest, as the sobs once again overtook him.

"Whatever do you mean, my friend?" Omid moved forward and knelt beside Erik, his hand moving to rest on Erik's back. It was not often that Erik allowed someone to see him cry. He knew something must be dreadfully wrong.

"Jenna found her way home," his said miserably, as his eyes stared off into the darkness. "She is truly now a lifetime away."

"What?" Omid exclaimed in shock that Erik's theory had actually worked. "How?"

"I told her I was in love with Christine," Erik answered bitterly. "I *lied* to her to make her want to leave. Her mind must have done the rest—must have opened the door that led her home."

Omid stared for a moment at his friend. He found himself greatly saddened at Jenna's departure, but his sorrow did not compare to the sheer agony that was written on Erik's face. "Erik," he began, speaking in gentle tones. "This is what you wanted," he reminded him, hoping his words could provide some small comfort to his friend.

"I did not *want* this!" Erik's voice was a visceral shout. "I wanted *her*. I *loved* her." Growing quiet now, he added, "But I had to lie to her." Erik looked directly into Omid's eyes. "I broke her *heart*." Closing his eyes and shaking his head, he added, "You should have seen her eyes. They were filled with so much pain—and *I* put it there." He let out a heavy sigh. "My love *is* poison."

"No, Erik!" Omid was not going to let him get away with going down this dark path alone once more. "Do not listen to Bernadette! Your love for Jenna was the opposite of poison," he insisted fervently. "You *loved* Jenna, Erik. And she loved you too. But you sacrificed your own happiness for *her* life. Your love was not *poison*, Erik. She will *live* because of your love."

"I pray for that, Omid," Erik nodded, calmly, "that she will live a long life filled with joy. For the happiness she gave me, she deserves that."

"That she does, Erik," Omid agreed, for in the way she loved his friend, Jenna was truly an angel.

Omid rose, and reached out a hand to help Erik off the ground. "Come on, Erik, let's go. The performance has already started. You would not wish to miss Christine's debut."

Erik made no move to take Omid's hand, simply saying, "I am not going," as he stared at the murky waters of the lake.

"What?" Omid asked, startled. "Of course you are going."

"No," Erik said, matter-of-factly, "I am not."

Omid's eyes narrowed in confusion. "But Erik, *why*? You *trained* Christine."

"And I *used* her to break Jenna's heart," he stated.

"You used Christine's *name*," Omid began, trying to make his friend see reason, "because you knew it was the only thing that would make Jenna want to leave you, Erik. You did it for *her* sake. Do not punish yourself for doing the right thing. You are already suffering enough."

"I'm not going." Erik said again, his gaze unwavering.

Omid glanced at him a moment longer while realization sunk in. "You mean to hide."

"That world is not for me Daroga…" Erik began calmly.

"Of course it is, Erik!" Omid insisted with growing irritation. "You're just being a coward!" Omid saw Erik's jaw tighten against the cruel words, but he made no attempt to defend himself. "You pushed Jenna away—broke her heart, as you say—forced her to live a life without you, because you knew that if you let her stay with you—which was what she wanted more than anything—she would die. Yet you sit here in your sorrow, and once again you hide from the world."

"I don't want to go!" Erik seethed through clenched teeth.

"You have no right, Erik!" Omid spat angrily. "You cannot choose to shun the world after you forced Jenna to live in it! No matter how well-intentioned your actions were, Erik, you didn't give Jenna a choice! What makes you think *you* deserve one? You forced Jenna to live, Erik. Now you need to force yourself to live for *her*!"

Erik's voice was brittle and raw. "Without her, I don't know *how* to live," he met his friend's gaze with eyes full of pain. "Jenna *taught* me how to live, Omid. She taught me how to laugh, and how to hope.

She showed me I could share this miserable existence with another and make it…better. She looked at me and she didn't see a monster. I didn't have to be an angel for her, or…or a ghost. With Jenna, I could always be myself—the man she made me want to be. How do I go on, Omid, now that she is gone?"

Omid knelt again beside his friend, his tone softening at Erik's obvious vulnerability. "You do it one step at a time, Erik. You remember everything that she taught you, and you take a chance. You start by going tonight to that gala performance. Do it for Jenna. She *loved* you, Erik. She wouldn't want you to be alone in the darkness. Do it for Christine. She has worked so hard just to make you proud, Erik. You promised her that you would be there. Don't break your promise. Go to Box 5, Erik. Listen to her sing. Then go see her afterward and tell her how wonderful she was. Not as an angel, not as a ghost, but as the *man* that you are—the one you say Jenna made you want to be. You *have* to begin again, Erik. You have to—for Jenna. You are alive, Erik. Now *live*!"

With one final attempt at resistance, Erik countered, "What do you know of beginning again, Daroga? Of *living*? You have never again taken a chance at love after you lost your beloved wife. How can you tell me I must move on, when it has been years and you still have not managed?"

"Oh, Erik, my friend," Omid chuckled quietly, "the world has not stood still while you have been hiding from it. I do indeed have a special woman of my own. You have just never seen fit to look beyond your own secret existence long enough to notice." Erik looked up at Omid with surprise. "I had invited her to join us for the show tonight, but she has other duties to perform during that time."

Erik's eyes narrowed in annoyance. "You invited someone to join us in Box 5!? Daroga, what were you thinking?"

"She has been there before…" Omid let his voice trail off, giving Erik a sly wink as he stood up.

Erik stared at him a moment before asking "Antoinette Giry?"

"We have both experienced the loss of love, Erik, and are ready to try again. Besides," Omid raised an eyebrow and gave a brief smirk. "She is a *formidable* woman, Erik."

"I am aware, Daroga," Erik said dryly, rising to brush the dust off his slacks. "I find that I approve of this match," he added as they began to make their way toward the boat. "At least I know she will have no trouble cuffing your ears if you get out of line."

"It's one of my favorite things about her!" Omid agreed.

"Obviously, you give her cause often enough."

The two continued to banter as they ambled along the lakeshore. Erik was first to enter the boat, and as Omid was climbing in behind him, Erik opened his fingers and took one last, longing look at the cameo in his hand. He lifted his hand to his lips and whispered the words he never had the chance to say—"I love you Jenna,"—and placed the cameo in his breast pocket, so as to hold it close to his heart. Then, just barely giving Omid enough time to settle himself, he picked up the oar and they pushed off across the lake.

Opening night was a grand success. The sets and the costumes were breathtaking, and skillfully managed by the new stagehand. Herriot had made certain the orchestra sorted out their pitch issues, and their playing was truly inspired. Ballet Mistress Giry had finally whipped the ballet rats into shape, and her daughter Meg danced masterfully as prima ballerina. But of course, the shining star of the evening was Christine.

As Erik stood there leaning against the back wall of the box, slightly behind the curtain so as not to be seen, he could not help but feel his spirit lift a bit at the sound of her voice. She sang with the purity of the angels and the strength of a storm. She was glorious. She was wonderful. She was everything he had trained her to be, and so much more. She was perfect.

Despite the ache he still felt in his heart, his chest swelled with pride at the curtain call, when he saw the roses pile up at her feet. He had done it! The Angel of Music had lifted a poor seamstress from the depths and raised her to her proper place among the stars. Now the name *Christine Da'ae* would be the on the lips of all of Paris. With her magnificent performance tonight, her role as first lady of the stage would be secured.

When the applause had died down, all left the stage but Christine. Erik's eyes narrowed, this behavior being highly unusual. Christine walked forward and Erik's breath caught in his chest at the sound of her words, "The Maestro has indulged me to sing one final song for you tonight. It was a song taught to me by my teacher, who I think of as my Angel of Music. This is for him."

When Erik heard the lone piano begin to play the simple tune that Jenna had hummed to him, he felt his heart begin to pound. He had worked on this song with Christine only once—at their last lesson together—before Jenna's seizure had changed everything. He had scolded the young soprano that night, yelling at her out of his own feelings of fear and frustration, accusing her wrongly of not understanding the emotions in the song. When he had realized he'd been out of line, he promised her he would come back, that things would return to normal, but it was a promise he never kept. He'd felt that monitoring Jenna's health was more important than lessons with Christine. Though he would never regret spending his every remaining moment with Jenna, he did feel somewhat remiss that he had abandoned his pupil—and he never expected to hear her performing his song that night. When she opened her mouth to sing, he was unprepared for the flood of emotions that filled his soul.

She sang of happy days spent whiling away in love's embrace—but days that were long since over. She sang of longing and dreams of a lover's kiss—yet hopes that could never come to pass. She sang of a love that was never meant to be—yet one which had changed the lovers completely, irrevocably, and forever after. Her song was a goodbye, tempered with a memory that would forever tie, forever link two souls that never belonged together, but would never again be apart.

As the crowd erupted in applause after the final cadenza, Erik just stood there, staring, his face wet with tears. He would never stop thinking of Jenna, and her spirit would always be with him. He had to hope—he *had* to believe—that somewhere, across the years, she was thinking of him too, and realizing that what he did, he did for her. He prayed she somehow knew that he *did* love her and that he would always hold her dearly in his heart as the first woman who accepted him, the first woman who loved him, the first woman who taught him it was alright to be himself. And though they were from different worlds, never meant to spend forever together, he hoped she somehow knew that he would *live* because of her—not as an angel, not as a ghost, but as the man she made him see that he was—the man she made him *want* to be.

"Daroga," Erik said, still staring at the stage. "I need you to procure something for me."

❧

Erik waited in Christine's dressing room, pacing a bit back and forth. He knew that there were throngs of people who would wish to congratulate her on such a triumphant performance, still he could not help but wonder what could possibly be taking her so long to return to her dressing room. She had a ball to change for, after all. She should really make haste.

Erik heard voices outside the door, and the door handle began to turn. He cloaked himself in the shadows, watching her enter, still smiling and nodding the whole time she was shutting the door. When she had accomplished the act, she leaned back against it, letting out a deep sigh, and Erik saw her glance quickly at the dressing table where he was accustomed to leaving her rose. When she did not see it, he saw her head drop in disappointment.

This was it—the moment for which he had been waiting ever since the Persian had returned from his little mission. She was finally here, and she had come alone. It was exactly as he had hoped. Yet why was he so afraid? *This was what you wanted me to do, Jenna,* he said in his mind, wishing he could somehow throw his voice across the ages so she could hear him. *You always told me I should be a man to Christine—not a ghost or an angel, but a man. I truly don't know if I'm ready for this, Jenna, but I have to try. You taught me to be brave—to be myself. This is for you...my Jenna.*

Erik reached into his breast pocket and squeezed the cameo, drawing strength from its presence. He took a deep breath to steel himself and made his way out of the shadows. "Excuse me, Mademoiselle." Christine's head shot up, and she jumped a bit in fright, startled to find a man hiding in her dressing room. But Erik continued in that soft tone of voice that was so familiar to her, and when she heard him, her eyes lit up with joy. "Tonight I thought to deliver your rose in person. And to tell you myself, that you were magnificent!" *As you wanted, Jenna. Just as you wanted.*

"Angel?" she asked, as she took a tentative step toward him.

Erik smiled sadly, and shook his head. "No, Christine. That is not my name. I must admit I did deceive you when I let you refer to me as your Angel of Music. But I am not a heavenly being—I am only a man." *Oh, Jenna, I am not sure I can do this,* he thought, as he fought the urge to recede back into the darkness.

She moved a little closer to him, her hands trembling with

excitement and trepidation as she carefully accepted the rose that the mysterious man offered her. It was exactly like the others she had received, a perfect red rose with a black velvet ribbon 'round its stem, proving to her that this was, indeed, her beloved angel. She found that she quite favored his new method of delivery. Looking down at the rose in her hand, she murmured, "I have missed you."

Feeling horribly guilty, Erik responded stiffly. "I am sorry. I…have been detained." He closed his eyes and looked down, remembering just what had detained him, and he began to feel to pull of Jenna's loss tugging at his heart once more.

"I find then," she whispered, shyly, "that I am very lucky you are here now—very lucky indeed."

Erik cocked his head to one side to regard her face, as he asked her, "Whatever do you mean?"

"Well," she continued, her smile growing bright. "Apparently, my teacher is *both* man and angel, and as such, I see no reason why he cannot take me to the ball. For as an angel only has wings with which to take flight, a man," Christine looked down briefly as she said this, and Erik noticed a slight blush come to her cheek, "has arms that can guide me in a dance. And as it appears you are already dressed for the occasion," she reached forward with a shaky hand and gently caressed his mask, earning only the slightest of dumbfounded flinches from the man standing before her, "all that is left is for *me* to get ready."

Erik stared at her, eyes wide in disbelief. He stood before her, a man shrouded in mystery, face concealed by a mask, and she made no mention of it? He had just admitted to her that he had been lying—deceiving her about his true identity—and she responded by asking him to the ball? Jenna had begged him, had *urged* him to go with Christine to the ball. Was this real? Could this *possibly* be happening? Jenna had accepted him—could Christine be accepting him too?

"Yet, before we go," he heard her ask, "there is still one thing I need to know."

Ahhh, here it was, he thought to himself. The moment when his hopes would be dashed and he would be reminded that no woman would ever again accept him as his dear, sweet Jenna had. *I tried, my Jenna. For you, I tried. But it was not to be.* "And what would that be, Christine?" he asked, bracing himself to hear her answer.

"Your name. What shall I call you," she asked, light shining in her eyes, "If I can no longer call you my Angel?"

He swallowed the lump that had formed in his throat, and thinking of Jenna, finally answered, "I…I am Erik, Mademoiselle."

"Erik," she said warmly, reaching out and taking his hand. "It is so good to finally *see* you."

Absolutely dumbfounded, he warned, "Christine, though you have now *seen* me, there is still so very much that you do not know about me."

"Well, then," she smiled, squeezing his hand, "I shall be *delighted* to learn, my Maestro!"

Just then, a loud rapping sounded, and without further delay, her door swung open. In walked a tall, handsome man, formally dressed, with blond hair that reached to his shoulders and eyes that were a piercing blue. "Little Lotte, it is you!" he said, his voice a bit breathless.

"Lotte?" she questioned the intruder with confusion. "I haven't answered to that name in years."

"Christine, don't you remember me?" he asked, a laugh in his throat! "Surely you recall the day you lost your red scarf in the ocean, and I jumped into the water, fully dressed to retrieve it for you. I almost caught my death of a cold after that."

"Oh, Raoul!" Christine exclaimed, and Erik tensed as he saw recognition finally light her eyes. "What are you doing here?"

"Well, I *am* the new patron, Christine," the man said with pride coloring his voice.

"You're the Vicomte?" she asked in surprise.

"The very same," he sniffed a bit in the affectation of nobility, obviously a bit over-proud of his birthright. "Tell me, Lotte," as asked, continuing to ignore the fact that Erik was in the room, "Do you still have your red scarf?"

"Oh, probably somewhere, Raoul," she said, waving her hand in the air. "But I haven't worn it in years. I have a lovely black one that I favor now." Erik could not help but smirk a bit at the look of rebuff that appeared on the Vicomte's face. "Now," Christine said, pointing a finger toward the door, "Both of you, shoo. Erik," she squeezed his hand. "I will meet you outside—I'll only be a moment. Raoul," she turned to him, still holding Erik's hand, "Do be sure to find Meg Giry—the Prima Ballerina—at the ball tonight. I am certain she would love to share a dance with you. *I* shall be spending the evening," she glanced back up at Erik with a smile, "dancing with my Maestro."

40 FOREVER

Jenna put in her second earring and was slipping into her heels just as the buzzer rang.

"Would you get that for me, Red?" she asked the cat who was lazily grooming himself on the bed. *Mreeeeow*! was the only response she got. "I knew you were going to say that!" she retorted, rushing toward her apartment door. When the buzzer rang a second time, she asked into the intercom, "Who is it?" smiling, because she knew exactly who was requesting entrance.

"'Tis your escort for the evening, my lady," answered the jovial voice she knew so well. "Come to whisk you away for a birthday celebration filled with fine dining and high romance!"

With a quick chuckle, she responded, "Well, then, by all means, come on up!"

Jenna smiled to herself as she waited by the door for Chris to climb the stairs that would lead him to her apartment. In the six months it had been since her accident, he had been her rock, staying close to her while she was still in the hospital for observation after waking from the coma. He had gotten her through the grueling effort it took to strengthen her weakened muscles after her long stay in the hospital bed. There had been many nights when she was exhausted from the exercises and the sheer exertion that it took to walk, that he would eat dinner with her in the rehab facility, and then read to her afterward while she rested, holding her hand as she fell asleep. When she was released, he'd aided her in finding this very apartment, and on moving day, he'd barely let her lift a finger. She remembered how he had carried box after box up several flights of stairs, and as she and Aunt Penny unpacked and arranged, she had regaled Jenna with tales of the truly valiant efforts Chris had gone to on her behalf while she had been in the coma. "He really took Dr. Charleson out?" Jenna had asked, when her aunt told her of the fight that took place between Chris and the doctor she had always thought of as a sleaze.

"Broke his nose, and knocked out a tooth or two—all because of how he treated you," she confirmed. Penny had not been proud of her own involvement with Blaine, but Jenna understood all too well how easy it was to become caught up with the wrong man, especially when emotionally overwrought. Still, she was happy that the hospital had begun malpractice action against Blaine Charleson and had revoked his privilege to practice.

Once Jenna and Red had moved into their new home, she and Chris had begun dating. If she had thought he was special before, in the way he supported her and took care of her through the hard times in her recovery, as her "boyfriend," he was truly wonderful. Always there to listen, and to make her smile, she was clearly the top priority in his life. He was always sure to make time for her, even after working exhausting hours in the hospital. He was equally comfortable taking her out for a lavish night on the town or staying in to watch a movie while sharing pizza and beer—and a cat. He listened to her and he laughed with her, and for the first time ever, Jenna truly felt like a queen. *Well*, she heard that voice in her head, *not ever*... True, she had to concede, there had been one other time in her life when she had been treated like a queen. But she still wasn't certain if that time even been real.

Thoughts of Erik rushed to her mind, and just like that the pain of losing him was new again in her heart. Her relationship with Chris was sweet and romantic and wonderful—he was caring, he was patient, and he was accepting of her need to go slow, understanding the emotional trauma surrounding her medical ordeal. It should be so easy to fall in love with him. But memories of Erik kept holding her back.

Erik had been exhilarating and maddening and yet, at times, so very tender. Despite her efforts to hold herself back, she had fallen totally and completely in love with him. And yet, one look at the beautiful, unique eyes through which Chris gazed at her now, and she was reminded that none of it had been real. She had not traveled back through time, and opened a secret door to the darkly seductive home of a lonely genius. She had simply been lying in a hospital bed, allowing the suggestion of a song, and fragments absorbed from the reality happening around her create a magnificent dream to occupy her brain while it healed. There had been no cheeky Persian, no haughty soprano, no seamstress in search of an angel. If she thought hard enough, she could even recall moments that must have been slivers of the real world breaking through her mirage—like when the stitches simply disappeared from her head, or when she thought she heard a voice calling her from so far away. She remembered several instances when she had started to reach for reality, but she had been pulled back—always drawn back to the dream by Erik's song.

It had seemed *so real*, but it was only her imagination. Her feelings had been so strong, yet they were inspired by a fantasy. So how could she be sure if the feelings she was now beginning to have for Chris were true or if they were merely more fabricated illusions? It was all so confusing and unsettling, and when she thought about it too long, she found herself feeling dizzy—dizzy and wistful for a man who had never been more than a dream

Erik was real, her heart screamed at her. But her mind knew that could not possibly be true.

She shook her head to clear her thoughts of the impossible assertion when she heard the gentle knock announcing that Chris was there.

She was greeted by a huge bouquet of red roses, and a melodious voice saying, “Hello Beautiful.”

She giggled a bit, despite her melancholy memories, and took the roses from him, so that she could reach up and greet him with a kiss. “Hello, Hotty,” she returned, and stepped away from the door so that he could come inside.

When the door closed, she took a deep whiff of her bouquet. “Thank you, Chris. These are lovely!”

“Not half as lovely as you, Jenna,” he said, and his voice was low and hushed as he took the flowers from her hands and placed them on the kitchen counter behind him. He then wrapped her fully in his arms for another kiss, one that lingered until they heard the loud, *mreeeeeeeeeoooow* from behind them.

Chris pulled back and winked at Jenna as he dropped to his knees to greet the interloper who had emerged from the bedroom at the sound of his buddy's voice. “Hey Big Guy!” Chris said happily, gently scratching Red behind the ears.

“Oh, *now* you come out!” Jenna teased her furry companion. “Where were you when I asked you to get the door?”

*Mreh! w*as Red's simple reply as he began to purr in response to his former roommate's attentions.

Smirking, Jenna picked up the roses and took them to the sink, grabbing a vase from the cabinet and filling it up with water. She removed the florist's paper from the bouquet and caught her breath a moment when she saw that it was secured with a silk black ribbon tied in a bow. *It's just a coincidence*, she told herself. *Florists tie roses with ribbon all the time.* She swallowed once and placed the roses in the water, trying to ignore the aching in her chest as she carried them over to her dining room table.

"Now, they aren't a snack, Red." Jenna heard Chris forewarn the cat, who cheekily *mreowed* his response.

"That's right, Red!" Jenna chimed in, grabbing her coat from the entry closet. "I expect them to be intact when we return from our evening."

Red simply sat quietly, with his back turned away from them, which told them he was insulted that they would even suggest he might tamper with the roses—all the other times notwithstanding. These were birthday roses. He would at least let them live for…the night.

Chris rose to his full height, and took her coat from her, wrapping it around her shoulders as he pulled her back into his arms. "Are you ready for your birthday celebration, my dear?"

"I'd be even more ready if you'd tell me where we were going." She smiled up at him sweetly.

"Not a chance, Jenna," he answered, leaning over and giving her a quick kiss on the mouth. "This is to be a night full of surprises." He took her hand in his and led her out the door.

❧

Jenna's heart shattered into a million pieces, as she heard the final, mournful words from the unmasked Phantom on the stage. *No*, she thought, as her sobs grew even more inconsolable, *it wasn't supposed to be this way*.

Chris glanced over to her and tightened his arm around her shoulder. They had had a wonderful evening together—one about which he had fantasized ever since she was still lying in her coma. He had arrived at her door with a dozen roses, and taken her to dinner at a four star restaurant, and then presented her with front row tickets to Broadway's longest running musical. Though her smile had not seemed to reach completely to her eyes when she saw them, she thanked him profusely and insisted she was thrilled to be going to the show. She had long wanted to see the darkly beautiful musical, she'd insisted, and she'd seemed to enjoy herself during the performance. She had teared up during the sad moments, as most of the women in the theater had. But now, as the cape was removed to show only the mask remaining on the Phantom's throne, she was inconsolable, tears of absolute agony pouring out of her eyes.

"Jenna," he whispered, pulling her even closer, as she tucked her head into his shoulder. "Honey, what's wrong?"

"I just…" she tried to talk, though the crying was making it difficult. "Chris, please, just take me home."

Immediately after the curtain call, they made their escape, and Chris hailed a taxi to take them back to her apartment. Jenna sat silently staring out the window on the ride, and Chris sat there wondering what he had done wrong. He longed for nothing more than to make Jenna happy, and yet, no matter how hard he tried, there always seemed to be something that held her back, something that kept her from completely surrendering herself to the moment. Something that kept her from falling in love with him.

He remembered the days when she was in her coma, and he would spend long hours just praying that she would wake up. He'd sworn so many times that it didn't even matter to him if she shared his affections, that all he had truly wanted was her well being. But the truth was that it hurt. Since she had awakened, his feelings for her had grown. No longer did he have to be content imagining her smile and dreaming of her laughter. Now he could experience the beauty of both first hand, and he did everything he could to make them happen as often as possible.

And yet he had still not been able to tell her all he wanted to say. He had wanted so many times to tell her that he loved her, that there would never be another woman for him—that she *was* his forever. But though her kisses were sweet and he could tell she had deep affection for him, he could feel that for some reason she still held back. He told himself it was the trauma of the accident and everything that surrounded it, but what if he was wrong? What if it was simply that she didn't love him the way that he loved her? What if she never would?

He paid the driver and they walked the stairs to her apartment. Once inside, Jenna collapsed on the couch, staring off, unseeing, at the wall. Chris took one look at her, and turned toward the kitchen, returning a few moments later with two cups of tea.

"Your tea, my lady," he said, offering her a cup, seeing the tears once again spring to her eyes. He set the mugs down on the coffee table and knelt down in front of her, taking her hands in his. "Jenna, please tell me what's wrong," he pleaded with her. "Did I do something to upset you?"

"No, Chris!" she insisted right away, reaching out and brushing an unruly lock of hair away from his eyes. "You are everything that is perfect and right and wonderful. You have done absolutely *nothing* wrong."

When she finished, there were tears streaming down her face, prompting Chris to ask the question, "Then why are you crying?"

"Because..." Jenna took several deep breaths, trying to stop herself from shaking, before springing to her feet and declaring angrily, "Because it *wasn't* supposed to be that way." She began pacing back and forth as she poured her heart out through agonized tears. "He wasn't supposed to pretend to be an angel to trick her into loving him. He was a *man*, not an angel or a … a *ghost.* He deserved to be loved, to be *cherished—to* be told every day how wonderful he was. He deserved a woman who would *adore* him the way he adored her, not one who would drop him like a hot coal for the affections of a handsome *Vicomte!*" she spat out bitterly. "He deserved a woman who would look at his face and see beauty, not accuse him of being the monster he was already so quick to call himself." Jenna sat back down on the sofa, burying her head in her hands, as she whispered. "Christine was supposed to *love* Erik. She was not supposed to leave him alone in the dark."

Chris watched her weep bitterly into her hands for a few moments not quite understanding why the play had resonated so deeply with her, but knowing that he had a way to help with her sorrows.

"She didn't," he said, sitting next to her on the sofa, putting his hand gently on her back.

Jenna continued to sob, saying, "She didn't love him? Yes, that's clear."

"No Jenna," he corrected her quietly, "She didn't *leave* him."

Slowly, Jenna raised her head from her hands and looked over at him. It broke his heart to see her eyes so wet with tears—those beautiful eyes that were meant for laughing, never crying. "What…" she said, her sobs quieting to occasional hiccups. "What do you mean?"

Chris ran a hand through his hair and took a deep breath. "I can't believe I'm going to tell you this, Jenna," he began, looking sheepish. "It's not something I ever talk about, because I find it so embarrassing, but if it will make you feel better, then I will. But you have to promise not to think I'm some kind of mental patient, ok?"

"Chris," Jenna responded, once again, thinking of Erik, "I would never accuse *you* of being a mental patient."

He sighed, "OK. Well. Let me start by telling you that the tale of the Phantom of the Opera *is* true. But the play is not the correct story. Neither is the book or any of the movies. I know this, you see, because I am a descendant of the real opera ghost."

Jenna looked at him with eyes growing wide. "*What?*" she asked. "How is that *possible?*"

"See," he chuckled, turning a bit red in the face, "I knew you were going to think I was crazy."

"No, Chris, please." She touched his arm to encourage him. "*Tell* me."

"Well, Leroux had obviously heard about the strange events that happened at the Opera House in Paris—and he knew enough to know that the Phantom was responsible for some of them—but most of what he wrote was just sensationalized fiction, designed to enthrall the reader. He didn't know what *really* happened. *That* story—the *true* story—you see, was handed down from generation to generation in old family journals. When the play became so popular, my father actually got them out of storage and re-read them, and then he passed them on to me. The journals were written, you see, by Christine herself—who happened to be my great-great-great-grandmother. And her husband was the Opera Ghost."

"Erik…" Jenna murmured.

"Yes…at least that part is true," he continued. "And it was also true that Erik was horribly disfigured—and he *did* initially approach Christine by pretending to be the mysterious angel sent by her dead father, because he was afraid she would want nothing to do with him when she saw his face."

"He was afraid she would think him a monster," Jenna added, sadly.

"Yes," Chris nodded. "He was. But that all changed the night of her debut at the Opera Garnier."

Jenna's eyes lit up. "The night of her debut?"

"Yes. You see, according to the journals, he came to her in her dressing room that night, and he told her everything. That he was a man and not an angel, and then he gave her a rose—all tied up in a ribbon of black—like the roses I brought you tonight," he added, looking somewhat sheepish.

"I love them," Jenna smiled at him, putting her hand on his arm. "They're beautiful."

Chris smiled and looked down, "Anyway," he continued, "He took her to the ball that night."

"He did?" Jenna asked, her voice barely a whisper.

"Yes, he did. And from that night forward they continued their vocal lessons in person, and eventually, he brought her down to his home beneath the opera house, to coach her from there. The story goes that Christine was already half in love with him when she thought him an angel, but she lost her heart completely when she began to know him as a man. In her journals, she described him as sweet and gentle—to everyone, that is, except his best friend, a Persian not even mentioned in the play, whom he loved to tease mercilessly."

"Omid," she supplied with a smile.

"Yes," Chris chuckled, looking a bit confused. "How did you *know* that, Jenna?"

"I...heard the name...*somewhere* before."

"Hmmm. Anyway, even though Christine had fallen in love with him, as the story goes, it actually took *him* some time to reciprocate those feelings."

Jenna's eyes narrowed, "Really?"

"Yes. I know it seems strange, since the story everybody knows paints the Phantom as a love-obsessed lunatic who would do anything to win the girl, but my great-great-great-grandmother wrote that there was a sadness in Erik's soul that she found hard to break through."

"What happened?" Jenna asked in a hush, truly surprised by this turn of events. The only reason she'd left him was because he'd said he was in love with Christine. Yet, if she loved him in return, why would he hesitate?

"Well, everybody quaked in fear about the Phantom—who rarely did anything but perform harmless pranks, like leaving toads and spiders in Carlotta's dressing room."

"I see…" Jenna smiled and nodded, remembering her own role in those events.

"But after Erik had finally come clean with Christine, he really didn't do a lot in terms of haunting anymore. He was too focused on training her and enjoying her rise to fame. But little things continued to happen around the opera house, which made people believe the Phantom was still active. Most of these incidents were easily passed off as accidents, which is why Erik paid them no mind. It did not bother him when the curtain tore due to careless handling, or a trap door on the stage opened at the wrong time, making the ballet rats shriek about The Phantom of the Opera. It kept his salary coming and it kept Box 5 open for him when he wished to hear Christine sing on stage.

"One night, though, the auditorium's grand chandelier came crashing down, killing one of the audience members in the front row. When the chandelier's hanging mechanism was examined, it was discovered that the counterweight that held the great light fixture in place, had been tampered with. Suddenly, the mischievous ghost was a murderer."

"No," Jenna murmured, shaking her head, "Not Erik."

"It was at that point that a former employee made his renewed presence known…"

Jenna felt herself catch her breath. "Joseph Buquet? He came back?"

"That's… right," Chris affirmed, once again with narrowed eyes. "He did. Christine wrote that at some point, after she and Erik had begun seeing one another in person, he snuck back into the opera house and started hiding out there in one of the cellars. She and Erik understood at that point, that the little accidents around the opera house had not been accidents at all, and that while Erik had been busy training Christine and generally keeping out of the way, the drunk, lecherous former chief of the flies had started to cause mischief where the phantom had left off.

"But the realization came too late. Buquet was busy making certain that all the blame for the chandelier incident fell on the Phantom. He told the managers and the gendarme that he had seen the Phantom, and that the ghost was really just a flesh and blood man who wore a mask. He then shared the knowledge he had gleaned about the cellars from slinking around there himself, and he intimated that Erik's home was even deeper beneath the opera.

"And so, with the gendarme crawling all around the sub-basements of the opera house, Erik realized that his home was no longer safe for him, and he told Christine he was leaving France. But to his surprise, she insisted on going with him, telling him that she loved him, and that the opera could never be her home if he was not there with her.

"They left on a boat to America, and during the voyage, they were married by the ship's captain. They arrived in New York as husband and wife, but at Castle Garden—the predecessor to Ellis Island—when they were asked to give their name, apparently my great great-great-grandfather said, "Erik, sir," as he was not even aware of his own last name. The clerk, unfamiliar with French accents, wrote down the name Eriksson, and it stuck.

"Erik and Christine Eriksson lived out the rest of their lives in New York, in the house still owned by my father, along the Hudson River." He saw Jenna smile quietly when he said this, but since she said nothing, he continued. "Christine sang occasionally at the Met, but the majority of their time was spent raising their two children, a son named Gustave and a daughter" he paused, smiling at her, "named Genevieve."

Jenna gasped and asked, "Genevieve?"

"Yes," Chris nodded. "The story goes that Erik encouraged Christine to name their son after her father, but when they had a daughter, he insisted upon the name Genevieve."

"Why?" she asked, as her eyes welled up with tears, a thousand emotions coursing through her veins. He may not have loved her they way he loved Christine, but he *had* cared enough to name his baby girl after her.

Chris reached out and stroked her cheek with his knuckles. "My great-great-great-grandmother Christine wrote that he said it was the most beautiful, most *melodious* of all names." His voice hushed as he leaned a little closer to her. "I find that I agree."

Jenna reached out and cupped his cheek, and closed the distance between them with a quick kiss. "Thank you, Chris," she whispered when they parted, her forehead resting on his. "For telling me that story."

"Does it make you feel better, Jenna?" he asked her, stroking her cheek with his thumb.

"It does, Chris," she sighed. "I'm sorry I ruined our evening."

"No, you didn't ruin anything," he promised her. "The musical moved you. Your great compassion is one of the things that I…" he trailed off, as if reconsidering what he was about to say, but then decided it was time to finally let his feelings be known. "Jenna," he said, taking both of her hands in his, "You are *so* beautiful. From the moment I laid eyes on you, I wanted to get to know you. But I was always too shy. Then, when you were lying in that hospital bed, I…" he shook his head and closed his eyes, "I cursed myself so many times for not telling you how I felt about you when I had the chance. And here we are—six months into a relationship, and I am still holding back. I can't do it anymore, Jenna. I've got to tell you that I…" he paused and gazed straight into her eyes, saying, "I love you."

Jenna's mouth fell open into an O, and Chris continued quickly. "You don't have to say anything back. I know it's been…difficult for you, since the accident, and that you need time—and you can have as much as you need. But Jenna, I can't wait to say it anymore. I *love* you—so much. I love your sweetness, I love your laughter. I love your fire and your sense of adventure. I love your tenderness, and I love your passion. I love *you*, Jenna, with everything that I am, and I know that there will never be another woman for me. That is why," he took a deep breath and reached into his breast pocket, "I want to give you this."

He produced a flat, wide box that obviously held a piece of jewelry inside.

"Oh, Chris," she gasped, "You already did so much for my birthday, you didn't have to…"

"I know, but I wanted to. Besides, this was something I already possessed. You see, there is a tradition in my family, Jenna. Ironically, it dates back to my great-great-great-grandfather Erik. On the day his son Gustave was to be wed, Erik pulled him aside, and gave him a beautiful necklace to present to his bride. It was not something that had belonged to Christine, but nevertheless, Erik told him he had had it for a while. He said it was fitting that Gustave give it to his wife, as it was a symbol of love that was always new, and love that would never fade; a love that would give courage and support in the darkest of moments; a love that would bring out the best in you. So Gustave gave the necklace to his bride, and later, when their eldest son Charles was to wed, he was bestowed with the necklace to give to *his* bride. So on and so forth, the necklace passed down the generations through the eldest sons and the women they loved. I am the *only* son in my family, Jenna, and now I want to give this to you—because I know that my love for you will never fade, and it will always make me strive to be the best man I *can* be—for you."

He held the box before her, and with trembling fingers opened the lid. Inside, lay a beautiful cameo with a carving of a rosebud, just about to burst into bloom. Jenna felt herself begin to shake as she removed it from the box and held it tenderly in her hand. Though the black ribbon was gone, it was the very same cameo Erik had given her—the one she had placed by the shore of the lake when she left him. He had found it and kept it, and had turned it into a symbol of enduring love—the kind of love he had for Christine. Though it had hurt her, had broken her heart when he told her, she realized now, that if he hadn't loved Christine, she would never have been able to gaze into the beautiful eyes of the man who was now before her—the man whose love brought her back from her coma, pulled her through her recovery, and waited patiently for her when she was afraid to offer him her fragile heart. But now, seeing that everything had been real, knowing that Erik had truly gone on and lived out his life surrounded by love, she found the courage to do the same.

She brought the cameo to her lips and mouthed a silent "I love you"—one she wished could span the ages, so that Erik could hear it and know that, in a part of her heart, it would always be true. And then she looked up at Chris.

He was watching her with eyes full of hope, and when her gaze met his, he asked, shyly, "Do…do you like your gift, Jenna?"

She looked intently into his gaze, as she said strongly, "*You* are my greatest gift, Chris. And I *love* you. *So* much." She reached up and tangled her fingers in his soft brown hair. Slowly, she pulled his face toward hers, and gently, sweetly she kissed him fully on the lips. When they separated, a look of pure joy lit his eyes, and Jenna was humbled to know that she was the cause of such happiness. "And I love *this*, Chris," she whispered, holding up the cameo—the tangible evidence she needed to finally know for sure that she had not been dreaming. Her time with Erik had been real. "Will you please help me put it on?"

He nodded happily as he took the cameo and reached behind her with trembling fingers to fasten the chain around her neck. After he was done, he loosed a quiet moan when he felt her lips touch his again. This time, their kiss lingered and deepened, their arms wrapping around each other. When they parted, breathless and shaking, they gazed at one another, eyes glazed with desire.

"I will treasure it always," Jenna muttered, stroking his face with her fingers.

"As I will treasure you. *Always*, Jenna. Forever," he whispered soft and low. And then they were lost again in one another's arms. Forever had waited long enough to begin.

Chris awoke the next morning to sunbeams dancing playfully in Jenna's strawberry blond curls, her head resting peacefully on his chest. He reached out his hand to stroke her hair. It was like a dream come true. He had spent weeks watching her as she slept, but never before had her smile looked so serene, or her lips so enticing. They had tasted heaven last night in each other's embrace, and he could not resist placing feather soft kisses along her hairline, her eyelids, her cheeks as their passion played on his memory.

Jenna's face shifted upwards, and without opening her eyes, she caught his lips with hers, their kiss deepening, their tongues dancing in memories of their euphoric night. Jenna sighed as she felt Chris's body responding anew to their kiss, feeling desire beginning to spread within her own core. She reached below the blankets to rest her hand on his naked hip, pulling their bodies even closer together, and earning her a husky moan of approval. "Oh, my Jenna," he whispered as he kissed her even more deeply, and began to shift above her.

They heard a muffled *mreeeeoooow* as Red joined them on the bed, landing in between them. Startled, Jenna opened her eyes to see the remains of an apparently delicious red rose still in his mouth. "Red!" she scolded good-naturedly, "I told you not to eat them!"

"Well, to be fair, my love," Chris chimed in, placing a sweet kiss on her lips, "We haven't exactly gotten up to feed him."

"Well no," she agreed, kissing him back, "but *you* gave me those roses."

"I plan to give you plenty more roses, Jenna," he deepened their kiss a little more, tangling his fingers in her curls, "enough to last a lifetime."

"Mmmmmm," she sighed, pulling him closer, leaning her head back, as his lips began to slowly travel down her throat. "That sounds wonderful."

"Like heaven," he murmured.

Mreeeeeooooow! They heard again, and groaned at the sound. "But first," he said, chuckling to himself. "I'd better feed the cat." He sat up and reached for his pants, which had been lying in a heap on the floor with the rest of their clothes. Pulling them up, he looked over at her and raised an eyebrow as he asked, "Wait for me?"

Jenna snuggled more deeply into the bed and whispered, "I'd wait for you forever."

41 NOTES

Jenna stepped off the final stair and looked at the room around her. She rubbed her arms with her hands for warmth. It was cold and damp—as most basements were—and even *with* the benefit of the naked bulb above her head, the room was full of shadows. And boxes.

They had inherited so many boxes of *things* when Chris's father had decided to move down to Florida, leaving them in charge of the family home. While they were grateful for the extra room the house afforded them—especially with their first little one on the way—they had both agreed that something needed to be done about the multiple generations' worth of *stuff* down in the basement. It was a large space, and would make a great playroom if they could just get it cleaned out. So, while Chris was away at the Medical Symposium in San Francisco, Jenna decided to use her day off to begin to do just that.

Rummaging through the boxes was almost like going through a museum of the Eriksson family. Clothing, and books, old dishes and plates were just some of the treasures Jenna found. She enjoyed looking through the old photo albums that were also stored down here and seeing what the Eriksson family had looked like through the years. Page after page depicted running, laughing children—most with straight black hair or bouncy brown curls. Chris's mismatched eyes seemed to be a trait that was prominent in the Eriksson family through the years. Seeing those eyes appear in picture after picture made Jenna fondly remember their source.

Erik. Oh how thoughts of him still played on her mind. Her husband reminded her of him in so many ways every day, in his mannerisms, in his looks, in the things he would say. Chris even sang to her at night, as he strummed his guitar, his voice every bit as mesmerizing as Erik's had been. The similarities between them were almost eerie at times, and at first she had been afraid that she was attracted to Chris mostly *because* he reminded her of Erik. And though time had proven her wrong, and she had come to love and adore her husband for the unique, exciting man that *he* was, she could not help but note the likenesses between the only two men who had ever truly held her heart.

Chris had told her the story related in Christine's journals—and she had read them herself. Chris alone was proof that Erik had lived out his life with a wife who loved him and children who adored him—one of whom he'd named after her! As she reached down and rubbed her own slightly swollen stomach, contemplating the child that lay therein, she wished somehow she could talk to Erik—and tell him that she too had found happiness.

She recalled the last time she saw him—when he had told her that he was in love with Christine. How it had broken her heart at the time. She had fallen to her knees, unable to even look at him. And then he had walked away and she had never seen him again. She wondered what he thought when he'd returned home that night after the ball and found her gone. Had he realized she'd gone home? Had he worried about her at all? He may not have been in love with her in the same way she was with him, but she knew that he at least cared. *He named his child after me*, she thought. H*e must have cared at least somewhat.*

She wished she could tell him that everything had worked out for her—that she had made it back home, and that she was now married to the man of her dreams, who just happened to be his great-great-great-grandson. She smiled to herself, thinking of the coincidence. Erik had once told her that she should hold out for a prince. Because of Erik, she had found him.

Exhausted by all of her rummaging, Jenna sat down to rest. Her head fell back gently, and she was surprised to hear an echoey sound from the wall behind her. Jenna turned her head to look at it. It was just a plain white wall, like all the other walls in the basement. There were no identifying marks of any kind, or anything to make it stand out in anyway. She stood and walked a few feet and rapped against the wall with her knuckles. Here, she only heard a light tapping. She crossed the basement and knocked on the other wall. Again, only a very light tap, tap, tap ensued. She returned to her original spot and lightly hit the wall again. Sure enough, there was no shallow *tap-tap-tap*, but a resonant *thud*. As if there was open space behind the wall. As if it were hollow. *Hollow*.

An undeniable certainty came over Jenna. This had been Erik's house. He may have left the opera house, to live with Christine in the sun, but Jenna sincerely doubted he left all remnants of the Opera Ghost behind. It was too much a part of him. And he *was* a master architect. Surely he could have built secret places into his home. It would be just like him to do so. And the basement would be the perfect place!

Jenna looked at the wall again. Just a wall. Simple and unmarked. Except, now she saw, two tiny cracks that ran from the ceiling all the way down to the floor. They were almost imperceptible—and if she had not known what to look for, she never would have seen them. But she had lived with Erik—she recognized his style.

Jenna stood on her tiptoes and reached her left arm up to the level she'd often seen him do at the Opera House. She could see nothing there, but in this case, as with all of Erik's secret passageways, *feeling* is believing. As she pressed gently on the wall, she felt a small, fingertip sized section press inward—just slightly. A soft click sounded, and those floor-to-ceiling cracks got wider, as the wall before her shifted, revealing a door.

Jenna did not breathe as she entered the room that was now open before her. Dank and musty, with spider webs here and there, it was clear this room had been forgotten for years. It was not a labyrinthine tunnel, like at the opera house. It was meager room—barely larger than a closet—but it was obviously Erik's. There was a small writing desk, with what looked like a dried up ink pot and several fountain pens arranged neatly near the back. A small tinplate portrait sat on its surface in an oval frame. Jenna picked it up to examine it. It was Christine, years older than when Jenna had last seen her, with her hair pulled back in the old fashioned chignon that married women of the day would wear. She was seated in a high backed chair, a young boy with pitch-black hair standing by her side, an even younger girl with bouncy ringlets seated on her lap. *Erik's family*, Jenna thought. Now hers, too. She looked more closely at the girl who was her namesake. She smiled for the camera and Jenna was sure she saw that familiar upturn of lips that she loved so well. "Oh Erik," she whispered into the secret room. "I miss you." And though she loved Chris with all her heart, and she would not trade being his wife for anything in this world, she knew it was true. A part of her would always miss Erik. He would forever hold a very special piece of her heart.

To the right of the desk, along the back wall of the room, there was a large bookshelf. On one of the shelves was a violin, and Jenna smiled. Though she had not heard Erik play violin in her time with him, she was not the slightest bit surprised that he could. Oh how the walls of this old house must have rung with music, when the genius composer and his soprano wife had lived here. She wondered if Erik had taught his children how to play. Thinking of her own husband's musical inclinations, she was certain musical ability had run in the family.

On the shelves below the instrument were sheaves and sheaves of paper, tied together with string. Jenna picked up one of the bundles to find swirls of hand written notes gracing lined pages. Though she herself was not able to read the notations, she knew that these were the masterful workings of a musical genius. Erik's compositions! She examined the rest of the stacks, finding page after page of symphonies and concertos, all hand-written in Erik's signature scrawl. Amid the excitement of being surrounded by Erik's music, her heart ached just a little bit. She remembered the time when she'd asked him to prove his musical genius to her. In this room was more evidence than she ever really needed. She'd never doubted his brilliance. "Oh, Erik," she whispered again, recalling the times she would try to lure him away from his piano to spend time with her. "I wish I could hear you play just one last time."

Jenna looked down, and took a deep breath against the bittersweet memories that threatened to overwhelm her. That was when she saw it. A small box sitting on the bottom shelf. There was something about the solitary box, set slightly apart from the sundry stacks of Erik's musical masterpieces that called to her. She knelt on the floor to examine it more closely, brushing years' worth of dust off its surface.

The box was hinged and made of wood, and would likely have a bright shiny finish with a bit of polishing. On the top, the letter J was carved in swirly script that Jenna could have sworn was Erik's own. A gold clasp held the box shut, but it wasn't locked, so Jenna gently lifted the clasp and gingerly opened the lid. What she found inside made her catch her breath.

More papers, neatly stacked and tied together with a ribbon of black velvet—but these were not sheet music. They looked to be letters written on the very same folded over parchment on which Jenna had seen Erik write his notes to the managers. And her name was scrawled across the front fold of the letter on top.

Jenna removed the precious packet of papers and tenderly stroked the ribbon, before untying it carefully with trembling hands. She felt tears spring to her eyes as she unfolded the first letter and read the words inside.

Oh My Jenna,

How I long for you to be here so that I could hear your voice, look into your eyes and see your smile as I tell you the things I have to say. Of course, if you were still here, none of it would have happened—but that would not matter, because I would still have you with me, and I would have all that I need.

But you're gone, and all I have are my memories of you, and the cameo that you left beside the lake. Once again, Jenna, you left my rose behind. But this rose was meant only for you. I shall not be giving it away, dear heart. I shall keep it here, always, with the letters I write to you—my dear sweet rose that will never fade.

I find that I already miss talking to you, telling you my secrets, sharing with you my dreams. I lived my life alone, Jenna, with scarcely anyone to talk to, and yet my short time with you makes me crave someone to whom I can unburden my soul. Or perhaps it is just that I crave you.

I'm sorry Jenna. I am so sorry that I had to lie to you to make you leave me. Jenna, I love you—as I know you love me. I only regret that I never got to say it. But that *I could never do, because once said, I would have wanted to spend the rest of my life repeating it again and again—an endless refrain of love that I would sing only for you. I hope you know, my Jenna. I hope somehow, someway you will understand that I let you go because I* did *love you—and while I wanted so much for you to live in my arms, I wanted one thing more. Simply for you to live. If I was right, and it was true, that you were somehow in a coma back in your time, I would never be able to live with myself if something happened to you because you chose to stay with me. If you died…I am certain I would have died too.*

As it was, I did not want to go on living knowing I would never see you again. I saw nothing more in my future but to waste away for want of the love I had lost—the only love I had ever known in my life. But the Persian—he told me that I had no choice now but to live *for you, as I forced you to live for me. So…I went to Christine, Jenna. Just as you had encouraged me to do. And I did not go as the Phantom, or as an Angel. I went to her as myself—the way you always wanted me to. I introduced myself as a* man, *Jenna. And she didn't run from me! No, instead she took my hand and asked me to the masquerade ball, and she even chose to accompany me over an offer from the Vicomte. I was shocked. But you told me it would be that way, my Jenna. And it was only because of you and your love that I could find the strength to try.*

It was a wonderful party—watching Christine enjoy every moment of her well-earned success. She and I danced quite a few dances, and at the end of the night, I bowed to her and thanked her for a lovely evening. She bashfully asked if she would see me the next day. I assured her I would be at the next night's performance—that I would see her afterward.

And now I sit here, and I dream of what would have happened if you had been awaiting me when I returned—or what might have occurred if you *had accompanied me to the ball instead. I remember the night* we *danced, Jenna. I think of it all the time. The way your body felt pressed up so tightly against mine, as we glided across the floor. Well,* I *glided—you stumbled a bit, but it didn't matter. Your body in my arms was still the closest thing I had ever held to perfection. And when I could no longer stand even the smallest separation and I brushed my lips against yours, I was sure I had been granted admittance into heaven. Kissing you—*touching *you—was the closest thing to paradise that I had ever known, and when I think of how we would have completed that evening, if your health had not suffered…Jenna, I ache. I yearn for the warmth I would have found within you. I thirst for the sweet wine of your mouth and hunger for the taste of your skin. What secrets would we have spoken that night, Jenna? What questions would we have answered? You have awakened a desire in me, Jenna, that had long lay dormant. Even just thinking of you, I feel my body responding, my soul reaching out to you. Do you reach for me too?*

I will never know.

But one thing I do know is that I love you. And I miss you, my Jenna.

~~Erik

Jenna held the letter out before her with shaking hands, tears streaming down her face. He had loved her. Erik had *loved* her. He had written this very letter, missing her the way she missed him. She was taken back to the emptiness she felt inside those first days after she had returned from Erik's world. Even though she had had Chris to help her through, the pain in her heart when she would think of Erik was almost unbearable. Now, to know he'd known the same pain broke her heart anew. He had claimed to love Christine only to save her from an almost certain death. She should have known that his genius had led him to figure out that she was in a coma. Hadn't they even had a conversation about what might have happened if she'd been found in her car?

But yet, through the pain, he tried. By some miracle, Omid had convinced him to try to live *for her*. And he had *done* it. She shuddered to think what would have happened to him—to *her*—if he had not gone to Christine that night.

Pressing this first letter to her heart, Jenna reached inside the box for the next one.

My Dearest Jenna,

It has been a week since you've been gone, and not a day—not an hour—has gone by without my thoughts drifting to you. Are you all right, my Jenna? Are you safe? Was this maddening sacrifice well made? I miss you terribly, and every day is a struggle, but I continue to try because of you—as the Persian points out, I forced *you to live, so now I have no right to discard my own miserable existence—although at times I want to when the realization hits me that I will never see you again.*

My lessons with Christine help to ease the pain though, at least for a short time each day. Would you hate me if you knew, Jenna? Would you despise me for temporarily alleviating this incessant misery with Christine's sweet company? You were right again about her, my Jenna. She's known me to be a man for a week now. She has seen the mask, and has not asked any questions. She does not demand perfection—or the mythical being I thought I had to become simply to be in her presence. She does not hate me for lying to her. She seems to accept me, Jenna, which is strange, because I had once thought that you would be the only one to ever do that. Of course, she has not seen what lies beneath the mask—and yet, the memory of the way you drew me to you even then gives me hope that perhaps she will not immediately flee should the day ever come that she sees my face.

But know this, my dearest. Everything I do each day, I do for you. Just knowing that you are out there—somewhere—living your life as I endeavor to live mine gives me the strength I need to carry on. I hope you too have found a way to lessen the sting of our separation—just as I hope with all my heart that you know I love you.

~~Erik

Once again, the tears poured from Jenna's eyes. "I know, Erik," she said out loud. "I know you loved me." She closed her eyes and said a brief prayer of thanks to God for Christine. Even with the slight smart she felt at knowing Christine would eventually take her place in Erik's heart, it brought Jenna such relief to know that Erik was not alone. He'd had Christine, as she had Chris. She would never begrudge him that.

Jenna read through a few more of the letters that highlighted the progression of his relationship with Christine. How he continued to teach her—even bringing her down to his subterranean world so they could have fewer distractions while focusing on the music. Jenna smiled when he wrote *I was trepidatious to show her my home, but she thought it beautiful.* "Of course, she did Erik," she said out loud when she read that part. "It *was* beautiful." Every letter ended with *I miss you, Jenna,* and *I love you* even when it was clear to her that his heart was beginning to heal.

Eventually, she found the letter she was waiting for.

My Dear Jenna,

So much has happened since I last wrote, and how I wish you were here to steady my trembling heart and hand as I write this. Buquet, Jenna. He has returned! And I did not notice! I curse my own distraction, for not detecting him sooner. I curse myself for not killing him the night he almost hurt you. He did not deserve to draw another breath after laying one miserable finger on you. But now he has gone a step further. He has killed, *Jenna. He has marred* my *opera house with murder! And in so doing, he has implicated me!*

He dropped the grand chandelier, Jenna, right in the middle of a performance when my Christine had been performing on stage. Once again, he threatened someone so vitally important to me! Christine was fortunate and blessedly saved from harm, but a woman sitting in the front row of the auditorium was not so. As I stood with Christine in my sitting room later that night, calming her fears, I believed it to be an accident, but when the Gendarme finished their investigation, it was confirmed that the counterweight had been tampered with. That was when that sniveling rat Buquet dared to show his face once more—telling all about the Phantom, telling them that I was simply a man. He has even told them about the cellars, Jenna. He did not know enough to lead them directly to my home, but with the Gendarme in pursuit, how much longer can I be safe?

I told Christine goodbye tonight. I told her that I was leaving France, that I had to find a new home now that this one was compromised. But then an astonishing thing happened, Jenna. She said she wanted to go with *me. I, of course, forbade it, saying that she had to stay. France was her home and she had her career to think about. She could not leave it all behind because of me. Yet, she told me she did not care, Jenna! She said that I was her home, and she wished to go anywhere I went! My God, Jenna. She chose* me, *just as you once chose me. I had never dreamed to know that feeling even once in my life, and now I have known it twice.*

Still I told her she could not make such a life altering choice as that, as long as she did not know what I was behind the mask. And she asked me to show her. Jenna, it was as if I was hearing your voice once again in my heart. I was so sure she would run, that she would scream and call me a monster. I was even afraid she might reveal me to the Gendarme. She had the knowledge, Jenna. She could have done it.

But the memory of your reaction steeled my heart, and closing my eyes against my fears, I removed the mask. Do you know what she did? She cried, Jenna. Not in fear, but in sympathy. And she drew me to her and told me if I but said the word, she would follow me anywhere.

And so I did. I asked her if she would share the rest of her days with me as my…wife. I once dreamed of asking that question of you, and I beg you to forgive me this betrayal. But I know, my Jenna, that you would not want me to be alone, just as I pray every day that you *are not alone. Christine has helped me to heal—she accepts me as you did, and…she* loves *me. I know with her love I can be happy.*

I will strive to be a good husband to Christine. I think the time I spent with you will help me. And I know that I will still think of you every day and be grateful that you taught me how to love, Jenna. I will live because of you.

~~Erik

"And *I* live because of *you*," she exclaimed tearfully, and she knew it was true. If it had not been for Erik, she never would have emerged from that coma. She would have died, and never known the joys life had in store for her. But even before the coma, she had not really been living. She had given her heart recklessly time after time to men who did not treat her well—who did not love her for who she was. Erik had shown her that she was worthy of a prince—and then he had given her one.

If he had not married Christine—if he had let the agony of their lost love take over and resumed his reclusive ways—then she would not have Chris, and when she returned, the anguish would have overcome her. But by choosing to try—by choosing to *live* with Christine as his wife—once again, Erik had saved her. She brought the letter to her lips and kissed it, whispering, "Thank you, my Erik. Because of you, I have found my prince."

Jenna took a deep breath and tried to compose herself, although she was convinced it was a lost cause. There were only a few more letters in the box, and she wanted to get through them all. The next one was dated a year later.

Dear Jenna,

A year has passed since last I wrote, yet still I think of you almost every day. We are in America now, Jenna. We've settled in New York. Once I saw the river—your Hudson River—I knew I had found my new home.

It calls to me, Jenna. After so many years of living on the lake, I find its presence comforting. At night, after Christine has gone to sleep, I often come out and watch the waters as they rush to the shore, and I remember that it was these very waters that brought you to me and changed my life for the better.

Oh and how my life has changed, Jenna! Christine and I, we were married on the ship to America. I thought it best not to wait, so that her reputation would not be in any way tarnished. We found this home and moved in shortly after arriving. I was never so happy for the money that the managers had paid me. It made our transition to America so much smoother. We have a new home, and a new name, and in a few months' time, we will have a new baby. Yes, Christine is expecting a child, Jenna. I am going to be a father.

*I find it strange. I never thought I would find a woman to love me—to…*touch *me. And yet now I have a child on the way. I worry, Jenna. What if my child looks like me? What if my curse continues? But Christine assures me she would find any child of mine beautiful, and she would love him with her whole heart, never making him hide his face, or feel in any way ashamed. I believe her, Jenna. She is a good woman. She will be a good mother to our baby, whatever he or she may look like.*

I…love her Jenna. I truly do. My God, when I first said those words to you, and saw the look on your face, I never thought it would ever really be true. But…I do. She is kind, and compassionate. She never makes me feel like less of a man because of my face. And she has helped me laugh again. I find that in her I have found completion. I hope you have found that in your life as well, my Jenna. I wish it, and pray for it every day, that you are blessed with the love and joy I have found in Christine. You deserve no less, my Jenna. You deserve no less.

I wish you could be here to see my child, Jenna. And I wonder do you have children of your own? I know any child of yours would be beautiful.

I still miss you.

~~ Erik

Jenna smiled and rubbed her belly, where her unborn child grew. "Oh Erik, I wish you knew that this child I'm carrying would be carrying on *your* line as well." She thought of Chris's beautiful features that were so similar to Erik's in so many ways. "This child *will* be beautiful. He or she will make their great-great-great-*great*-grandfather very proud!"

Jenna reached in the box for the final letter. It was dated three years later.

Dear Jenna,

Life is wonderful. I know it has been awhile since I last wrote, but it is because my life has been so full. Christine and I had a son, Jenna. She named him after her father, Gustave. He is so beautiful. With pitch-black hair and a bright, joyful smile, he is exactly how I would have looked if I had not been born disfigured. He has my mismatched eyes, but set in his exquisite face, they do not seem a curse. He is two and a half years old, Jenna, and already he sings and reaches for books. In the evenings, I sit with him on my lap at the piano. He plays a little like you right now, Jenna, (I'm sorry, dear friend. I couldn't resist.) but one day, he will fill concert halls with his masterful music. Or he will build magnificent buildings. Or he will do whatever else it is that sets fire to his heart. The world is open to my son, Jenna, in a way it was never open to me. And I will see to it that he has every advantage, every benefit that I never had. He already has the benefit of a wonderful mother. And now, a beautiful sister.

Christine has just given birth to our second child. It is a girl this time, Jenna, the most exquisite one I have ever laid eyes upon. Also, the most bald. But she has eyes as blue as the sea, and I can envision brown ringlets running down her back one day. Since Christine named Gustave after her father, she told me I could name our daughter anything I wanted. And so I called her Genevieve. Because it is the most beautiful and melodic name I have ever heard. And because it belongs to you.

None of this would have been possible without you, Jenna. I look around at my home in the sun, at my wife, and my beautiful family, and I am amazed that I should call it my own. I know I would never have emerged from beneath the veil of the ghost if it had not been for knowing and loving you. You told me to be a man, Jenna, and you made me want to be a good one. And I will always love you for that. And now, I honor you with my daughter. I will do my best to raise her to be as kind and as spirited—and as fiery as you. She already screams just as loud! I just wish you could hear her!

~~Yours, Erik

Jenna sniffled as she folded the final letter—the final words Erik ever wrote to her. Oh, how her heart swelled with joy at the way his life had turned. How grateful she was that he had not been alone in the dark—that he had found love again with Christine. There had been times, over the years, when she had felt guilty for loving Chris so much. It almost seemed a betrayal of her feelings for Erik somehow. But knowing he had found happiness she no longer felt that pang of guilt. She could love Chris freely, just as Erik had loved Christine. She only wished there was a way she could tell him—that she could let him know that everything had worked out for her—and that his choices had unknowingly shaped her own life.

Jenna set all the letters back in the box, and replaced it in its spot on the shelf. She was certain she would be back to reread them again and again, but first, there was something she had to do. She ran upstairs as quickly as her swollen, pregnant feet could carry her, and sat down in the office she and Chris had set up on the first floor. She reached into the drawer and removed a sheet of paper and a pen…and began to write.

Jenna found an envelope and sealed the letter inside, writing the name Erik across the front. The day had grown dark while she sat and read Erik's last words to her, but still, she took the letter and walked outside to the riverbed behind the house. The world had changed so much since Erik had occupied in this same spot, gazing out across the choppy waters, thinking of her. But tonight, across a century, their hearts were still united.

Jenna took the envelope and pressed it to her lips, sealing it with a kiss that she hoped would span the ages. "I love you, Erik," she whispered, and she let the letter go. It fluttered from her hand and drifted down into the Hudson. She watched as it teetered a bit at first, on top of the bobbing waves. And then, finally, it succumbed to the water, sinking beneath the surface, until it slipped out of sight. Jenna reached up and clutched the cameo that even now hung around her neck. "Forever," she whispered as she gazed out into the dark waters. And then she turned and walked inside.

The Persian walked into the sitting room using the passageway by the kitchen. It had been years since he had seen his friend, and truly, he was looking forward to the upcoming trip. He was eager to see how Erik and Christine were coming along. *Two* children of their own now! He recalled the delight his gruff friend would take in spending time with his own dear Aziz. Still, caring for two children at one time? Erik must be out of his wits on a daily basis! Omid found that the thought made him smile.

He had had the urge to visit Erik's old home while he and Antoinette had been packing their final bags. He did not know whether it was a sweep of nostalgia, or something else that had drawn him to venture once more beneath the opera house, but venture he did, and now he stood once again in Erik's domain.

The house looked the same as it always had, Erik not having had much opportunity to clear things out before he moved. But it was lacking his presence, it was lacking his force. The Opera House without its ghost was just a theater, no longer the seat of splendor it once was. No more chandeliers fell, no more notes appeared, and Antoinette had long ago stopped depositing the Phantom's monthly salary in Box 5. They no longer even staged operas here any more. The auditorium was now used strictly for ballet. While that made Omid's new wife and stepdaughter very happy, Erik would be appalled. *If* he cared. The Opera Garnier no longer held his heart. Christine had a firm grip on that now.

Omid walked along the edge of the murky lake, remembering a night—which now seemed so long ago—when a crash in the cave led them to find an angel. Oh, they did not recognize her as one that fateful night. They thought she was an escapee from the asylum! But the change she brought forth in his friend—she must have been a miracle. If not for her, Erik would still be here, languishing in loneliness, *dying* a little more with each passing day. But Jenna taught Erik how to live, and Omid would forever be grateful for it.

Something white and crumbled on the lakeshore caught his eye. He approached it curiously, and knelt down to see what it was. An envelope, wrinkled and worn, with the name Erik scrawled across its front. Omid lifted it in his hands, and felt a surge of excitement run through him. The envelope was filthy and battered, made of much thinner paper than Omid was used to seeing. It looked different from any other envelopes he had seen in his day, and it was completely out of place just lying here on the lakeshore, just as *she* had been. It didn't belong, just as *she* hadn't. But Omid had the feeling that this letter was exactly the thing Erik needed—just as Jenna had been.

Omid carefully opened the envelope. He knew he would pay for this later, but Erik always found something to complain about—

might as well earn his lunatic friend's ravings this time. An amazed smile spread across his face as he read Jenna's heartfelt words of love to his friend. It was astonishing to him, how closely intertwined their fates were—one to the other—how the universe had endeavored to keep them connected. While he was truly happy that things had worked out so well for both Jenna and Erik—and while it was clear that they were both madly in love with their respective spouses—he imagined for a moment what their lives would have been like if they'd ended up together. They would have been magnificent!

With a happy sigh, Omid put the letter in his breast pocket, eager to deliver it when their boat arrived in America. But there was one last thing he had to do before he left. He sauntered over to Erik's liquor cabinet, certain that he would have been too distracted by the events of his last days here to hide the Cognac. Sure enough, there was a bottle inside. As Omid reached for the amber liquid with a laugh, a piece of paper fluttered to the floor. Bending, Omid found one of Erik's customary notes, written on heavy parchment. Unfolding the note, Omid guffawed as he read, *Enjoy, you thieving Persian!*

He felt a sense of completion wash over him as he made his way out of his friend's old home, for what he knew would be the last time. He paused at the passageway by the kitchen, and looked back one final time over the lair. This place, just as the Opera Ghost himself, would fade away into oblivion. It would become the stuff of legends—a story for the ballet rats to titter about in the dark, a seat of mystery that brave men would seek but never find. The opera house would guard its secrets well, but Omid knew the real treasure that had been revealed on the shores of this lake—the true story that played out within the lonely walls of this musical kingdom. It was the one about the angel that fell in love with a ghost and turned him into a man. And his world was never the same.

Omid took a deep breath, saying a final goodbye to Erik's dark domain. And with one last smile, and a tip of his hat, Omid closed the secret door.

42 HAPPILY EVER AFTER

"Oh Young Master," Antoinette said, as she knelt down to ruffle the wispy black hair on the little boy's head, "You are so much like your father!"

"Oh don't give the poor kid a complex, Annie!" Omid teased his wife, earning an eye roll from the father in question.

"Omid!" Antoinette glared at him, rising to her full height. "Remember your manners!"

"No worries, Madame Javed," Erik interjected to the woman whom he had always held in the highest regard, "I am well aware that he has none."

Shaking her head at the hopeless pair, Antoinette once again turned to Gustave and asked, "Dear Sir, would you be so kind as to escort me to your mother and sister? I find I have had enough of these two...*gentlemen*...for the moment."

Erik smiled down at his son, who seemed a little uncertain as to what to do, and crouching down to look him in the eye, encouraged him gently. "Go on, Gustave. Take Aunt Antoinette to see Mama and Genny. It's alright."

The little boy reached out his hand quietly for the older lady to take, and led her from the room.

"Fine young man, you have there, Erik." Omid remarked, as soon as Antoinette and Gustave were out of view.

"Yes..." Erik agreed, leaning against the stone fireplace, arms folded in front of his chest. "Parentage notwithstanding, of course."

"Now, Erik," Omid quipped, making his way to the small liquor cabinet at the far side of the room. "I am sure that Christine is an excellent mother."

"Mmmm..." a rueful smile tugged at the corners of Erik's mouth as he watched the Persian help himself to a snifter of brandy. Some things, it appeared, never change. "That she is. A wonderful mother. And wife."

Omid looked back to his mysterious friend. Yes, Omid agreed, Christine must be a wonderful wife. For the change in his friend was astonishing. Though still on the thin side, Erik appeared to have gained a few pounds, so that his figure did not look quite as gaunt as it once had. The stern furrows of irritation and the hard set to his jaw that had always given the visible side of his face a rather sharp appearance had softened into lines of laughter and an almost kindly countenance. His eyes, which had so often seemed guarded, uncertain and defensive, appeared alight with happiness, and it did Omid good to see such a transformation in his friend. Truly, the love of a good woman had done wonders for him. "You are happy, my friend." Omid stated, rather than asked, since the answer was so obvious. He took a seat in Erik's new reading chair, taking a small sip of his drink.

"I am very happy," Erik admitted, the smile on his lips now genuine and warm, rather than sarcastic. "The people here seem a bit more accepting of my…" his voice trained off as he gestured toward his mask. "It seems that if a person can pull his own weight, the neighbors don't really seem to care much what he looks like. I am composing again, and I have sold a number of my compositions to the local opera house. And the children… and *Christine*…they are such a joy to me." Omid noted how Erik's voice seemed to hush as he uttered his wife's name. It had been about four years since they were married on the passage over to America, and he was still so enchanted…

"Whoever would have thought it possible, Daroga," Erik continued, taking his own seat now on the sofa across from where his friend sat, "that I could be a father? A *husband*?"

"I always knew you had it in you, Erik," Omid answered, his voice plain, with no hint of jest. "And so did Jenna."

"Jenna?" Erik said the name with a hitch in his voice. It had been years… "What makes you mention her?" he asked.

"Do you ever think of her, Erik? Do you remember… ?"

"I do," he said with a wistfulness in his tone. In fact he thought of her often. Some mornings, when he was graced with his wife's first gentle morning smile, or rewarded by his son's peals of shrieking laughter as he tickled him mercilessly after dinner, then his red haired visitor would spring to mind. It was at those times that he would remember how thankful he was that she made him realize what a thrill it was to smile and laugh. And now, whenever his beautiful baby girl would tightly squeeze his finger, as she gazed with wonder into his eyes, he would occasionally recall those first tentative times when Jenna's fingers had reached for his hand, and taught him that his touch was *not* poison—a lesson Christine had enthusiastically furthered through the years. Jenna was to thank for so much of what was now his. If it had not been for her teaching him how to live—how to *love*—he would never have reached out to his beautiful Christine, preferring always to remain a shadow, instead of a man.

"What do you think ever happened to her?" Omid asked, taking another sip of his drink.

"I can only hope," Erik said, earnestly, "that she has somehow found the same happiness that I have. She was right all along about Christine, Daroga. I never needed to be an angel for my wife. She completely accepted me for who I was, right from the start—just like Jenna once did. I can only hope Jenna has found love and joy—since she made those same things possible for me."

"I was down in the lair the day before we departed—" Omid began.

"Down in *my* lair, Daroga?" Erik asked, incredulous. "Whatever for?"

"I wasn't really sure myself, Erik, until I got there. Something was calling me there, making me visit just one last time."

"Was it the lure of free alcohol?"

"Yes, I found the bottle you left—along with the note. Thank you." Omid smiled, as Erik shook his head. Then, quietly, Erik asked, "How did the old place look, Daroga?" He braced himself for the worst. He knew that when he left, the Gendarme were hot on his trail. He was uncertain as to the fate of his old home.

"It was a little dusty," Omid answered, putting his friend's mind at ease. "But beyond that, it was the same as always. It appears that even with that cad Buquet's assistance, no one was ever able to find your lair."

Erik let out a breath he realized he had been holding in and nodded. He was gratified to know that his secrets were still hidden.

"Are there any of your old possessions that you would like me to ship over here to you, Erik?" Omid asked.

"No," Erik answered without hesitation. "There is nothing I need from my old life anymore, Daroga. The only treasure of any importance to me from the Paris Opera House accompanied me when I left, and became my wife on the passage over to America." Erik smiled proudly as he thought of Christine, and the new life they had forged together.

Omid looked at his friend and smiled, before reaching into his breast pocket. "While I was down there," he continued his tale of his time spent in his friend's old home. "I also found this." He held out a small, battered envelope that had Erik's name scrawled across the front.

Eyes narrowed, Erik reached for the note. "What is this?" he asked, examining the strange missive in his hand.

"I found it along the lake shore, in the back cavern." Omid explained, as Erik's eyes shot up to meet his. "It's from Jenna."

Erik felt the breath leave his body. "Jenna?" he whispered, in confusion. "But how…?"

"Read it Erik." Omid encouraged gently.

"But, Daroga," Erik sputtered, "I fail to understand how… "

"Your fates are *connected*, Erik. They always will be. It was no mistake that she showed up on your lakeshore that night. Now *read* it." Omid urged again, knowing all would be clear if Erik just read the words written by the first woman who loved him.

Erik looked down again at the strange communication from the woman who had given him the courage to change his life—the woman whose encouraging words had replaced the corrosive abuse that had, for so many years, plagued his soul, preventing him from truly living, making him choose to hide away in the bowels of the Paris Opera House. *Jenna*—no longer his, but still so dear to him. He took a deep breath as he turned the envelope over with trembling hands, intending to break the seal, only to find that it had already been broken.

"You read my mail!" he looked at Omid with accusing eyes.

"I would hardly call it mail, Erik!" Omid dismissed his friend's irritation with a wave of his hand, and another sip of his drink. "It was lying on the lakeshore in a home you had vacated years ago!"

"My name was on it," Erik hissed.

"Still is, in fact," Omid pointed at the appellation scrawled on the front of the envelope. "Now are you going to read it, or shall I summarize?"

When Erik only glowered at him, Omid rose with a smile and said, "You know, I think I am going to find Antoinette and your lovely wife. I have yet to meet your darling daughter."

"Good idea, Persian," Erik seethed, icily. "Down the hall, third door on the left."

"Thank you for the directions," he said, making his way to the door. As an afterthought, Omid shot back a joking, "Should I keep my hand at the level of my eyes, old friend, as I traverse your domain?"

"Couldn't hurt," Erik snapped.

Once alone, Erik lifted the flap on the back of the envelope and unfolded Jenna's letter to him.

My Dear Erik:

I have no idea if you will ever read these words. It would take a miracle. But if there's one thing that my time with you has proven, it is that miracles do *happen. You were a miracle for me, my dear.*

First of all, thank you. For everything. For taking a chance with Christine, for marrying her, for naming your daughter Genevieve. Thank you for loving me enough to send me home. You have no idea what that one act has meant for me. It was indeed a sacrifice well made—never question that!

You see, by yet another crazy twist of fate, I came home to the most wonderful man already taking care of me. His name is Dr. Christopher Eriksson, and he is your great-great-great-grandson. And after months of missing you and wondering if you were even real, I realized that I had fallen in love with him—the real and everlasting kind of love only dreamed of in fairy tales. We are married, Erik, and we have just moved into your house by the Hudson. The family has kept it all these years. I am carrying Chris's child, my friend. I hope my baby will be as handsome as my husband—who looks so much like you, Erik. Chris is brilliant like you, as well, and he loves to play the guitar and sing me to sleep. He would make you so proud, Erik. He *is my prince.*

By taking a chance on love, you gave me *a chance at true happiness. By continuing to live your life, Erik, you truly* were *living for me. And I live a joyful and happy life every day with my Chris, because you first took that chance. And while at one time, I too yearned to share my life with you, I could never begrudge you your happiness, Erik. It led to such happiness for me, but even more importantly, I* love *you and wanted so desperately for you to be happy. I am so glad you are no longer alone in the darkness. You deserve the light, my Erik.*

And you have always *deserved to be loved.*

One more thing, Erik. It took some time, but I finally realized it was ok to love Chris back when he presented me with the cameo pendant that you first gave me. It proved to me that everything you and I shared had been real—that I was not truly a mental patient. Erik, don't let it linger in a box forever. Give it to Gustave to give to his wife. It will find me if you do, and I promise I will never *again leave your rose behind. I will wear it proudly for the rest of my days in honor of the two extraordinary men who have loved me. I cannot believe I have been so incredibly blessed.*

Goodbye, my Erik. Please know that I think of you often, and that you will forever own a piece of my heart.

I love you.

And I miss you too.

~~Jenna

For long moments, Erik just stared at the note in his trembling hands. How was it possible? Could it be real? Could she really have somehow gotten a letter to him from across the ages? Could this all be an elaborate joke played by the Daroga? No, he had no indication that the Persian entertained a death wish, so he knew *that* could not be the case. Plus, how could the Persian know about the box? About the cameo? From the tone of her letter, it seemed she had read the letters that he had written, and still had hidden in his basement lair—the very letters he had penned when his mind screamed out for someone to listen the way she had always listened to him.

She said that she was married to a descendant of *his*. She said his name was Christopher, and that he was a doctor. Erik's lips curled at the thought that a man in his line was now dedicated to saving lives, just as, for so long, Erik had been intent on ending them. How on earth, through all the years, and all the distance between them, could their fates still be so intertwined that she would have found an offshoot of his own family tree—a tree that began with the love he shared with Christine? A love Jenna herself had encouraged and made possible.

He remembered the moment he first understood the depths of Christine's love. He had told her he was leaving France—she had begged to accompany him. While he desired it more than life itself, he first insisted she know who it was to whom she was promising her loyalty. He had shown her his face, fully expecting her to run, and yet, she drew him to her, and said to him the words he desperately longed to hear.

"*My Erik, my angel,*" she addressed him tearfully, caressing his face with her hands, drawing him to her. "I *love* you—and *only* you. If you but say the word, I would follow you to the ends of the earth and back. *You* are my home. You are my *heart.* My *Erik.* I cannot be whole without you."

Erik caught her lips with his then, feeling as if his heart would burst from his body. When they at last parted, both tearful and gasping for air, he looked deeply into her cerulean eyes, and holding her hands in his, he knelt on the floor before her. "Say you'll share your life with me. Each day. Each night. Each morning—"

"Oh Erik!" she interrupted him, with a sniff and a giggle. "Tell me you love me!"

"You know I do," he whispered breathlessly, knowing without a doubt that his words were true. "Christine, I love you." He leaned forward and scattered soft, sweet kisses along her eyelids, her nose, her cheeks, repeating the endless refrain after each one. "I love you, I love you, I love you."

"Oh, Erik," she exclaimed joyfully, finally joining his lips once more with hers, to seal her promise with a kiss. "I was born to be your wife."

When they parted, full of joy, full of hope, Erik gazed into the beautiful eyes of the woman who would become his bride. On a whim, he removed the onyx and gold ring he wore on his pinkie, and placed it firmly on Christine's left ring finger. "You are mine, as I am yours, Christine. And soon, it will be binding, before God and in the eyes of the law."

Tears of joy glistening in her eyes, Christine exclaimed, "I love you, My Erik, *my angel.*"

"Your *man*, Christine," Erik corrected her. "Your *man* for now and always."

"Both man *and* angel, my Erik." Christine kissed him lightly on the lips. "For truly, I have found heaven in your arms."

Erik pulled her close to him then, and kissed her again, pulling away only when he felt that their kisses were about to push them over a precipice he did not want to cross before they were wed.

"Let me take you back to your room," he said, holding onto her shoulders and looking into her eyes with a smile. "We need to leave quickly—there is a ship to America leaving tomorrow night. You should pack what you need."

"You *are* everything I need, Erik," she declared, reaching forward to give him another quick kiss.

Erik kissed her back, relishing the joy he felt at her words. When they once again parted, he chuckled and murmured back, "You might also want some clothes," wishing fervently that she did not pack too many. After all, once they were married, there would not really be much of a need.

"Well, maybe just a *few* things…" Christine answered, her reddened cheeks revealing that her thoughts had followed a similar course. They left then, so Erik could return her to her room for the last night they would spend apart, for the next evening, they left the Opera House under cover of darkness.

Erik said a bittersweet goodbye to his little Samineh, charging the Persian with her care.

"You will care for my Little Lady, Daroga," Erik commanded, as he held Samineh in his arms, stroking her lovingly on the head. "You will see to it that she is spoiled and given the life of luxury to which she is entitled."

Omid rolled his eyes and reached out for the cat. "I shall commission her a diamond collar, Erik—just like the Shah's felines used to wear."

"It would be a start, Daroga," he quipped, giving Samineh a final squeeze, before handing her over to her new guardian.

Omid accepted the kitten, bringing her to his face to look in her eyes and say, "Hello, my little Fifi!"

"Don't you dare!" Erik hissed.

Omid chuckled and tucked the kitten securely under his arm. He then surprised Erik by pulling his friend into a one armed hug. "I'm going to miss you."

Erik stiffened, feeling awkward and uncomfortable by the Daroga's display of camaraderie. Still, he reached up one arm and gave Omid a graceless pat on the back. "I…shall miss you too, Daroga," Erik said, clearing his throat and awkwardly stepping out of the embrace. "Thank you…for everything over the years. I think I have not always displayed the proper…appreciation for your friendship."

"Oh, who needs appreciation," Omid asked cheerfully, trying to mask the sadness he felt at his friend's departure, "When you have given me alcohol?"

"*Given* you alcohol?" Erik questioned with a scoff. "You downright stole it, Persian."

"You stole it first!" Omid reminded him with a chuckle that earned him a roll of Erik's eyes. Sobering a bit, he added, "Be good to her, Erik. And be good to *yourself*. Never doubt that Christine loves you."

"I cannot doubt it, Daroga," Erik answered with a smile on his face. "She is giving up *everything* for me."

"Then give her everything back," he advised, grasping Erik firmly on the arm.

He looked Omid squarely in the eyes and nodded, "I plan to spend the rest of my life doing just that."

Erik smiled, remembering how he and Christine had furtively made their way to the Daroga's waiting carriage, and after a final, tearful goodbye to Madame Giry and little Meg at the docks, they boarded the ship that would carry them to their new life. Once out in the open waters, Erik sought out the Captain and explained that he and Christine wished to be wed. They spoke their vows beneath the stars, with the sound of the waves keeping pace with their beating hearts, and soon they were pronounced husband and wife. Christine elected to go back to their cabin as Erik paid the captain and took care of paperwork.

Afterward, Erik had taken a few moments to simply stare out at the ocean before returning to his room—the room he would now share with his wife. He knew he shouldn't, but he could not keep his thoughts from turning to Jenna. He had once dreamed that the fiery haired beauty would be his wife—and that they would share all that was new and wonderful together. He had thought, once he'd lost her, that he would never again find a woman to love the way he loved her—or find one who could possibly be moved to love him. But now, he had Christine, the angelic songbird who had touched his heart that first night he saw her, so long ago, crying in the chapel. He had longed to reach out to her then, but he knew now, that if he had not first met Jenna—if she had not first loved him, and taught *him* how to love—he never would have had the courage to do so. He would still be a faceless, nameless angel to Christine, but now he was the man who would share, her life, her dreams, her…*bed.*

He took another silent moment to thank Jenna in his heart, for making this perfect life possible for him. And then, inhaling a deep calming breath, he turned to join his beautiful bride in their room.

❧

Christine had changed out of her dress by the time Erik arrived. She was sitting on the bed, back turned to him, wrapped in a white dressing gown. The soft glow of candlelight danced on her chestnut curls, and Erik found his heart pounding at the sight. He silently shut the door behind him, turning the lock, before gliding over to stand in front of her. Wordlessly, he tipped her chin up, so that he could look in her eyes, as he gently brushed his knuckles along her cheek. "You are so beautiful," he whispered, tucking a stray curl behind her ear. "My bride. My *wife*."

Christine's eyes closed, part from the pleasure of his touch, part in anticipation of what was to come. "My Erik," she whispered. "My *husband*." She opened her eyes and gazed into his, with love and wonder, and…not a small amount of trepidation.

Erik picked up immediately on her nerves. "My love," he whispered, taking his place beside her on the bed, grasping her hands in his. "What is wrong?"

"I…" Christine lowered her lashes, as pink traveled across her cheeks. "I am so nervous…" She still did not look at him, as her inexperience in matters between husband and wife mortified her and made her certain she would be unable to please her husband.

Erik gazed at her, so innocent, so afraid, and felt his heart swell even more in love for her. Again, he tipped her chin up, forcing her to look at him. He cupped her cheeks in his hands, leaning forward for a few quick, gentle kisses before he asked, "Do you trust me?"

"With my life." Christine answered, adoring the way his hands felt on her cheeks, his lips felt brushing against hers.

"Then do not be afraid," he murmured as his lips trailed now to her neck, and he relished the soft sigh he heard escape her mouth. Working his way back up to once again taste his wife's lips, he looked her directly in her eyes and implored, "Trust me," as his fingers traced the edges of her robe until he found the sash. His eyes never left hers as he gently untied the knot that closed her robe, and, delicately separated the layers of fabric, pushing them off her shoulders, leaving only her shift, translucent in the candlelight, to shield her from his hungry eyes. "Christine," he moaned his approval, leaning in once more to blaze hot, burning kisses on her throat, "you are exquisite."

"Oh Erik," she leaned her head back, giving him better access to her sensitive flesh, "Your touch is divine."

Allowing himself to get a bit lost in the moment—this first, heady moment with the woman he would adore for the rest of his life—Erik pulled her closer, crushing her form against his, tangling his fingers in her rich mane of dark curls. Their kisses were deep and yearning, and when Erik used his tongue to part his wife's lips, Christine moaned when she felt him delve inside, tasting, drinking the sweet wine of her passion. Nearly delirious from his mouth's attentions, Christine felt her hands working their way beneath his waistcoat, kneading the muscles of his back through the thin fabric of his shirt.

Erik pulled back from the kiss to once again look into Christine's eyes, now darkened to a midnight blue with her desire. "Trust me," he begged again, in a deep, rumbly plea. Christine nodded, unable to make any other reply, and he began to push the straps of her shift down below her shoulders, until her two pert and perfect breasts were revealed to him. "Oh, sweet heaven," he murmured as he leaned forward and worshipped each flawless mound with his mouth. When his lips encircled one nipple at the precise moment that his fingers squeezed the other one, Christine let out a pleasured cry, which was the most delightful music to Erik's ears. "My little songbird," he moaned into her breast.

"Oh, Erik," she gasped, a ragged moan, arching her body against his, while maddening new sensations traveled through her body, awakening wants and needs she never knew she had. "I don't…," she groaned again, as his hand moved down her side, "I don't…Ooooooo." Her head fell back once more, as her eyes closed against the rising tide of heat coursing through her body.

"Yes, my angel?" his voice caressed her with his calming, silvery tones, as his hand began to stroke her leg, pulling her skirt away as it did so. "You don't what?"

"I don't," she groaned a final time, "I don't know…what to do."

"There is much to learn, Christine," he murmured, leaning in to place feather soft kisses along her cheek. "For *both* of us." He pulled away to once more look her deep in the eyes. With his arms firmly around her, he asked a final time, "Do you still trust me?"

"Yes," she breathed, trembling from the urgency he was inciting within her.

"Then we shall teach each other." And then he claimed her mouth with his own, as he lowered their bodies to the bed.

The next morning, when Christine had awoken, it was to the soft, dulcet tones of her husband singing her a love song, his fingers delicately stroking her hair. Her head was resting on his bare chest, and his arm was holding her firmly to him. She had never felt happier. She inhaled deeply, taking in the scent of her beloved before opening her eyes, and gazing up at him. "Erik," she whispered, as a happy smile played on her lips.

"Ahh, Christine," he murmured, as he bent his head and kissed his wife fully on the lips, drinking in the joy and the pleasure of their joining once again. Last night had been the most ecstatic night he had spent in his life. Again, and then again, he had found fulfillment in his wife's arms, and from the encouraging strains that had spilled from her lips, he was assured that he had given her pleasure as well. "I love you, Christine," he whispered, when their kiss ended. "I love you so much. If I say it a hundred times every day for the rest of my life, I could never express the amount of love that I feel."

"Well Erik," Christine giggled. "I'd be willing to let you try…" She tangled her hands in his sleep tousled black hair and drew his maskless face to her for a deep passionate kiss—one that spoke of the depths of her own satisfaction in their union and a strong desire for more. When they were breathless, Erik broke the kiss, and gazed down at the beauty who lay beside him once more. "Are you hungry, my sweet?" he asked, wanting to meet her every need.

"Yes, Erik," she pulled him to her again, and kissed his lips sweetly before adding, "For you, my husband."

With a guttural growl, Erik gathered her into his arms and devoured her mouth with his, fanning the flames of their passions for the first—but not the last—time that day. It seemed that with Christine, finally, he had discovered the true magic of being, simply, a man.

Erik emerged from his reverie, and ran a loving hand over the letter one last time. "Thank you Jenna," he whispered. "Thank you for giving me the courage to pursue my beautiful Christine…for the amazing life I now have…thank you."

Suddenly, he heard his wife's sweet tones as she snaked her arms down his chest from behind, leaning in for a kiss to his cheek before asking, "What are you doing in here all by yourself, when we have guests?"

Erik smiled and let out a quiet chuckle. "I am just remembering, my darling."

Christine's eyebrows wrinkled, "Remembering what, dear?"

"Well," Erik began, with a sigh, pulling her around to the front of him, so that he could settle her firmly on his lap, "If you must know, dear wife, I was remembering our wedding night."

A slight blush played on Christine's cheeks. "Ah. I see," she said with a smile. "I guess it was our wedding night when we last saw Omid and Antoinette."

"Mmmmmm…" he agreed, nuzzling her neck as he hugged her closer. "That was the last time we saw them, as well as the first time we…"

"Erik!" she giggled, pulling a bit away, in an effort to calm herself after his attentions. "Stop! I have already promised our guests some lunch. I only came to see if you would join us."

With a groan, he loosed his hold on her, allowing her to rise from his lap. "Oh, all right," he capitulated. "I'll behave."

Christine looked at her husband once more, amusement flashing in her eyes. Winking at him, she responded, "Only for now, my dear." Suddenly, she noticed the piece of paper on his lap. "What do you have there, Erik?" she asked.

"Oh this?" he looked down at the letter from Jenna, still resting on his lap. "It is a correspondence from an old friend, very dear to my heart, whom I have not seen in what seems like a lifetime. Omid delivered it."

"Oh," Christine responded. "Is it *good* news?"

Erik smiled, folding the letter once more and placing it in his breast pocket. "The best." He rose from his chair, and placed his arm around Christine's waist. "Come, my love," he said, as they began to move toward the dining room. "Leaving the Persian unsupervised was *not* the best of ideas. By now, I am sure he has finished every last drop of Cognac in the house."

Christine rolled her eyes and gave her husband a gentle swat on the arm. "I love you, Erik," she chuckled, struck at that moment with great affection for her husband.

"As I love you, my darling Christine." He leaned down to kiss the top of her head, and they made their way to their guests.

"Erik," Christine murmured as they walked together.

"Yes?"

"You know those events of our wedding night you were remembering earlier?"

"Mmm hmmm…" Erik responded with a wicked smile.

"I'm going to remind you later."

ABOUT THE AUTHOR

J.M. Smith has been a long time fan of The Phantom of the Opera, and Erik has always held a very dear place in her heart. She lives with her husband, two children, and *very* vocal cat (who bears a rather striking resemblance to a certain feline character in this book!) The Secret Door is her first published work—but hopefully not her last.

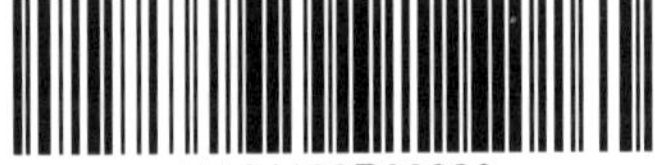

Made in the USA
San Bernardino, CA
16 August 2014